"You're Some Lady!"

He turned to her. "We're five miles from the site. Nobody else is coming here today."

"Jason, you're crazy. . . ."

The desert wind raced through the still car as he leaned over and coaxed her mouth open and touched his tongue to hers. "Undress," he commanded.

Silently, Amanda watched as he pulled off the expensive silk tie and tossed it into the back seat, unbuckled the slim alligator belt. His arrogance took her breath away.

She could hear the cackle of some desert creature as her pulse became a drumbeat, then a hundred drumbeats, spiraling downward through her body. Slowly her dress drifted to the carpeted floor of the car. . . .

DESIGNS

Iris Johnson

A JOVE BOOK

DESIGNS

A Jove Book / published by arrangement with
the author

PRINTING HISTORY
Jove edition / March 1987

ISBN: 0-515-08902-8

Jove Books are published by The Berkley Publishing Group,
200 Madison Avenue, New York, NY 10016.
The words "A JOVE BOOK" and the "J" with sunburst
are trademarks belonging to the Jove Publications, Inc.

PRINTED IN THE UNITED STATES OF AMERICA

PART ONE

chapter 1

THE Mediterranean villa on the east end of Long Island commanded a sweeping view of the Atlantic Ocean. The pool pavilion, in Palladian style, opened to a marble terrace. A suntanned man in his mid-fifties stood on this terrace on a windy afternoon, in a six hundred dollar burgundy robe and two hundred dollar silk pajamas. The money meant nothing to him. His sensitive skin screamed at anything less luxurious.

The man's name was Byron Moore. He was a man of crushing power in the art world, a man of privacy and mystery. He smoked an unfiltered Camel cigarette as his tormented eyes squinted at the bright daylight. A wet, warm wind blew into his face.

"Byron . . ." came a young girl's voice from inside the pavilion.

He ignored the voice. He regarded the ocean almost with disappointment, as if it had not turned out the way he'd ordered. His hair was iron-gray and hugged his Roman skull in a short layered cut. His face seemed hammered out of bronze. Yet the face was aging, and the throat was no longer firm.

He crushed the cigarette against an archway and dropped it to the marble terrace. A servant would retrieve it. Byron Moore never cared where he dropped things. Beneath his robe and pajamas, his body moved sinuously and suggested the strength of steel cables.

"Byron . . . ?" came the girl's voice again.

"Coming," he said. A faint smile creased his face. He looked with finality at the sea and the scudding sails. It looked flat like a Van Gogh painting, with thick layers of sea and sky and white rings of sun. Byron turned away from the view with the same indifference he had felt when he dropped the cigarette.

The pavilion's interior was dramatic and classic, with deep mottled walls and a terra-cotta floor. The dark wicker furniture was covered in white fabric. Keystoned arches formed a palisade around the room. Byron looked at the girl on the wicker chaise.

She was sixteen and she wore a blue bikini bathing suit. Wheat-colored hair framed her child's eyes. She was lengthy and lustrous, her flat belly glistening, her legs glowing with suntan. Her young breasts made curved shadows. She was a delicious creature, slim and unself-conscious.

Byron appreciated her with motionless eyes. "What do you want?"

"I'm bored."

"Why don't you swim?"

"I'm tired of swimming." Her voice was querulous. A pack of cigarettes lay on the table next to the chaise. A glass half filled with ice and Tequila Sunrise stood next to the cigarettes.

Byron moved into the coolness of the pavilion. "You're tired of swimming," he repeated. He sat on the edge of a wicker chair at right angles to the chaise. He touched her painted toenail with his thumb and forefinger, erotically massaged her foot and calf. She smiled and purred.

His words iced over. "I want you never to say you're bored. You've got a brain. You've got imagination. You should be able to live with yourself, alone, in a barren room. And you should be entertained there, every single moment. I *told* you all this."

The girl looked annoyed at the lecture. She reached over and worked a cigarette out of the pack, lit it with a Bic lighter. "Yeah, you told me."

He touched each of her toes in succession, making her shiver. "And you didn't listen. Just another teacher, just another lecture. You ignored me. You sloughed me off."

"Okay, okay, I'm sorry."

"No you're not."

His fingers wrapped themselves like small snakes around her calf and he twisted her foot violently. She screamed in surprise.

"Jesus—"

He held her foot in its twisted position and the girl arched her back, panting. Her eyes swam with pain.

"Byron, come on—"

"This is entertainment," Byron said. His face was dark with exertion. "I've snapped you out of your boredom. Are you bored now, Heather?"

She had dropped her cigarette onto the terra-cotta floor, where it smoldered. Her hands clawed at the wicker arms of the chaise. "It hurts . . ."

"Suppose I break it," he said. He twisted harder, and she screamed. Her head snapped back and she bared her teeth. He put cruel pressure on the tortured leg.

Her eyes pleaded with him through a film of tears. "Please let me go. Please."

"Should I break your leg?"

"No."

"Why not? The pain would be exciting. It would be something different."

"I don't want it broken," she said. Her voice had weakened from the pain.

"You don't?"

"No."

"Why not?"

"Oh shit . . . "

"Why not?"

"I don't know . . . please . . ."

"Are there things you want to do with this leg?"

Heather glistened with sweat. She nodded.

"What things?"

Her head thrashed from side to side, wordless.

"Talk to me, Heather."

She managed to raise her head slightly. "Swim."

"Swim?"

She nodded.

"You said you were tired of swimming."

"No, I'm not . . ."

"What else would you do?"

"Walk . . ."

"Yes?"

"Ride a bike . . . dance . . . swim . . ."

"You said that."

"Go bowling . . . oh Jesus, *please* . . ."

Byron's face was dark with blood, his neck roped with veins. "Look at that," he said. "Look how many ideas you have."

He released her foot and sat back in his chair, shaking and short of breath. Heather slumped in the chaise and cried. Her sobs punctuated the sound of the wind.

Byron let her cry for a while. He did not retrieve the burning cigarette on the floor. He watched Heather patiently. Soon, she turned her head to one side and lay on her cheek, her fist at her mouth.

"Finished?" he asked.

She nodded.

"Do you want to go home?"

She shook her head.

"Do you want your parents?"

"No."

"Next time I'll break your leg."

She said nothing.

"Are you bored, Heather?"

She shook her head. Tears welled again in her eyes.

Byron stood up, shocked at the cramp in his legs. It was not easy to get out of a chair anymore. He seemed horrified at this. Saying nothing, he walked toward an archway, this one facing landscaped gardens. Behind him, Heather gingerly rubbed her twisted leg.

Byron reached into the pocket of his robe and took out a folded magazine page. He unfolded the page and looked at a color photograph of a woman. There was some text as well, but it had been wantonly torn, making it unreadable. Byron had wanted only the photo.

The woman in the photo looked about thirty and might have been a fashion model, except that her eyes were too intelligent and impudent, her nose just slightly off center. Her face glowed with expertly applied makeup and with character. She leaped off the page. She was wearing a bone-colored dress and a champagne scarf and a rakish hat. She was smiling, the sudden, startled smile of a celebrity caught by the camera. The background was a blur of cityscape. The woman looked lean and healthy like someone who played tennis.

Byron held the magazine page gently because it was tearing at the folds. He looked long and hard at the photo. The wind rustled leaves outside.

"Amanda," Byron whispered.

He could hear Heather's ragged breathing behind him. He turned to look at her. "Boredom?" he said, only half to the girl. "You can't imagine boredom. Not the cancerous horror that boredom is to me. Do you know I'd be willing to dynamite this pavilion, just to watch the colors of the dust. When your life becomes dreary, so dreary that you treasure nothing . . . but you can't possibly grasp that. Not possibly."

He folded the magazine page lovingly and put it back into his pocket. He unknotted the sash of his robe, let the robe fall from his powerful shoulders to a wicker loveseat. He unbuttoned his pajama jacket and took it off. His torso was knotted and muscled, the deep chest matted with white hair. Heather watched him with hypnotized eyes.

"But even with that much boredom," he said, "you can still find something. Even if it's only one thing, only one worthwhile project. I created a masterpiece once, and it was taken from me. Some works you don't let go. Some works you keep. I'm going to get this one back."

He stepped toward the chaise. Heather sat up and winced in pain. She reached behind her without shyness and undid the halter of her bathing suit. The bra loosened and she slipped it from her body. Her breasts came free, the nipples rosy in the afternoon light. There was an angelic quality about her slim nakedness.

Byron could no longer become aroused by the teenaged girl. Only by framing the magazine photo in his imagination could he grow and hunger. Amanda was his obsession now. She kept him from suicide, from murder, from berserk violence. *You will come back, Amanda,* he thought calmly.

Driven past restraint, Byron cried out hoarsely and covered Heather's urgent body with his own.

The soaring, airy banquet hall in the Tennyson Tower in downtown Atlanta was an appropriate place for Jason Turner to receive an architectural award. After all, Turner Associates had built this commercial skyscraper and helped make Helen Tennyson even richer.

The coiffed heads of beautiful women and the tanned faces of rich men turned upward and smiled as hundreds of hands clapped. On the flower-strewn dais, Jason Turner grinned boyishly and held the glinting award over his head, as if it were the Stanley Cup. His media-idol face glistened with perspiration under the hot lights, his black moustache damp.

To his left and right, the elite of the architectural world formed two applauding arrows pointing at Jason. He was the nexus, the blazing light. But the room crackled with an undercurrent of jealousy. They applauded, but they didn't like it.

Jason tensed under the pressure of his own performance. He had gotten drunk on scotch in the Pump Room earlier while romancing several bankers about the Pueblo Project, and the prime rib dinner had not settled the alcohol in his blood. He could feel his heart pounding.

Finally, the applause slackened, and Jason set the trophy amid the water glasses and soiled cutlery. The base of the award made a grating sound as it rubbed against bread crumbs on the white tablecloth.

Jason looked out at the faces, many of whom he knew. But they sure as hell didn't know *him*. He was struck with a terrible pang of loneliness, which passed, like the throb of an old wound. He knew he cut a gorgeous figure on the dais, in a custom-tailored tuxedo. The formal wear adored his body, and his suntan was honestly come by. His startling blue eyes invited and teased the bejeweled women of Atlanta.

He fondled the warm metal of the award, which was an abstract design in silverplate. He made sure his voice was steady before he spoke into the microphone.

"Well, this is a surprise," he said, and grinned at the laughter and applause. "Look, I'm not into giving speeches. This has been a beautiful night. We're all feeling good here. It's a gorgeous room, right?" The applause and laughter had a jeering edge this time. "And on behalf of Turner Associates I want to point out that this room was done by Orrin Davis. Orrin, are you here, partner?"

There was the obligatory turning of heads as a balding man stood at his seat and waved shyly at the applause. Jason clapped loudly at the dais, then took a sip of ice water. He realized he was being an asshole. He was too drunk for this public event.

He looked down at the award, touched its rim with the ball of his finger. "This is for the WestCorp Building in Phoenix," he said. "Most innovative commercial building of the year. I'm very grateful for this award. Of course, it has to be carved up into lots of pieces and shared with a lot of people."

He surveyed the crowd, pausing at foxy ladies. There was one, a redheaded reporter for an architectural magazine, who was signaling with green eyes. She wore peach chiffon and had deep, beautiful breasts.

"Turner Associates employs the most accomplished and creative people in the business today," Jason said. "And I mean that, folks. Look, if we put up the most innovative building in *any* year, it's because of the creative force field that exists in our offices . . . it comes from all the brains . . . one big energy field, like a fucking generator, and it powers all of us."

He stopped, terrified at his blunder. He could see the shock and delight in their eyes. Sweat rolled down his jaw. "Okay," he said, and took another sip of water. "On behalf of Turner Associates, thank you. Every good building makes the planet a little better. That's our main business now. Making a better planet." *Jesus, sit down.* "Anyway, thanks."

He raised one hand to wave at the crowd and hesitated, not sure if he should remain standing. There was a crack of applause on the dais, and clapping from the audience, and then the people swept out of their chairs and stood, and he saw a blur of rings and bracelets, a galaxy of eyes and smiles.

He waved and smiled and held up the award again and flashbulbs made lightning. The chairman of the banquet tugged at Jason's arm and coaxed him back to his seat. The applause seemed to fade and then grow loud again as if the audience were spinning round and round.

Some official of Atlanta got up to speak. Jason saw his porcine profile in the light. The man's pores all seemed open and his skin glowed blue. *Christ,* Jason thought, *I'm sick.*

He got up and excused himself and sidled behind the seated dignitaries. He left his award sitting in the bread crumbs.

From the men's room, Jason went out on a terrace that overlooked sloping meadows leading down to a manmade lake. The lights of Atlanta wavered in early spring heat. Jason felt dizzy. He hated straight liquor, but that's what businessmen drank these days and Jason was one hell of a businessman. *And a fraud as an architect. But they'll never know that.*

He heard someone come out onto the terrace, and he turned. It was the lady reporter. She looked sculpted by the moonlight.

"Are you okay?" she asked. She had a lilting drawl.

"Yes. Thanks."

"You caused a stir by leavin'."

"I'd've caused a worst stir by staying."

She smiled, and her eyes twinkled. "Please don't think badly of Atlanta's banquet facilities. Maybe it was jet lag."

"Probably. What's your name, angel?"

"Sharon Brannigan. I write for *Architect's World*."

It was an elite, expensive magazine published on heavy coated stock. Turner Associates work had been featured more than once. "An Irish magnolia," he said.

She smiled again and moved gracefully to the railing of the terrace. She leaned provocatively toward the meadows below and her eyes looked toward the city. "I'm sweet and fiery," she said.

He felt better now, having gotten rid of some of the poisons. He was in his element here, on a moon-drenched terrace with an exciting lady. Speaking of which, he wondered briefly about Amanda Gray and decided to ask Sharon about her. He took a pack of cigarettes from his inside pocket and tamped one out. "Do you smoke?"

"Yes, I do."

He smiled and offered her a cigarette, which she took with tapered fingers. She smelled of Guerlain. He lit her cigarette and their heads tilted close in the illumination. She exhaled richly and threw back her head. Her mane of chestnut hair swirled excitingly.

"It's like being part of the underground," she said. "You don't dare smoke out in the open anymore."

He smiled and lit his own cigarette. "You have to do it in the company of other sinners."

Her laugh was throaty. "Mr. Turner, I find you a fascinating man. Have you ever been told that by a woman?"

"Name's Jason," he said. "And yes, almost constantly."

She laughed more spontaneously. Her teeth glinted in the moonlight. Smoke swirled from her nostrils. Jason looked unabashedly at the smooth mounds of her breasts revealed by the low neckline of her dress. "Handsome and clever," she remarked. "Unusual combination."

"Handsome and *straight*," he said. "Even more unusual."

She stared for a moment, then guffawed. She turned away and shook her head. "Wonderful," she murmured. "You deserve your reputation."

His memory kicked in. "Which reminds me, why isn't

Amanda Gray at this bash? She's the hot name in interior design this year."

Sharon's eyes cooled momentarily. "She's somewhere in the Orient, I think, designing an embassy. Why, do you know her?"

He tapped ash over the railing. "Nope. She's an interesting lady and I'd hoped to meet her."

"Ah." Sharon visibly recovered her initiative and said, "Jason, can I offer you some of the city's hospitality? I know a few adult nightspots—meanin' cool jazz and low lights."

He caught her eyes, sophisticated and vulnerable, and felt the anticipation warm the inside of his skin. "Your car or mine?"

"Mine," she said softly. "They won't let your car in my private garage."

He stepped toward her. She came into his arms meltingly and her mouth was hot and waiting. He held her passionately and her tongue probed and promised as her long fingers excited the back of his neck.

They stepped apart. Her eyes and nostrils were wide. "On the other hand," she said huskily, "you might prefer brunch."

He laughed pleasantly and guided her toward the terrace door. This would be nothing new, but it would anesthetize the pain for another day.

chapter 2

IN the shadow of green mountains, the city of Kulong shimmered with human bodies and Japanese cars. Kulong was the capital city of Bahru, a shaky U.S. ally in Southeast Asia. Because Bahru was strategically important, a new diplomatic residence had been built high in the mountains, and because of that residence, a striking woman in a linen suit and white hat strolled the thronging streets of Kulong. She walked alone, but didn't seem aware of danger; in fact, she had the air of a savvy buyer strolling the aisles of a trade show. Yet the woman did not seem arrogant. *Enjoyment* was the word an onlooker would use to describe her long-legged stride, her smartly tailored ensemble, and her fine-boned, quick-eyed face. She was enjoying herself: enjoying her fashionable and tawny beauty, enjoying her exotic surroundings, and enjoying her work.

Through designer sunglasses, Amanda Gray saw textures, colors, and shapes. Around her swirled native Bahrundians, Chinese, and Indians, some in flowing native dress, many in Western shirts and slacks. Small autos choked the narrow street, honking in a deafening squall.

Amanda drew many stares, for she moved with elegance, and she was taller than most of the natives. She was also dressed too stylishly for this rundown area, but she was shopping for ideas, not for luxuries. She liked the attention, but felt nervous.

It's all those old Charlie Chan movies, she thought. She smiled to herself and stopped to look at hanging baskets in a dark little shop. The squat proprietor scuttled up to her and began jabbering.

"No, no," she said. "Just looking."

She ran her sensitive fingertips over the woven baskets, as her creative brain conjured applications for the straw. The residence of U.S. Ambassador Michael Curtis was a modern glass and wood composition that she had decorated as a mountain lodge rather than in traditional embassy style. Already, she'd placed exquisite Oriental sculptures amid glass panels and white oak.

Amanda enjoyed a shiver of ego. The residence was brash and controversial. Her design had been written up. She was on the map, even if it *was* in the middle of a rain forest.

She looked up and noted the afternoon sun descending. Time to hail a cab back up the mountain. She didn't want to be in this neighborhood at sunset.

She held up a basket. "How much?" she asked.

The proprietor exploded into chatter and Amanda shook her head. "No, I don't understand you. Please . . ."

Dimly, she was aware of shouting on the street, but there was so much noise that she hadn't paid attention. Now she heard shrieks and she looked.

For a moment, she saw nothing unusual. Then a woman in a sarong pointed and screamed. Heads turned. Amanda saw a boy, perhaps eight or nine years old, pop out from between taxicabs and sprint toward the curb.

Amanda couldn't make out why everyone was shouting. The boy ran a crazy pattern in and out of the crowd and turned into a blind alley. Amanda stepped out onto the sidewalk to see where he'd gone.

She heard a man shouting in English, and the sudden familiarity of language made her snap around. A big man, dressed in a rumpled summer suit and straw hat, was running toward her. He was screaming, "Stop the son of a bitch!" over and over.

Amanda looked back and forth, at the alley and at the man. Why was he chasing the kid?

Amanda moved to intercept the man, and then she saw that he brandished a pistol in his right hand. She didn't believe it for an instant. *Dear God, he's going to kill the boy!*

Her heart trip-hammered. She looked into the alley. The boy had run into a wall of stacked baskets. An irate merchant pinioned the boy's wrist and gesticulated angrily. Even if the boy wriggled free of the merchant, he'd run right into the man with the gun.

People had gathered. The armed man loomed at the alleyway, only a few feet from Amanda. "Little animal!" the man screamed, and aimed the pistol.

"Hold it!" Amanda snapped. The man looked at her, startled by the sound of her English. He kept looking, captivated by her glamorous appearance.

Amanda tried to breathe but heat filled her mouth. What did she do now? She studied the man. He was over six feet tall, maybe two hundred and fifty pounds, and sweating profusely. His hands were puffy and pink. The details burned into Amanda's senses.

"What's going on?" she asked inanely.

The man gestured with the pistol, which stopped her heart. "That little prick lifted my wife's pocketbook. Just pulled it off her shoulder. I think he broke her arm, the little shit."

Amanda's eyes could not leave the gun. "Okay, but why don't we get the police?"

"Come on, honey," the man said. "I'm American. You think these baboons are going to do anything? I'm sick of these little yellow monkeys laughing up their sleeves. Maybe a bullet in his balls'll show him we're not pushovers."

The man's violence washed over her like ocean waves. She became acutely aware of the people surrounding them. If he shot the boy, the mob might tear *her* apart. *Just talk to him, Amanda. Somebody should be here soon.*

"I know you're angry," she said. "I can understand that. But you can't shoot him."

"Why not? You think they have any laws here?"

Now Amanda noticed the uniformed policemen at the perimeter of the scene. Their own guns were drawn. Amanda wet her lips, felt moisture pool between her breasts. Goodbye to *this* dress. "Listen," she said to the man. "I don't even know your name. Mine's Amanda Gray."

She managed what she hoped was an alluring smile. The man looked off-balance. "I'm Jack Weiner," he said.

"Nice to meet you, Jack."

She sensed that she was calming him, or at least confusing him. He was mostly bravado. Probably he was not used to attractive women being friendly. He was probably crude and loud and a bully back wherever he came from.

Okay, you pathetic jerk, she thought. *Put down the gun.* "Maybe we can get a drink somewhere and talk this out."

"Oh no," Jack said, shaking off his weakness. "*After* I shoot the bastard."

Great, Amanda thought. *Now what?*

Amanda heard a change in the volume and tone of the voices around her and turned her head. She saw the police escorting the boy through the crowd, toward an official car down the street. Her eyes flew to Jack, whose face slowly registered that he'd been suckered. *My God, he's going to shoot me.*

But a loud honking drew Jack's attention as well as hers. Amanda murmured with relief as she watched the black diplomatic limousine flow through traffic. Several cars veered onto the sidewalk to make room.

The rest happened in quick, disjointed images. The back doors of the limo opened like sprouting wings and men in sunglasses and dark suits crouched behind the doors and leveled guns at Jack. "Drop it!" one man yelled in English. "We'll blow your head off!"

Jack stared at the car and the men, suddenly deflated. He seemed a lumpish sack of rice as he stood at the alleyway. He mumbled, "Yeah . . . sure . . ." The pistol slipped from his swollen fingers and clattered on the pavement. Amanda shut her eyes and gasped, expecting the pistol to discharge.

The men from the limo rushed through the colorful crowd and one of them shoved Jack toward a police car that had pulled up. Jack looked back at Amanda, his eyes showing that he felt betrayed, his adventure over. The other man from the limo picked up the gun and followed his partner.

Michael Curtis came to Amanda from the limo and put his arm around her shoulders. "Are you okay?" he asked.

She nodded and smiled at him. He was a trim, attractive man in his early forties with thinning brown hair and tortoise-shell glasses setting off a tanned face. He wore his light-weight suit gracefully.

"He didn't hurt you?" Curtis asked.

Amanda shook her head. She felt fine, better than she would have guessed. In fact, she felt excited and aroused. "No, I'm great. Just get me to the car."

He helped her through the crowd and she leaned gratefully into his body. She heard cameras whirring and wondered if any news services were capturing this. Then she ducked down and slid into the spacious back seat. Air conditioning cooled her face.

She sat back, and Curtis slid in beside her and shut the door. She asked, "Where's Jack?"

The diplomat tapped on the glass panel to signal the driver to move. "En route to the American Embassy. I want you to lie down for the rest of the day. You can testify tomorrow."

"Thank you," Amanda said.

He glanced at her as the limo inched through the streets. "In fact, how about some dinner up at the house?"

"I'd like that," she said, and watched the crowds glide away. She felt a growing rush of excitement. She had acted quickly, thought fast, dealt with terror. She could perform under pressure. That was good to know, finally.

After dinner, Amanda and Curtis sat on redwood chaises on the roof deck of the lodge, looking down on a vista of rain forest. Amanda wore a light flowered sundress and sipped coffee with anisette. Her senses burned with the damp greens and violets of the jungle. She imagined tigers and exquisite butterflies, and she listened to the chatter of monkeys.

Curtis swirled the ice in his gin and tonic and looked at her with curious eyes. He'd changed into a silk shirt, slacks, and loafers, and Amanda liked the way he looked. Her breasts and thighs began to tingle pleasantly, and she let the evening's liquor speed through her blood and arouse her.

"I wondered," Curtis said, "how it feels to sit here, in your own creation."

She smiled. "It's a rush. I guess it's like seeing your own paintings at a gallery. Very big ego boost."

"You deserve it. I love this place."

"Thank you."

He settled back in his chaise with a subtle assumption of power. "I feel good being here," he said. "So does Maryanne. She worried that we'd be stuck in some old dump."

Maryanne was Curtis' wife. "You might, if you get transferred to Europe."

"I know." The sun flared for a moment just above a distant mountain, and the peak looked black and shaggy. "But I don't intend to be an ambassador forever."

"You almost lost your credentials today."

"Don't remind me." A white-jacketed Malaysian servant slid open the glass door to the deck and whispered to Curtis, who waved him away. The servant withdrew. The shriek of monkeys grew suddenly loud.

Curtis swallowed more of his drink and sat up, straddling the chaise. Amanda glimpsed his chest beneath the open shirt. "You were cool as ice," he said.

"No problem."

They both laughed, aware of the sexual tension. He said, "Are you always that slick?"

She leaned back, aware of her perfumed body beneath the thin dress. "I wasn't slick at all."

"You handled it beautifully. Gave me a chance to get there before we had a full-scale incident."

"Well, I was trying to avoid a full-scale bullet in my neck." She watched the setting sun shimmer like molten gold. The rain forest turned black against the sky. "Actually, I've become soft. I used to be a real hellion when I was a kid. I ran *into* danger."

"I know," he said. "I guess we've all read about your past. I'm as fascinated as anyone."

She could actually feel herself bristling. "Michael, please. It's so damned boring."

"Sure. I'm sorry."

"Oh, damn," she said, and looked contritely at him. "I didn't mean to jump down your throat. But you can imagine how often I've been hounded. I want to put it behind me; I want to be accepted on my own terms. As a designer, as an artist, not as the ex-mistress of Byron Moore."

He nodded. "Of course. It was a long time ago."

She forced a laugh. "Not *that* long ago. Don't get insulting."

He returned the smile, showing white teeth. He was in shadow now. Soft electric lights came on magically, casting a russet glow. The mountain peaks stood out in silhouette against a deep vermilion sky.

"I think of you as ageless," he said.

"What a diplomat," she quipped.

But the quip died in her throat. She'd been looking with emotional wonder at the changing sky, alive to its color and intensity. For an instant she thought it was a trick of the sunset, the way the mountaintops burned with a fiery corona. Then she realized it was no trick. She stared with horror as the blackness curved up from the mountains like arms, shutting off the light. Pain exploded behind her eyes.

No, she thought. *Not now . . .*

"Amanda?"

Had she screamed aloud? It didn't matter. Only the blindness mattered, the blindness that crushed her eyes like an iron mask, that sucked the breath from her lungs, that pushed her heart through her ribs. She felt her fingers clawing at the thick air, trying to tear it away . . .

Curtis' hands were on her shoulders, his breath at her cheek. "Amanda, what is it?"

The sky was there again! *Thank God!* She blinked furiously, and tears flooded her eyes. She sat up in the chaise, clutching Curtis' forearm.

"Amanda, what happened?"

She shook her head. "Nothing. It must be the excitement. Delayed reaction. I couldn't breathe."

"Do you want a doctor?"

"No. Thank you. I'm fine, really."

She patted his hand, looked bravely at him. His eyes searched her face. He looked so grim that she wanted to laugh. But she couldn't laugh. This wasn't the first time. She couldn't ignore these symptoms much longer. She had to see a doctor, she had to think the unthinkable. But it couldn't be what she dreaded. Not when color and form and line were her life.

She drew a steadying breath, feeling her pulse normalize. She disengaged her hands from his arm, leaving him standing over her. "Thank you again, Michael. I'm sorry to cause you so much trouble."

"No trouble at all." He returned to his chaise, but didn't sit. He picked up his drink from the aluminum drum table and took a healthy gulp. He seemed jolted. "This has been a pretty adventurous assignment for you."

"Yes, it has."

"Oh—which reminds me." He took a slip of memo pad paper from his shirt pocket and glanced at it, over the rims of his glasses. "There was a cable for you today. From Turner Associates in New York. They want to see you next week about something called The Pueblo. Is that a new project?"

Her blood paused and the night seemed to swell inside her. "The Pueblo?"

"That's what it said."

She forced her voice to remain steady. "It's a hotel and convention complex that's going to be built in the Southwestern desert. I'd expressed interest in doing the interiors." She took a sip of her coffee. "I imagine they're interviewing every designer in the business."

"Sounds exciting," he said.

She looked out at the gathering night. "Yes. Yes, it is exciting. It's something I want very much." It was *everything,* not something. It would put her name in lights. It would carve her fame into rock. It would fulfill every artistic and power-mad dream she'd ever dreamed.

She couldn't be going blind. It was exhaustion. It was nerves.

She belied the stormy emotions inside her with a cool, graceful smile. She stood by the railing, dangerously near a precipitous drop. "This has been a very eventful day," she said. "Thank you for dinner. I enjoyed it."

"So did I," Curtis said, disappointment edging his voice. "With Maryanne in Singapore and only workmen here, it's pretty boring."

She looked long and hard at him. He would be dull and comforting in bed. A healthy American boy, well schooled, ambitious and articulate. He'd played football in college. He was finely muscled, and he cared for her.

And she needed to have a man touch her tonight, and kiss her in dark, secret places. She was afraid and aroused. And he was married, and required his wife for his career. That was the kind of man Amanda wanted, all right. No strings. No love.

No love ever.

She shook off the self-pity and put down her coffee. They were encircled in darkness now, the day's heat steaming upward from the jungle. She went to Curtis, who waited with trembling wonder. She wrapped her cold hands around his warm neck, tilted her head and kissed him passionately. He accepted the kiss passively at first, then responded. His hands came uncertainly to her back, then moved to her waist. She pressed her groin tightly to his, and felt him bulge against her. Her breasts swelled, her nipples tight against her dress.

She smiled at him and her fingertips toyed with the hair at his ear. "Do I get diplomatic immunity for this?" she whispered.

He smiled back, with boyish joy, and pulled her close.

Jason stepped out of the private elevator into the elegant reception room of Helen Tennyson's skyscraper office suite.

Eleanor, Helen's ice-blonde secretary, looked up from behind her rosewood and ormolu desk. "Hi, Jase. She's waiting for you."

"I guessed," he said. She looked seductive in an open-throated skirt, but his most devastating smiles did not penetrate her.

"How is it outside?" she asked.

"Hot. Is she in the salon?"

Eleanor smiled impishly. "No, the sauna."

Jason cursed silently but vowed not to look upset. If Helen was playful today, it was better than her bitchy moods. He fixed the knot in his silk tie and strode past Eleanor into an archway flanked by brass and crystal sconces.

He moved without pause through the salon, with its violet-wood molding and parquet floors, and through the draped doorway to the bath suite. The suite was computer-controlled, done in makeup-foundation tones, and softly lit. Jason noted that the elegant tub was filling itself with temperature-controlled water.

"Hello, Bill," Jason said, trying not to feel like an idiot.

"Hello," came the grating voice synthesizer. "Miss Tennyson is waiting for you. Please remove your shoes."

"Eat my dick," Jason said pleasantly.

"I don't understand," the synthesizer replied.

Jason grinned, then kicked off his Bally wingtips and said, "Thank you, Bill," which was the correct input for the computer to open the sauna door.

The rosewood door slid open and Jason stepped into the steam-filled cabinet. The door closed behind him as ferocious heat blasted his face. He was bathed in deep red light, and heard water dripping and hissing on rocks, against a background of soft music. He said, "Hello, Helen."

Helen Tennyson lay naked on a towel-covered table, the track lights highlighted her glistening back and rounded ass. When she raised her patrician head, her breasts swelled invitingly. Helen was forty-six years old and richly preserved, her body ripe and full and taut. Her skin glowed cherry red. Her eyes gazed at Jason from beneath serpentine lashes. They were topaz eyes, and they smoked with power. A straight nose set off a full, red-lipped mouth. Her raven hair, shot through with gray, was wet, and hugged her skull. Later, it would be coiffed by a private hairdresser. She would be powdered, manicured, and dressed. Helen Tennyson did nothing for herself.

"Jason," she said with drenching sweetness. Her voice was musical and throaty. Helen intimidated everyone.

"What's up?" Jason asked. He suffered the heat silently as his Chereskin suit wilted.

"Amanda Gray," Helen said.

"What about her?"

"She's hot news."

"I've heard."

"I've looked at what she did with that diplomatic lodge in Bahru. Very innovative, very couragous. Do you agree?"

"Sure."

Helen laughed. "How in God's name would you know, Jason?"

"I've read the journals."

"Yes, dear, but you don't *understand* them. You're not beginning to think you're really an architect, are you?"

"Is the comedy necessary?"

She raised herself more provocatively. "Jason, you were a bore at the awards dinner in Atlanta. I wish you wouldn't say more than I tell you to say. You have one purpose and one purpose only, and that is to seduce people for me. You are the most talented seducer I have ever known. Your personal charm, your face and body, have earned millions for me. You can make a kickback or a rigged contract sound like a holy quest. That's what I pay you for, Jason. You *pretend* to be an architect because it's useful and it disarms your prey, but you are *not* an architect and you must not run off at the mouth. Catch?"

Subtly, her voice had flattened and harshened and her eyes had turned to flint. She commanded vast sums of money and battalions of bankers and politicians. She could break Jason in half, because without her, he owned nothing but his shame.

He breathed slowly. "What the hell are you lecturing me for?"

"I thought it was necessary."

"It's not."

She smiled. "Well, good. The Pueblo is underway, dear boy, and it's my little masterpiece. I'm having enough trouble with those asshole Indians out there. I need you badly on this one. Don't get drunk again on the job and don't go public with your ignorance."

"I'll try."

Helen gazed levelly at Jason. "I think Amanda Gray might be good for The Pueblo. I cabled her in Bahru and arranged a lunch. Wine and dine her. Find out if she has the right stuff. Sign her up if she does. I want that filly in my stable. She fascinates me. Byron Moore's little slavey, out on her own. Do you know he has another teenager?"

"Who?"

"Oh Christ, Jason. Byron Moore. What happened to your intensive reading program?"

"I don't follow scandals."

She chuckled. "You *are* a scandal, sweetheart. Look at you. Drenched to your silk underwear, looking at my tits and buns. Rather compromising for the President of Turner Associates. Suppose I was taking pictures of this?"

"Without your wrinkle cream? I doubt it."

She hissed, like an adder stepped on. "Get out of here, Jason. I was going to let you lick my pussy until I came all over this table, but forget it now."

"I'm crushed," he said dryly.

"Get out."

He turned, but her voice stopped him like a thrown dagger. "Jason."

"Yes?"

"If you like Amanda, you can have her for a while. I think the coupling would be useful."

"Go to hell." He swallowed his rage and humiliation and said, between his teeth, "Open up, Bill."

Nothing happened.

Helen laughed. "I changed the program. Tell him you want to suck my ass."

"Go fuck yourself," he said.

"Would if I could, dear, but you'd still be in here *schvitzing*. Go on, give the password."

Jason exhaled. "I want to suck Helen's ass."

The rosewood door slid open and Helen's insulting laughter followed Jason back into the bath suite. The door closed, shutting off the laughter. Jason tore his handkerchief from his pocket and mopped his dripping face.

He put his shoes back on and retraced his steps through the salon and into the reception room. Eleanor looked up at him, poker-faced. "Want to use the washroom?"

"No," he said. He looked at Eleanor. "Don't you ever want to kick her teeth in?"

Eleanor smiled smugly. "No. But then, she's very nice to me."

He smiled, understanding. "I hope you give each other a disease." He took some satisfaction in Eleanor's intake of breath and boarded the elevator before she could respond. As the upholstered door whispered closed, he shut his eyes and worked methodically to cover the truth about his life with enough lies to get him through the day.

chapter 3

THE offices of Amanda Gray Designs were sheathed by the reflecting glass of a Manhattan tower, but inside, Amanda's personal flair made the space her own. This morning, she strode purposefully through her reception area, past panels wrapped in blue and beige fabric.

"Hi, JoAnne," she said brightly to the receptionist. "Any calls?"

JoAnne smiled. "Not yet."

Amanda whipped off her rakish hat and shook her hair. "Well, if it's Turner Associates, just patch them right through."

"No problem," JoAnne said.

Amanda smiled once more to assure JoAnne that her sense of humor still held sway, but of course she fooled nobody. The office was hyperkinetic with preparations. The big Jason Turner lunch was three days away and Amanda's butterflies had become Japanese movie monsters.

Amanda continued through the office suite. Her gray V neck cotton dress showed sleek legs in Bendel sandals. She *felt* confident. She knew how good she was, and how good her people were. But Jason Turner was a kind of icon. This was not an easy week.

Especially with nightmares about going blind.

She swore fiercely, and poured herself a steaming mugful of coffee from a "first aid" station in the corridor. She popped in on Lacey Coleridge, her Creative Coordinator (she had enjoyed making up titles for everyone). Lacey bent over her drawing board, and Amanda first saw a cascade of soft, straight hair against a white cotton jumpsuit.

"Not done yet?" Amanda said.

Lacey looked up, tossing back the hair fetchingly. She smiled with real warmth. "Hi, boss. How goes it?"

Lacey's eyes gleamed in a cameo face of exquisite beauty. She wore a white chain necklace which set off her bare throat and shoulders. Her skin was smooth and evenly suntanned.

"Mild hysteria so far," Amanda said. "How about you?"

"Take a look."

Amanda came around the desk. Lacey was working on a desert palette carried through in fabric and furnishings. She'd pinned swatches to the drawing board, set out cacti and other succulents in plastic pots on her desk, and had done watercolors of lobbies and individual rooms. Lacey was gifted, with an intuitive sense of line.

Amanda bent slightly to study the sketches. "Go with it. Do a lobby."

Lacey looked up. "For real?"

"Why not?"

"We don't know what Turner is planning."

Amanda sipped at her coffee. "Look, hon, I've always worked one way. Show 'em what you can do. He can throw out our lobby, but if he hires *us,* that's the point."

Lacey nodded. "You got it."

Amanda fingered some of the swatches. "One thing. Consider the desert at night, too, not just the earth tones. Get some deep blues, some greens, scales of a Gila, eyes of a snake. Get *under* the rock, okay?"

Lacey nodded again, and quickly jotted some notes with a pencil on a yellow pad. "Got it."

"Any backtalk?"

Lacey shook her head. "No."

Amanda knew she'd criticized Lacey's work, and always got knots in her stomach when she had to do that. But people told her she had a knack for being nonjudgmental and nonthreatening. She exhaled, glad Lacey was not offended.

"Okay," she said. "Try for a series of finished drawings, color charts, the works. I'd like to take home a portfolio tonight if possible. Don't kill yourself and don't skip lunch."

Lacey leaned back in her chair, catlike and stretchy. She toyed with her pencil and said, "Are *you* going to have lunch?"

Amanda smiled tiredly. "I've got some yogurt in the fridge."

"How about going out? Celebrate everything. The embassy, The Pueblo. Get psyched."

"It sounds delicious, pet, but I'm about as psyched as I can get without throwing up. Anyway, it was a diplomatic residence, not an embassy."

"Everyone's calling it an embassy." Lacey's face slipped a little with disappointment.

"No. It's much more intimate. Very romantic, in fact."

"Was the ambassador sexy?"

Amanda smirked and sipped more coffee. "Oh, pretty sexy. *I'd* make a pact with him."

The snap of Lacey's pencil was so sudden that Amanda's coffee slopped over the rim of the mug and onto the custom carpet. Lacey tightened her mouth and looked foolishly at the two shattered pencil halves in her hands.

"Are you okay?" Amanda asked.

"Yes." Lacey sighed angrily and slammed the pencil halves into her wastebasket. She put her hands over her eyes briefly and then in her lap. "Sorry."

"Don't apologize," Amanda said, "I hope I'm not making you all insane with this Pueblo thing."

"No," Lacey said. "It's me. I've gotten into old movies at two A.M. Why I don't get a VCR and tape the damned things . . ."

Danny Rosetti came into the office at that moment and stopped dead as his quick eyes took in the emotional tension. "Uh oh, did I pick a bad time?"

Amanda smiled, glad of Danny's intrusion. "No, Danny. We're just being exhausted and overwrought."

Danny pushed a hand through coal-black, tightly curled hair and shook his head. "I'm *past* overwrought. I came lookin' for you because I've got the bid all worked out, I *think,* and I want your okay on it. No big hurry."

Amanda stared at him and they both laughed. She threw her arm around Danny's broad, shirt-sleeved shoulders and squeezed him close. "You're marvelous. I don't know why I don't go to bed with you."

"He's engaged," Lacey said.

Danny looked with irritation at Lacey. "It was a *joke*."

"How defensive!"

Danny realized he'd overreacted and shook his head sheepishly. Amanda kissed his cheek, which was rough from a bad shave, and smelled his Old Spice. Danny Rosetti, she thought, might be the only male in the interior design trade who used Old Spice. But then Danny was an accountant, not a designer, a boy from the streets of Flatbush who'd used his fists and his brain to work his way through college and into a glamour industry. Danny rolled with the punches, sometimes came up bloody and bruised, but wouldn't back down. Amanda loved him like a crazy brother who reminded her of herself as a kid.

"I've got time to look at the figures," Amanda said. "They'd better be good."

Danny shrugged. "They're competitive. We can't lowball them and then make it cheap."

"No," Amanda concurred. She sighed, sipped coffee. "I'm really edgy about this. I keep thinking that Helen Tennyson is famous for getting low bids from firms who want to be linked with her, and how some of those firms went bankrupt." She could feel her blood racing. "This is not productive. We know Helen Tennyson is no saint, and we know she can make us number one." She patted Danny's cheek. "Don't worry, baby. We won't prostitute ourselves."

Danny flashed a smile. "I don't mind prostitutin' myself, I just want to get paid for it."

Amanda tousled her hair. "Well, I'm glad to see you got your prurient mind off your fiancée. I thought I was going to have to write you off after you got engaged."

Danny shrugged. "Hey, you know how it is. You get engaged, you go shoppin' all the time. She's pickin' out bathroom towels today."

Lacey swiveled in her chair. "I suppose you wipe *your* hands on your pants."

Amanda caught the rage behind Lacey's bantering and made a mental memo to have a heart-to-heart with her. "All right," she said. "Danny, ply me with your budget. Lacey, get the brush moving. We have a presentation to make."

Lacey sighed and said, "Right-o," as she returned to her drawing board. Amanda followed Danny into the corridor. Her nerves and brain cells were gearing up for lunch with this powerful and unknown man. Nothing could stop her from proving herself.

Once Amanda knew she had a job to start, she eased into her rituals the way she eased into a bubble bath. She never had to think about what to do; it all came naturally, including the procrastination at the start. She had to hit the sidewalks first, to clear her head and start the creative solutions cooking. That meant a brisk stroll along Fifth Avenue just to soak up the expensive ambiance. Today she left her apartment in a beaded sweater and silk pants, not a working outfit, because she knew she wasn't going to work. She was freeing her spirit, tuning up.

Already, as she strolled purposefully past reflective windows and listened to the grind of traffic in the streets, she was working. Her eyes, amber looking from dusky gold powder shadow, gulped colors, textures, and shapes—from the hot frocks in designer store windows to the silvery prisms of Steuben's display, she saw with an artist's vision. Always, even as a screwed-up kid, Amanda had seen more than anyone else. When a thundercloud moved over a summer sky and the sun lanced golden highlights against the gray, she would cry out with the beauty of it. When a cherry-red pickup truck passed under a yellow and pink sunset, she felt pain along with the creative glow the scene created for her.

Her desire for creating beauty had only gotten worse. Or better? Sometimes she wasn't sure. There wasn't any rest, for certain. As long as her eyes were open, they saw the world richly and intensely. As long as her tapered fingers touched fabric, their nerves felt ridges, bumps, silkiness, and grain. Her skin differentiated between warm Gulf breezes and stinging Canadian wind; between densely-crystallized snow that fell dry and sugary, and fat, wet snow that folded over the nose; between heavy summer air that seemed laden with pollution, and brilliant winter air that could shatter like glass. Amanda's senses pulsed, reacting to every stimulus. It was like always being on mind-expanding drugs, without the crash and without the hurt.

So Amanda took her long walk, stopping at some favorite discount houses and vintage clothing stores, and even a couple of designer showrooms where she knew and patronized the big-name designers. She had bright, warm hellos for the salespeople and she tried on loads of scarves and belts, because when she began a big commission, she loved to mix and match different shapes and colors.

Back in her apartment, ignoring the sweeping view of the park, she sat on a high wooden stool and sewed beads onto a tunic, saying to herself, for the first of hundreds of times, "I must get started on this thing." This was also part of the ritual. She would circle the job, warily, like a cat stalking a bird—well, no, the job wasn't really her prey. Maybe *she* was the bird. She'd learned not to worry about it because it always mysteriously worked. She spent part of the afternoon at her kitchen table planning a menu for a small dinner party she was giving for some friends. Crudités, she decided, with yogurt dill sauce, and possibly a selection of crepes. She was wonderfully efficient with these domestic chores when she was faced with a big job.

Naturally, planning a menu meant shopping at the butcher, the greengrocer, and the florist, or maybe an early morning jaunt to the flower market. And, looking ahead, there would be a languorous and enjoyable hour or so alone in the apartment searching out cunning containers and arranging the flowers. God, with a little ingenuity, she could avoid working on the Pueblo presentation for weeks. This part of the ritual would go on for a day or two, and all the time Amanda's creative brain would be simmering, the ideas heating up.

Finally, in a self-denigrating rage, she picked up the phone one morning, flicked her hair back behind her ear, and called Turner Associates to see if she could get hold of some information about the site and landscape. That mattered. Level of site, the fall of the ground, the hard landscape of walks, drives and terraces, and the soft landscape of whatever grass and shrub layer there might be, though this would involve desert plants—it all made a difference. And while she was on the phone, she asked about plans. "We'll send over a kit," the cool-voiced woman said on the other end.

"I was hoping for some blueprints, axinometric drawings, renderings," Amanda said. "Something more than a press handout."

"Everything you need will be in there," the ice woman said.

Sure it will, Amanda thought as she hung up. Turner didn't want any designer knowing too much at this stage. Well, she could project from the kit, whatever was in it.

Now Amanda flicked on one of the fluorescent lights in her work area. At her professional drafting desk, she took sheets of stick-on memo paper and scribbled notes to herself. *Lighting,* said one, with three question marks. *Reception Areas,* read another, *Lounges, Central Service Area.* She sharpened pencils and laid out her drafting tools, thinking in pulses now, in flashes of memory. She remembered to ask about conference rooms, kitchens, and bedrooms, and she prepared a vertical dimension chart so she could plan for standing mirrors, cupboard heights, chair heights, and doorset heights. On another sheet of paper she listed bathroom fitting problems, where she would have to know dimensions.

She needed ten minutes to become totally absorbed. That evening she skipped supper and hardly noticed the daylight on the walls turn from brilliant gold to dusty orange to blood red to blue-black with slabs of moonlight. When she did glance over to rest her eyes, she saw a milky moon afloat in a royal blue heaven over the park and the night-ribboned city. The respite reminded her that her head pounded and her body screamed for sleep.

She managed to do another hour of work, taking out of her files the phone numbers of her favorite fabric and furniture houses and plumbing suppliers. She clipped the addresses to her notes so that they framed the drafting table. Before she undressed for bed, she remembered to write *Saunas?* on another pale yellow memo sheet and stick it to the notes on conference areas.

Her next walk in the city found her in raspberry blouse and brown suit with midcalf skirt, a very businesslike ensemble. She browsed the showrooms, fingering bolts and noting what woods and metals and laminates were being pushed. She looked for desert ideas, but with half an eye, and vaguely hoped that she wouldn't see anything she loved already out there. Amanda put a premium on creating her own looks, rather than buying ready-made. She looked over pure tones, tweeds, and red lacquer things that might be interesting in a conference room. She was dutiful, checking seating at Casa Bella, fabrics at Brunschwig, some Japanese cocktail tables at Lorin Marsh. For no particular reason, she looked at antiques at Newel's, and dropped into the D&D Building to see wallcoverings at First Edition and the new collections at Artebella. Everywhere she was greeted with warm arms and warmer smiles, because Bahru had gotten terrific press and of course everyone on the street knew that Amanda was in the running for The Pueblo.

It made her feel terrific, though she knew this was only the beginning, just a stroll-through to get her designing sense attuned. She'd have to check the showrooms in Florida and California and Europe, the art galleries, the auctions, and the estate sales. There'd be many days of window shopping before any notions took root, because she first had to conceive of a look, and a texture and a scheme. But it was helpful to know what was being shown, and to renew her acquaintances.

In her office, she made up files for The Pueblo: color and materials, floor coverings, wall coverings, ceiling coverings, lighting, furnishings, tableware, and works of art. She made another file for graphic design, knowing that it looked impressive to present the client with a distinctive logo. She assigned the files to her staff for preliminary research and reports, and she huddled with Lacey on every aspect. She stood by her office window and looked out, seeing the cityscape as an abstract, jazzy painting as she breathed slowly and felt the knot tighten in the center of her stomach. She hated doing auditions; now she could go only so far, because she had to come up with a presentation, but she knew that her best work came after revision and trial and error. Well, this *was* an audition, whether she liked it or not.

In the days immediately following, Amanda became short-fused and given to odd outbursts. Frequently she emerged from her office and said things like, "Smoked glass panels, chrome-framed movable," or "Tweed panels in green. No, not green, rust. Or both." Lacey and the others on Amanda's staff knew it was a good idea to jot down these ravings but not to pursue them unless Amanda brought the notions up again in a more lucid way.

Amanda lay in bed, her eyes glowing in the darkness, her body tense and needing a massage. She thought that designing was a lonely business, as she supposed any kind of art was lonely. It wasn't like clothes designing at any rate, with the zoo-madness of shows and fitting rooms. The designer madness expressed itself in insomnia, with swirling colors and shapes taunting her. Thousands of details mocked her, and places to visit, calls to make, appointments to arrange. But the rituals had taken their expected course and her skin breathed The Pueblo. Now she would ruin a dinner party if she tried to give it, and she wouldn't make it to the flower market or to Balducci's to buy groceries. Now that she had her steam there'd be no new frocks, no finds at auctions that her dressmaker would whip into knock-'em-dead outfits. Not for a while. Fourteen years earlier, on Byron Moore's estate, Amanda had learned to turn her obsessive need to redecorate the world into a career and an art. She was no less obsessive today, as success swept in her front door and lit up her life.

Amanda was frightened as the time neared for the presentation. She was famous for all the wrong reasons, and only just becoming respected for the right ones. She needed The Pueblo to show everyone that she was for real, that she mattered for herself. It would be another way she could make her life pretty, scrape and sand and strip away the ugliness and refinish her reality. But still, beneath the stomach knots and the headaches and the compulsive snacking on Peanut Butter Cups, and the hard driving office afternoons, Amanda loved to do this. Designing made her feel wonderful.

The files bulged in her office, stuffed with watercolors, sketches, clippings and notes. With great anticipation and joy, Amanda spread them all out and began the job of collating and choosing, of putting together the one set of pictures, plans and proposals that would sell her to Turner Associates and make her the woman to design the interiors of The Pueblo. Lonely it was—at least this part. But nothing, she believed, could also feel warmer or better.

Jason Turner picked the restaurant, a festive place called The Market in the four-story skylit atrium of a midtown tower. After an hour of unhinged rummaging in her double closet, Amanda chose a flowing silk blouse in hot jasmine over a deep blue cotton skirt. She marched into her hairdresser for a summer cut, and he gave her blunt layers with lots of volume and movement, and a hint of wave.

On the morning of the lunch, she had JoAnne phone Turner Associates in the guise of a client asking for Jason. When JoAnne buzzed Amanda that Jason had left for the restaurant, Amanda left her office building and took a cab across town. The summer day was hot but dry, with high white clouds against the blue sky.

Amanda took two deep breaths before she followed the captain into the bustling restaurant. The bright colors and multiplane fiberwork sculpture complimented the banquette seating. *Very nice*, Amanda thought, grudgingly.

She looked at Jason Turner from behind, and grew clammy. She considered herself a tough kid inside the chic shell, but he scared her. She'd seen pictures of him, and knew he was heartstoppingly gorgeous, but in person he was even more exciting. He wore a dark blue suit and sipped what looked like scotch and water. She liked his thick dark hair and his profile. Not a Barrymore face, but good-humored and fetching.

What I love about me is my cool head, she thought wryly. Well, it paid to know that she was vulnerable to his secondary male sex characteristics.

He looked up as she approached the table. "Hi," she said.

"Hello." He stood up, extended a sun-browned hand. She took it. Her eyes locked with his, and his were a beautiful sapphire blue. They twinkled playfully at her from beneath thick eyebrows that matched his moustache. His smile made apples of his cheeks.

"I'm glad to meet you, finally," she said.

"Same here. I keep hearing about you."

He motioned for her to sit. She set her portfolio against the banquette and adjusted her blouse collar. The captain said, "Would you like a drink?"

"San Giorgio with a twist of lime."

The captain left. Jason smiled. "No drinks with lunch?"

"Not when I have to talk business."

Jason regarded the diluted scotch swirling around the ice cubes in his glass. "We're not going to look at sketches today," he said.

She felt the wind knocked out of her. "Oh?"

"This meeting is for me to learn your approach, your outlook, your personality."

"The sketches show that pretty well."

"You show it better. I want to find the *person* behind Amanda Gray Designs."

"L'homme c'est rien, l'oeuvre c'est tout."

His eyes twinkled anew. "You've got me."

She battled the fury churning inside her. "The man is nothing," she translated, "the work is everything."

"You," he said, "are not nothing."

He lifted his glass in salute. She was annoyed by the sense that he was performing, and that he had staged this performance, with the same lines, many times. His magic weakened her, but she knew he was casting a spell.

"Thanks," she said. "But I'm a little unhappy. My people put in lots of overtime coming up with a presentation that I think is a knockout. I'd like you to see what we do."

"In time," he insisted.

She exhaled as the waiter brought her bottle of San Giorgio and an ice-filled glass garnished with lime. He poured the sparkling water into her glass and said, "Would you like to order?" He had an Italian accent.

Amanda sipped at the water and pondered her next move. "What's good here?" she asked Jason.

"I'm having the Porterhouse steak," he said, and glanced up at the waiter. "Medium rare. And a fresh spinach salad." He handed up the velvet-clad menu.

And I can figure out my own lunch, Amanda thought murderously. She picked up her menu with clipped, ferocious motions.

The waiter proved gallant. "If I may suggest the stuffed boneless chicken legs and thighs, filled with a ragout of chicken, wild mushrooms, and livers."

"Sounds marvelous," Amanda said gratefully. "I'll try it."

Jason said, "I'm sticking with scotch, Amanda. Would you like some wine?"

"I'll have a glass of Chardonnay."

The waiter nodded and took away the menus. Amanda linked her fingertips and smiled icily at Jason. "So. What is it you want to learn about me?"

"You're angry," he said.

"Yes. I am."

He leaned slightly toward her, enough to be threatening but not enough to be intrusive. "If I looked at your sketches, and I thought they were wonderful, what would I know? That you can do great sketches? Why you and not someone else? Are you egocentric enough to think that sketches can overwhelm me?"

"I think my ideas are better than most others, yes," she said hotly. "I think that you could tell that."

"You're avoiding the question," he said. "Are the drawings in that portfolio dramatically better than any I've seen so far?"

"How would I know that?"

"Can you *assume* that?"

"It's a ridiculous question."

"It's a pertinent question. This isn't a cereal box contest where you color the clown and win a bike. This is the most ambitious hotel project ever conceived. We're talking about a self-contained city. The Pueblo will have its own airport, its own hospital, a legitimate theater, a post office, a lake. Amanda, don't show me pictures. Show me that you're bold enough, interesting enough, remarkable enough, to carry out this concept."

He leaned back, perspiring slightly. Amanda knew for sure that he was all hocus-pocus and razzle-dazzle, and that this was unprofessional ego-tripping.

But she knew something else, something that troubled her. If Jason Turner was a shark that was fine. She had handled sharks. But underneath the smile and the intimidation, behind the jeweled eyes and the cleft chin, there was another Jason Turner. And that second Jason Turner emitted a profound sadness.

Ridiculous. How could she see that in ten minutes? She was making it up, wanting him to be decent because she was attracted to him. But Amanda had a special sensitivity, and she saw two Jason Turners.

She let her pulse throb a moment before responding to the *first* Jason. "I think," she said, "that this is a phony approach. You want to avoid looking at my work. Maybe you're just tired or bored. I can understand that. I'm small potatoes to you. But I work very hard, Mr. Turner, and I'm very, very good. I thought that was why you cabled me in Bahru." She felt her emotions taking over, and let them. "I'd rather be in an honest cereal box contest than in a personality pageant that's a bunch of baloney. All I can show you at lunch is that I'm intelligent and that I have a pleasant disposition. So if you're not going to discuss my work, and we're not going to accomplish anything, I'd just as soon not be polite for two hours."

She felt her eyes moisten, but she controlled it. She knew she was trembling. She hadn't been this angry in a long time.

Jason regarded her with shock. And at that moment, the waiter returned with their lunch. As they both sat in deathly silence, the waiter uncovered the dishes and placed them on the table. The aroma of shallots destroyed her. Jason's steak sat in its ruby juices, looking wonderful. The waiter put down her wine and a second scotch for Jason and hurried away.

Jason looked down at the food and then looked at her. A puckish smile animated his face. "That's going to be a big doggie bag, Amanda."

It took an instant, but she exploded into a helpless laugh. "I'm sorry," she said. "You were being such a bastard that I lost control."

He pursed his lips. "Nobody ever dumped on me like that. You realize you blew the whole thing."

She nodded. "Yes."

"Was that bright?"

She shook her head. "No."

"Why the hell didn't you play the game?"

"I don't know." She found herself drowning deliciously in his gaze. "You just rubbed me the wrong way."

He looked at his scotch. "Women don't generally tell me off."

"It *was* stupid." She sighed, and took a sip of wine. "What now?"

"What do you think?"

"I think I'm going to be a grown-up girl and have lunch with you, and then go back to my office and try to tell my people that I lost. I'm not looking forward to it."

"Kills your day."

"It more or less kills my year."

He laughed. "I'm really turned on by you."

She looked up sharply. "I'm going to need clarification on that."

He gestured with his hand. "Let me have the portfolio, Amanda. I'll look it over this afternoon. And I'll have a firm answer for you by tomorrow morning."

She felt her stomach heave and then a rush of giddiness. "Is there another shoe?"

He chortled. "Let's eat lunch, Amanda. And let's talk about what we do for fun. Do you play tennis?"

"Yes."

"Go to shows?"

"Yes."

"Sail?"

"Yes."

She was smiling. He smiled back. "Maybe we can do all of that together."

"I'll let you know," she said recklessly.

He carved his steak, forked some into his mouth. He spoke as he chewed, which she found delightfully swinish. "What do you like about me so far?"

She gazed at him with open passion and now, for the first time, she felt the warmth in her groin and breasts that signaled sexual arousal. Not just electric response to his good looks, but honest hunger. She fantasized him naked, and found the fantasy too steamy. She became intensely aware of her open throat.

"I like that you call me Amanda and not honey," she said. "And I like that you haven't asked about Byron Moore."

She noticed the flicker of danger in his eyes at that, but it passed so quickly she ignored it. "So I'm doing okay."

"You're doing pretty good *now*."

"I'm crazy about you."

"I can understand that."

They laughed, and the rapport was like warm sauce on good food. Amanda felt the glow of the wine, and looked into the mountain sky of his eyes. The roller coaster ride ended with relief and a kind of adolescent thrill in her heart.

At ten-thirty that night, Amanda's phone rang. It was Jason. "I *love* it," he said. "You couldn't be more special. How about a sail and lunch on my boat? Thursday at twelve?" She just nodded with the phone at her ear and said, "Sure." He added, "Bring a bathing suit," and hung up. But Amanda got no sleep that night.

chapter 4

JASON picked up Amanda in her office at eleven. Amanda left the afternoon's work in Lacey's care and smirked obnoxiously as JoAnne's eyes stripped Jason. His candy apple red Maserati waited at the curb.

"God, taking off at midday," she said, in the passenger seat.

"Workaholic?" He smiled behind his aviator sunglasses.

"Yes."

"Type A," he said. "I'm Type B."

She glanced at him. "Did I just fail the blood test?"

His smile widened. He wore a striped cotton shirt in navy-blue, and white shorts. She studied his arms as he drove. His biceps were sharply cut, his skin deep brown, with fine golden hairs. Well, of course. No doubt he sunbathed and pumped iron. Type B, indeed. To herself, Amanda hummed the *Jaws* theme.

Aloud, she asked, "Where's your boat?" They headed over the Queensborough Bridge, the traffic light at this hour.

"Montauk."

"You're joking."

"Nope." He gunned the engine impressively. She could feel the red metal of the car heating her skin.

She was tighter than wet rawhide in the sun. God, she hadn't been this nervous with a man in a long time. But she had never been a quick lay in exchange for business—if that's what this was all about. And why had she agreed?

She looked out at the iron latticework of the bridge, at the vista below of sun-shattered river and black smoke curling from red factories. The top was down and a hot rush of city wind stung her nostrils.

"We'll make it in a couple of hours," he told her. "Can you hold out for lunch?"

"Sure." Breakfast had only been at six-thirty. She'd gone to work in a soft white blouse and pedal pushers but she'd packed shorts, top, and bathing suit in a canvas tote. She'd had insomnia thinking about today and about this man. He'd been pompous and imperious so far, but she liked him. The *second* him. Which really made a lot of sense.

"There's a little island," he said. "About five miles off Montauk. My buddy and I own it. No electricity, no water. But it's got a neat cove."

For the exchange of services. And I can't wait.

Off the bridge, he drove under the elevated tracks with shadows of iron curling over his face. He turned down Van Dam Street and entered the Expressway. Once on the wide, white road, he stepped hard on the gas. The Maserati roared through its headers as it sped through Queens.

Amanda put up a hand to protect her hair, which blew anyway. She watched his skin move over his musculature as he shifted, watched his eyelashes flick the sunglass lens when he blinked. She imagined how his tongue would feel in her mouth. Concentrating on lust helped her butterflies.

"Are we there yet?" she asked.

On the way, they stopped at a Howard Johnson's off the expressway. Amanda used the bathroom and Jason bought cokes for them. She liked stunning the suburban customers. He moved with athletic grace. He took off his sunglasses and rubbed the bridge of his nose. Oh, was she ever hungry for him.

She took a calming breath as they went back to the car. In the parking lot, they drew stares. She recalled the lovely part of their lunch, the laughs and the chitchat.

They reached Montauk after one, and drove straight to the yacht club, where he left the car to be parked. He bought Amanda a Gibson at the bar. He had a Heineken. He nodded toward the big window and showed her his boat. It was a 120-foot sloop, clad in gleaming mahogany, its cabins hidden by bronzed windows. She smiled into her drink and felt moisture in the hollow of her throat.

"I'm starved," she said.

"Lunch is on board."

"Good."

Her body ached from the long ride. He was trying to soften her up. Car trek to torture her body, then drinks and seduction. He was so damned practiced, so polished. Was she the thousandth pretty lady to pass through this bar onto that boat? For a moment, Byron's face stared at her, and his cold fingers squeezed her arms. She shuddered and nearly cried out.

"What's wrong?" he asked.

She shook her head. "Nothing." She drank the rest of her Gibson, feeling the ice cubes clink against her teeth. She put down the glass. Polished. Don Juan. And *still* there was that other man, that man she needed to find and touch.

"Come on," she said.

He flipped money at the bartender. His eyes were masked behind the sunglasses. She'd messed up his timetable.

His yacht was christened *The Argonaut*. Excruciatingly clever, she thought. Jason and the Argonaut. Well, he did possess Grecian beauty. Not Grecian sexual tastes, she hoped. Christ, she was getting giddy.

She stood at the rail of the yacht, with gray-blue Atlantic water sliding underneath and the sun burning her shoulders. She'd stripped off the city clothes in a cabin and put on the beach top and white shorts over her bathing suit. She liked the way her breasts filled this suit. Her skin tingled as she imagined herself naked in front of him. Him naked in front of her. She was happy and scared.

She tasted wine. The fruity Beaujolais had gone nicely with the cold stuffed lobster and crusty bread. The air was heavy with salt and the stink of fish, and the water blinded her.

He joined her at the rail. "How was lunch?" he asked.

"Great."

"Really?"

She looked at him. He'd slipped a white cotton jacket over the shirt, and his feet were bare. He had shapely feet, and light hair on his legs. "I ate it, didn't I?"

"I prepared it."

"What?"

He flashed a dimpled smile. "I made the stuffing and did the lobster early this morning."

She popped a small laugh and leaned on the railing. Seagulls screamed and wheeled. "You cook?"

"Yep."

"Do you have a restaurant stove?"

"Something wrong?"

"No, nothing's wrong. I hoped you weren't another one of those trendy guys with restaurant stoves and woks."

"Did you have a bad experience?"

"Oh *Christ*." She glared, then softened. "I'm sorry. The pressure is killing me. I'm crazy for this job. Doing The Pueblo—it's my dream, it's everything. You're the man I have to impress, and I don't know what the hell you have in mind."

She bit her lip as her eyes blurred. He covered her hand with his. So warm. "Look, Amanda. I love the sketches. There's no more selling for you to do. I like *you*. You've got incredible eyes, you know that? They're like green fire. I wanted to be with you. That's all it is."

She felt her face pulsate. She couldn't read his eyes behind his sunglasses. Her eyes didn't feel incredible, they felt burnt out. "You sound so sincere," she said.

"Like I'm handing you a line?"

She nodded.

"Sorry. I can't help my reputation."

"Be straight, Jason. I'm vulnerable."

"Good. Want dessert?"

"What is it?"

"Cheesecake and coffee."

She listened to the throb of the engines. "Did you make the cheesecake?"

"I even milked the cows."

She smiled and grabbed the brass pole with both hands. She leaned her sunhot cheek against the brass and smelled metal against seawind. "Okay."

"Thanks."

She felt terrified and euphoric. She hadn't loused up her shot at The Pueblo. She also hadn't deciphered her feelings. He was under her skin, but she didn't know why.

His island was scrubby, the sand textured with tiny polished pebbles and dried debris. It smelled of pine. The wind came strong and stiff from the west, blowing heat and sun at Amanda. She'd taken off her clothes on the boat and stood barefoot now in her bathing suit. Sea blue with multicolored stripes. She was almost blushingly aware of the high cut at her thighs and the plunging neckline.

The yacht was moored at the leeward tip of the island, out of sight. Jason walked to where she was. The sun loved his trained body. He wore a startling white bikini that bulged temptingly between his thighs and molded his rear. He squinted into the distance, minus sunglasses. His eyes were dark pools, his damp, fragrant hair glistening.

She let her eyes run deliciously over him. He was no musclebound oaf. His length, his meaty leanness, showed an active man. Running, racquetball, swimming. The works.

"Come here," he said gently. She squeaked through the sand and winced at broken shells.

He slipped an arm around her reddened shoulders. "Neat, huh?"

She saw flat pewter ocean and distant, greenish Montauk, the lighthouse white and angled. "It's pretty."

"It makes me . . ." He searched for the word. "Mystical. It's like a ghost ship coming to me, picking me up. I'm the survivor, but I don't want to go back."

"That's not a terrifically original image."

"Well, it's how I feel."

"Then go for it." She smiled. His skin felt hot against her. Everything about his allure warned her off. Christ, this guy probably used bronzing gels and skin scrub and had massages. He was so toned, so faceted and sinewed. He smelled broiled and sweet. She wanted his suit off, she wanted his brown nakedness unbroken. She wanted to see his balls, his cock, feel it, hold it. *Damn!*

He took his arm away and leaned against a scrub pine. He pulled a pack of cigarettes from the waistband of his bikini and lit one with a Bic. He tucked the cigarette and lighter back in the waistband, flashing an instant of groin. He inhaled richly.

"You think I bring a girl a week to this island," he said.

"I hadn't thought about it."

"Sure you have."

"Sure I have."

They were quiet, and the feelings flowed through her, heated her skin from inside, hurt her heart.

"I'm fascinated by you, Amanda," he said.

"Thank you."

He expelled smoke through his nostrils and laughed. "Shit, there's not a thing I can say to you."

She smiled. "I'm sorry, Jason. You're too beautiful."

His eyes flickered. His chest was cut crisply, deep and wide. "You're different," he said. "You're ballsy."

"Don't be obnoxious."

"And smart."

He came away from the tree. He took another drag on the cigarette. "I'll level with you, Amanda. I know what you said at the restaurant, but I want to know about you and Byron Moore."

Shock and fury washed through her. "You've got to be kidding," she said. "That's why you came on to me? To get off on my childhood, like all the deviate men I've had to live through?"

He threw the cigarette butt into the sand, where it smoldered. "No. But it's in my gut."

"Screw off."

His eyes never left her. "Talk to me, Amanda. What did that old shit have that made you love him?"

"None of your business."

"Come on, Amanda. You want to please Helen Tennyson's architect, right? You had Byron Moore in court. You were front page news. Tell me about it. How did you get free of him?"

Her blood cells were doing a conga line up and down her arteries. "Take me back home, you bastard."

He placed his hands on her arms. *Sizzle sizzle.* "I really need to know, Amanda."

She looked into his murderous eyes. Oh God, it hurt. "There's no big secret, Jason. I was sixteen, and my adoptive parents were icebergs. I was a stinker."

"How?"

His hands slid to her shoulders, and subtly, with strength that only hinted at what it could do, he drew her closer. An inch of summer air separated them. "Every which way," she said. "We knocked off houses, we dropped acid, we had orgies in the woods. Every kind of teenage horror you can think of."

"Christ," he said huskily. "You stand here like a damned goddess and tell me that. What gave you manners, Amanda?"

"You're really a piece of shit, aren't you?"

"Yes."

Holy cow, here he came. Off guard, she shut her eyes, and his mouth covered hers. His tongue was thick and warm, and he thrust gently and expertly, finding the corners of her mouth, the ridges of her teeth, the pathway to her throat.

She interlaced her fingers behind his neck and rocked her head back and forth under his. His hands pressed the small of her back, moved up to her shoulder blades. She felt her muscles contract and relax under his fingers.

She wet her lips and looked deeply at him. "Leave me alone, you son of a bitch."

"How did you get free of Byron Moore?"

She blinked twice. "What?"

"How did you get free?"

"You're still on that?"

"Yes."

"You're crazy."

"How did you get free of him?"

His fingers deftly unknotted the strap around her neck and she felt the bathing suit loosen. She was trembling. "He knew my parents. He always visited, and one day he made them an offer. I'd live with him and he'd straighten me out."

"And you agreed?"

"Yes, I agreed."

"Why?"

"Stop it, stop it." She lunged for his mouth again, kissed him hard. He forced her head back. "Answer me."

She'd been right. Two Jasons. And this second one was terrified of something and she held the key. If she listened carefully, she could hear the deep rumble of the boat's engines. Jason pushed down her bathing suit, exposing her breasts, and then her waist. She began to hyperventilate. Her breasts felt swollen, pulsating.

"Answer me," he said.

"Oh God . . ."

She watched him cup one breast and press it. Felt the pressure of his palm on her tender skin. She shook her hair back and said, "You know what happened. You read the stories. He straightened me out. I became his mistress. He put me through art school. Damn you."

"More."

"No."

His mouth pursed over her nipple and his tongue roughened it erect. His hand moved down to her belly and she convulsed. He was at the first fringe of hair. His fingers plunged, came back wet. It burned. She tangled her hands in his damp hair and her eyes hung on to his curved copper back. She was drowning, burning. This was not afternoon delight. Jason was inside her skin, hurting. This wasn't working. Too much feeling, too much feeling . . .

He left her, looked at her. "You stopped."

"That's right."

"How did you get free of him?"

A sad rage dulled her heart. "I didn't need him anymore. At the time, I needed him very much. I needed the discipline. I needed to be beaten up, and chained to the bed."

"Shit . . ."

"That's right. Until I studied, or whatever he wanted me to do. Are those the details you want? I've spent years trying to wipe it out. I can sleep without Valium, sometimes, and that's a big thing, Jason. Does it turn you on?"

He exhaled with self-loathing, stepped away, and lit a second cigarette. It was done. Nothing would happen. She saw him through a wavering film. "It was a stupid come-on," he said.

"It sure was," she said. "I hope you live to see your looks fade, Jason. So you can't crap on women this way. Decency and sweetness are nice traits in a man, also."

He forced a smile. "That's twice you've bawled me out."

"Well, you don't learn anything."

He smoked in silence for a moment as she stood half-naked and ashamed. "You've been through hell."

"Are you trying again?"

"No."

"Yes, I've been through hell. A long time ago. I'd like to go back to the boat now."

She pulled her bathing suit back over her breasts and reached behind her neck to tie it up. Jason stepped forward to help, cigarette jiggling from his lips. She looked up at the humid sky and battled her frustration. Her body was on fire.

He said, "Amanda, let's have dinner tonight."

"I have work tomorrow."

"Here in Montauk. Hell, it's probably six o'clock already."

She couldn't help smiling. "I'm still digesting your gourmet lunch."

"We'll go to Gurney's. Crab claws and champagne. We're celebrating, remember?"

"Drop it, Jason."

"Come *on*, Amanda. I screwed it up. Give me a chance to make it good."

She spun to look at him. His face was aglow with sunset, his body hammered brass. "For Christ's sake, *why?* What does it matter?"

"Because I need to make you like me. I need that."

She fought for breath. His words went under her bathing suit, into her vagina, around her throat. Sincere? Could she ever know?

"All right," she said.

"All right what?"

"I'll have dinner. Otherwise, you won't drive me home."

"Great. Let's shower."

She lingered in the sudden chill, and the desolation of the island. The distant lighthouse threw a yellow searchlight into the violet fog. She was alone with him. And with herself. She had nearly made love to him, had wanted it so much. He'd ruined it. A man who *never* ruined lovemaking. And a lady who never got involved. And the both of them had screwed up their first date.

She took his offered hand and pushed a strand of hair out of her eye as she walked in the sand with him. Red waves lapped at the mud.

chapter 5

A Rolls Royce Silver Shadow drove Byron Moore and Heather between the gates of the West Hills Sanitarium in Westchester County. Climbing yellow roses lined the driveway, and drifting clouds of pink azaleas framed the white antebellum mansion.

Byron looked out the tinted window and gestured with one hand. "Look at that," he said huskily. "The beauty . . . my God, my God . . ."

Heather was frightened by his intensity. She drew her bare knees up to her chest and her sneakers scuffed the upholstery.

"It's pretty," she said.

He exhaled sadly. The Rolls stopped in front of the mansion. "This house was built in 1725," Byron said. "Neglected after the Civil War. Bought by the Clifford family and restored. Amelita Clifford designed the gardens. Ten thousand pansies are grown from seed every year. Do you *care*, Heather?"

She shrugged. "I guess so."

He looked at her with disgust. "You stupid bitch."

Instinctively, Heather's hand flew to protect her face. "Don't—"

"I'm not going to hit you. Why don't you open your mind? *See* things!" He put his hands on her cheeks, and held her face lovingly. His eyes scorched her face. "You're blind. Do you understand that you're blind, Heather? Your spirit is crippled. Listen to me, baby. There are such wonders . . ."

Heather trembled under his hands. Byron kissed her puzzled mouth. Her lips parted for him, and her tongue flickered. She shut her eyes and her hands covered his.

Byron whispered, "Stay here. You can't come with me."

She nodded, and nuzzled his hand.

Byron got out and slammed the door shut. Heather sat in shadow, curled and quiet, as she watched him walk up the stairs to the portico.

A few moments later, Byron walked in the gardens behind the mansion with an expensively dressed doctor. "Is she walking outside?" he asked.

The doctor was a thin-faced, stocky man with florid cheeks. "By the lagoon."

"No new problems?"

The doctor glanced abstractedly at the screen of oaks and pines. "There's pain, of course, but she doesn't know yet that she has a tumor."

"Don't tell her."

"Of course not."

Byron lit a cigarette. "How long will it take?"

"A few months. It won't be long."

"Will it be ugly?"

The doctor looked at him. "It's always ugly, Byron."

Byron regarded the doctor with contempt. "You assume I don't give a damn. She means a great deal to me. She's beautiful, and for her to die in such a disgusting way . . ."

"We can make it easier for her. She'll die with dignity."

"You don't comprehend dignity."

They emerged above parterred gardens, overlooking scrolls of Podocarpus hedges and multicolored beds of pansies. A white latticework belvedere overlooked the pure blue water of the lagoon.

Byron paused and let smoke curl from his lips. "This is magnificent," he said.

"Yes."

"Henry, you have no appreciation of this. It's nice to you because it cost a lot of money."

The doctor chuckled. "Well, nobody has *your* taste, Byron."

Two women appeared now on the belvedere; one was a nurse dressed in white. The other was a slender, stately woman of fifty. Byron said, "*You* should be blind, Henry, and she should see. If I had the medical knowledge, I would slice out your eyes and give them to her."

The doctor snorted. "Well, I'm sure glad you're not a doctor, Byron."

Byron drew deeply on the cigarette and crushed it on the path. He walked fiercely down the slope and through the riotous gardens, up the steps to the belvedere. Short of breath, he stood with one hand on the white latticework rail.

The blind woman turned her head. She wore stylish sunglasses, and her pale hair spilled to her shoulders. She was dressed in a linen T-shirt and skirt with a white spencer jacket. Sensibly fashionable, as he'd taught her to be.

"Who's there, Alice?" the blind woman asked the nurse.

The nurse looked anxiously at Byron, who shook his head. "Another patient, Mary," the nurse said. "I think he wants to be alone."

Mary nodded. "Oh. All right."

Byron watched her. She looked so elegant in this setting, like the spirit of a mistress long dead. Her skirt drifted in a gust of wind and she put her hands in the pockets.

"It's a beautiful day," Mary said to the nurse.

"Yes it is." Alice was young and buxom, her sandy hair tied in a ponytail.

"Is something the matter?"

"No," Alice said.

Mary's face clouded. "Is something wrong with that other patient? Go on, if he needs you."

"Nothing's wrong." Alice glared at Byron. "I'm a little tired."

"Then why are we out here? I can sit on the portico or lie down for a while."

"It's fine, Mary. I don't mind, really."

Mary turned up her face to catch the wind from the lagoon. "The writing is going so slowly today."

"It'll come."

"I can't seem to sit down and get at it. These headaches are getting worse."

Byron smiled sadly. Mary had written several novels, haunting and gentle. Byron had used his influence to have them published and Mary now had a small but loyal following. None of her readers knew that the author was blind, or terminally ill.

"The sunshine feels marvelous," Mary said. "It warms my blood."

"That's good," Alice said.

Mary laughed. "You don't have to respond to everything I say, Alice."

"Whatever you like."

"Uh oh," Mary said. "You're really getting upset. Please, let's go back. I've got to force myself to work anyway, and you need some rest from *me*."

"I'm sorry," Alice said with feeling. "I didn't mean . . ."

"No more talk," Mary insisted. "In fact, it might be nice to leave this other gentleman to his solitude. Is he still here?"

"Yes."

"Should we say hello?"

"I don't think so."

"Okay. We'll tiptoe past, then, quiet as mice."

Mary offered her arm. Alice guided Mary past Byron. Byron watched her as she passed, observing the clean lines of her body, the patrician beauty of her face.

He stayed on the belvedere until Mary and Alice disappeared around a curve in the path. He lit a second cigarette, then, and smoked it in lonely silence, while he watched the water.

He finished the cigarette and flipped it into the lagoon, where it hissed and sank. With no backward glance, he turned from the scene and walked briskly back to the mansion to say goodbye to the doctor.

Byron slid into the back seat of the Rolls, next to Heather, and slammed the door. The driver started the engine and the car moved luxuriously down the path. Heather sat in a corner and looked at Byron with wide eyes. She touched his arm.

"Be still," Byron said.

Heather withdrew her arm as if it were injured, and held herself tightly.

It frustrated Byron that Heather would never have vision. More than once, he had confided to Amanda some of his own blazing comprehension. "To *know*," he said intensely. "To look into the sky and understand it. Sometimes you have a stunning vision, Amanda, where you can see the earth floating against the night in its wrapper of air, all of it blue and white. Then you see from the earth, and you know it's the same sky and you've seen it from both sides. You know you're breathing ozone and oxygen but a few miles up there's nothing at all to breathe. It's just an air tank, a limited supply. Sometimes I can't breathe at all when I think about it. Do you *get* all this?"

And Amanda—*only* Amanda—would nod quietly in the gathering dusk and hold his hand tightly and say, "Yes, I understand."

She did understand. Perhaps Mary had understood too, on a more basic level. But Amanda knew what Byron knew, and saw what drove him to the brink of madness again and again. Heather was blind stupid. She never thought or cared about anything or anybody older than yesterday. She thought Byron was a hunk, and exciting because he was an older man, and she luxuriated in the things he gave her. Realizing it didn't make Byron feel better. What did it make him, an aging roué? A painted gigolo content to be suckled by a nymphet?

He needed more. He'd always needed more, which had moved from nothing to everything. As a tough, sullen kid in the Bronx, he'd ranged the hot, war-empty streets and screwed up in high school. The principal would call him down and lecture him. "You're smart, Moore," he'd say, "smart enough to go to college. Why do you throw it away?"

Byron, the flint-eyed, taut-skinned teenager, would only turn his handsome face aside and shrug, angering the principal. There was no stern father at that point to knock sense into the fresh kid. Byron's father was a drunken wife-beater who worked in the fish market. He'd come home at night stinking and roaring, and plunge his brawny arms and red face into the sink full of water. It was never quiet or pleasant when he was home. He cursed his poverty all the time, and if one of his kids crossed him, he opened the child's face with the back of a hand.

Byron knew, from the time he was four, that his father abused his wife. Even now, Byron could remember stinking summer nights, lying in a sweat-soaked bed or out on the fire escape with the clash and belch of city noise, and hearing his mother's screams of pain, and the rhythmic, fleshy thump of fist against skin. Even now, Byron could hear the grunt of his father's breath and smell the liquor. He could remember shivering, even in summer heat, and crying until his body trembled. His hatred for his father became a reason for living. Often, Byron would sass the huge man, or get into trouble at school, just so the bastard would paddle Byron's ass until it bled. Byron proudly and defiantly wore the livid bruises, the shut and swollen eyes, and the fractured bones. They were his merit badges, and his training scars. He required the pain and the terror, so he could grow.

Sometime before Byron reached thirteen, his father disappeared. Byron's mother told the neighbors that her husband had enlisted in the service. Byron stood one fall night in slanting moonlight and smashed his fist into a brick wall again and again until the hand was pulp. He had been cheated of his revenge on the man. As Byron's hand slowly healed, he nursed his frustration. He'd never hated being poor; he liked the heat and danger of the streets, the noise and stink of crowded tenements, the smells and tastes of pushcarts and shops. He worked as a newsboy and a candy butcher at the movie theater. He made deliveries for local junk dealers and watched some of them grow rich in war profiteering. He ran errands for gangsters, who were amused at the lean kid's daring and resourcefulness. Byron didn't scare easily and boredom was his enemy; he stripped the library shelves of books and read everything, whether he understood it or not. He bolted down history, literature, science, and art. His life of poverty provided ample opportunity for action.

No, it was not the poverty that gripped his chest and shut his throat in anguish. It was the lack of control over all the nights he could do nothing to protect his battered mother and brother and sister; all the days he could not escape stifling schoolrooms. He saw how the gangsters and politicians made things happen their way. He saw how bulldozers tore down whole neighborhoods when a distant man named Moses snapped his fingers. He saw how fat, cigar-smoking union bosses crooked a pinky and began or settled strikes. He saw how the billionaires who lived in the splendid estates on Long Island determined how millions of lives would be spent. Though he despised school, Byron became a fervid student of history and sociology. He comprehended what he oberved, and saw how the life of the streets was controlled by what happened in granite office buildings and limestone mansions. He saw that money could bring powerful men to their knees and raise up scum. He learned that everything could be sold and that people could be made to want anything.

At the same time, the complex and tormented young man developed an appreciation for art; art, after all, represented control over color, line, and nature itself. He could draw swiftly and competently, though he never took the time to study or perfect his technique. He would stand for hours and watch buildings go up. He'd study moldings, cornices, and gargoyles, patterns of brick, the geometric designs in courtyards. Sometimes, not knowing why, he'd hop a subway train and visit museums. He caught stares from uniformed guards, but never spoke or caused trouble. He just wanted to sit on stone benches in marble halls and gaze at framed oils. If no guard was nearby, he'd run his fingers over sculptures. In some primitive way, he understood the concepts of art. He saw the art in life, made connections between events, put random happenings into patterns. Byron did not know he was highly gifted; such terms were not used then for children. Not until years later did he know that his I.Q. was nearly 200.

He only knew that as he passed his adolescence, his frustration grew like a ravening cancer. His sullen defiance became violent at times. He'd pick fights, often with gangs of boys. He fought like a dervish, often whipping four or five opponents. Sometimes he got kicked and mauled so badly he needed days in the hospital to recover. He welcomed the humiliation and pain. With every joint aching, he'd strut into the gutters and ask for it again. Soon none of the toughs would bother him; he was crazy, and a crazy man was too dangerous to fool with.

Girls adored Byron. They couldn't resist his dangerous, brooding handsomeness, his tortured eyes, his muscular body, or his inarticulate rage. He was the clenched rebel who would, in a few years, find embodiment in Brando and Dean. He accepted the easy caresses and frightened lips of local dolls, with cold indifference. The sex relieved him physically, but he became disgusted with the clinging and whimpering of the girls afterward. Sometimes he grew angry enough to hit them, and he found that bloodying their mouths or blackening their eyes made them even more devoted. This reminded him of the stupid, masochistic devotion of his mother to his father, and Byron began to hate all women as useless, pitiful dopes.

But one day, he saw a girl in the Metropolitan Museum of Art, and pursued her. She was fine and delicate-boned, a beautifully dressed woman in her twenties. Her hair was immaculately coiffed, her lips a pert slash of red, her eyes intelligent and amused.

Byron opened a conversation with her about the Delacroix paintings they were viewing, and the girl stared at him, first with ill-concealed laughter and then with riveted interest. She invited him for lunch, and he accepted. By late afternoon, they were naked in her Park Avenue bedroom and her cool ivory hands stroked the length of his street-dark skin with panting excitement. For the first time, Byron felt emotional response. His heart pounded and he flushed with perspiration. She pushed him down into sheets softer and whiter than anything he'd ever seen, and she tutored him in the arts of lovemaking, until vermilion sunset flooded the windows. Byron climaxed in minutes the first time and turned away, red with shame. She consoled him and coaxed him with her hands and mouth to ecstasy he had not thought possible. She showed him how to fuck her with control and finesse, and he showed her what it was like to be assaulted by a jungle cat. She seemed to want that the most.

He spent the night with the rich woman, and in the morning she awakened him with the smell of eggs and bacon. He sprang up, nude and hard, and looked at her in her robe, smiling domestically at him. In a rush, he felt nauseated and used. His hands lashed out and she screamed in surprise as the pan flew from her hands and clanged against a wall. Egg yolk stuck to the floral wallpaper. He left her rocking back and forth on the bloodstained rug. He walked the streets near his home for hours, trying to comprehend. He knew then what kind of woman he needed and that hurting would always be as important to him as loving.

Danny Rosetti swallowed the last of a can of beer and shook his head, doglike. He was in Southhaven Park on Long Island, on a hot, cloudless Sunday. With a spatula, he overturned hamburgers on a rusted charcoal grill. His yellow tank top and jogging shorts hugged a muscular, powerful body. His shoulders were ridged with pink sunburn. Around him, children shrieked and radios blasted rock music.

A vivacious, dark-haired girl came over to Danny with a plate of franks. "Here," she said. "Put these on, too."

Danny snorted. "What are we feeding, the fifth regiment?"

The girl laughed. She was lean-hipped and small-breasted, with a sinuous grace. Her striped top and shorts showed smooth, dark skin.

"Everyone's hungry," she said. "What can I tell you?"

"Jesus." He picked up each frank with his thumb and forefinger and threw it on the grill. Smoke poured up in thick columns. Danny tossed the beer can into a close-by garbage pail and grabbed the girl around her waist. "When do we get some time together?"

She kissed his mouth. "Probably never."

He sighed. "I don't like big picnics. Too noisy." He glanced around. "Who the hell is playing that radio?"

"Oh, who cares? There's eight million people here today. Enjoy it."

"Sure." He looked at her with comical disgust. "Terri, I'm being a terrific guy, but when we're married, screw the family picnics. Except *our* family."

"Oh, are we having a family?"

"Sure. I figure three kids."

"You do?"

"Absolutely. Two boys, then a girl."

Terri leaned provocatively against him. "What if I want to go to work first?"

He flipped the burgers. "You don't have to work. I'm doing terrific at Gray Designs."

"Boss likes you, huh?"

"Give it a break."

She threw her arms around him. "You have no sense of humor."

Danny nodded. "I know, I know. There's been a lot of pressure with this Pueblo thing. I had to refigure costs six times already and it keeps changing. Amanda's acting like a bitch. *Damn* it, that radio's a pain in the ass."

Danny looked around, and saw the two teenaged boys with the radio. They were ropy and unkempt, one in a black T-shirt, one in an undershirt, both in faded jeans and sneakers. "Whose side of your family are *they* on?" Danny asked.

Terri glanced over. "I don't know them. I guess they wandered in from somewhere else."

"Yeah, the men's room. We reserved this picnic ground, right?"

"Oh, Danny, don't worry about it."

The flames crackled under the burgers and franks, and Danny began to flip them onto the waiting platters. "Yeah, okay. Let's go eat this stuff."

Each carrying a plate of cooked meat, they headed for the long picnic tables. They passed close to the teenage boys, and Danny clenched his teeth.

One of the boys said, "Nice ass, baby."

The boys laughed a dirty laugh. Terri drew in a breath and held Danny's arm tightly. Danny kept walking as the boys sniggered. He put down the platter of hamburgers on the table and said, "I'll be right back."

"Danny . . ."

Danny headed for the boys, with a throbbing pulse in his head. He saw the boys looking at him with snide expectation. Danny's temper quickened his walk.

He reached out and gripped Undershirt's arm, yanking him off the table. In the same motion, he spun the startled boy against a tree. Danny wedged his forearm under the boy's chin, and pressed hard.

"You got a big mouth, scumbag."

Undershirt's chest heaved, trying to get air. T-shirt came off the table and grabbed Danny around the neck. Danny heard Terri's scream. He knew a crowd had gathered. T-shirt was strangling him. Danny managed to turn around and heave backwards to crush T-shirt against the tree. He jerked forward and slammed back again.

T-shirt's grip loosened. Danny ducked out, pivoted, and lashed out with his fists. T-shirt put up his hands but never got the chance to fight back. The boy's nose split open, gushing.

Then strong hands were pulling at Danny. He strained against the arms, cursing. T-shirt was restrained by other men. Danny heard voices telling him to cool it.

Finally, the red fury subsided and Danny caught his breath. His knuckles pulsed with pain. T-shirt was being hustled away and Danny thought he saw Undershirt too.

Terri was at his side, trying not to cry. "Danny, you asshole."

Danny glanced at her. "Nobody opens a filthy mouth to you."

She shook her head. Then she gently hugged him, trying to find uncut places to kiss his face. "They didn't hurt me," she whispered. "You can't be crazy like that. My Uncle Joey's trying to convince the park patrol not to throw us out."

He tasted warm blood, and spat it on the ground. "Throw *us* out? And not those dirtbags?"

"You were looking for a fight," she said. "You wanted a goddamn excuse." She stopped herself. "Your company is in the news, Danny. You can't get into fistfights."

Danny knew she was right, but he was too emotional to give in. "I grew up on the streets. I learned you have to kick ass. You think I'm an animal, go to hell."

Jesus, he was yelling at her. In front of her family. He said, "Shit," then stalked over to the big barrel that held cans of soda on ice. He dipped his head into the barrel and scooped ice water over his battered face.

He picked up his head, and wiped his eyes. "Do I look bad?" he asked her.

"You look horrible," Terri said. "You're all cut up."

Her face was suddenly streaming with tears. Danny put his swollen hands on her arms, and she went rigid. "Get the hell away."

He moved his hands onto her shoulders, around her neck. Her hair was hot from the sun, and smelled of charcoal. He kissed her wet cheek. He kissed her eyelids, her chin, and her mouth. She kissed him back, softly, then urgently. Her arms went around him.

He brushed her hair with his hand. "I'm sorry. Okay? Listen, I went nuts. It's cookin' all those hamburgers. I got smoke poisoning." She looked at him with glistening eyes. "I love you, Terri," he murmured. "I love you more than my life."

Finally, she stopped crying and smiled at him. "I can't take you anywhere."

She laughed through her tears. He smiled back. "Let's eat the goddamn hamburgers," he said.

chapter 6

FROM the airport, Jason and Amanda drove to the site of The Pueblo. Amanda sat in the passenger seat of the Olds Cutlass and looked at Jason through her sunglasses. Nothing had been said about their first date. They'd had dinner that night, and cut it short because they'd run out of conversation. Jason became withdrawn and drove her home in silence. She remembered being miserable.

Today was business—a visit to the site so she could get ideas. Jason had not talked on the plane, so she'd read magazines and looked out at the clouds.

"How far?" she asked him now.

"About fifty miles once we get out of town."

She looked out the window. Sun-baked streets slid past, with their commercial buildings, signs, cars, people. Then neat residential dwellings, and then, suddenly, they were in open desert and the sky was enormous and overpoweringly blue.

"So empty . . ." Amanda murmured.

"Look," Jason said. "I'm sorry."

Her head snapped around. "What?"

"I'm sorry about what happened in Montauk. It was a lousy start."

She wondered how to react to this sudden overture. She had smothered her feelings for him, which was like pinning a bird who wanted to fly. She watched her hands in the lap of her white belted dress. Her body strained against the cotton.

"I'm not upset about it anymore," she said.

"Good." His voice sounded unsure. He looked businesslike in a tan cotton suit, but she remembered his nakedness underneath, his long muscles and burnished skin.

The car burned up miles on the wavering ribbon of road. In the distance, rugged mountains swept up from the flats. The horizon glimmered in the relentless light.

"Rain," she said softly.

"Say again?"

She smiled. "Rain makes the shapes of the desert. It rushes down the mountains and bites into the rock. Rain and wind. And the sediment makes alluvial fans at the foot of the mountain. Do you use shapes in your thinking? I do."

"You've researched this," he said.

"I should think so. Haven't you?"

He smiled. "I'm intuitive."

Something gnawed at her, but eluded her. She returned his smile. "I guess it was a stupid question. You have computers and hundreds of experts to research an area. Geologists, meteorologists. I've read about *you*, too."

He adjusted his sunglasses. "I'm impressed."

"No." She weighed the risks. "I think you're angry. What is it, Jason? What's eating you up?"

He chuckled. "Now *you're* getting nosy."

"All right, yes. I'm nosy. Goddamn it, Jason, we almost made love. I wanted you. I *know* lots of women want you. I know it's nothing new. But it's important to *me*."

Jason didn't answer, but she knew he was thinking about her. They drove on a dry lake floor, past rock and gravel tinged with saltbush and mesquite. Sand gusted across the natural pavement, blown by wind that polished and rubbed the desert smooth. The blazing heat refracted light and the sky shimmered like ghostly water on the road.

"I got crazy," he said, finally. "Thinking of you and Byron Moore."

"Why?"

"Because he's a sadist. A drooling, abusive son of a bitch who likes to own people. I couldn't stand the thought of him owning *you*, and making you do disgusting things."

Her heart jumped. "I don't know what to say, Jason. It's wonderful of you to be so angry, but you'd just met me."

"I know."

"How did you know *I* wasn't abusive and disgusting?"

"You're not."

"Well of course not, but you didn't *know*—"

"This is stupid."

He gripped the wheel convulsively. She could smell his tension. "Okay, I won't push it. I don't even know what we're talking about. You know, I was a little disappointed, too. I thought you were horny because I looked good, not because I was once tortured. I've been through that too many times. There are sick men out there. It can be scary in a bedroom, alone with a sick guy."

"Do you know a lot of men?" he asked.

Oh Jesus. She leaned back against the seat and shut her eyes, then looked at him. "Is this going to be a bad scene?"

He smiled. "I'm being jealous."

"Oh." She shifted sideways to see him better. "I was promiscuous twice in my life. Before I went to live with Byron, and just after I left him. I'm not promiscuous now. I have boyfriends, but I don't pick up men in bars."

"You were pretty eager with *me*."

"What are you saying, that I'm a slut?"

"You sure acted like one."

"My *God*. I don't *believe* this. You didn't take me to that island to make it with me?"

"You could have refused."

She made an exasperated noise and faced front. "You're an asshole."

"Yes," he said agreeably. "But let's stay with *you*, Amanda. Admit that you were seducing me out there. Your eyes said it. Your body said it. You wanted to ball me from the moment I picked you up at your office."

"And *you* wanted prayer and fasting?"

"Never mind what I wanted. You made an assumption about me. And you said yes before I asked."

The nasty truth kicked her under her ribs. "What is all of this leading to, Jason? Are you a closet evangelist?"

That made him laugh. He looked at her, fully, for the first time since they'd boarded the jet. His look made little eddies in her stomach. He turned back to the road.

"I am thrilled that you're having a good time," she said.

He laughed again.

She exhaled in loud fury and crossed her arms over her chest. He chuckled infuriatingly to himself. Then he worked a cigarette from his shirt pocket and lit it as he steered with one wrist. He tossed the burnt match out the window.

"You won't believe me if I'm straight with you," he said.

"Try it."

"I liked you as soon as you said hello. I liked you more and more every minute after that. You're attractive. You're sexy. You're smart. You're talented. You're a hell of a lady."

She melted like ice cream on the back porch. "I still don't know where you're coming from."

"From a long, long exile," he said with fervor. "I mean, this wasn't fireworks or violins. Just a realization that I felt something I hadn't felt for a long time. I wanted to be with you, Amanda. I was a wreck when I opened your portfolio. I prayed to God your sketches were great."

Calm, Mandy. This is not happening. "Jason, if this is a line—"

He licked ash from his lip. "Does this mean you're interested?"

"You're so smooth. How in hell do I know what you're saying?"

"You want rough? I'll give you rough." He made a grotesque, leering face, and growled, *"I loves ya honey, I loves ya!"*

She stared at him, then laughed. She put her hands to her face. "This is sunstroke. It has to be."

Her throat ached, and her stomach had dropped out a few miles back. She looked helplessly at Jason and let her feelings bubble up and spill out. She hungered for him now, and hung by a thread of self-control.

"I care for you, Amanda," he said quietly. "I need some time with you. I need to know you. Will you spend some time with me?"

She nodded, crazy-happy. When he looked at her, she laughed and said, "Yes, I'll spend some time with you. Why didn't you say all this before?"

"Because it was too soon. I wanted to protect my rear."

"Leave your rear open," she said. "And the rest of you, too."

"Don't make me stop the car here."

"Why not?"

"Because we'll die, you jackass."

She leaned over and kissed his cheek and his ear, then sat back, pounding with need. She'd have to keep this in perspective.

Perspective my ass, she thought giddily. *I've got The Pueblo and I've got him. What the hell can go wrong?*

"Jesus Christ!" he yelled.

Her eyes snapped open. "What is it?"

"Look."

Amanda adjusted her eyes to the unexpected scene. She saw a big sign announcing the site of The Pueblo. Clustered around the sign were Indians. Some wore brightly colored shirts, beads, and feathered bonnets. Others were dressed in everyday shirts and jeans. Cars and pickup trucks were parked nearby. The Indians held handpainted sheets and signs.

"Is that the site?" Amanda asked.

"Outskirts of it. Helen said there might be trouble."

"You knew about this?"

"Well, Helen usually handles it."

"Does she turn hoses on them?"

Jason didn't reply because they had reached the Indians. They were mostly young, teens to late twenties. Jason rolled down his window and smiled pleasantly. "Good morning," he said.

A stocky Indian leaned down and his face filled the window opening. "Where you folks headed?"

"Pueblo site."

"We'd rather you didn't go there. We're trying to get people to stay away."

"Why?"

The Indian grimaced, a mockery of a smile. "Take too long to tell you, jack. The Pueblo is going to divide our land, destroy the desert, and kill any chance we got of getting out of poverty. We have some stuff you can read."

"Sure," Jason said. Amanda began to be worried. There were about twenty or thirty of the Indians. The signs and banners said things like NO WHITE MAN'S HOTEL and PUEBLO WILL BURN.

The Indian leader got some mimeographed sheets from another man and passed them through the window. "Here. Now turn around and go back."

Jason tossed the sheets in the back seat and put out his cigarette in the ashtray. "Well, I have to look things over out there. I appreciate your problems, though."

The Indian grimaced again. "You're going to be a hard case."

"Just doing my job."

The Indian stood up and spoke to the others in a native tongue. A teenager kicked the door on Amanda's side. Amanda gasped. Several Indian youths sat on the hood. Others lounged on the rear fenders.

The Indian bent down again. "My people are really mad," he said. "We've been out here all morning, in the sun. Can't get any media coverage. You don't want to get us pissed."

Amanda said, "Jason . . ."

"Quiet," Jason told her. She saw tiny globs of perspiration on his temples. He said to the Indian, "Now, what will you do if I don't listen? Turn the car over? Beat us up? What kind of headlines do you want?"

The Indian stopped smiling. "Look, man. You're not going out there. We're serious, man. Turn the car around."

Amanda's blood pounded. The Indians blocked her view. She felt suffocated; her skin crawled. "Jason, don't be macho."

Jason tapped on the steering wheel. "I have work to do, Amanda. These assholes don't employ me."

The Indian hissed. "You bastard—"

Jason stepped hard on the gas and the Olds lurched forward, throwing off several Indians. But more Indians poured into the path of the car and Jason had to jam on the brakes. "Shit," he swore.

A rock struck the rear window of the car, making a cobweb of shattered glass. More rocks thumped against the car. The Indians began to push the car, side to side. Amanda saw sticks in some hands. "Oh my God," she whispered.

A drone cut through the noise of shouting outside the car and grew louder. Amanda tried to see outside but couldn't. The windows were cracked. But the rocks had stopped. Now she heard shouts. The drone became a whistling roar that shook the ground and made the Olds vibrate.

"What in God's name is it?" Amanda said.

"Chopper," Jason yelled.

Amanda watched sheets of dust whip up outside the car, and in the haze, she saw Indians scattering. The roar was deafening now. Amanda heard the whipping sound of rotors. Now she saw the helicopter, dimly, about fifteen feet away. It was a red and white Bell, with the monogram HT in gold.

"Is that Helen Tennyson?" she asked.

Jason smiled thinly. "Yeah. The cavalry." He lit another cigarette.

"Thank God," Amanda said.

"Oh, come off it. She was *supposed* to meet us here. She knew about this demonstration. She knew she was going to break it up. She's probably been up there the last half hour, planning her grand entrance."

"You sound bitter."

"Not me."

Now the dust was settling in reddish folds, letting through patches of blue sky. The helicopter stood like a giant locust in the desert.

"Come on," Jason said.

He shut off the engine and pushed open the door. Amanda got out on her side. Her legs nearly collapsed as she stood in crushing heat. Her eyes searched for some clue about what was happening. Then she saw the second chopper, this one from the sheriff's office. "Jason," she cried out. "Look!"

He nodded. "I didn't think she'd tackle them alone."

Uniformed police officers, in pilot sunglasses and Stetson hats, had rounded up the Indian dissidents and guarded them with drawn guns. Some of the Indians were choking. The door of the Bell helicopter opened and a tall woman stepped out, so incongruously glamorous that Amanda drew a startled breath.

Helen wore a flared pinstriped shirtdress and her head was wrapped in a white scarf; movie star sunglasses with white frames adorned her nose. Her lips were vibrantly red. She looked around with superb disdain, then stepped onto the desert.

"What an entrance," Amanda said.

"She comes out of the bathroom like that."

Amanda looked swiftly at him and smiled. He squeezed her hand.

Helen Tennyson walked to where Jason and Amanda waited. She smiled perfunctorily and said, "Nearly got your ass handed to you, Jason."

Jason drew on his cigarette. "Can't you keep the rabble out?"

Helen laughed. "We try, dear. Are you Amanda?"

Amanda felt off-balance, like a schoolgirl before the prioress. "Yes."

Helen extended a tapered hand. "Sorry to meet you so dramatically."

"Well, I'm glad you're here."

Helen smirked. "You see, Jason? People *like* me to be around."

She patted Jason's cheek, then abruptly plucked the cigarette from his lips and dropped it. She crushed it under the heel of her shoe. "You're chain-smoking now, do you know that?"

Jason breathed a last wisp of smoke from his nostrils. "It's the pressure."

"My ass." She strode away, to where the police officers guarded the Indians. Amanda tried to signal Jason with her eyes, but Jason didn't see.

Helen studied the Indians, especially the leader who had threatened Jason. She said, "The ones in the warbonnets must feel like absolute jackasses. The rest of you are just sleazy. Now listen: if you threaten my people again, or try to close off my work site, I'll have you arrested, or shot down. Is that clear enough, or do we need smoke signals?"

"Jesus Christ," Amanda whispered.

Jason sucked at his teeth. "Helen likes the aggressive approach."

The Indian leader's forehead throbbed. He said, "You're trying to get us riled up. Forget it. We know the score. We're not stopping. This hotel is not going up."

Helen sighed. "Dedication to the cause. Well, feel free to carry your signs and jerk off. But don't try to interfere. You ought to touch base with your own chiefs. At the last tribal council, it was agreed to work *with* us."

There was derisive laughter, and some cursing. The leader said, "White woman, our tribal council sold us out a long time ago. *We're* the voice of the red man now. And we tell you that your equipment will burn and your workers will be found with their throats cut. *You're not coming in.*"

Whoops greeted this outburst, and impromptu war dancing. Helen trembled visibly. She turned to the nearest police officer. "Get them out of here," she hissed. *"Now."*

The cop looked unhappy with the situation. He began to shout at the Indians to go to their cars and trucks. The Indians kept up the noise for a while, but slowly began to drift away. A lot of fingers were thrust at Helen's retreating back, and a lot of filthy words were flung across the sand.

Helen returned to Jason and Amanda. "This wears me out," she said. "I thought this kind of shit was over years ago."

"Maybe they have a legitimate gripe," Amanda suggested.

"Oh, fine," Helen snorted. "A bleeding heart. My dear, you can listen to their gripes if you like. You can personally service every one of their braves. Just do your job."

Amanda stared, in shock. *Control yourself,* she thought. But she said, "I don't think you have any business talking to me like that."

"I don't?"

"No, you don't. I'm a professional, not your office girl."

Jason said, "Okay, girls, let's not bicker. Too nice a day."

Helen's eyes snapped to Jason. "Oh shut up. I can handle this twat."

Amanda said, "That's about it. My ambition doesn't extend to making a jerk of myself. You can find another designer."

"Wait a minute," Helen said. She took off her sunglasses, revealing smoky eyes. "I'm sorry for the outburst. I'm not a nice lady. I'm distracted by this Indian problem. I'm behind schedule and over budget. All in all, it's been lousy. So I dumped on you. I might dump on you again. If you can live with that, and realize it's absolutely impersonal, I'd like you to stay on. You're about the best I've seen."

Amanda reeled under the perfumed onslaught. This woman was superb. *Of course she is. She controls an empire.* "All right," Amanda said. "I can't say I *want* to quit. I've been dreaming of this. It's just not the way I'd imagined it."

"I know," Helen smiled. She replaced her sunglasses. "It should have been an elegant lunch at Lutece. But this is how it is. At least you've seen me in the raw. And this Indian bullshit is not your problem. You be the artist. In fact, once you've seen the rock pits, stay the hell away from here. We've got a magnificent office suite for you in town. Pamper yourself. You'll find a very generous expense account in your name."

Amanda had to get away from this lady. She was being snowed under. "Thanks," she said. "Don't worry about me."

"I won't." Helen checked her Piccard watch. She glanced over to make sure all the Indians had driven away. The police chopper was making ready to take off. "Well, I've got a meeting in Chicago, so I'm off. Get back in the car so you don't die in the updraft. Nice to meet you, Amanda. You seem a chaste spirit. Try not to violate her, Jason."

Helen turned and walked back to her helicopter. Jason said, "Get in the car," and moved toward the Olds. Amanda waited one more moment, to watch Helen Tennyson. She shivered with a frightening chill.

Jason started the car as Helen lifted off, and he sent the speedometer past sixty. Amanda said, "Jason, could you clarify your relationship with Helen Tennyson?"

"Meaning what?"

"She's horrible to you, and you don't say anything."

"What should I have said?"

" 'Go to hell.' You're not working for her; you design buildings for her. She needs *you*."

"That she does."

Amanda watched the cactus and creosote roll by. The nightmare was over, but the adrenalin kept coursing through her blood. Her pulse kept pounding. Her terror of being killed just now had turned to helpless desire. Her breasts ached, and her thighs tingled.

"I wish I knew what was going on," Amanda said to him. "I wish I knew you."

He swung the steering wheel and pulled the rattling Olds off the road. It thumped and creaked on the rockbed until he stopped.

He turned to her. "We're five miles from the site. Nobody else is coming here today."

"Jason, you're crazy. . . ."

But it was exactly what she wanted. He opened the door on his side, letting in the desert wind. "Open your door," he said.

"I thought we'd die if we did this."

"I didn't want to do it then."

"So you lied."

"Yes. Open your door."

"Jason, we can drive back to the hotel—"

"Open it."

She nodded, and pushed open her door. The wind raced through the car, heating them. He leaned over and his breath reached her an instant before his lips. He coaxed her mouth open and touched his tongue to hers. His hand molded to her throbbing leg and moved under her dress to her groin. Then across the rim of her panties.

"Take off your belt," he told her. "I want to get at you."

She clamped her fingers in his hair and nipped at his chin. "Figure it out," she teased.

He hooked his fingers in the blue and yellow belt. He yanked her against his body. "Undress."

She gasped at his strength. He let her back down. With shaking fingers, she undid her belt and slid it off. The dress loosened. Jason pushed the white cotton up her flanks, over her naked breasts. With one hand, he cupped her breast and squeezed. His lips were at the nape of her neck, and his tongue explored the warm cave of her ear. She stroked his hand, pushing it harder against her breast. She swelled to fill his palm.

He sat up and she crossed her arms to lift the crumpled dress over her head. She could hear the cackle of some desert creature. She let the discarded dress drift to the carpeted floor of the car, and she writhed in her panties. Her skin stuck to the leather of the seat.

"Now you . . ."

He undressed with swift movements, unknotting his silk tie and whipping it from his throat. He unbuttoned his plaid cotton shirt, baring a tempting inch at a time of dark brown chest. He shrugged off the jacket and tossed it into the back seat. He unbuckled his thin alligator belt with a yank and unzipped his trousers. She felt her blood banging in her neck. The memory of his gleaming skin and arrogant beauty took the wind from her lungs.

She felt her body grow inside, pushing against her skin. "Touch me," she pleaded.

Suddenly he was naked, and she saw him complete, smooth and tigerish. He pushed her down on the seat and she braced herself against the open door with one arm. Her other hand cushioned her head. She closed her eyes against the blinding sun. His powerful arms went around her waist. He tongued her nipples, first one, then the other, teasing each into erection. His lips and his silken moustache dwelled between her breasts, then below them, dropping sweet kisses on every inch of her skin. He paused below each rib, brushing with his lips, making small circles with his tongue. She panted as she spread her legs apart and his chest pushed down on her vulva.

"Yes," she breathed. "Please. Please."

She saw nothing but the impression of swirling red sun against blackness. The universe was Jason's mouth and his damp tongue, now swirling in her navel, now lacing her belly, now hovering at the first fringe of downy hair.

She let out a long, sobbing cry as his fingers parted her and he sucked gently at her throbbing sex. Ecstatic pain spiraled and she pulsated at his touch. His tongue tip was an artist's brush, plunging into her wet recesses, painting her with her own juices. He suckled her organ, then kissed, then swirled, faster and faster.

Her pulse became a drumbeat, then a hundred drumbeats, spiraling down through her body and spurting through her legs like liquid fire. She flooded his mouth and heard herself screaming.

Her eyes fluttered open, but she saw only a blur. She reached blindly for him. "Jason . . ." she mouthed.

She forced him back, upright against the seat. She lifted her leg over him and straddled him, so that her thighs locked against his buttocks. Her hands draped his powerful shoulders and her fingers pressed his tense muscles. She touched her lips to his and tasted herself. His hands caressed her ass, curving to the tender flesh. She filled her eyes with the rigid manhood jutting from the dark thatch between his legs.

She had no strength. She pressed lightly on his tip and felt herself split over him and slide down. He filled her thickly and with oiled smoothness. She kissed him passionately as she rotated her hips, forcing herself against him again and again, rubbing herself into new orgasm.

She threw back her head and hung onto his shoulders as she rode him harder and faster. Gasping, she could feel him quiver and hear his own grunts of pleasure. A ball of flame burst open in the pit of her stomach and exploded downward in white heat. His knotted back went rigid under her fingers. Every beautiful muscle tightened at once, and his hands dug hard into the flesh near the base of her spine. She cried out as he convulsed, and licked her lips as his warmth coursed through her. He throbbed ever more gently, and then not at all.

She couldn't sit up anymore. Tenderly, she climbed off him and they both lay down on the seat, so that her cheek rested on his belly, and his head lay pillowed in the crook of her thigh. She felt wind rush over her sex. She toyed with his earlobe.

"It was so beautiful," she said.

"You were very special."

She smiled, her eyes peacefully shut. "I love your body. I love the sensation of each muscle against my skin."

"Your skin is like an infant's skin."

She wanted the love talk. She wanted him. She'd learned to know ecstasy and pain from Byron, but this was different from anything she'd known before. She'd never known it could happen this way, with so much beauty.

"We'd better get moving," she said.

"Yes. Let's go right to the hotel. I want to be in bed with you all night, loving you over and over and over."

"And I want to make love to *you*," she whispered. "I want to fill my mouth with you. . . ."

She opened her eyes and looked at him and they both laughed with coltish delight at their lust. "I'm going to know you, Jason," she said. "I'm going to know you inside out."

"And I'm going to know you too, Amanda," he promised. "Even if it hurts."

She felt a cloud chill her. "No," she said with urgency. "It won't hurt. It can't hurt when we feel like this."

He devoured her with diamond-bright eyes that scorched like the sun. "I'm glad you came into my life," he murmured.

"So am I," she whispered back. And foolishly, but gratefully, she wept.

The explosion of relief inside Amanda made her limp and giddy for a long time, and released her creative energy. Little tongues of fire lapped at her breasts and thighs as Jason drove on to the site, and her senses became heightened. She could smell animals and birds on the wind, and the blue sky made her eyes ache. She realized this was a little adolescent, but she wasn't going to argue with herself. She had become, she supposed, a little cynical about sex in recent years, using it as a relief from tension and some kind of reassurance of her attractiveness. She hadn't been made to feel brand new for a long time.

And now she did. *All right,* she told herself, now back in Bradley. She began to make phone calls to resorts throughout the Southwest. *All right, he's gorgeous and I wanted him right from the start and it was exciting to have him*. She could understand that. But she'd made love to gorgeous men before, some of them icily narcissistic, some of them warm and giving. It had been kicks but not like this.

"Arizona Biltmore," the voice said, and Amanda tapped a pencil eraser on the table as she asked for a night's lodging.

No, not like this. She dialed again after noting the reservation on a sheet of hotel stationery. This time she called The Wigwam in Arizona. And she let herself get dreamy and hopeful. Infatuation felt nice, if that's all it was. Boy, she could use some infatuation to allay the ambition and fright that fueled her.

She wound up making reservations at six southwestern resorts, the most famed and elegant resorts in the region. Amanda was not going to fly straight back to New York. She'd stay at each of these hotels to soak up their ambiance, and to see how they'd solved certain design problems. For a foolish moment, she considered asking Jason to make the tour with her, but she shook her head at the notion. Jason would keep (*I hope, I hope,* she added). She was on fire with The Pueblo now, after her brush with violence and her skirmish with Helen Tennyson. And her consummation with Jason.

Amanda spent the next two days at the site of The Pueblo, making swift, agile sketches with colored charcoals on a big sketch pad. She lugged a Minolta and took ten rolls of color film, capturing the desert from every angle. "The setting is fantastic," she told Jason, who watched her with interest. "You've got breathtaking mountain passes and a lake—but you're building a lake, aren't you?"

"Sort of expanding the one that's there," Jason said, as he adjusted his aviator sunglasses. His tan shirt billowed in a brisk, dry wind.

Amanda raised the camera to her eye and composed more shots. Her hair blew relentlessly and she kept pushing it out of her eyes and mouth. "You're going to have a real landscaping challenge," she said. "Bare desert means starting from scratch."

"But it means we can do what we want," Jason said. "Wait until you see the golf course against the desert."

"I can imagine." She rubbed her eyes and enjoyed Jason's golden profile against the white sky. "Bahru was incredible for landscaping. You had plunging mountains and lush foliage. What a difference here."

"I'll bet," he said. He seemed to be observing her.

Amanda felt a small ripple of worry in her heart, and it annoyed her, because she felt so good. She couldn't pinpoint the source of the worry; it had something to do with Jason.

Those two personas were there again, that ghost behind the man. "You don't sound excited," she said.

"I'm not."

"I guess that explains it."

He smiled winningly, which melted her. "When it gets this big, Amanda, it gets to be business. We have armies of meteorologists, landscape architects, geologists, all computerized to the teeth. We generate models, we crunch numbers, and the armies march in and build. Watching you take snapshots and draw pictures is a kick for me. I do my planning on a high-resolution screen. If you have enough pixels, you can draw anything. Take out a tree, put in a bush. Change the color of the facade." He sidearmed a pebble down a slope. "A few weeks ago, I had the whole Pueblo standing right here. As real as a photograph. Three dimensional, any viewpoint."

"I know," Amanda said. "God, I wish we could afford that kind of setup. We're limited in what our equipment can project. And anyway, I like drawing the site; it stimulates my thinking about color.'

"Go to it," he said.

Her mind chafed at her emotions, as she agonized over a decision. For a long moment, the wind sang in her ears. "Jason," she said, "I'm visiting some resorts on the way home. Come with me."

"Where?"

"Tahoe, Camelback, Sun Valley—all the big ones. Just a night or two at each. I've been to some of those places before, but I want to absorb ideas and avoid being repetitious. I don't want to be away from you, not now."

He gathered her close and lit her up with a quick and passionate kiss. She gripped his hard body. "I don't know if I can," he said. "It's pretty crazy. How about if I keep a copy of your itinerary and catch you along the way?"

She fought disappointment and felt foolish. "Sure. It was a stupid idea."

"No, it was pretty smart," he said. "And tempting."

"Bull," she said. She walked away from him, despising her blunder. She hated to make mistakes.

But the son of a bitch called her up when she was at the Arizona Biltmore and asked if he could join her. Ironically, she was totally involved in sketching and note-taking, and in talking shop with a prizewinning British designer who was staying over. But Amanda was determined to keep their flame alive, so she said "Sure, come on up."

Jason found her viewing Camelback Mountain from the golf course and asked her why she didn't play a round instead of just standing there. They teed off and at the second hole, a gruff male voice called out, "Jason Turner! What in hell are you doing here?" The voice belonged to a tanned, gray-maned investment banker who'd done business with Turner Associates and who'd played golf and racquetball with Jason. He was golfing with his partner, and they made a foursome. Now Amanda had the chance to watch Jason in action, and she was astonished at the difference in his behavior. When she talked designing and architecture to him, he clammed up and acted frightened. Now, talking loans and market shares, he cranked up the charm and crackled with energy.

He's a first-class con man, she thought. He had these two potent businessmen laughing and nodding like mailroom clerks being visited by the boss. Amanda kept her amusement to herself, and enjoyed the looks she got. The two bankers were trying to figure out the relationship between Amanda and Jason but Jason gave them nothing to work on. These men knew who she was and why she was visiting the Biltmore, but that was it.

Amanda nursed a childish anger at Jason's smooth expertise, and vindictively shot three strokes under his score. Later that evening, in the Aztec Lounge, she sipped a cold Margarita and said, "You were impressive."

"So were you," he said. She looked coolly sensuous in black and white cotton by Yves St. Laurent, and he lounged in Norman Hilton linen. They attracted discreet glances and murmurs as tension flickered like summer lightning between them. He studied her curved throat and she said, "It turns you on, doesn't it? The jungle hunt?"

"Sure," he said. "What turns *you* on? Drawing pictures?"

"What does that mean?"

He sipped his scotch with a look of distaste and stole looks at the gold-leafed vaulted ceiling. "If you want The Pueblo, you want the big time. Otherwise you would design summer homes for Hamptons matrons. You're checking out hot resorts, because you want to design the hottest. You didn't get this far by staying in your studio."

"Oh oh," she said. She licked salt from the rim of her

glass. "You're defensive, Jason. You know how I got this far. My God, the whole world knows. It was in the papers long enough. How Byron set me up and how I walked out on him and would I make it without him? I had two-martini lunches, sure, and played tennis with the right partners and even lost sometimes. I know what to do. And I like it, to an extent, especially when I score on someone who's powerful and knowledgeable. It's a rush. But drawing pictures is the biggest rush. Knowing that this place, that The Pueblo, is going to be mine, that I'm going to make it live—that's better than closing the deal."

"Is it?" he said with arched eyebrows.

She laughed. "Come on. That's not what I meant."

"I didn't think so. I'm lost with you, Amanda."

She leaned toward him and covered his warm hand with her cold one. "Don't be lost. I'm not remote."

"Remote enough for me." His eyes reflected the Aztec jade light and his skin was sunset gold. Amanda hungered for him, and enjoyed feeling light-headed. She let the pulse in her hand throb against him.

"What is it you don't understand, Jason?"

"Can't put my finger on it."

"Oh, I bet you can," she said shrewdly. "But you don't want to say it. I'm not being inscrutable right now. I'm expressing my passion. I love to design. It's that simple. I love to shop, to go to auctions, to draw . . . that's what came out of my nightmare with Byron Moore. That's the *only* meaningful thing that came out of it. The celebrity, the money, all that went to my head at first, but I got bored with it."

"I can dig *that*," he said.

"And what's left? After you're sick of talking into microphones and looking into lenses and seeing yourself on glossy magazine pages? For some people, nothing is left. For me, there's designing. What I loved at the start, watching a space come together and work. That feeling still catches in my throat."

He smiled. "You sound like a kid."

"I'm still a kid in some ways," she agreed. "Sometimes the willful and vicious kid I used to be."

"Sounds dangerous."

"Best beware my sting," she said. She finished her Margarita, the ice clicking against her teeth, and put down the glass. The sun's last rays flooded the room and made tableware flare like golden artifacts. Amanda felt washed with romance and excitement, and troubled to her toes by secrets.

"Let's get out of here," Jason said intently. "I want to be alone with you."

She eyed him languorously. "I think you want to be alone with yourself, mostly."

"Don't psychoanalyze."

She sighed. "Okay. I'll enjoy this. But I wish sometimes our conversations could be two-sided."

"I'm a better listener," he said.

She shook her head and smiled softly. Somehow he'd dampened her enthusiasm, and she felt frustrated and disappointed. This was no way to run a love affair.

chapter 7

BACK in New York, Amanda stayed after hours to work on The Pueblo, and Lacey Coleridge volunteered to join her. The ladies went out for a quick supper of Tuscan summer salad, with warm Italian rolls and strawberry shortcake. For fun, they split a bottle of white wine.

Amanda watched the sun go down from her office window, and the evening became filled with creative juice and warm companionship. Or maybe it was just that she was crazy in love with Jason.

Amanda fought a goofy smile as she sketched and leafed through photos and plans. The women worked in Amanda's private office. An oil-and-acrylic farm scene, painted by Amanda, hung over the custom credenza.

"Lacey," Amanda said, with her lips around a pencil. "Let me see the architect's drawings again."

"Sure thing." Lacey picked up the drawings from a glass-topped table. Her cotton tank and pull-on skirt clung to her swanlike body. She shook her hair behind her neck and brought the drawings to Amanda.

"That's terrific," Lacey said, as she looked down.

"What's terrific?" Amanda glanced up, then at her sketches. "Oh, these. I'm just doodling."

"Well, it's brilliant doodling."

Amanda smiled up at Lacey. "You're superb for my ego."

Amanda squeezed Lacey's hand and blew a stray hair back from her forehead. Her white top, with ribbons of lace, felt scanty in the air conditioning, and she shivered.

"How did it look?" Lacey asked abruptly.

"What?"

"The site of The Pueblo."

"Oh." Amanda shrugged. "Rocky. It's really barren out there, but it was a kind of wild beauty. This—" She tapped the drawings with her pencil. "—is going to look monolithic on that land."

"Exciting?"

"Imposing, for sure." She used the pencil as a pointer. "See—Jason's designed four distinct bays, even though it's one structure. He's got three skylit atria separating the bays, and two of them are full height. The third one is only on the second and third floor. I see that one as a planted garden."

"Sounds neat."

"I think so. The atria are going to be big and dramatic. But about eighty percent is rooms and conference areas. He's got copy centers, auditoriums, all kinds of amenities. And each bay has got separate elevator banks, support systems, and reception. The building's being done in a white granite with recessed windows—*portales,* they're called."

"Clever."

Amanda leaned back in her blue executive chair. "It's clever, all right. I guess I can see why some of the Indians are upset. It's going to dominate the desert, especially with the new lake, and the air strip, and the satellite buildings. It's going to have its own power generating station and reservoir, and local highways are being widened."

Lacey perched on the arm of Amanda's chair and casually draped a slender arm around the back. "Sounds a little pushy."

"Doesn't it? And Helen Tennyson isn't exactly Buckminster Fuller. Those Indians were *sore.*"

Lacey looked down at Amanda. "I'm glad you got out alive."

"So am I, honey."

Lacey rubbed Amanda's shoulder. Amanda felt tired, but driven, and maddened with desire for Jason. Seeing his designs only heightened the hunger.

And heightened the awful, nagging doubts.

Something was off-center, and had been from the moment she'd met him. There were still two Jasons, and her love for him could never be open and sunny until she cut through his smokescreen.

Ah well, the long weekend would give her time for that. Probing could be fun.

"You're grinning," Lacey said.

Amanda wiped off her smile. "Sorry. I was daydreaming. Let's get back to this—"

The phone jangled, causing Amanda to gasp. She paused, with one hand at her breast. "Jesus," she whispered. "Who is *that*?"

Lacey scooped up the receiver and curled the wire around her slim wrist. "Amanda Gray Designs."

Lacey's brows knit as she listened, and she held out the phone. "For you. Mr. Kleinman?"

Amanda sat upright. "Kleinman?"

"Is something wrong?"

"Well, I don't know," Amanda said, as she took the phone. "He's a private investigator."

"*Mandy!* What . . . ?"

Amanda didn't respond. She could feel her heartbeat rev up as she put the phone to her ear. "Andrew?"

"Hi, Miss Gray. Sorry to call you so late. I tried you at home."

"No, I'm at the office. What's happened?"

She instinctively picked up a pencil, and pulled over a memo pad imprinted with her name. She made nervous loops on the paper.

"Well, I think I've made some progress." There was the muffled sound of paper being shuffled. "I've come up with the attorney who handled the adoption. A Randolph Malone."

Amanda swallowed to keep breathing. "That's fantastic! Does he know—?"

"Well, I haven't talked to him in depth. But I think he might want to cooperate. He's been disbarred, in a sewer scandal, and he's bitter."

"How much does he know?"

"I'm not certain," Kleinman admitted. "But I'll give you the number and you can set up a meeting."

"Fine." Amanda wrote down the name of the attorney, and a phone number. "Why is he bitter?" she asked.

Kleinman cleared his throat. "He's bitter at Byron Moore, Miss Gray. He thought Moore would help him in his hour of need."

"Byron—?"

"Looks like Mr. Moore knew about you earlier than you thought, Miss Gray. He may have had some involvement with your adoption."

Amanda shivered as a deathly chill went through her. She said, "Thank you so much, Andrew. Please stay on it."

"You bet, Miss Gray."

Amanda hung up slowly and looked out at the shadowed office. She could feel millions of lights burn into her flesh. The skyscrapers seemed to break loose from their foundations and fall toward her. She was cold, and terribly frightened.

"Mandy—?"

Amanda's head snapped up, and she saw Lacey's face. She smothered Lacey's hand in both of hers and said, "Oh, God, I'm so sorry. I must be scaring you half to death."

"Yeah, kind of."

"Forgive me. I'm fine, really."

She released Lacey's hand and got up. She went to the bank of bronze-tinted windows and looked out at the urban darkness. Her pulse throbbed.

"Can you tell me what the call was about?" Lacey asked.

Amanda nodded, her back to Lacey. "I suppose I can, now. Could you pour us some ice water? It's in the fridge."

"How about something stiffer?"

"I don't keep anything stiffer."

"I do."

Amanda turned. "You keep liquor here?"

Lacey flushed. "Not liquor, just some grass. I thought . . ."

Amanda waved her hand and smiled. "It's all right, I'm not prudish. The water will do fine."

Lacey breathed a relieved sigh and busied herself at the portable refrigerator, pouring ice water from an Italian milk glass pitcher into two paper cups. She brought one cup to Amanda and sipped from the other.

Amanda took a long, cool drink. Her mouth was burning. She perched on her desk, pushing aside the litter of paper. "I hired a private investigator about a year ago, to try to find my real parents."

Lacey sat in a lounge chair, crossed her legs primly. "Hey, that's super. Lots of adopted people do that now."

"I know. I had especially good reason. My adoptive parents hated me. They showed it every way they could."

"Tell me about it."

Amanda shook her head. "No. I'm not going to go into it here. I couldn't handle it now. Maybe over a long lunch, in daylight, when I'm stronger."

"It's all right, Mandy. You can let it out."

Amanda smiled. "Oh, I know. That's what scares me. I'm not ready to let it out yet. Holding in all the hate made me strong. Made me want to succeed." She looked at Lacey with blazing eyes. "I wondered why in hell they took me. Why they wanted me. Why they kept me. So when I grew up, and when I got away from Byron Moore, when I got my act together, I hired Mr. Kleinman. He's very good, and very discreet."

"And he's been investigating for a *year*?"

"More or less." She finished the ice water. "Blind alleys, dead ends. It isn't easy normally, but my adoptive parents had covered their tracks. They wanted me never to know. So I kept paying Mr. Kleinman and I told him I *had* to know."

Lacey tilted her head and watched Amanda with liquid eyes. "You never told anyone."

"There was nothing to tell. Until now." She took a long, deep breath to steady herself. "Now Kleinman has found the lawyer who handled the adoption. And it looks like Byron Moore was involved." She shook her head in wonderment. "I can't pretend to be shocked. It seemed strange that he entered my life just when I was a helpless teenager. Where did he come from? Why me? It was always shrouded in mystery. Now it turns out he was waiting for me. Or he abandoned me and came back. It sure answers a lot of questions."

"And asks a lot more."

"Oh, definitely." Amanda stood up, crumpled the cup, and dropped it in the wastebasket. "But I've got a lead now. I look forward to meeting with Mr. Malone." She put her hands on her hips. "Well, I'm sorry, Lace, but I think I'm going to be pretty useless for more work tonight. Let's clean up."

Lacey stood up also. "I can keep going."

"You are not staying in this building alone. We are going to go downstairs in the elevator together and try to make it alive to our cars. Come."

Lacey nodded, her eyes never leaving Amanda. "I understand."

"Thanks. I wish I did. I really wish I did . . ."

She felt the hysteria sweep over her so suddenly that she was unprepared. Her hands went to her face and her body was shaken by long, ripping sobs. It was more release than sadness, but the emotion rocked her. "Oh God," she wept. "Oh God, all those years, all those years . . ."

Lacey crossed the carpeting and her arms went around Amanda. Amanda gave herself to the embrace, leaning against Lacey's shoulder. Lacey's hands stroked Amanda's back and massaged her neck. Her lips whispered near Amanda's ear. "It's okay, it's okay. Mandy . . ."

The attack subsided and Amanda felt weak. Her eyes burned. Her neck was hot, her blood racing. "Thank you," she said to Lacey.

"No thanks . . ." Lacey breathed. Her hands tightened against Amanda's shoulder blades and she pressed urgently against Amanda's body. Her breath grew rapid and her lips grazed Amanda's throat. "No thanks . . ."

Amanda's pulse shot up as she realized what was happening. *No,* she thought in panic. *Oh my God . . .*

She fought to make her rational mind work. Gently, she lifted her hands and held Lacey's wrists. She disengaged from Lacey's embrace and held the other girl's hands tightly in her own. She locked into Lacey's wild, animal eyes and spoke in soothing tones. "You're wonderful," she said. "I really needed the comfort and you were here. Thank you."

She watched Lacey's eyes comprehend and grow terrified, then ashamed. *Please, please don't hate me,* Amanda thought. *I should have seen it.*

Lacey averted her eyes and struggled to control her breath. She murmured, "It's okay, it's no problem."

Amanda turned Lacey's head back with a firm hand under the girl's chin. "You're a good friend, Lacey. I'm glad I have you."

She smiled with reassurance. Lacey nodded, but her face was drained of color. The exquisite bird was wounded to the heart.

"Let's clean up the mess," Amanda said. "It turned out to be a rougher night than we'd planned. I think we can both use some rest."

Lacey nodded again. Amanda began to gather the papers on her desk and tuck them into manila folders, which she filed in a designer filing cabinet. Lacey threw away discarded memos and a broken pencil, but her movements were desultory.

She stopped, and watched Amanda work. Her humiliation turned dark and swollen. She'd made a dreadful blunder, allowing her own need to take away her reason. Yet she hated

Amanda Gray at this moment, more savagely and profoundly than she'd ever hated anyone. *I gave myself to you,* she thought hysterically, *and you threw me away . . . you threw me away . . .*

Amanda exhaled and pushed back her hair. She smiled gently at Lacey. "Ready to go?"

Lacey barely nodded. "Yes."

Flanked by stone pilasters, Byron Moore made a rare public appearance. He was at the Metropolitan Museum of Art to kick off his exhibit of rare Chinese art and sculpture. Dressed in a gray silk suit, Byron smiled tensely as he was bathed in flashbulb light.

The curator of the museum, a tall, stooped man with horn-rimmed glasses, waved for quiet from the media people who jostled below the makeshift platform. Around the vast room, in glass cases, the Treasures of the Forbidden City gleamed: sinuous ceramic dragons, blue and white pottery, *blanc de chine,* a carved and gilded wooden throne, and much more. The curator blinked under the glare of TV lights and his upper lip perspired.

"Ladies and gentlemen," he said, "we're proud and excited to host this exhibit. It's one of the most fabulous shows we've ever had. And we must bow to this man—to Byron Moore—for bringing it here."

The curator clapped lustily and there was warm applause from the crowd. Byron acknowledged the ovation with a slight bow.

But most of the reporters and columnists looked past Byron to Heather who stood off to the side in a blue rolled-collar blouse and pleated skirt. She looked sophisticated in an upswept hairdo. The reporters murmured in delighted shock at Byron's flaunting of his underage mistress. Meanwhile, fawners and sycophants crowded around Byron: city politicians, doyens of the art world, and business bigshots. They shared Byron's spotlight, but Byron and Heather owned it.

Owned it, yes, and they hated his guts for it. They liked to portray him as a crude power-broker polluting the rarified air of the art world. It made them feel better. But Byron knew art, and people, and that was how he'd amassed a fortune in the billions and ruled galleries and museums. It was hardly a challenge now for him to convince the newly-friendly Chinese government into releasing its treasures; after all, Byron owned the largest art auction house in the world, and he was in a position to put Chinese treasures on the market and pump millions into official coffers.

Inside, he laughed. They said he'd made art into a commodity, like pork bellies. Bullshit. It had always been a commodity. Half of these aesthetic assholes had never read their history books. For most of human history, art was created for pragmatic reasons: religious icons, symbols of royal power, decor. Only recently had art been thought of as worthy for its own sake. Even then, a painting or sculpture was a tradable item, its value in the boosting of a reputation. What Byron Moore had done was to make the dealing more efficient.

When he began, the art boom of the 1980's was years in the future. The sudden volcanic eruption of money, the realignment of assets, the birth of thousands of new millionaires, hadn't begun. Art sedately and routinely passed into a few private collections or museums. Artists made their reputations slowly and played by the rules. Auction houses coveted their lofty status as tastemakers. The seething boy from the Bronx, with his City College diploma in hand, was in no position to challenge this establishment, or even to buy a valuable painting.

But he *was* in a position to smell and observe and listen, and to feel the pulse of postwar America. He saw the soldiers swarm back to the U.S.A., hungry for homes and stable lives. He saw developers raze the potato fields on Long Island and land across America. He saw cars, back in production, clog the roads, and he saw that new highways would be laid, longer and faster than anyone had ever known. Byron sensed change and with the small inheritance left by his mother, and the additional cash he persuaded his sister to kick in (his brother had been killed in the Ardennes), Byron bought land on Long Island and sold it back to developers. With his profits he bought into a company that put up soft drink stands along roadsides, and convinced the management to make the stands into quick-service restaurants.

Within a year, Byron became a manager in the company, then a vice-president, and made deals with Turnpike Authorities in ten states to provide the refreshment areas for new roads. The profits became much greater, and Byron kept his keen eye on the booming suburbs. He sniffed out the coming dominance of the shopping mall and bought key land where roads would go through. His carefully cultivated friendships with city and state commissioners provided the inside information. Byron also bought into three department store chains and convinced their managements to open several branches in new shopping malls. He played his game from several angles, investing in the land, the real estate itself, and the products purveyed in these locations.

Nobody quite knew how Byron built his fortune so quickly. At a time when corporate bigshots rose ponderously through the ranks, wearing gray flannel suits and kissing ass, Byron behaved like the venture capitalist who would become commonplace thirty years later. He stayed unencumbered and moved swiftly and ruthlessly. Years of not having had given him the drive and energy to run others into the ground. His natural intelligence enabled him to outwit and outmaneuver smart men. His physical strength and charisma propelled him into private offices and left skeptics mesmerized. Soon his success generated its own life, and nobody stepped in his way. The fact was, nobody knew where Byron would appear next, so he couldn't be blocked.

He invested his money diversely and well, and now he began to buy and sell art. He gathered a small but remarkable collection, specializing in impressionist works for no reason except that he was able to get his hands on a lot of it, and a unified collection had value. He attended hundreds of auctions, learned about pre-sale estimates, reserves, guarantees, and bidding strategies. He found himself embarrassed by cannier collectors, saddled with white elephants, and shouldering big losses. But he withstood the jeers and setbacks and kept learning. Soon he could bid subtly and cunningly, and he posed a threat to the old guard. Paintings were stolen from Byron's collection, or vandalized. Fires were set at his new estate in the Hamptons, and in his art galleries. He tripled his security and bulled his way forward.

Along the way, he increased his riches. He formed partnerships to buy valuable ranch properties out west, and then sold out for huge profits. He made bids for companies that built stairways, made towels, and milled paper. He financed oddballs with exciting ideas, sometimes taking a bath and sometimes midwifing the birth of a bright new company. He bought oil stocks and knew enough to dump them before the glut of the 1970's. He opened art galleries along the Eastern seacoast, joined the boards of trustees of museums, and began to exert a real influence in the art world. Byron did not simply make a lot of money; he used the money to shape the situations he wanted.

Once he owned galleries and controlled museums, Byron began the next phase of his dominance. He searched out promising artists and nursemaided them, often breaking the genteel rules. In the early 1970's, Byron sensed the coming realignment of assets in the United States and abroad. He studied the disruption wrought by OPEC, and the crumbling of old verities in business. He watched merger fever climb, and considered the invasion of computer technology. He saw the emergence of young magnates, hungry for instant status. One road to status lay in collecting art, especially new art by hot new artists. Byron provided these hot artists. He found them spray-painting graffiti, sleeping on roach-infested cots in Village flats, drenching canvases in bold colors and angry shapes. These crude, obnoxious young men and women would never have made it into the posh galleries of old-time collectors, but they made it into Byron's galleries. He walked the dark, urine-wet streets of Soho, the Barrio, and the East Village. He found these *enfants terribles* in their lofts and cellars. He withstood their tantrums. He paid them thousands of dollars for their work, and recreated them as superstars.

By this time, major banks were financing art collections, and Byron got the banks to unload for the new artists whom Byron wedded to desperate collectors. The new art patrons grew viscerally excited about owning the works of mercurial new talents, and Byron could make a spray-paint vandal into an international pet within months. Byron put on startling shows, to which blacks and Hispanics came in limos. Their jazzy, hopped-up paintings might land in private collections or turn up at auctions, but always the unseen hand behind the success was Byron Moore's. He had conquered the art world.

The final step was the buying out of the Richardson Auction house with a bid of $125 million. Byron combined with seven friends on the deal but retained control. The auction house had been floundering, managed by old blood. Byron made aggressive changes and within a year the house was operating in the black. Vicious accusations flew, chiefly that Byron was devaluing priceless art by inflating the value of mediocre stuff. After all, there was a limited supply of truly great art, and a growing hoard of rich, hungry collectors.

Byron's solution was to pump up the prices on secondary pieces just to keep everyone happy.

Byron said "Bunk!" and kept on making money. He enjoyed being a patron of the arts and helping museums make vital acquisitions. He exposed frauds, founded a repository of written materials about art, and conducted glittering fund-raisers for worthy projects. From his mansion in Southampton, Byron Moore cast a giant shadow over American art and the international art scene. Very few people knew the extent of his holdings or how many boards he sat on as a silent partner. Everyone knew he was one of the richest and most influential men in the world.

And they despised him for that. But he had done it step by step, with no flash and no magic. He'd made money and used that money to make more. When he had enough, he'd used the money to indulge his passion. He had never exorcised his hatred of his father or the need to hurt the man. He had never been able to share his success with his mother. His sister, who still reaped her share of the profits, lived in France with her diplomat husband and never spoke to Byron. He was alone, as he'd always been alone, but he was no longer powerless. He had taken control of his world. Today he presided over an art show that would draw thousands of trendy gapers, and he had arranged the show. There was very little he couldn't have.

Very little except Amanda. Once again the frustration spread through his chest, and gnawed at him. Once again he was a boy on a fire escape, his knees drawn into his chest, shivering at the blows and screams inside. Once again he needed to hurt, to quiet the demons that screamed inside his head.

The curator spoke again into the microphone. "These treasures from ancient China have never been allowed outside the People's Republic. But Byron Moore visited China last year and charmed the ruling government into loaning the exhibit for an American tour. Nobody knows how this man does it, but we're sure glad that he does!"

There was another burst of applause, and the curator urged Byron to step forward. Byron placed his hand around the mike stand and his diamond-bright eyes pierced the audience. The others on the platform masked their envy. Heather fidgeted with a catalogue.

Byron spoke in a resonant and commanding voice. "The

Chinese officials were very cooperative. They are justly proud of the treasures of the Forbidden City—which is the inner section of the Imperial Palace of Peking, where the emperors conducted their daily affairs. I hope that art students, sinologists, and the general public will come and be inspired by this show. Thank you."

He stepped back, to a third round of applause. He fled the relentless pursuit of video cameras and mikes. Byron Moore was a deeply private man, hounded by scandal. He barely spoke in public, and when he did, a lot of film was shot.

The curator stepped back to the microphone to answer questions about availability of tickets, how long lines would be handled, and how the exhibit was going to be displayed. Businessmen and art pundits shouldered each other to get close to Byron and bask in the aura. They shook his hand and offered congratulations. Byron nodded politely.

A dark-haired female reporter edged out of the pack and approached Byron. "Mr. Moore,' she said, "can we hear from your young lady friend about *her* reaction to this exhibit?"

A stunned hush fell and the men around Byron seemed to shrink back. Eyes turned to Byron. Byron glanced at Heather, whose face whitened. He looked blandly at the lady reporter and said, "Heather is studying art, not public relations."

"What about *private* relations?" the reporter persisted. "We hear that the young lady is more than a student. Any truth to that?"

There were audible gasps at the woman's effrontery. Byron's cheekbones reddened. His lips curled into a thin smile. "What's your name, young woman?"

"Penny Jessup," the reporter said pertly. "Cable News."

"Well, Penny, I've heard that *you* are something *less* than a journalist. Any truth to *that*?"

There was a snicker of mirth from Byron's groupies. The woman paled and retreated into the crowd. Byron walked over to Heather. "I'm going to have the car come around," he told her. "Wait in the lobby."

Heather nodded, chewing her lower lip. Byron squeezed her arm reassuringly. Heather hurried under a vaulting archway, and a burly man followed her at Byron's eye signal.

Byron turned back to his press conference, needing a cigarette. His mind was far from Chinese treasures or idiot reporters. He thought about Amanda, and of the latest photos he'd cut out of magazines. Amanda, who had achieved fame for her diplomatic residence in Bahru, and who was now designing the interiors of The Pueblo.

He glanced idly at the terrazzo floor, his mind burning. Such a long way for her to come! So lovely, so successful. There were even hints of a blossoming romance between Amanda and Jason Turner himself.

Byron's chest swelled with bitter impatience. He needed her now, just as he needed the smoke. He could have these pieces of Chinese art. He could have the adoration of these magnates and art critics. He could have the media. It bored the life out of him. He wanted Amanda. His creation. He needed Amanda to whimper again as he rode her, naked, with a chain yanked tight around her white throat. He needed to listen to her pitiful screams. He needed to see her bleeding, rolling back and forth in a fetal ball.

He needed her to need *him*.

More flashbulbs popped and Byron stared coldly at them. Nobody in the museum suspected that, behind Byron's public facade was a possessed man tracking Amanda's every move and closing in on her, day by day.

The first move would come this weekend. He looked forward to that night, and so he endured this day.

chapter 8

AMANDA drove her midnight black Trans-Am vengefully over the Triborough Bridge. Her smoke-toned ensemble matched the smoke of the sky. She sighed and pushed her windblown hair away from her face. Thank God her eyes were hidden by sunglasses. She knew her gaze was murderous and it wasn't smart to gaze murderously at New York City motorists.

Dinner with Jason, she thought, *will make me feel better.* That's why she was heading home early. He'd phoned and asked why he hadn't heard from her. She'd apologized. He'd suggested dinner and she'd offered to cook.

"Cook?" he'd echoed.

She'd grinned into the phone. "Yeah. I'll make a summer stir-fry and a lamb shish kebab."

"Okay. I'll bring the wine."

She thought ahead to their evening together. They'd share dinner and then make long, languorous love in her very own bed for a change. Maybe they'd grab a midnight snack and look out at the quiet night all spangled with streetlights. Then back to bed until noon. So why was she miserable?

Amanda changed lanes with a clash of gears and passed a meandering station wagon. The New England Thruway stretched drearily ahead, the summer trees in the distance dark and heavy. Humidity made her perspire. A strand of feathery hair tickled the corner of her mouth.

The date did *not* excite her, and that was the damned problem. It was overwork, partially. It was also Lacey. Amanda cursed the exquisite little bird for being in love with her. Lacey had not come to work for a couple of days after their crisis, and now that she was back, she put out enough coldness to make ice.

Then there was Helen Tennyson, whose wildly incongruous descent into the desert still rankled, despite Helen's expensive stroking. Mandy Gray had not been a submissive kid. She used to fight, often in school corridors, and she usually drew blood. Maybe she was chic and civilized now, but her gut still twisted when she was dumped on.

And when Jason, with his super body and gorgeous eyes, took that kind of treatment, Amanda had to wonder. She could feel her blood pressure soaring. She wanted to shake Jason by his well-developed shoulders and demand to know what secret he harbored. She also wanted to know what Byron Moore had to do with her adoption. She also wanted to become famous for her work on The Pueblo, and to stop going blind. No *wonder* she wasn't horny tonight.

Her exit waited just ahead. Amanda changed lanes and cut off a Cadillac, who gave her a long, furious horn blast. She hung her arm over the doorsill and with one tapered hand steered the Trans-Am onto the exit ramp, anticipating her stint in the kitchen. The thought made her a *little* excited.

She noticed a dark blue Mercedes parked just off the ramp, but she didn't expect to see a man in a suit step out and wave her over. Amanda reacted instinctively to the sudden event. *Cop,* she thought, and jerked the Trans-Am to a bumpy stop on the shoulder.

The sudden stillness unnerved her. She heard birdsong and distant radios, and the steady *whip-whip-whip* of cars flashing by on the highway. She tapped her fingernail on the wheel. What the hell had she done wrong?

The man walked over to her car and smiled. He was tall and powerfully built, like a pro football player, and his suit was expensive. He was no cop.

"Miss Gray?" he said politely. *They always talk politely before they rape you,* she thought insanely.

"Who are you?"

He leaned down. "I'm Todd. You're to come with me."

Amanda's hands constricted around the wheel. "What are you talking about?"

"You've been invited to dinner."

Cute, she thought. "I appreciate your creativity, Todd, but I already have a dinner date."

"It's not going to be kept."

Amanda bowed her head. Anger swirled in her chest like a little typhoon. She looked up, pushed back her hair. "Look. I think you're nice-looking, Todd, but don't press it."

Todd nodded, as if he'd expected this. "Miss Gray, you really have to come with me." He reached under his suit jacket and Amanda glimpsed the chamois holster just an instant before he drew the .38 revolver. It was a Smith and Wesson police model. If he wasn't a cop, he was a bodyguard.

Amanda stared dumbly at the gun. Stupidly, she recalled fat Jack in Bahru. "I don't get this."

"Please get into my car," Todd said.

"If I leave my car, it won't be here in the morning. . . ."

"It'll be picked up and taken to your garage."

"Why are you doing this? Do you want money?"

"I'm just an employee, Miss Gray. You're not having dinner with me."

She looked at him sharply. Who was setting this up? Todd opened her door and she was exposed. She let her fingers slide from the wheel and eased herself out of the bucket seat. She stood stiffly on the summer grass. This was totally unreal.

"The other car," Todd reminded her, gesturing with the gun. He held it so that passing motorists could not see it. Amanda looked wildly at the houses just beyond the trees. She saw the familiar traffic light turn from amber to red to green. Cars stopped and went. Routine.

"Let's go," Todd urged.

"I'd like to make a call," she said. "The man I was going to have dinner with . . ."

"Don't be stupid," Todd said.

His voice froze her blood. Her heart ached for Jason, and she felt tears spring to her eyes. She walked the short distance between the cars and Todd opened the back door of the Mercedes for her. She settled into the soft upholstery. As Todd shut the door, she noticed a plexiglas partition between the front and rear seats. Todd got in on the driver's side and there was a sudden, loud snapping noise. Central locking system.

Todd gunned the Mercedes and pulled off the ramp. Amanda looked with desperate longing at her Trans-Am, abandoned on the grass. The Mercedes turned left at the light and crossed the overpass, then drove back onto the Thruway heading toward the city. Amanda fixed her gaze on the back of Todd's head. She refused to look back, or to think about what might happen.

Todd drove carefully as night fell, and they reached the heart of Manhattan an hour later. Amanda stared at the lights and movement and guessed that they were heading for the Pan Am Building where the heliport was. A few moments later, she knew she was right. Todd pulled the Mercedes to curbside at the magnificent old archway under the building, and another suited man met them to take the car. At that moment, Amanda knew for certain that her own car *had* been garaged for the night, and that this was no college frat stunt or bizarre random event. Somebody with money and clout wanted her and had the resources to get her. Brief hope surged inside her. Maybe it was Helen Tennyson.

Todd kept a firm grip on her arm as they rode the high-speed elevator. They emerged onto the roof and Amanda fought vertigo. "Hey, look," she said, "I can't handle this."

"Sure you can." Todd remained relentlessly polite. Amanda grew fiercely dizzy at the proximity of the chopper, outlined in strips of luminous color. The rotor tips made zigzag patterns against a mosaic of lighted office windows and plunging glass canyons. Everything spun and Amanda nearly swooned against Todd.

"You really *do* have a problem," Todd commented.

Amanda said. "I wish my boyfriend were here to break your head."

Todd smiled. He walked her across the windy roof and helped her into the passenger seat of the helicopter. A pilot sat at the controls. Todd patted Amanda's shaking leg as she leaned hard against the seat. "Have fun."

"Screw off," Amanda said thinly.

Todd laughed, and shut the chopper's door. Amanda sucked in a long, terrified breath. The pilot pulled back on the throttle and Amanda felt the helicopter lurch and lift. "Christ," she groaned. But under the acrophobia, she thrilled at the chasms of light and the deep, phosphorescent violet of the evening sky, smeared with bands of red and black.

Fifteen minutes later, she knew what was happening. The chopper was heading east across Long Island, following the Expressway. The helicopter dipped south at Riverhead, and the muffled whirring of the rotors and the suffocating darkness jarred her into comprehension. Only Byron Moore could have been this elaborate and efficient. Her first reaction was tumultuous anger, an urge to fight the pilot and crash the chopper in a fireball.

But beyond the anger was terror. How easily he'd gotten to her after so many good years. Her supposed freedom had been an illusion; he was unstoppable. She looked out at the light-spattered land against a rain-thick sky. She thought bleakly of Jason, ringing her doorbell again and again, asking neighbors, finally leaving in puzzled fury.

"Bastard," she cried in a low voice.

The pilot ignored her outcry. Now she saw the solitary estate, far from the backbiting of Hampton snobs who trained thoroughbreds for their daughters and dug ponds that sank. Dramatically illuminated against a black ocean, the Georgian mansion enslaved its beach. She'd never seen it from above, but God she remembered it. Her insides twisted and contracted, folding into her soul.

The pilot brought the chopper down on the seaward side of the mansion and came to rest on a brilliantly floodlit landing pad framed by lawn and shrubs. The engines screamed as Amanda sat rigidly, not wanting to get out.

The chopper's door opened and another of Byron's men extended a hand to Amanda. On the ground, she wobbled. She smoothed her belted pants and straightened her jacket. The rank smell of the sea assaulted her. In the profound silence that followed the engine's cutoff, she could hear the slow, rhythmic rush of waves on the beach.

She saw Byron at once. He stood dramatically on a balustraded marble stairway, bathed in light from the house. She was struck first by the whiteness of his hair. It had been darker when she left him.

"*Amanda,*" he smiled.

"What's this about, Byron?" Her voice nearly betrayed her. Christ, she'd thought some strength had accrued after all this time, some semblance of toughness. Wrong. She was naked and vulnerable. Every nightmare came rushing back, like demons out of Pandora's Box.

He descended the stairs lightly. "You look fantastic. Just fantastic."

So did he. He wore a double-breasted linen suit, with a soft cotton shirt and silk tie. Elegant and continental, the man belonged to his estate. And she stood facing him in the salty wind in her work duds. He'd always been good at power plays.

"I had a dinner date," she said. "You could have phoned if you wanted to talk to me."

Byron smiled, lizardlike. "I didn't want to talk on the phone, Amanda. I wanted you here. You wouldn't have come on your own."

"No."

"Well, then. Were any of my people rude?"

Amanda shivered as the wind touched her perspiration. "No."

"Good. Come inside, Amanda, won't you? I have drinks waiting, and a wonderful dinner."

"I don't want to have dinner with you."

"You have no choice. You know that you can't get off the grounds."

Her stomach heaved. "How long are you going to keep me here?"

"As long as I like. Come, darling. You'll get cold standing there."

He turned and went up the steps, swallowed by the glorious whiteness of the mansion. Amanda's hands curled into impotent fists. She tossed her hair, which was rapidly being ruined by the salt. Hunger made her dizzy. It had been two hours, or more, since she'd been kidnapped by Todd. Jason would long be gone.

I won't cooperate, she promised ferociously. He'd have to kill her.

Drinks were served in a ground-floor oval room that Byron had redone in yellow. The sofas had been recovered but the chimneypiece and the 18th century French furniture were the same as she remembered. He'd changed the artwork, of course. The walls now displayed American originals.

Byron stood by the white overmantel. He sipped a scotch and water and his eyes burned smoking craters in Amanda's flesh. Amanda gratefully drank her wine and let the warmth slowly numb the backs of her hands and her ribs.

"You wear clothes stunningly," he said.

"Thank you."

"But then, you do *everything* stunningly. I've followed you, Amanda. I clip pictures. You carry yourself with authority and grace. Your face is wonderful. You really take care of yourself."

She flushed. "What are you trying to prove, Byron?"

"Prove? Nothing. I'm just *gloating,* for God's sake. I created a masterpiece. I am so goddamned excited at being close to you. I have never seen you look or smell or sound this marvelous.''

Amanda pushed a strand of hair away from her eye. His power seized her heart. She remembered everything. ''I'm happy that you're pleased.''

''Ecstatic. How do you *feel*?''

''Pretty lousy.'' She looked at him. ''I don't like being kidnapped.''

''I mean generally, Amanda. Is your health all right?''

He asked the question with macabre intensity as if he'd poisoned her. She felt chilled. He couldn't possibly know about her attacks of blindness. She said, ''I feel fine.''

''Tremendous.'' He swirled the ice in his drink, like a nervous sophomore at a school dance. He moved from the chimneypiece with catlike suddenness and sat at the edge of a sofa. He gazed at her with proprietary lust. She could smell his imported Danish cologne and his sweat under it.

Amanda looked at her glass as it caught the light from the fireplace. Byron said, ''I've had the cook prepare a salmon mousse and fresh Long Island duckling in cherry sauce. I've brought up some fine wines from the cellar. God, I've dreamed about having dinner with you again.''

She shook her head violently. ''I haven't,'' she said. ''I'm annoyed as hell. How dare you pull a stunt like this?''

''Is this going to be a tantrum?''

''No. But when you let me out of here, I'm going to the police.''

He laughed. ''That's no way to get back on my good side. You ran out on me, baby, and I'm offering the olive branch. Don't be a bitch about it.''

She stood up, with an abrupt scrape of her chair, and cradled her glass between moist hands. Her clothes felt stale. ''What will you do, Byron, lock me in my room again? I'm a big girl now. People will look for me.''

She was hyperventilating. Byron said, ''You can try to make this into a cheap melodrama but it won't get you anywhere. I've grown older too.''

''Not old enough.'' She could feel her jaw clenching. This was madness. His power was still hypnotic and crushing. A middle-aged degenerate should be hideous and drooling, she thought, not more sexually potent than before. Not able to penetrate her defenses, not able to break her down again.

She heard him get up and come to her. She sensed his

breath near her neck. "You're hungry and tired," he said. "And you were scared pretty badly. I'm sorry I couldn't let my boys tell you what was happening. You might have attracted attention."

"You know it." She moved away and stood under a massive chandelier.

"Let's have dinner."

"Go to hell."

He sighed. "Good old Mandy. Spirited as always. Shall I eat while you watch?"

The room blurred for an instant, as the memory of his cruel punishments sliced her like sharp knives. "Do what you want."

"What I *want*, Amanda, is to have dinner with you. I want to be with you again. I want to talk to you about what we are now, and what we might be."

"Is this a proposition?"

"It's a dinner."

She turned, rocked by his closeness. She remembered his broad, iron body and could visualize his smooth skin beneath his clothing. She instinctively shied away from the raw power in his eyes, but she looked compulsively at his sinewed hands. She remembered every finger of those hands impressed in her flesh; her body cringed at the memory.

"Byron, for heaven's sake, let me go home. You can't accomplish anything this way."

"I think I can."

"Why?"

He drank his scotch as if to quench his impatience. "Because you're very special, very important to my life. It was wrong for you to go away."

"Because it hurt your ego?"

"It hurt my soul, Amanda."

"You have no soul."

"Don't get smart."

"I *got* smart. That's what you won't comprehend. You made me know myself, Byron, and then I knew *you*, and the game was over. *Damn* you." She squeezed her glass too hard and it broke in her hands. The sudden cold wetness made her cry out. She held out her hands in horror and looked at the oozing weals of blood and dripping wine. Shards of glass glittered on the carpet, staining the yellow plush deep crimson. "Damn you . . ." she sobbed.

She spun, panic-stricken, and ran through the house as he cried "Amanda!" after her. Her memory knew the rooms and hallways and she was soon at the rear doors, and then outside, on the marble stairway. She heard her silver shoes click like a telegraphed distress signal as she plunged down toward the overlook. A fine misted rain stung her cheeks. She smelled fish and her breath rattled in her throat.

She heard his footsteps behind her. She whimpered as she ran, past grillwork and plant-filled urns. There were mocking lights far out on the black sea, winking green and red and white. Amanda stumbled and wrenched her ankle. She cursed and viciously kicked off one shoe. She bent down to take off the other one.

"Stop running," Byron told her.

She cursed and straightened up, leaning against a wet tree trunk. Her eyes filled as she stared at him, shadowed and threatening. His linen suit seemed luminescent in the darkness. "Leave me alone," she said.

"Why in hell are you running?" he demanded. He seemed honestly outraged. "It's not ten years ago. It's now. I'm different, Amanda. It's time for us to be together again."

"No it isn't, Byron. I'm through with you. Accept it. You have your new play doll. Can't you be happy with her?"

"No," he said. He didn't seem offended by her words. "I can't be happy with that kind of thing anymore. I found that out. See, Amanda? I'm capable of self-examination, of changing. Whatever I did to you, whatever I used to be, I love you. I never stopped loving you. Did *you* stop, Mandy?"

Amanda fought for her breath. "I don't love you, Byron. It wasn't ever love. It was dependence. God, we've been through all this. You're not feeling love now. You just want to possess me again. You're bored. You don't comprehend love."

"Teach me."

"Byron, you're afraid of getting old. All your money can't buy you any more years. It's okay to feel that way. Human men have feelings and fears. Just be human, will you? You've got all the money on earth to fight your depression. You don't need to chain me up again."

He curled his hands over her shoulders. The contact made her muscles spasm. "I don't want to do that. There won't be any more . . . bad things. I want to marry you. I want to share all I've got with you, or it means nothing. Please believe that I care for you. I'm going nuts over this."

Her heart thudded against her breasts. If he didn't take his hands away, she'd faint. "Byron, there's no love. It's over."

"It isn't over."

"Yes it is. I'm not playing dumb. I asked for what happened to me. And you transformed me, whatever else you did. You made me like myself and find myself and God, I'm grateful for that, Byron. And I can forgive you for everything else, even bury it. But it doesn't make me love you."

"You *did* love me."

"Maybe . . . for a while."

"Then you can't turn it off."

Amanda threw back her head and her hair made a cushion against the rough tree bark. She licked her lips, tasting salt and wine. "Byron, this is crazy. It makes no sense."

"It sure doesn't make sense to *me*, Amanda. I remember you, curled by my feet, so soft and pliant. I remember your eyes, crying while I held you. I remember how you pushed back my hair with such deep affection. The way you smiled when you first saw me in the morning. Grateful to God that I was there. You *needed* me."

Her blood slammed against her skull. "Yes, I needed you. For a time, Byron. And the time ended, and I didn't need you anymore, and that's okay, too. It doesn't take away from what you did, or what you are. I was part of you, but that time is done. Let me go, Byron. Please."

Byron's hands moved like snakes down her arms, making her shiver wherever he touched. "You've got a boyfriend now, haven't you?"

"Yes."

"That pretty architect."

"Oh God, Byron, stop watching me."

"New life, huh? New loves?"

"It happens, Byron."

"Not to *me,* you treacherous bitch!"

She shut her eyes and her throat closed in anticipation. His hands pushed her hard into the tree and flew to her throat. Her wind was cut off as his hands crushed her neck. His body scraped her. She felt his tie against the bare skin above her embroidered camisole. Then he let her go. Her eyes opened and stared at his contorted face.

"I've made a fool of myself," he rasped.

"No . . ."

"Don't humor me, goddamn it! I can handle kings, presidents, anybody in the world. Bend them and break them. Not you. I can't be close to you and be rational."

"I'm sorry for you, Byron," she whispered.

He turned and looked out to the rainswept ocean. He slammed his fist against the tree. Then he jammed his hands into his trouser pockets. "You're going to have dinner with me," he said suddenly. "That much I assure you."

"All right," she murmured.

He turned back to the sea. "You've got to come to me willingly. You've got to want me. It won't work this way."

She said nothing.

He pushed a hand through his hair. "Wash up. You can go home in the morning."

Disappointment flooded her, but she agreed to this compromise. "Okay."

He looked at her with bleak eyes. "In the morning."

She nodded.

"After dinner, I'll have you shown to a bedroom. The chopper will be here before breakfast. You won't see me. But it's got to be different the next time we meet, okay?"

"Sure."

"Sure, sure, sure. What the hell are you, a parrot?"

She exhaled, unable to stop trembling. "What do you want me to say, Byron?"

"Not a damned thing. Just be in that dining room, and behave yourself." He walked away briskly, turned, and pointed at her. "Next time will be different. *Different,* Amanda." He whirled, and kept walking.

Amanda sank onto a garden bench. Her neck throbbed. One of her barrel earrings had loosened and she fixed it. She smoothed out her sleeve. For a few moments, she stared mutely out at the fog. Then she gave herself to hysterics, bending over and wrapping her arms over her head as if warding off rain. Her shoulders heaved. Good God, he'd done nothing to her, *nothing,* and she was in shreds. What a fool she'd been to think she'd found any freedom. It never came easy for Mandy Gray, and it never would.

Finally, the crying ended, she put her shoes back on and walked numbly to the mansion.

chapter 9

SOMEONE pounding on his door brought Jason out of a thick sleep. He tried to call out that he was coming, but he had no voice yet. It took him six minutes to sit up and bury his cobwebbed head in his hands. The knocking continued, and he heard a woman's voice. Jason took a deep breath and let the mirrored bedroom come into focus. He had a disgusting headache. He remembered drinking Margaritas last night as he listened to jazz tapes and cursed Amanda.

He felt like an asshole now. When was the last time he'd acted so childishly over a woman? So far he'd loused up everytime he crossed paths with this fox.

"Cool it!" he rasped now. He stood up and stumbled barefooted to his closet. He knotted a velour kimono over his pajamas and padded through the sprawling apartment to the front door.

The knocking started again in a sudden tattoo. "Who the hell is it?" Jason growled.

"It's Amanda."

Jason stopped between a limestone horse and a floor-to-ceiling abstract painting. The implausibility of the moment threw him. "It's eight in the morning," he said inanely.

"Please let me come in." Her voice sounded hollow.

Jason fought the headache, which had settled over his right eye. Anger flowed as he unlocked the door and opened it. He stared at Amanda, who seemed to sway on the threshold. She wore a three-piece ensemble that she usually wore to work, and she looked like shit.

"What's going on?" he asked.

Amanda looked at him with wonder and gratitude, then grabbed him and pressed hard against him. She burrowed deep into the hollow of his throat and cried. Jason wrapped his arms around her, first managing to shut the door. He held her with amazement.

"Jesus," he said into her hair. "What the hell happened to you?"

"Nothing," she said. "Just hold me."

"Not without an explanation."

"Give me a minute."

He exhaled tiredly. "Well, I'm not going anywhere."

Amanda used Jason's bathroom to wash her burning face. She looked with loathing at her pale visage in the mirror. She was certain her clothes smelled. Her hair was a hopeless cause. But she hadn't taken time this morning for a makeover. A maid rousted her at seven from a broken sleep. She'd taken enough time to wash up and put her clothes back on, and she'd nearly run outside.

The chopper waited on the pebbled beach beside a slate-gray ocean. She'd actually cried out with relief as the helicopter lifted and banked sharply over the estate. Amanda refused to feel safe until she was deposited on the roof of the Pan Am Building. She'd taken the elevator down and hailed a cab.

She found Jason in the dining room. Her designer's eye appreciated the mirror-lined walls and recessed lighting that defined this sophisticated apartment. She would have expected no less from Jason Turner. What she *didn't* expect was to find him in pajamas. That touch of hominess gave him a boyish quality that she found endearing.

He sat, unshaven, at the art deco table, and sipped coffee. "Did you eat breakfast?" he asked.

She shook her head as she sat down.

"Have coffee," he said, gesturing at the pot on the table. "I'll scramble some eggs.'

"You don't have to go to any trouble."

"Well, *I* have to eat something. I'm not going to let you watch me."

Amanda smiled and said, "Thanks. You're pretty super to do this for a lady who stood you up."

"Damn straight." He went into the kitchenette to cook. Amanda watched his robed back as he broke eggs into a bowl, whisked them up with milk, and expertly scrambled them. She felt tears welling up at the domesticity of the scene. Christ, she was falling apart.

He brought the plates of eggs, with toast and preserves, to the table. Amanda tore into the food with unladylike hunger, and Jason watched her with bemusement. "Slow down," he said.

Amanda looked up at him sheepishly. "I'm sorry," she said. "These are delicious."

"Laid them myself."

She laughed, and felt a delicious runnel of well-being wind through her veins. There was a rightness about this scene that made her want to get weepy and make promises. Jason toyed with his eggs and observed her closely. His hair was mussed and his whiskers black and rough. He looked lived-in, Amanda decided, his handsomeness muted. He would age well.

He said, "Are you going to tell me what happened last night?"

"No."

"Why did I know you were going to say that?"

Amanda sipped her coffee and studied two Japanese bronze candlesticks on the breakfront. "I was detained from getting home . . . a friend. I know that sounds ridiculous."

"Just suspicious."

"I know." She sighed. She ached with wanting him. Last night had set her back ten years, at least. Byron had played with her, shown her that he still could control her life. It wasn't a pleasant feeling.

"I stood at your front door for half an hour," Jason said. "I'm not used to being made a fool of."

"I'm sorry."

"You don't sound sorry."

"Well, I'm sorry for that, too." She turned aside as her eyes filled. The eggs had turned cold in her plate.

"Amanda," he said, "why did you come here?"

"To apologize."

"You could have apologized by phone."

"I didn't want to."

He stood up and began to clear the table. Amanda pushed back her chair. "I'll help."

"This won't take long." He took the dishes to the sink and put them in, running water over them. He wiped out the frying pan with paper towels. Amanda worked on her second cup of coffee, which managed to jangle her nerves more than they'd been jangled before.

Jason returned to the table. Amanda remembered the warm silkiness of his skin when he'd made love to her in the desert. This wasn't the same man. She'd only dreamt that she could accept the risk of loving him.

"What's the story?" Jason asked. "I can't waste time with crazy women. Is it some kind of pathology with you?"

She gave him a filthy look. His eyes were the color of mountain lakes on a winter morning. "What if I *am* sick?" she asked.

"See a therapist."

"I've seen a few."

"They didn't help. Want a Valium?"

She laughed softly. "I'm past that. Have any Thorazine?"

"Jesus, Amanda."

"I love shocking you." She drained her cup. "Jason, forget me. You only think I'm fascinating because I was Byron Moore's kept woman."

"That's not the only reason I'm attracted to you."

"I know." She stood up, purposefully. "I don't know if it's any use, Jason. Why bother? I'm thrilled to be designing The Pueblo. Maybe we thought we were obligated to have an affair. What's the difference?"

"What do *you* want?" he asked.

"I want to be left alone." She touched a blue and white Japanese porcelain dish.

"No you don't," he said.

"Well, I can't have obligations, Jason. I can't have responsibilities. Look what happened last night. I can't guarantee that I won't stand you up again."

"You said somebody detained you."

"That's right."

"Same person going to do it next time?"

"Maybe."

"Are we talking about Byron Moore?"

She nodded.

She could feel the rage inside him, though he didn't exhibit it. He lit a cigarette, then came to her, exhaling smoothly from his nostrils. "Why didn't you say so when you came in?"

"Because you got paranoid the last time we talked about

him." She pushed back a droop of hair. "What does it matter, Jason? Are you going to punch him out?"

"What did he do to you?"

His face had gotten so intense that she laughed. "Nothing," she said. She held out her bare arm. "See, no whip marks. No burns."

"I don't get off on the humor, Amanda." His words snapped, like switchblades opening. "I don't really give a shit if you want to be a pervert with him. But don't play it both ways. Don't hang me up to play games with Moore and then come here for breakfast."

"I won't," she snapped back. "Come off your high horse, Jason."

"Give me an explanation I can live with. Stop being a mystery lady."

She made a sarcastic noise. "*Me?* Look, hon, *you're* the boy with the secrets. You rule the architectural world, but you kiss Helen Tennyson's ass. You never explained that to me."

He sucked on the cigarette. "Kissing ass for business reasons isn't a mystery, Amanda. Trotting off with a sadist *is*."

"I had no choice," she said. "I told you that."

"He kidnapped you?"

She realized that it sounded ludicrous. "More or less."

"Is this a joke?"

"No."

"Did you call the police?"

She felt her nerves splitting. She put her hands to her face and shut her eyes. "No, I didn't call the police. He gave me dinner. They can't arrest him for that."

"But he got you there under duress."

"He certainly did."

Jason shook his head and gave up. "I don't understand you, Amanda."

"You shouldn't expect to."

"What do you want? Can you state it simply?"

"I want to square last night with you," she said, holding back the flood with difficulty. "Then I want to go home and shower and sleep."

"And not see me anymore?"

She heaved an angry sigh. "I didn't say that, Jason. This is a hell of a time to ask for commitments."

"I guess it is." He doused the cigarette in an ashtray. "You can use my shower if you want. I have no new clothes for you."

"I thought you'd have an emergency wardrobe," she said.

"My women bring their own. Don't try to be cute when we're in a lousy mood. Want me to send your clothes around the corner? My cleaner does good work. He can have the whole outfit freshened up in an hour if I ask him."

Amanda felt newly itchy as she thought about her clothes. Of course saying yes would shoot her whole exit scenario to hell. "If it's not going to take all day."

"I said an hour."

"Okay. Is there a place to run my underwear through the wash?"

"Want me to do it?"

"No."

He grinned and went back to the dining room to finish cleaning up. Amanda went into the bathroom and shut the door. She glanced at the lock and ignored it. She slipped off her jacket, slacks, and top, with a series of relieved sighs. She stood for a moment in bra and panties, openly surveying herself in the mirror. She watched the swell of her breasts against the soft bra cups each time she inhaled. She ran a finger along the milky skin. Her face looked like hell from crying.

She slipped off her undergarments quickly and turned on the water. Somehow Amanda had expected Jason's shower to be equipped with the most fashionably kinky sprays and attachments, but it was unadorned. Beautifully tiled in black, the shower enclosure wrapped her in hissing solitude. She threw back her head and gave herself to the needle spray and the rising cloud of steam.

Her body contracted under the massaging fingers of hot water and she opened her mouth to let the drops splash on her tongue. She doused her hair and squeezed it between her hands. She began to feel clean. Only her memory of last night remained filthy. Byron was around the bend, of course. She'd laugh in vindictive pleasure if he weren't so dangerous. She knew he wasn't done with her. What did she do now, pack a gun in her car and keep the windows rolled up?

She shuddered and cursed at the stupidity of it. The bastard only needed to hire gunmen to pick her up whenever and wherever he wanted. He had her under surveillance. He'd let her out on a leash and now he'd yanked it back.

"*No,*" she spat. There had to be a way to get free. She wouldn't be his property again, not after she'd found her life. It had been nearly ten years! She'd built her new life like a good, sturdy house, and he *couldn't* break down the door.

She heard the bathroom door open and saw a human shadow. For an instant, a Hitchcock nightmare stopped her heart, but then the frosted door slid back and she saw that it was Jason. He was naked.

"I haven't showered yet, either," he said.

She only nodded. He stepped in and closed the door. Her eyes lapped up his body from neck to shoulder to chest to waist to crotch to legs. His musculature was more at ease in the morning, and there were wonderful little juttings of bone where joints meshed. The shower wet down his chest hair. His moustache dripped. His eyes asked for her through a film of water.

"Jason . . ." she breathed.

Again, he knew exactly what she needed. He took a bar of fragrant soap and a sponge from a shelf and began to lather her body. He did it wordlessly, beginning with her throat, working down her shoulder blades and her back, making small circles down her spine. He babied her rear end with the sponge and then turned her with one hand. He soaped each breast separately, and the sponge made little meringue peaks on her nipples.

He washed her ribs and her belly and worked the lather gently into the cleft between her thighs. Then he put the sponge back on the shelf. Her skin had erupted into a thousand fires and a self-generated orgasm already tingled in her groin. His hands replaced the sponge now, palms flat and firm. Her body glistened, soapy and tender.

She twisted and stretched to pick up the sponge and pushed him a step back with her fingertips so she could wash him. She rubbed the sponge over his chest to make the hair curl. She laughed at her artistic efforts and bit her lip as she continued, reaching behind him to soap his back. She lingered at his waist, circling slowly, using her hands to rub his buttocks. She moved the sponge silkily under his balls and up his shaft and he became fully erect. She curled one hand around his lathered organ and slowly moved her hand up and down as she watched his eyes become feral.

He locked one hand around her wrist to stop her. She dropped the sponge to the shower floor. His face angled over hers and she shut her eyes. His tongue stabbed to her inner cheek and the roof of her mouth, and his hands crushed her shoulders. He maneuvered her against the tile and his wet skin slipped and squeaked against hers. She realized with a savage thrill that this was not a prelude, but all of it, right now.

She welcomed it. She braced herself, her buttocks pushed up against the tile; he flexed his knees and smoothly penetrated her. She whimpered and flung her arms around his neck. "I need you . . ." she whispered.

As the steaming water sluiced over their bodies, carrying away soap in foaming rivulets, Jason filled her with long, even strokes. She sought his mouth and his neck. She parted her lips and smiled with closed eyes as she felt herself climax. She stroked his thighs, loving the hard, knotted muscles there. She urged him on, wanting every ounce, for reasons she didn't want to deal with at the moment.

She felt the wrenching spasms weaken her legs, mingling with the water. Jason groaned and slumped against her as he came, and she dug her nails into the skin of his back, whispering for him to give her more. She hadn't felt so good about making love in too long a time.

She smiled and hugged him, then kissed him. "It was gorgeous, and prefect," she said.

"Your body is like no other woman's," he told her. "You know how to please a man."

"I just respond to *you*," she said graciously.

He watched her for a moment, under the streaming water. His eyes seemed to change color, like opals. "Finish up," he said. "I want to shave."

"I wish you would," she jibed.

"We can go to the park for lunch. I want to spend the day with you."

She nodded happily. "Okay."

He placed his hands on her shoulders, and her nipples grazed his chest. "What about us, Amanda?" he asked. "How do we define ourselves?"

"I love you," she said. "That's how."

"I can't say that yet," he said. "But if it's ever going to happen for me, it's going to happen with you."

"Don't expound on it," she said. "Let it happen."

"Byron Moore won't grab you again."

She hugged him, gloriously alive to his skin. "Don't worry about it."

"I'm not afraid of him."

"Good," she murmured into his ear. "Let's not talk about it."

Jason was silent, then stepped back. "See you soon," he said, and kissed her mouth. She held the kiss, then released him.

He slid open the door and pulled a fluffy bath sheet from a rack. Amanda reached for the bottle of shampoo on the shelf and closed the door. Her legs felt deliriously rubbery. Her body sparkled from the lovemaking and she thirsted for more. It had solved a lot of conflicts inside her. Right now, she didn't want to imagine the complications. Maybe, for a while, she could fool herself into believing Jason, even into believing that he could protect her from Byron. Angrily, she massaged the shampoo into a lather.

"What I like about the park," Amanda said, "is the juxtaposition."

"Of what to what?" Jason asked. His head lunged to lick melting ice cream from the rim of his cone. Amanda smiled at this, adoring the way he looked silly. She also liked the way he drew dreamy stares dressed as he was in his black double-breasted blazer and white linen trousers.

"Of the park to the city," Amanda replied. "Contrast always excites me. You take a magnificent forest and it's—well, breathtaking. But put trees and hills and rocks against glass towers and concrete grids and . . . it's just mind-blowing. Each part becomes more intense, more achingly beautiful."

He looked at her through his sunglasses. "I could listen to you talk that way for hours."

"Thanks," she said dryly.

"No mocking," he assured her. "For real."

She popped the last tiny cylindrical pieces of her cone into her mouth and her tongue separated the cool white ice cream from the sticky cracker. Immediately, she was ravenous with thirst. The April sun washed down from a blinding blue sky, the kind you hardly ever saw in New York. Amanda's eyes looked at office towers beyond the tree line, and watched white clouds float through the glass, wavering and undulating. "Are you still doing glass?"

Jason bit into the ice cream and puckered. His eyes flicked to the tower Amanda watched, and he shrugged. "When it's called for. We try to tell some clients that stone is more appropriate sometimes. Not every company needs a glass tomb."

That made her laugh. "Good line," she said. She shut her eyes briefly as the fresh wind ruffled her hair. She felt fresh and relaxed after her erotic shower, and her clothing had come back crisp and fragrant from the cleaner. "We did the King Henry in Houston. Incredible hotel. Three towers, five hundred rooms. The concourse is a city in itself."

"I know you did it," Jason said. "We checked your credentials."

She watched a small group of joggers puff by. "We worked day and night on that. Couldn't crack it. Finally, we went with the glass, and let the sky flow through the entire place. Soft blues and grays and violets, with some greens and whites. We gave it the illusion of open sky, the feeling of space. We used entire trees in some of the open courtyards. As many glass and metal artifacts as we could find. We got warned about it. They said it would be so cold and forbidding that it'd be a glass prison. But I think it worked pretty well. The warmth came from furnishings and the trees, and lots of reds and yellows at ground level where we carried through the idea of the earth."

She felt a small shiver of remembered joy. She impulsively linked arms with Jason. Around them, city people dressed the park: upscale young couples in fashionable togs taking lunch breaks. Nurses with kids. Even the inevitable dowagers with dogs. There were cyclists and runners and lovers on every rock and lawn. There were boys and girls, gay men, and gay women. They thrashed and writhed more openly than Amanda remembered doing in public, but maybe she was getting old.

The scene filtered through her emotions and restored some balance. In this bright urban setting with the reassuring sound of traffic in the muffled distance, Amanda could believe that the episode with Byron was a bad dream, that she hadn't been kidnapped to his estate and propositioned anew. For the first time since that awful night, her nerves had stopped throbbing. She began to feel ownership of the city once more, and of herself. Jason helped, even with all of his damned secrets.

"Let's sit," Jason said. "I'm sweating."

"Out of shape," she chided.

They left the path and found an unoccupied hillock. Amanda sat gingerly on a flat outcropping of rock. Her hair blew wildly across her face and she looked rapturously at the skyline beyond the trees.

Jason watched her as he took out and lit a cigarette. It took him a few times in the warm wind. "Juxtaposition getting to you?"

"Always did," she said. "A black-topped road winding through the desert. A gorgeous Mercedes parked on the rim of a canyon. Each thing makes the other more beautiful." Her heart paused for an instant and her memory tipped dizzyingly backward like an amusement park ride.

"What's up?" Jason asked. He sipped smoke from his cigarette.

"Contrast," she said in a small voice, not knowing how to tell him what she was remembering. "A white T-bird against a black night, and kids puking on million dollar lawns."

"Huh?" he said.

She shuddered inside and looked at him with veiled eyes. She smiled. "I've puzzled you."

"Is this a game?"

She shook her head and pushed back the blowing strands of hair. "No. Although I'm kind of glad it happened. Payback time for your deep dark mysteries."

He exhaled smoke and held the cigarette like a dagger. He sat with one leg bent sharply, the other loosely draped over the rock. She imagined his musculature under the trim clothing. "You are really obsessed with that, aren't you?"

She felt silly. "I guess I am. I'm nosy and demanding. I don't like when people hold back on me and get away with it. I don't like that I don't know you completely."

"That generally takes a lifetime."

"I don't have a lifetime."

"Terminal disease?"

That caught her by the throat. "No," she said, too sharply. *Oh, come on,* her mind chided at the same time. *Even if you're going blind, you're not dying. Except that it's really the same thing.*

"Talk about cryptic," Jason said. "You're talking in hieroglyphics. I say things innocently and you choke up. You have weird memories that don't make sense. And of course you kick me in the groin if I bring up Byron Moore."

A jet flew across the sky, bisecting it. The roar broke up on the wind and reached them like sonic rain. She said, "I wish I had secrets to keep about me and Byron. But none of it was secret. He kept his sadism from the public for a long time, but it came out eventually. It only made him sound more fascinating."

"Nothing's come out," Jason insisted. "Except rumors, sensationalist stories, gossip. You never went to court or the press."

"They came to me. Often. Yanked it out of me like teeth. *You* knew about it."

"I know what I've heard. I know that the story of how you got free of him, of everything he did to you, is still inside your head."

"I'll tell you, eventually," she promised. She curled her hand around his neck, which had become hot from the sun. "I'm not ready yet. Not because I can't speak about it, but because it just isn't right. I'd feel dirty, like I was describing a rape to a cop. I remade myself, Jason. Well, maybe Byron remade me, and I helped. I always worry about giving credit where it's due. But I'm a recently born again woman and I'm falling hard for you, and I want you to fall for me."

"It's possible."

Her eyes misted. "Good. But for *me,* for the recent Amanda. Not for the little shit I used to be, not for the girl who was debased and abused and recreated by a megalomaniac. I don't want sympathy or fascination with horror or anything like that to be part of it."

He ground out the cigarette on the rock and drew her close to him. She leaned against his chest and burrowed her head into his neck. "You sound like Nora," he said.

"Nora who?"

"Nora in *A Doll's House*."

"The Ibsen play?"

"Uh-huh." He kissed her lips. "She went through this thing of not telling her husband her big secret because she wanted to save something for when she was old and ugly so he'd still love her."

Amanda raised her head and wiped her eyes. "So you're literate, too. No end to your depth."

"We had to read the play in school," he said gruffly. "But it stuck with me. We all do it. We save something in case we run out of things to do or say, to make someone like us."

"And you think I'm doing that?"

He looked at her and the sunglasses were like the glass in the towers, with the sky dark and glossy in the lenses. "All this crap about the new Amanda sounds a little desperate. There's no new Amanda. You're who you are, babe. You can tell me about your horrors or not, but they shaped you."

"Is this a two-way street, this analysis?"

He turned away, not embarrassed, but stuck. "Probably."

She pushed back her hair again and took a tissue from her purse to daub at her wrecked makeup. She smelled cooking and tree sap and pot in the air. The wind rushed pleasantly through new, shivering trees. "So we haven't made much progress."

He got to his feet gracefully. "Come on, let's get going."

She let him help her up. "It was a nice walk, Jason. A nice lunch, and a good time. Really."

"Yeah, it was okay."

She pushed her hands under his arms and pressed her body against his. "I'm still falling for you. Even if you want to be bitchy right now."

"What do you want me to say, Amanda?"

"That you'll keep your options open."

He smiled impulsively and hugged her. "You're about the best option I've had."

"Good."

She kissed him for a long time and even liked the cigarette taste in his mouth, which she usually despised. He stroked her hair. He'd grown under his pants; she got to him all right.

"So," she said. "Secrets are on hold, but we continue with the social calendar."

"Okay," he agreed. "We have the ground breaking for The Pueblo coming up."

"I'm excited," she said. "Are you?"

"Always excited," he said coolly. "A new Helen Tennyson masterpiece."

"But I'm here this time."

"Right." His cheeks appled again. "That makes a difference."

Helen Tennyson circled the red-upholstered chair where Lacey Coleridge sat. She marveled at the purity and romantic beauty of the girl, innocently luscious in a white blouse and burgundy skirt. Helen's fingers paused only a hairsbreadth from Lacey's shimmering hair. She found her heart fluttering.

"I'm so glad you came to talk," Helen said. "I enjoyed looking at your work. You're a talented designer, with a real future."

Lacey's amber-flecked eyes watched Helen as she moved. Helen was perfectly aware of Lacey's awe and played on it. This magnificent conference suite, with its travertine floor and fountain, intimidated most visitors.

"Thank you," Lacey said.

"Were you surprised when I called?" Helen asked.

"A little. I didn't know you were watching me."

"Talented people are always watched," Helen said. She dared a light pressure on Lacey's shoulder, and felt the girl shrink. Helen's body swelled beneath her crisp suit.

"I'm flattered," Lacey said.

"Be more than flattered, dear. Be aggressive and ambitious. It's always good for people like me to know who supplies the real ability in a company."

"Oh no," Lacey said hastily. "Don't think that it's me. It's Amanda. She's brilliant, really. She taught me most of what I know."

"How very gracious of you." Helen sat in a white divan and crossed her legs. "Amanda is just a bit tardy with some of her designs. I think I'm getting a little impatient with her being out of the office."

Lacey colored so richly that Helen drew a sharp breath. The girl turned away.

"What's wrong?" Helen pressed. "Did I say something upsetting?"

Lacey recovered. "No. I'm sorry."

"Listen, dear, if something is going on in that office that is going to affect *my* project, I want to know. Is there?"

Lacey looked with cold fear at Helen, clearly trying to make a decision. Helen made certain her own face showed encouragement and trust. The dramatic furniture and lighting did the rest. Lacey said, "I think it's great that Amanda has found romance, but it's kind of slowing us down."

Helen felt the blood rise in her neck. "Romance?"

"*You* should know. It's your big architect."

"My architect . . . ? Oh, you mean Jason *Turner*?" Helen's eyes widened.

"That's who Amanda talks about all the time."

Helen felt her heart skip merrily. Jason had certainly taken her hint. If Amanda Gray got dippy enough, as most girls did over Jason, the bitch would remain pliant. So *that* was taken care of. And *this* dear creature was horrendously jealous. Helen had intended to court Lacey simply to train her as a spy within Amanda Gray Designs, but since the child despised her boss for screwing Jason, Helen could play on that jealousy.

Helen stood now and smiled sympathetically. "Don't be too harsh on your boss. Wait until *you* fall in love, and see what it does to your work ethic." Helen noted Lacey's discomfort with amusement. "Still, it doesn't excuse laziness or malingering, not on *this* job. I'll give Amanda a call."

Lacey looked up with terror. "Don't tell her . . ."

"Please," Helen said. "Give me credit. Why would I want to get *you* in trouble? I want you right where you are, working on The Pueblo. I like to know where my future creative geniuses are coming from."

Lacey smiled. "Thank you."

"And of course, future creative geniuses keep mum about my discreet head-hunting, okay?"

"Absolutely."

"Good. And now, sweet thing, I must kick your butt out, since I have business to attend to. But I *do* want a nice, leisurely lunch very soon."

Lacey stood, smoothing her skirt with a winsome hand. "That would be nice."

Helen smiled winningly and held Lacey's eyes captive for a moment. The girl lowered her gaze, unable to look for too long into the eyes of this American empress. Helen appreciated the deference and embraced Lacey. She kissed the girl's cheek, feeling light perspiration against her lips. "My secretary will show you out. I *will* stay in touch."

"Goodbye," Lacey said softly. "Thank you." She hesitated, then hurried like a startled fawn from the suite. Helen watched her, and tapped a Cross pen against the edge of her desk. She grew physically aroused at the manipulative possibilities, and oddly annoyed at the liaison between Jason and Amanda.

chapter 10

AMANDA prepared for her meeting with Randolph Malone as if for a first date. She brushed her hair several times, smoothed her blouse and skirt, fussed with her makeup. She drove to the address Andrew Kleinman had given her, a shambling lumberyard in Babylon, Long Island, with a makeshift wooden walkway leading from the parking lot to the office.

Calm, she told herself uselessly. Slinging her bag over her shoulder, she stepped into the small, dank office. A leathery man behind a formica counter looked up from his *Daily News*. He smelled of tobacco. "Yeah?"

"Hi," Amanda said. "I'm looking for Randolph Malone. I have an appointment with him."

The man's eyes stripped her with open crudeness. Amanda's kind of woman never came into this grungy universe. He fought a leering grin and called out, *"Randy?"*

Amanda ran her tongue over her lips and let her eyes roam. The office was filthy and cluttered, the counter awash in puddles of coffee. The cheap Kentile floor felt gritty under her heels. A flickering light fixture cast garish illumination. This was an ugly, cold place that reeked of ash and mildew.

A second man came out of a back room. He was bulky and balding. Coffee stained his white shirt. His tie was yanked down. A sheen of perspiration made his pink skin glisten. "Yes?" he said.

"Mr. Malone?" Amanda asked.

"That's right."

"I'm Amanda Gray."

Malone nodded. "Okay," he said. "Come in the back."

The lanky man watched Amanda with prurient interest, and gave Malone a pointed look. Malone uttered a small sigh and opened a swinging half door for Amanda. She felt her skin recoil at the drabness and dirt.

The back room was for storage, with a peeling desk and a few chairs the only furniture. Amanda sat in a wooden chair with a torn green cushion. Hot, pale sunlight struck the grimy window with blinding brightness. Malone rummaged in the drawers of the desk for a disposable lighter, and lit a cigarette.

Amanda began to feel irrational anger at Malone's slovenliness. He wore faded slacks that wrinkled around his work shoes. He smoked his cigarette nervously. Finally, he pulled a chair away from the desk and sat down. "I can get you a can of soda from the machine," he said.

"No, thanks."

"I guess this is pretty unpleasant for you."

"I didn't come here for glamour."

"I know." He spat tobacco shreds and tapped the cigarette in a glass ashtray that spilled over with butts. "I was a little surprised when your P.I. found me."

"He's very good."

Malone's eyes blinked rapidly. "I'd better put some paper towels on that chair. You'll get your clothes dirty."

"Don't worry about it." She leaned forward slightly. "Mr. Malone, I know this must be embarrassing for you. I don't want to disrupt your life. I just want to know about my real parents."

She felt cruel and selfish barging in on this broken man's purgatory. Malone swiveled aimlessly in his chair. "I don't mind you being here," he said. "I haven't been close to a classy woman in a long time." He grinned mechanically. "Don't take that the wrong way."

"I won't."

He stood up. "You want to know about your parents."

"Yes."

"I can only tell you about your father. The P.I. mention that?"

Suddenly, Amanda was afraid. She clutched her handbag spasmodically. She felt absurdly out of place in this dirty office. "Go ahead."

Malone sucked on the cigarette. "He's dead. Been dead for three years."

She lowered her eyes. "I see."

"He was a gardener, Miss Gray. I don't know how that strikes you. I mean, you're a fancy lady."

Her eyes looked up, fiery. "I don't care what he was."

"Well, he was a gardener. He worked for Byron Moore at the time of your adoption."

She felt her heart lurch. "Oh?"

"Out on his Hampton estate. He was pretty artistic. He landscaped the grounds, supervised the staff. His name was Tom Crawford." Malone softened as he thought about the man. "Sensitive soul. A sweet man. You would have liked him."

"How did he die?" Amanda asked.

"Accident." Malone crushed out the cigarette and coughed as he settled into the chair again. "He left Moore years ago. Right after he gave you up for adoption. Started his own landscaping business out in California. Did pretty well. He was run off a mountain road by a drunk driver. Your father's truck went over a cliff, exploded, and burned. They never found the drunk."

Amanda listened with detached grief. It was as if Malone had described another man, a stranger. She hadn't known what to expect, or how she would feel. She was disappointed to feel so little.

"What an awful death," she said softly.

"Terrible," Malone agreed. "Such a nice guy, too. He never cared about himself. You liked his watch, he'd give it to you." Malone studied her. "You look like him, around the eyes and mouth. I don't mean to be forward."

Amanda smiled. "No, that's all right. It's nice to know I look like him. Do you have a picture?"

Malone shook his head. "Never had one. I guess your P.I. could dig one up. I'm sorry it's bad news."

She sighed. "I expected bad news. I'm glad I know his name." She stood up, unable to sit. She ran her finger down the handle of a rake that hung on a pegboard. She thought of the lawns and shrubs and alleys and gardens that had defined her world for those crucial years. Her father's work and she never knew it. Byron never told her. "So," she murmured, "the gardener gave me his artistry."

Malone's face creased in puzzlement, then cleared. "Oh, right. You're a designer. I guess it was in the genes."

"Yes, it had to be. His sense of color, his sense of design. I took my first inspiration from those gardens. He was with me, guiding me. God, I'm happy to know that. It gives me a sense of continuity and a past. Thank you, Mr. Malone."

"Glad I could help. Sorry I never said anything before, but it's been kind of lousy for me these last years."

"I don't blame you for anything." She turned and looked at him. "Who was my mother?"

Malone shook his head. "I don't know. The thing is, your father wasn't married to your mother. Not that it was a quickie or anything dirty. It was a real love affair, at least the way he told it. But she was society, and they couldn't marry. I guess that happens."

"Yes, it does," Amanda said. She moved closer to Malone. "How did you learn all of this?"

Malone's eyes retreated. "Don't get pushy, honey."

"What are you scared of?"

Malone laughed defensively. "What are you, playing detective?"

She bowed her head, took a breath. "I didn't mean to. I just wondered how you knew."

Malone lit a second cigarette with a lot of fumbling. Amanda waited with badly concealed impatience. Malone said, "I was an attorney out on the East End. Had some important business clients. I did negligence work and some corporate law. Dabbled in family practice with my partners, but got out of it. I was pretty sharp. I don't know what happened to my partners. I think they hooked up with another firm in Smithtown. . . ."

"Mr. Malone—?"

"Sorry." He smoked more vigorously. "Your father got my name from listening to Byron Moore's cronies. He came to me and told me about his baby, and how he had to get her adopted. It all had to be black market."

"Why?"

Malone shrugged, looking off into a private distance. "Well, if the mother was an important lady, the kid would be a scandal. Anyway, Tom was a wreck. He was in tears, I remember. I don't think he wanted to give you up."

Amanda's eyes filled. "Why did he?"

Malone eyed her with contempt. "He had to. I told you that. Jesus, what do you want from me, lady?"

"What you know," Amanda said, keeping her voice steady. "I've been searching for a long time, to find out who I am. Don't hold out on me now."

"Come off it," Malone said. He took a drag. "You're a

big interior designer. You live in an expensive world. What is this, a game for you?"

"It's not a game," she said. "But I want to know where I came from."

"I told you that."

"Part of it. Are you afraid of Byron Moore?"

Malone crimsoned. He put out the cigarette and stood up, smelling of sweat. Amanda could hear the door open in the front office, and male voices. "Look, Miss Gray, what can *you* do for *me*?"

She was startled. "I can pay you for information."

"I wasn't talking about money."

"What, then?"

"How powerful are you?"

"I don't understand."

"I think you do." Malone went to the door and wrapped his hand around the doorknob. He paused, near tears. He said, "Damn it," softly, under his breath. He stared at the blistering door, suffering. Amanda was moved by his emotion.

"Did Byron Moore do this to you?" she asked gently.

He snorted. "Look, I'll tell you the truth. I had the idea that you could get back at him for me. It was stupid. I have fantasies sometimes."

"So do I."

He turned and studied her. She trembled under his gaze. "How old are you?"

"What?" she said.

"Thirty?"

"Something like that."

He smiled. "I remember you as a baby. That makes me very middle aged."

She smiled sympathetically. "I guess it does."

"You know, I threw your father out of my office. I was a real snob in those days. I wanted to scrub down the furniture after he left. A gardener, in *my* office. Who the hell did he think he was?" Malone shook his head. "I had no heart, Miss Gray. Just greed."

"I wasn't very nice myself, when I was younger."

"Who was?" He left the door and leaned against the desk. Trucks roared by outside. A fire siren wailed. Malone folded his arms across his belly. "What are you doing, feeding me lines to keep me talking? I was a lawyer, honey. I know all the tricks."

"Good for you. Why don't you tell me what's on your mind?"

"Sure." He scratched his whiskered cheek with his fingernail. "I'd like to make love to you. Right here. Right now. Your body is driving me up the wall."

She forced her expression to remain neutral. "Well, that's direct."

He laughed. "You wanted it."

"Yes, I did."

"It's not likely to happen, is it?"

"Not voluntarily."

He shook his head. "It takes this kind of thing—you coming here—to really make me grasp what's happened to me. I could have lived in your world, Amanda. Mind if I call you that?"

"No."

"Mercedes. Town house. All of it. I figured it was coming my way. First in my class at Brooklyn Law, aced the Bar on the first shot. Plush job on the Island in a week. *Zoom*. Then Byron Moore walked into my office, a day or two after your father walked out."

"And?"

"Boy, you're anxious. Maybe I ought to push my luck, see what you're willing to give."

"Forget it."

Malone seemed to deflate. "I'm scared to death, Amanda."

"I know."

"You're sharp as hell. Your mother must have given you that. Your father was lovely, but dense."

"You're rambling."

Malone coughed. "You want to know about Byron Moore? He made me wet my pants, just by walking in. He looked around like he was going to have the place torched. It was in his eyes."

Amanda said, "I know what his eyes can do."

Malone looked at her with a bemused expression. "What gives a man that kind of power? Money?"

"No," she said. "He gets money because he has the power. It comes from inside. It's some force that makes others helpless. He can be charming, and even loving, but when he becomes twisted, he just breaks people and hurts them some more."

Her words trailed into sudden silence. The dingy office

seemed to bake under the late summer heat. Malone said, "He told me to arrange the adoption, that he'd finance it. Anything it cost. Plus a bonus for me—fifty grand into a private account. And a chance to work for him, even a chance to break into politics. He was persuasive, Amanda. He even located your adoptive parents."

Amanda's lungs seemed to swell inside her body, suffocating her. "*He* found them . . . ?"

"I just had to get my secretary to prepare the papers. I was hot for a few years. Until I challenged the town bosses and ran for Suffolk County Executive. I played rough. I exposed some bigshots in a sewer scandal. I figured I had Byron Moore behind me."

Malone tugged at his lip. He seemed surprised to be talking about this. "They came after me. Moore forgot I was alive. I waited for him to get me out, and they ripped me to shreds. They owned the papers, the cable stations, everything. They had dossiers on me. They dug up my past crimes. A little jury tampering, a little fee splitting. Fact that I once incorporated a business run by gays. It goes on and on. I woke up with the disbarment proceedings started. Naturally, I had to pull out of the election. I was washed up, cleaned out, disbarred, and all alone when they got through. I got a job in this yard through a former client, once I stopped drinking. My wife left me during one of my binges. She won't let me see my kids. I think about trying to get back into law, but I'm too old." He looked at Amanda, and made a gesture of hopelessness. "See, Byron didn't destroy me. He just forgot me."

Amanda exhaled and realigned the handbag strap on her shoulder. "I'm truly sorry," she said. "I don't know what to say to you."

"Nothing," Malone told her. "When your P.I. called, I decided to talk to you. I don't know, I guess I had some stupid dream that you would go punish the son of a bitch. But he screwed *you* pretty good, didn't he?"

"Once," she said frozenly.

Malone smiled. "But you're not going to get him, are you?"

"I'm not in a position to get him, Mr. Malone. I just wanted to know about my parents."

"So you know. Now what?"

"I try to find out about my mother. And why Byron Moore wanted to place me with the Grays. I think I have a pretty good idea why. It doesn't solve any problems, but it answers some questions."

"Well, glad I could help." Malone clenched and unclenched his hands, and Amanda could sense his bitter fury.

"I'll see that you're paid for your time and information," Amanda said. "You deserve that much."

"I deserve more than that, but I'm not going to get it. Why don't you leave? This has all made me feel crazy angry again."

Amanda nodded. Malone opened the door for her and she shuddered a little at his sweaty nearness as she left the room. Somehow it seemed wrong that revelations about her life should have been made in this dusty room.

Amanda returned to her car with a headache that throbbed under the afternoon sun. She sat behind the wheel and toyed with the sunvisor, trapped in bitter emotion. She felt so many things—grief for the father she never knew, outrage at the drunken killer who took his life, hope that she would find her mother. Running like an ominous current beneath all these feelings was the presence of Byron Moore, whom she now realized had been in her life from her infancy. She was *conceived* in his household, and he arranged for her rental to the Grays.

Until he was ready for her.

And he watched, and waited, as she grew up.

She cried out and brought her fist down on the wheel. It was too terrible to contemplate. He had taken her from her father, forced Tom Crawford to give up everything he loved, only so Byron Moore could have a slave, a pet, a thing to abuse and hurt and crush.

Amanda gunned the engine and pulled out of the parking lot onto the main street. Out of the corner of her eye, she saw a green Aries idling across the street, and realized that the car had been there when she arrived. Genuine terror coursed through her chest, like a thrombosis, as she comprehended. She was being watched. Like in a goddamn police movie.

She drove quickly, recklessly. She needed to be near Jason now, to be loved, and to think.

When she got back to her office, Amanda phoned her ophthalmologist for an appointment. She intended to keep the appointment. If the news was going to be rotten, then she had to know before she became deeply committed to The Pueblo. As tight as the grip might be on her heart, as incredible as the excitement might get, she had to honest. The *thought* of blindness, the horrible nightmare of losing The Pueblo and everything that came with it . . . well, if she was going to lose her eyes, none of it mattered.

So she made the appointment, and sat down in her chair behind her executive desk, and let hysteria wash over her. The work had really piled up. There was the condo of a Manhattan art world couple, a condo that had belonged to an heiress who'd given it an English country house look. Now Amanda had to redo it to accommodate a modern art collection and *not* tear the place apart. And there was the old farmhouse on Long Island's East End, with the endless entrance corridor. And the gloomy kitchen in the Brooklyn Heights brownstone. These were bread and butter commissions, with real people as clients.

Amanda sat back and stared at her fabric-covered walls and the original art that hung there. She wore a big silk organza shirt and navy blue pants, and her hair hugged her face and loosely touched her back. The Pueblo was going to change her life. She felt it happening, and at the same time that she lusted for it—the fame and money and endless excitement it would bring—she hung back, terrified. The condos and farmhouses and brownstones had defined her life as a designer. The hotels and office buildings and embassies had ushered in the next chapter, and she'd never been entirely comfortable working on that scale. Rooms. She did rooms best, one at a time.

The phone rang and she took the call. "Oh God," she said apologetically. "Of course, two o'clock. Yes, send them in."

She gracefully rose from the chair and parted the drapes to squint down at the street scene. A reporter and photographer from the *Times*. A special Sunday supplement on decorating. All the major designers to be interviewed, and Amanda Gray scheduled for today. She'd forgotten. It happened more and more often.

The *Times* people were lovely; a healthy and slim redheaded girl with a sweet smile, and a stocky, moustachioed photographer who kept shooting through the entire interview. The girl asked Amanda about her most challenging problems and how she solved them.

"The most challenging problem," she said, "is how to

make it beautiful and how to make it work. You have to know the lifestyle of the client, you have to know what's going to be done in the space. You can create a room for *Architectural Digest,* but can it be lived in? Is there an art collection, and what kind? Lots of entertaining? Formal? Informal? Then you sometimes run into conflicts. The client wants a look, but the look won't be practical. Or it will mean construction and the client doesn't want the expense."

"How do you deal with stubborn clients?" the girl asked.

"Whoa," Amanda said with her best smile. "Careful of the wording. Clients are never stubborn, only demanding." The interviewer laughed. Amanda said, "Design is control. You take a space and you make it say what you want it to say. You color it, mold it, decorate it. Whether you choose an African mask, two roses in glass jars, a Victorian birdcage, paintings by Motherwell, Picasso, or Degas, you're shaping that space. I never liked the decorator's word 'statement.' I don't make statements. I control space. The client is part of what that space is all about. Her personality, her movements, her needs . . . well, they make demands, too. I don't *handle* clients, I design with them and for them."

"Did you always want to control space?" the girl asked.

Amanda sat graciously on her desk and tilted her head for the camera. "Almost always. I didn't realize it until I was nearly twenty, but I guess that I had a built-in need to alter what I didn't like and to create what I did like."

"Did Byron Moore bring out that need, or did he just provide the teachers?"

Amanda bristled, as she always did, but the question wasn't unfair. "It was in Byron's home that I began to perceive the desire for designing. Naturally, Byron was able to provide expert training and my first opportunities."

"And he set you up?"

Amanda's lips thinned and her eyes iced. "Didn't I just answer that question?"

The girl flushed. "What are some of your current projects?"

Tired and angry, Amanda quickly highlighted some of the jobs she was working on, and sat for another set of pictures. When the *Times* people left, she had to take two aspirins. They hadn't asked her about The Pueblo, and probably would have if she hadn't attacked them. But they should have known better. It was long past time to stop being ghoulish about Byron.

Amanda sat down again at her desk, trying to summon the energy and the mood to work on her projects. She had to finish them before she plunged into The Pueblo; that would consume her, and her clients did not want assistants doing all of their work. There was that life change she feared and wanted. After The Pueblo, she would never be a chic designer for upscale individual clients again. A branch of Amanda Gray Designs might handle single dwellings, but she would become a major force in the design world. She sensed that, and what scared her was that she felt no regret. Was her need for control that voracious? Apparently so. Homes were only the beginning for Amanda. The drugged, rebellious teenager who somehow suspected that she could alter her landscape had made progress. Byron had unleashed big-time demons.

She would be on Jason Turner's level. Maybe Amanda Gray Designs would even be swallowed up by Turner Associates, which would make Amanda one of Helen Tennyson's playthings. That was probably the plan all along. Well, it was flattering. If Helen wanted to own Amanda, that meant Amanda was good. And wasn't that what she'd longed for? To be recognized for her own talent, not for her bondage to Byron Moore? Here was the recognition, folks. Amanda would design monstrous spaces, and her color choices, furnishings, artifacts, paintings, fabrics, and lighting designs would become part of peace conferences, corporate takeovers, major sex scandals. History in the making, against Amanda Gray's backgrounds. Maybe an Amanda Gray wall would influence a Soviet premier's decision. An Amanda Gray knicknack might catch a president's eye. How megalomaniacal.

Just at the moment she'd learned how insidiously and totally Byron Moore had controlled her life, Amanda dreamed savagely of controlling so many others. God, she needed Jason now, to bring her down before she went crazy. She shivered inside. And she knew she wouldn't keep her doctor's appointment.

chapter 11

AMANDA returned to a hectic schedule and didn't get to see Jason until she jetted out west for the ground breaking ceremonies. It was only when she saw him near the reviewing stand that she realized how emotionally wrecked she was.

She called his name, and he turned, smiling. Amanda fell in love with him again as she admired his lean handsomeness in a double-breasted gray suit. He outshone the local politicians like the brightest star in a constellation. She made her way through the thronging visitors and clasped his hands.

"God, I missed you," she said.

"I've been miserable," he replied. His smile softened and his eyes gave back desert blue. A soft, dry wind brushed her hair, which gleamed in the afternoon sunlight. Her smart tweed separates, worn over a fuchsia notch blouse, complemented Jason's executive look.

"I need to talk," she said.

"Problems?"

She nodded. "Lots of things messing up my mind. How are you at listening?"

"I don't think I could listen for very long," he said mischievously. "Unless you wear a nun's habit."

She smiled. "You're impossible."

"Just improbable," he said. "How do you like this hoopla?"

He gestured with his chin. Amanda released his hands and her eyes swept the vista of dun-colored buttes brushed with green sage and the violet mountains. The deepening sky was edged with thick white clouds. Her artistic sense appreciated the contrast of majestic loneliness against the small city of trailers, vans, and grandstands.

Music blared from a local high school marching band. Amanda liked their garish gold and red uniforms as she listened to the brass sounds surge and fade in the wind. TV cables snaked across the desert from air-conditioned trucks. This was a photo-opportunity crowd: politicians, businessmen, tribal chiefs, and media darlings. Amanda noticed the gray-haired officers of several major corporations, and a reclusive Texas billionaire who swallowed up oil companies or greenmailed them into submission. A tanned Senator grinned into the cameras, practicing for his coming Presidential run. Amanda smiled wickedly. Never mind the sharks, she thought. The killer whales were out to circle Helen. A little shudder ran down Amanda's spine. It was still scary playing with maneaters.

"It's what I wanted," Amanda said. "The excitement. The circus."

"You don't sound happy," he observed.

She looked hopefully at him. "I *am* happy," she said. "And I'm depressed. It doesn't make sense."

Jason casually lit a cigarette and his eyes squinted. Amanda thought that he looked like a cowboy in a cigarette ad. He said, "Anticipation is always better than the event."

She smiled. "You come up with such original thoughts."

"I was trained to be a cliché," he said.

She slid her arm through his and leaned against him. "Be serious. I need understanding."

"Forget it, Amanda. I don't begin to understand you."

"I'm not that difficult. I just want things that have no name. I thought this was it. I put every egg into this basket, Jason, every ounce of hope and work. But suddenly I'm not confident. And I'm not sure this is what I *should* be doing."

They watched as visitors filed slowly to their chairs on the reviewing stand. Trucks plumed dust as they roared through the area. TV cameras were adjusted. "What do you want *now*?" he asked. "At this moment?"

"To succeed." she admitted. "And yet I'm scared of succeeding. Scared of reaching my goals. Scared of not being fulfilled."

"Maybe it's you," he suggested. "Maybe you just don't think you deserve anything good."

She stiffened at his direct hit. "Give me a break."

He shrugged. "Enjoying success takes a healthy ego. I think you work night and day to prove to everyone that you're worthwhile and even when everyone says you are you doubt it. Considering what you went through, I don't blame you."

Amanda bit her lip and felt the wind scour her face. "You're too perceptive," she said.

Jason threw his arm around her shoulders and whisperingly kissed her blowing hair. "Well, maybe I *do* understand you."

She trapped his hand in hers and pressed his fingers to her lips. "Just stay with me," she asked. "Let me care for you."

He dropped his cigarette and crushed it with his heel. "You want to prove you can do that, too."

"Don't be flip about everything."

"Sorry. I'm getting pissed at myself now, and taking it out on you."

"Why?"

His smile lifted his moustache. "If you want my secrets, you have to tell me yours."

She lowered her eyes and shook her head. "Not yet."

"Not even what's bugging you as of a few days ago?"

Another head shake. "No."

"Visit from Byron Moore?"

She looked up. "No, not that."

"Then what?"

She moved away from him. "Don't press me, Jason. I'm not ready to talk about it yet."

"Not to me, anyway."

"Oh, Christ, don't be a baby."

He rubbed his fingertip along the bridge of his nose and flipped her a noncommittal smile, then walked away, toward the grandstand. She called after him "Jason!" but he didn't respond. Bastard. Well, she'd had her chance. She ached to spill her guts about her dead father, and the bastard who hurt her for so many years, and how mixed up she was. But she'd clammed up and played martyr and he'd taken a hike. So what did she expect? Better luck next time.

Now it was too late for self-recrimination. Amanda found herself herded by uniformed troopers to the grandstand. Her seat was a folding chair, rope-tied to others in a row. Amanda sat between strangers, a man and a woman who seemed to be politicians. The woman wore perfume that was too heavy for the open air. The man kept mopping his pink face with a crumpled handkerchief.

Her mind wandered as the ceremonies began. The high school band played "The Star-Spangled Banner" as Amanda stood and looked out at a whipping American flag held by the color guard. There was a selection of marching band pieces, including a disco version of Stravinsky's "Firebird" complete with a young twirler and her flaming baton. Amanda found it all endearing.

She looked over to where Jason was sitting with Helen Tennyson and her party. Helen also shared the dais with the governor, an Indian chief, and several local officials. Amanda noted that Helen had wisely avoided looking like the high priestess of tacky glamour. Instead, she caught the sun in a white georgette blouse and black skirt. The high collar of the blouse set off Helen's neck and her peppery hair was combed out in a youthful, almost ingenuous style. The woman knew how to present herself for any occasion.

Amanda dutifully applauded when Helen was introduced and stepped to the bank of microphones. The wind toyed with Helen's notes, flapping the pages as she held the lectern. She looked infuriated at this. Amanda could read vengeance in the woman's eyes as she talked of gutting the desert and erecting her Taj Mahal.

"Under this desert sky," Helen said as her words were torn by the wind. "will rise The Pueblo—a self-contained, self-supporting complex that will become the business and entertainment center of the Southwest. Everything that the Sun Belt represents—booming economy, high technology, bright future—will be embodied in this project. Computer-controlled, The Pueblo will be an 'intelligent' complex, monitoring its own functions and providing the most up-to-date amenities. Every business suite will be equipped with its own mainframe computer, linked by private phone lines to every important bank and corporation in the world. Convention rooms will be state-of-the art media centers, with multibank video, stereo, film, tape, and holographic photo-presentation capabilities. Elevators will . . ."

Amanda grew bored. The concepts were thrilling, of course, and Amanda loved high-tech toys, but her mind rebelled at the speechmaking. Her legs itched under her skirt, and her skin itched under her blouse. She kept looking out at the undulating land and the ragged horizon. Night waited like a patient wolf just over the ridges. The ceremonies had been programmed for evening to avoid the killing heat of midday. Now, the wind turned cooler, and violet haze wreathed the grandstand. Spiky black shadows bisected the yellow earth-movers and bulldozers.

The earth seemed to whisper to Amanda, pleading and warning and clutching her throat with undefined longing. She was an East Coast girl, a suburban hooligan transformed into a chic designer, and this crushing vastness frightened her. She gazed at Jason as he sat with feigned interest next to Helen's empty seat. Amanda lazily recalled his naked skin against hers, his powerful organ deep inside her, his lips grazing at her breasts. She shivered with desire.

Jason was now part of whatever she longed for. She'd never given much thought to her plans before. She'd pursued success and proven her talent. She'd triumphed as Byron Moore's Galathea. Yet somewhere deep in her well-groomed body, a hurt and frightened little girl cowered. The carefully doctored wrist scars had disappeared; the dependency on drugs and liquor had long since been conquered. The broken ribs had healed. But Amanda knew the little girl lived within her, waiting for her to get drunk enough, to get lonely enough, to hate herself enough.

She shuddered and looked hard at her gold bracelets to remind herself that she was fashionable and refined. Now was not the time to court suicidal fantasies. Helen finished her speech and Amanda clapped lustily. The cameras swept the audience and the band played.

Now Jason was introduced and Amanda rested her chin on her fist as her eyes caressed him. The mikes and cameras loved Jason. For the first time Amanda realized how much charisma he exuded in public, and knew why he had become America's most well-known architect, inspiring wet bottoms in girls from coast to coast.

She hardly heard his words. She preferred to hear the sound of his voice and to look at his rugged elegance from afar, knowing that she would mesh with him tonight, naked and hot. She dreamed, open-eyed, of kissing him, tonguing him, feeling the plunging sensations as he entered her. She dreamed of lying in his arms afterward, kissing his morning whiskers, prying open his mouth with her tongue. She bit down hard on her lip as a molten warmth spread through her loins and she decided to quit having fantasies here.

Jason was giving the signal now for the equipment to roll. He gestured dramatically, silhouetted against the inflamed desert, and headlights flared from the big machines. Motors coughed and rumbled, then roared like mythical lions, and the yellow behemoths lurched forward on monstrous treads and tires. The audience cheered and applauded with big, greedy smiles, like Politburo chiefs at a Russian military parade. The old Indians wanly smiled, their black eyes unreadable. They'd sold out their tribes for trinkets.

But Amanda clapped too, thrilled as the rumble of machinery vibrated in her chest and stomach. She shivered at this display of raw power, though if she raised her eyes to the horizon, she could watch the desert dwarf this puny show. She didn't want to see that. She wanted to watch the great steel scoop come down with a metal screech and thud into the caked earth. Again and again the scoop pounded the crust until it cracked. Now the shovel dug deep, filled its maw with rocks and soil, lifted high in drooling salute to Jason and Helen. Dust and gravel spilled from between the yellow teeth as flashbulbs made summer lightning.

Somewhere beneath all this din, Amanda thought she heard a thump. She looked around quickly, her eyes confused by all the movement. She shut her eyes for a moment and pressed the lids with her fingertips. A burning sensation alarmed her. She'd been staring too hard at Jason.

A woman screamed. Amanda opened her eyes and blinked through a film of tears. Her muscles tensed at the high-pitched voices. Someone yelled "It's burning!" Amanda tried to find the voice. There were more screams.

Now she saw the flames. Nearly invisible in the afternoon light, they licked at the lower tier of the grandstand, making the air waver with heat. Dignitaries stumbled ungracefully as they jumped out of folding chairs and backed away from the fire. Amanda's gaze flicked to Jason, who still looked at the steam shovel. He hadn't heard this localized commotion.

She gasped as she heard a second thud. This time the flames jumped up in front of her. She fell backwards against her chair and felt a sharp pain in her thigh. She cursed foully. "What the hell is going on?" she asked the man near her.

"Thing's on fire," he said.

Amanda listened to her blood pound, but kept her head. She looked sharply to her left and saw that visitors were being escorted from the burning platform by troopers. Amanda shuffled into line behind a man in a blue suit.

Another thud made her head jerk up and she watched new flames roll over the tier below her. There were more screams. Somebody was firing something at this platform, deliberately setting it ablaze. Amanda tried to see through the thickening black smoke and orange fire.

Then a man screamed *"Look at that!"*

Amanda couldn't locate the voice, but she looked in the direction the crowd was pointing. A souped-up Trans-Am roared across the desert floor in front of the grandstand; inside the car, a man set something afire and leaned out the window. It took a moment for Amanda to make sense of the bizarre scene. Then her heart paused as she recalled the Indian dissidents attacking Jason's car.

The flaming arrow was loosed, and sailed toward the grandstand as Amanda watched with horrified fascination. There was an unreality about the frozen moment; it seemed part of the ceremony, another baton-twirling act. Then came the thud and the spurt of flame. Now the grandstand was fully ablaze and the crackling paper noise drowned out even the engines of the earth moving equipment. A wall of heat struck Amanda and her throat closed shut, filled with toxic smoke. The flames melted the resins in the wood, releasing a foul stink. Amanda panicked now; this wasn't funny.

She was being pushed hard by the people around her. Bodies rubbed against her and she heard their scared breathing at her ears. She was being carried along as if by a swift river current. Her shoe heel caught in a chair leg and broke off. She cried out in surprise and pain. Limping, she felt her skirt tear. Heat licked at her back. She fought savagely to keep her wits. She'd faced a gun barrel in Bahru and Byron Moore in his mansion. She could certainly face *this*, long enough to get out. *Then* she'd have hysterics.

With abrupt relief, she felt herself lifted and guided by powerful hands. "This way, ma'am, don't panic, just keep movin' along."

God bless the troopers. *I apologize to all the cops I hassled in my youth,* Amanda thought feverishly. The hands moved her to solid ground and she staggered through the curtain of smoke. She hugged herself, shaking violently. Around her, chaos ruled. People were running, the way they ran in video reports of riots, but this was real life. Amanda focused on the

Trans-Am, which was screeching around in wide circles. There were other cars, too, with raised rear ends and booming exhausts. Amanda could hear yelping from the cars, like movie Indians. And backfires.

No. These weren't backfires, they were shots! Amanda tensed, in expectation of being hit. A man slammed into her as he lurched past, and she fell backwards, tripping in the dust. A faceless man in a white Stetson steadied her.

"You okay?" he asked.

She stared at his moon face, and nodded. "Yes. Thanks."

"You'd better get out of here," the man said. "Those bastards are shooting at us."

Amanda looked again at the mad road race of circling cars, half hidden in clouds of red dust. *"Why?"* she asked in a whisper.

The man was gone. Amanda heard a huge explosion that made her scream. She saw one of the earth movers sink, as if to its knees. Amanda looked again at the cars, or tried to, but they were masked by black smoke. The Indians were shooting at everything; even the earth movers.

Everything mingled now; screams and shouts, thudding feet, explosions, searing flames. Amanda stood still, absurdly paralyzed. Glass and metal shattered as bullets spun through the air and ruptured windows and fuel tanks. Amanda smelled the sudden sweet odor of gasoline. *"Jason!"* she screamed.

A trooper loomed in front of her. "Get moving!" he snapped. "Behind the platform."

Amanda nodded. His voice pumped blood into her legs and she moved. After two steps, she stopped and bent to take off her shoes. Feet encased only in pantyhose, she began to run, not thinking about the jagged rocks and hard earth that punished the soles of her feet.

Her lungs burned as she ran, along with others, in a grotesque foot race away from the billowing flames. Shots whistled through the air. Amanda tried to find Jason. The air seemed clearer now. She could see the sky, and the mountain ridge. Maybe this was safe ground. Maybe she could stop for a moment . . .

The sound of a tremendous explosion slammed into her spine and lifted her off the ground. She felt herself flying, split with raging pain. The concussion thudded against the air like a struck drumskin, and the sky seemed to ripple in accordion folds.

She fell, her knees taking the jarring shock that sent fire shooting into her thighs. She spread her hands instinctively and her wrists absorbed the next jolt. She knelt for a moment, trying to comprehend. One of the fuel tanks must have gone up. Amanda's instinct for survival blocked out any speculation about Jason. She knew she had to keep moving. She began to crawl.

Pain overcame her. Dizziness crushed her mind and she sprawled on the ground, her cheek tickled by sage grass. She heard her breath come shallow and rapidly. She raised her head, looked up at the blue sky, and as she looked, the sun swelled, bloated, and became a swirling fireball, spinning towards earth.

Another explosion, she thought.

But there was no explosion. Just the red ball, whirling and whirling, and a black corona, thickening as the red narrowed. It was like an iris closing on a camera. Then there was only black.

Amanda sat up, fighting nausea. She heard the riot somewhere behind her, the running feet and screams and gunshots. She smelled gas fumes and flames and desert wind. But she couldn't see. The blindness had come again, but this time it wasn't going away. *No,* she screamed silently. She tried to control her breathing, but she had lost control.

She heard herself whimper as she stood up. She swayed, unable to steady herself. Her knees throbbed with pain and her wrists felt swollen and useless. Bile rose in her throat. She cried into the wind, turning her head back and forth like a wounded bird. Darkness pressed against her skull, crushed her eyes to jelly behind her lids. Somehow the blindness slithered, like a black worm, down her throat and shut off her windpipe. Somehow it spread into her chest and squeezed her heart. Somehow it cracked each rib and shattered her pelvis and buckled her legs. The blindness imploded within her, folding her again and again into herself.

She screamed insanely, her hands clawing at her face. She felt her nails puncture her own skin and rip backwards. She couldn't stop herself.

Finally she toppled, but hands caught her and spun her into a fierce embrace. "Amanda," came Jason's voice. "For God's sake, what happened?"

She couldn't speak. She cried piteously against his chest and her hands grappled for his shoulders. Her face burned where she'd torn herself, and she prayed to die. Jason stroked her singed hair and kissed her bleeding face and whispered to her, but none of it could help.

Amanda sat up in the hospital bed, her arms wrapped around her knees. She wore an azalea pink velvet robe, trimmed with lace and ribbon. Jason had brought her the robe from her hotel room, along with the petal pink nightgown she wore beneath it. "I'm sorry to make you run errands," she'd told Jason. "But I woke up in a lot of hospital rooms when I was a kid and I got to hate those flimsy little gowns."

Jason only nodded.

Now Amanda moped as morning sunshine bleached out the walls. She recoiled at the chemical stench that defined all hospitals. "Thank God it's a private room," she said as her lips brushed a velvet sleeve. "I couldn't stand a suffering roommate."

Jason stood by the window, looking out with the sad eyes of a caged tiger. His blue short sleeve shirt and white twill slacks cried out for action. Amanda gazed at the curved thickness of his biceps and the sculptured planes of his chest under the cotton. His strength calmed her. But he looked upset, and that made Amanda feel even worse.

"How am I?" she asked. "The doctors won't tell me anything."

Jason turned to her, and the intense sunlight threw half his face into shadow. "You have bruised knees and wrists. You cut up your face pretty well, and you inhaled some smoke. Nothing serious. You'll be out of here by this afternoon."

"Terrific." She sighed, blinking back foolish tears. "And what about my going blind?"

Jason's own eyes reached out to her. "They couldn't see anything wrong, Amanda. I know you said you've had these . . . episodes before, and I told them that, but they seemed to think it was hysteria."

"Did they take tests?"

"Not in the E.R. They suggested you see a specialist. We talked about that, too, you and I."

She shook her head and her hair swept against her shoulders. "I know. Maybe it *was* hysteria."

Jason pulled over a bright plastic chair and sat down. "You had good reason to be hysterical."

Amanda's malaise sapped her will to think, but a spark of

curiosity still burned. "What went on? I've been out of it since last night."

Jason smiled reassuringly. "They had you on tranquilizers."

"Oh, no. I hate being a fool in public."

"You weren't foolish, just shaky. Anyway, the medics don't make judgments."

She looked dryly at him. "They don't, huh? I'll tell you some stories sometime. But, hey, tell me what happened yesterday."

Jason's eyes seemed to harden, like cooling steel. "Papers and TV are having a ball with it. Remember those protesting Indians we ran across?"

"I'll never forget."

"They've got a leader now—but not the one they wanted. A kid named Peter Deal, but he calls himself Lone Dog."

"A renegade Indian?"

He shook his head and reached for the cigarettes in his shirt pocket. He withdrew his hand as he remembered where he was. "No, a criminal. There are legitimate Indian reps who are against us. This guy is a dangerous son of a bitch. His rap sheet includes armed robbery, assault, drugs, rape, and harassment. He's been a pain in the butt for the tribal leaders as well as the cops. Now he's into social reform."

Amanda studied him. "You sound sore."

He gave a shrug. "I'm the one who has to handle it."

"Why?"

"I troubleshoot my own projects. I charm away objections and smooth over problems."

"Since when does an architect do that?"

"Since I design for Helen Tennyson." Jason moved to her and touched her hair. She shivered at the movement of his strong fingers. "I'm good at public relations. That's why Helen made me rich and famous."

"What about your talent?"

He smiled. "Lots of talented designers. Only one superstar. Look, let's talk about the Indian uprising, not about me."

Amanda felt the wall go up between them. "Sure," she said. "As long as you keep touching me like that, you can talk about anything you want."

That brought a twinkle to his eyes. "You scared me, Amanda. When I found you, I thought you were really hurt. Your face was a mass of blood."

She shuddered and became aware of the burning in her cheeks. "I guess I panicked. So much for my cool head in tight situations."

"You got away from the fire."

"The cops got me out." She shook her head to stop him from stroking her hair and settled back against the propped-up pillows. "I fell apart, Jason. I don't like that. It really gets me upset."

"Who said you were supposed to be Wonder Woman?"

"I *used* to be tough."

"You used to be a juvenile delinquent. Running around with a gang of rich snots isn't being tough. Tough is being all alone, with no options, and surviving."

His words unnerved her. "Good sermon."

He sat on the edge of the bed and his mouth hunted her lips. She shut her eyes and he kissed her. His hands burrowed under her nightclothes and curved warmly over her damp breasts. His fingers traced slow paths down her sides and paused at her cleft.

"Jason, stop," she whispered. "Not here."

He kissed her again, harder. He imprisoned her face between fierce fingers and forced her eyes to see him. "Don't try to make me open up," he said. "I don't want to spill my guts to you."

"I didn't ask."

"You ask with every blink of your eyes."

She managed a smile. "I'm sorry. I'm trying not to real hard."

He sighed heavily and sat up. He grabbed a cigarette from his pack and stuck it between his lips. "I have to smoke," he said. "I'll be back when I finish."

"Sure."

He stood up and looked down at her. "Lone Dog and his boys ruined about fifty thousand dollars' worth of heavy equipment. He left a note on one of the flaming arrows. If we don't lay off The Pueblo, he's going to burn us out. The cops think he's got a lot of firepower stashed away. He and his gang know the desert. They can stay on the run, strike fast, get away. They can cause a lot of damage."

Amanda's lips burned from his kiss. "What are you going to do?"

Jason took the cigarette from his mouth. "I'm going to persuade the authorities and the tribal chiefs to bring that boy down. He's got a lot of misguided sympathy, and the Pueblo is the big taco, baby. We don't go backwards in this life. There's never enough money or women or good times. Helen wants her Pyramid."

"What do *you* want?" she asked.

"I want my cigarette. I have no long-range goals, Amanda."

He walked out of the room and Amanda remained propped against the pillows, suddenly drained. Her heart thudded and her head ached. *I'm in love with him,* she thought wonderingly. He'd come so close to revealing himself just now. Jason held powerful secrets, maybe as powerful as hers. The beautiful hunk had feelings, all right. He was as trapped behind the beefcake as freaks were trapped behind their deformities.

Amanda pressed the button to summon a nurse. Her face was on fire. She didn't dare look into a mirror and see the gashes. Her eyes turned toward the window. She could vaguely see glass-walled buildings and pale sky.

The nurse came in, a heavy, sweating woman. "Yeah?"

"My face hurts badly," Amanda said. "Can I have something?"

"I'll check with the doctor."

The nurse left and Amanda shut her eyes. Scarlet helixes and blue fireballs spun against her inner lids. She blinked and felt her universe focus on her eyes. Her artist's eyes. Her dying eyes. Oh, she was going blind, all right. She knew that. But she didn't want the medical facts. She felt overwhelmed by terrible threats to her happiness. She had come so far, so fast, and held a golden sun in her hands. Now the sun had turned black, and the night had turned cold, and only her love for a man she didn't know kept her going.

She clutched at that love and savagely promised to win this fight and never, never to be a loser again.

PART TWO

chapter 12

AUTUMN came to New York with pale sunshine and sweet rains. Amanda said a small prayer of thanks for the sunshine as she trekked up Third Avenue to shop for fabrics. The daylight struck her newly cut hair, and she shook it back, liking the way she turned heads. Her printed glen plaid suit complemented a crisp white blouse and a black bow at her chin. The shoppers here knew who she was. Amanda could taste their envy.

She smiled to herself as she went into *Michael Lowy Designs*. She said a cheery hello to the salespeople and waited regally on the vast floor filled with fabric bolts as Michael Lowy himself strode up to greet her. "Amanda," he smiled, and grabbed her shoulders to kiss her. His feather-light form wore a European suit perfectly and his huge eyeglasses peered at her. Amanda offered her cheek cordially.

"Hello, Michael. How are you?"

"Lousy. I've got some virus thing and I can't even hold down soup. What can I show you?"

She laughed softly. The nape of her neck crawled with the stares of other designers who browsed amid chintzes, taffetas, and brocades. Amanda's fingertips burned from rubbing fabrics and her eyes ached from memorizing colors and patterns. It had been a long morning, with a brief lunch at a yogurt and salad bar. She'd have to call it a day pretty soon.

She sighed as Michael led her toward the back rooms. Of course she kept thinking about her eyes. She woke up each morning staring wildly. She carried eyedrops. There was a ritual afternoon rest with cool compresses, and she wore sunglasses even on cloudy days. Talismans to delay the horror. So why didn't she just see Dr. Fabiano? Well, because the potential truth was unbearable. If she could put it off one more day, have one more day of designing . . .

When, she thought, *do I stop being a victim?* Each time she believed she'd found her strength, she did something weak. And Jason, who was going to snatch her from the pits, chain-smoked and behaved like a fugitive. Which left Amanda, again, with her back against the wall, fighting shadowy armies.

"Look at this," Michael cooed. "Would you believe these are vinyl wallcoverings? I dare you."

Amanda ran her fingers over what looked like Indian cotton in a rough-textured weave. "It does feel natural," she said. "How do they do it?"

"Incorporate natural fabrics and colors," Michael said. "We have linens, wools, everything. I think this is your desert look. Scrubable, low upkeep, and you won't see it in every Holiday Inn."

"Well, that's good to know." Amanda smiled. At least here she was in control. They all knew that she was designing The Pueblo, and that she'd be spread across the pages of every architectural journal and every woman's service magazine in the world—complete with names of fabric houses and furniture showrooms. Amanda Gray was the lady to court.

Well, it felt good, Amanda decided. And if Helen Tennyson was keeping an eye out for Amanda, and if Byron Moore was haunted, then maybe she *had* arrived. The price of success, she thought ruefully.

Amanda sat at a long table and leafed through massive volumes of wallpaper samples. "I like these undiluted tones," she said. "This sapphire blue is very fresh, and I like this rose, and this apple green and apricot. I assume this is all designed for crossover coordination?"

"Of course," Michael said. "But I thought you were more interested in desert tones. That's why I wanted you to see the natural classics collection."

Amanda looked up. "You think in clichés, Michael. That phony Indian cotton looks exactly like what it is—phony Indian cotton. Have you ever spent time in the desert?"

"Yes I have."

"Have you ever made *love* in the desert?"

Another shopper turned at this. Michael's eyes panicked beneath his glasses. "What?"

She turned up the corners of her mouth in amusement. "Then you don't really know what desert tones can be." She tapped a finger on the wallpaper book. "*This* is the desert. Clear tones. Pure cotton, pure wool, pure linen. I'm doing the most important lodging in the country, Michael."

"Okay, okay, I get the idea."

"Great." She leaned back in the stuffed chair and brushed a fingertip against her upper lip as she studied the samples. "These positive-negative color prints—can they be coordinated with the clear tones?"

"Sure."

Amanda considered. "I don't know. I'm really seeing pure tones for this. No geometrics, no prints at all. I know that's dangerous."

"But daring. If you could bring it off—"

She glanced up at him as he hovered. "Don't fawn, Michael. Just get me some more books."

"Sure," Michael said wearily. "You know, you don't have to be a bitch about it."

Amanda sighed. "I'm sorry. I hear what I'm doing and it isn't me. I've been under pressure."

"Well, I can imagine."

"No you can't."

"Has it been that bad?"

She made a sour face. "Worse. I really *do* need to see those books. My nerves are shot. You're my last stop today."

"Ah," Michael said greedily. "In that case, you get super service."

He strode away and Amanda shut her eyes and pressed her fingers gently against her eyeballs. White stars spun against blue lightning. Her head pounded and her feet were on fire. Well, this was her dream. Shopping, sparring with the showroom owners. Of course it was more fun installing what she'd designed than creating, which was just plain hard work. But this was the part she loved most.

Still, it was great to be in Manhattan, great to be making outrageous money. Not that being rich was an end in itself. She'd always had enough money to spend. That had been part of the problem when she was a kid; too much money and too little love.

But now, she had money and at least a strong maybe on the love. The blindness was probably exhaustion. So nothing was really as bad as it seemed. Except for the yawning emptiness in the pit of her soul.

"Books!" Michael announced as he dropped them on the table with a thud. Amanda pulled the top book off the pile. The soft fluorescent light bathed her hands in whiteness as she began to flip pages, suddenly awash with ideas as she responded to the colors.

An hour later, Amanda walked out of the showroom back into the pale sunshine. Her body ached from sitting, and she squared her shoulders as she strode down the avenue, watching the sun blaze against glass walls and make blue pools of shadow in sunken courtyards. *Keep going,* she told herself, as she was jostled and hemmed in by thousands of strangers. *You'll get it together any day now.*

Helen Tennyson marched into the conference room in the Municipal Center in Bradley, Arizona, with every intention of breaking balls. Her red blouson jacket shouted with rage and authority, and her dark hair framed a face paled with anger.

The circular conference table, set beneath a raised ceiling section, was already crowded with men. Helen didn't bother to say hello, but simply took a chair. A white-haired man in a blue suit turned to her and said, "Hello, Helen. Sorry about this mess."

"You'd damned well better be sorry," she said. Her eyes swept the assemblage, recognizing the mayor of Bradley, a state senator named Halsey, a police captain in tan uniform, and several attorneys. A toxic cloud of cigarette smoke already hung above the table.

Helen was handed xeroxed copies of reports, which she placed neatly in front of her without a glance. "I want an update on everything," she said. "I am so pissed off, you can't begin to know."

The men coughed and murmured to each other. The white-haired man next to her said, "Why don't we get right to this, gentlemen? We've got to know what's happening, because we're all getting killed in the media."

The mayor of Bradley, a rawboned, pepper-haired man in a shapeless brown suit, leaned forward. "I don't see where *you're* gettin' killed, Mr. Ledda. You're not running for office this November."

Helen rolled her eyes. "My God, is *this* what I have to look forward to? Backwoods politicians covering their asses?"

"Now *look,*" the mayor shouted, "if this woman does not keep a civil tongue—"

"Aw, Christ," Senator Halsey grumbled. He was a big man who sweated all the time. His dark gray suit was custom-fitted, and his sandy hair was thinning.

The mayor looked at Halsey. "*You* think she's in line, Ed?"

"I don't *give* a damn," Halsey said. He picked up his cigarette and took a deep drag. "I'm looking at an explosive racial situation in my state. I'm looking at the potential loss of millions of dollars of revenue and the potential loss of political support from bankers and businessmen. My life is flashing in front of me. Helen's got a right to be sore."

The white-haired man was Dan Ledda, Helen's attorney. He clasped his hands in front of him on the table. "Boys, why don't we deal with facts and leave emotional outbursts for later?"

Ledda gestured at the uniformed police captain, a muscular, crop-haired man who looked like a Marine drill instructor. "Why don't we hear the official report of what happened at The Pueblo site?"

Helen touched her fingertips to her eyebrows. "Yes, I'd like to hear that report." Her perfume, subtle and expensive, lent the masculine room a sweet redolence.

The captain took a pair of eyeglasses from a worn case clipped to his shirt pocket, and slipped them on. He glanced at several official reports in front of him. He read in an uncomfortable monotone. "At four o'clock on September 15th, Gregory Curtin, a foreman for McCarville Construction, went behind a trailer at The Pueblo site for a cigarette." The captain looked up and gestured vaguely. "This is all from Curtin's deposition."

"I gathered that," Helen said. "Go on."

The captain lowered the report. "I don't have to listen to this, ma'am. I don't work for you."

Helen sighed wearily. "No, you certainly don't. But you do work for this city. And you have some responsibility to protect the people who live and work *in* the city. Since you totally failed to exercise that responsibility, I think you ought to act like a man with an apology to make."

The captain's face darkened, and he appealed to the mayor. The mayor said to Halsey, "Look, Ed, this is ridiculous."

"Helen," Halsey said, "I know you're upset, but insulting everybody in the room isn't going to help."

Helen sat more stiffly in her chair. "My foreman was

beaten nearly to death,'' she said. ''My equipment was vandalized. Pipe bombs were planted. Three security guards were hospitalized. One of them may go blind. And on your local television station, I had the thrill of seeing a videotape made by this shithead Indian . . .''

''Damn it, Helen!'' Halsey cried.

''Oh, shove it up your ass,'' Helen snapped. Her eyes blazed. ''I watched this little shit tell me that his gang would cripple and kill as many people as it took to get me out of here. Not to mention destroying every piece of equipment on the job. Now this was really fine editorial judgment. What kind of half-assed news director puts that kind of crap on the air?'' Helen pointed tremblingly toward the door. ''I had to walk into this building through a mob of ragpickers and junkies who were *demonstrating* on the steps, cheering this Indian turd as a champion of the oppressed. You *bet* I'm steamed. I want to know what the police are going to do about giving us protection and putting that scumbag in jail.''

Helen lit a slim brown cigarette with shaking fingers and sat back in her chair. The men at the table fidgeted and some muttered angrily. Ledda looked down at his knuckles as he spoke. ''Helen, you ought to know that the gentleman across from you is Richard Juan, a Navajo attorney representing the tribespeople in this area.''

Helen's eyes darted to the tall, olive-complected man in a blue suit and maroon tie. ''Well, Mr. Juan, I'm glad you're with us. If you're representing the tribes, you must be very anxious to help us catch this sleazeball.''

Ledda sighed hopelessly. Juan essayed a smile and tented his fingertips. ''I'm not a fan of Peter Deal's,'' he said in a rich voice. ''He's a criminal, there's no doubt about it. But he has support because he says what a lot of our people are afraid to say.''

''Like what?'' Helen asked.

''Things about poverty, drunkenness, illiteracy, drugs. We're in pretty bad shape, Miss Tennyson. I won't go into the whole history of it—''

''Thank you.''

Juan smiled again. ''But the problems are there. We're a racial minority, and an oppressed one. A lot of our people just want to make ends meet and stay out of sight. They're tired of betrayals. But some of our people want to make it better. We want to run for office. We've been working on several reclamation plans for our grazing lands, plans to make us self-sufficient. Plans to integrate us with our society. These are long-range plans, of course. It won't be easy to change things. . . ."

"Mr. Juan," Helen said. "I'm not really interested in this stuff. Could you make a point?"

"Jesus Christ," the mayor said as he shook his head. Juan flushed, but kept his composure. "All right," he said. "If The Pueblo is built, right on the border of our reservation, it will cut us off forever. It will destroy our grazing lands. It will create new slums. It will evict marginal people from their homes and farms. It will be an oasis for the very rich and powerful. Those Indians who don't starve or commit suicide will go on welfare or become migrants. The complex as it's designed will blight the natural landscape and spoil the ecosystem of the desert. It will alter population density and have far-reaching consequences due to new roads and airfields. This is a pure money deal, to benefit the powerful and their political pets."

"I see," Helen said. "And what are you doing about it?"

"We're fighting," Juan said. "We're filing injunctions and seeking restraining orders. But that takes time and we're running out of time. We're going to lose, as we always do. It creates a sense of despair and impossible frustration. Peter Deal has come at the right time for desperate people."

"Oh." Helen touched her fingertips to her red lips. At that moment, the door to the conference room opened and Jason strode in, brisk in a tan suit, his hair glistening from the heat outside.

"Hi," he said airily. "Sorry to be late. I was talking to my construction people."

"That's all right," Helen said sweetly. "That's what you're supposed to do. Sit down, Jason."

Jason ignored her condescending tone and greeted some of the men at the table with handshakes and a shared word. He took an empty seat next to Senator Halsey and busied himself lighting a cigarette. "What did I miss?"

"Absolutely nothing," Helen said pointedly. "This gentleman here is an Indian lawyer." She seemed to find the concept hilarious. "He's fighting us in court. Did you know about this?"

"I'd heard there was opposition," Jason said neutrally. "But I assumed all the preliminary legal stuff had long been taken care of. Dan?"

Ledda pushed a hand through his hair. "We thought it had. But resistance has continued. There'll probably be a settlement."

"A settlement?" Helen said. "You mean we'll *pay* them? For *what*?"

Ledda gestured toward Juan. "For what he mentioned."

"*Bullshit,*" Helen spat. "That means we acknowledge that he's right. Jason, are we destroying the desert's ecosystem? Creating Indian slums? Sending swarms of migrant workers out to die?"

Jason's temples trickled with perspiration. "Not that I know of."

Dan snorted. Helen smiled. "I didn't think so. Dan, I think you ought to consult with me before you agree to any settlement with our red brothers."

Halsey put up both hands. "Okay, enough. I've had a bellyful here."

"When *I'm* ready," Helen snapped back.

"Goddamn it," the mayor shouted, "when did she become our boss?"

The shouting became general, and Helen seemed to drink it up like a nourishing vitamin cocktail. Jason's mouth turned up in a rueful smile. He allowed a brief thought of Amanda, which refreshed him. His blood pumped faster as he prepared for his coup. He usually got a charge out of controlling a situation; it helped him forget that he was the most jerked puppet of all.

"Right," he said quietly. He reached beneath his jacket and drew a .38 revolver from a shoulder holster, mentally thanking Amanda for the idea, which she'd given him when she'd recounted her abduction to Byron's mansion. He leveled the gun at the assemblage and waited as they realized what he was doing. The police captain went for his own gun but Jason said, "Don't try it, I'm a crack shot." The captain leaned back, looking dyspeptic. Helen gazed at Jason with rapt admiration.

The table quieted and the men sat tensely, not certain of how to react. Jason's heart thumped as his adrenalin flowed. It felt good to hold the gun, and for a delicious moment, he fantasized about shooting Helen between her eyes.

"I bought this gun," Jason said, "because I need protection. No psycho Indian is going to beat the shit out of me when I'm on the job. It's a shame that I have to work under these conditions."

Ledda said, "Jason, I appreciate the object lesson, but I think pointing that gun at us is a criminal act."

"Bet your ass," the captain said.

Jason sat back and smiled. "Well, I wouldn't want to be a criminal." He pulled the trigger, and even though he knew nothing would happen, he felt a surge of power roar through his blood. He winced at the loud click and enjoyed the gasps around the table. He chuckled and replaced the gun in the holster. "I wouldn't point a loaded gun at anybody," Jason said. "It wouldn't be rational." His eyes narrowed and his face became deadly serious. "And it isn't rational to allow a juvenile delinquent to threaten a major project or to get air time on television. We're all reasonable people. We have interests at stake. Captain, you would have booked me if I'd loaded this gun."

"I might book you yet, wise ass," the captain said.

"But Lone Dog has injured several people and destroyed expensive equipment. Can we expect the same zeal for law enforcement?"

Halsey poured a glass of water from a copper carafe. The captain removed his glasses and said, "You think we don't want him? We have a whole situation room set up just to track this bastard. But he knows the desert better'n any cop. He's got lots of friends who'll hide him, and lie for him. We go down to South Bradley and roust the bars and they all clam up. He could be in the back room of Nate's Cafe, but we'll never know."

Jason finished his cigarette and ground it out in the ashtray. "Put on more men. Bring in outside help. You let this job be sabotaged, Senator Halsey's ass is on the line. Senator Halsey is on important committees. Lots of federal funds ready to be cut off. Things could get very cold in the Sunbelt."

The mayor made double fists. "Is this what it comes down to? Threats?"

Halsey sucked on his lower lip, looking tired. "It always comes down to threats, Burt. The man is right. Captain, this boy has got to be stopped."

"And no TV coverage," Helen added.

The captain said, "I have no control over that."

"The mayor does," Helen said. "And Senator Halsey does. There's to be no more publicity for that clown. I want double security at my building site, or triple if that's what it takes, and not at my expense. What I have to pay to replace equipment is going to cost this city and this state. And if anything goes on television it's going to be my foreman and my guards and people are going to see what our heroic tribesmen do to get their way. Mr. Juan, I can assure you, there won't be a hell of a lot of nationwide support for your cause."

Juan's jaw worked in rage and frustration. "You don't think we *have* a cause, Miss Tennyson?"

"No, not really. Of course, I don't care much if anybody else wants to get involved. But you might want to assist in bringing in our bad little Indian boy if you want to have *any* hope of success."

Juan said nothing. Ledda spoke. "Well all right. I think we're agreed. We're all pretty outraged at Lone Dog's effrontery. We're frustrated at his ability to slip through police nets, to strike at our people and equipment at will. The cost overruns are mounting and the banks are becoming nervous. I think increased security is a must, and increased effort to capture Peter Deal. I think we all regret being ungracious here, but it *is* an unnerving situation."

"I don't regret anything except the stupidity of others," Helen said.

Ledda smiled. The meeting broke up, the men gratefully standing and stretching. The captain huddled with the mayor while Senator Halsey collared Juan and Ledda. Helen quickly went to Jason, who smoothed his suit jacket.

"I loved it," Helen said.

"Did you?"

"Absolutely beautiful. You continue to be a treasure."

"I'm happy about that, Helen. I was thrilled to see you lose control."

She made a rude noise. "I have no patience for these bullshit sessions. I'm going to have Dan's balls on a plate for talking settlement with Tonto over there. What's *with* these Indians all of a sudden?"

Jason shrugged. "We're destroying their homes and damaging the land. Nothing new, but you're particularly obnoxious about it."

Helen smirked. "Jason, you sound concerned. Is your heart bleeding?"

"I have no heart," Jason said. "You cut it out."

Her eyes hardened at his flippancy. "Well," she said with a quick sigh, "how is little Amanda doing?"

"Little Amanda is in New York, shopping," Jason said. "She's very good at it, from what I hear."

"Glad to know somebody is competent. Is she generating good publicity?"

"Best kind," Jason said. "Magazine articles, talk show appearances. When did a *designer* ever make a talk show before? She's special, and beautiful and charming on camera."

"Super," Helen said. "Looks like Byron Moore molded a great little piece of ass. *Is* she?"

"Is she what?"

"Great in bed," Helen said. "You *are* sleeping with her on a regular basis, aren't you?"

"None of your business."

Helen checked her Cartier watch with affected aloofness. "Oh, of course not. Don't let the affair get too syrupy, dearest. Keeping her stuffed and mounted will keep her content, but I wouldn't want love to bloom in the desert."

"Why not?" Jason asked. "I've been in love before."

"I know," Helen said. "And anytime you threatened the franchise with emotional instability, I moved you somewhere else, like a good pawn."

Jason's chest constricted. "That's right. I recall all your little moves. Paying them off, scaring them off."

"Well, I'm very good at what I do," she said. "I just like to remind you that I have no intention of giving you up. You're too terrific. So enjoy Amanda's pussy, but don't gaze too deeply into her eyes. I don't trust her."

Jason looked playfully at Helen. "You're worried about her, aren't you?"

Helen blanched only momentarily. Her smile was deadly. "No. I only worry about Indian boys who cost me money."

She patted his arm and strode away to speak with Ledda. Jason smiled bitterly. He wondered how strong his feelings would grow, and what would happen when he pulled out the truth, like he had his gun, and leveled it at Amanda, and Helen, and himself. *Bang bang*, he thought icily. *Everyone dies*.

chapter 13

AMANDA wriggled closer to Jason and her hands played along the wide sweep of his shoulders. She darted her tongue into the rim of his ear and stroked the nape of his neck. He moaned gratefully and one powerful arm held her tightly in the mussed bed. Her belly fluttered as it brushed his groin and she rubbed her cleft against his thigh, moistening his skin.

She raised her head to look down at his shadowed face. Small fires still burned throughout her body, unquenched even after the sexual flood of their reunion. She hadn't suspected how ravenous she'd been for him until now.

"Jase?"

His eyes flickered. "Hm?"

She trailed sweet kisses over his face and neck. Mingled smells of his shaving soap, cologne, and sweat made her heady. "Lord, I missed you."

"Missed you too, babe."

Her fingers lovingly pushed back tendrils of his hair. "I'm burning with ideas," she said. Her voice was husky from lovemaking. "I ordered tons of stuff in New York. Fabrics, wallcoverings, carpeting. I think you'll like it."

"Can't wait," he said sleepily. She bent her head and brushed her lips over the swell of his biceps, then bit into his wrist. He smiled and tugged at his unkempt hair.

"I love you," she sighed. He hugged her close and she sought his mouth. The kiss turned long and passionate and she moaned deep in her throat. She felt him thicken against her vulva.

"Yes . . ." she hissed, and moved against him, urging. He

began to breathe more raggedly and his fingers pressed into her shoulders. His tongue touched her inner cheeks and explored the roof of her mouth. She shuddered at his expertise. Sometimes it bothered her, when she remembered to think about it. Was she just another violin to be played by a bored virtuoso? *At least am I a Stradivarius*? she thought giddily.

Jason assumed command now. He pushed her back on the bed and nuzzled her throat. He was growing his morning beard and the rough whiskers raked her tender skin. His hands cupped her breasts and his thumbs rubbed her straining nipples. He suckled her avidly. She tangled her hands in the hair of his chest. This was not going to be a long rhapsody of sex; it would be a coda.

Jason's hands moved down to span her waist and then to the tangle of curls between her thighs. His fingers rubbed her throbbing clitoris into madness. She gasped and her eyes flew open. She saw a grid of silver light and black shadow on the ceiling and heard muffled cars outside. The crumpled sheet was drenched against her spine as she arched to receive him.

He parted her and filled her. He felt hot. She groaned and grabbed his neck. He thrust rhythmically and she seized his hips to help control the rhythm. She went a little mad with the rapture of it, as she always did. Christ, it was something to realize that there *was* a difference when you found a special man. It was great to open her emotions and feel vulnerable and girlish. Jason made her feel this way, and nobody else had. Not Byron, not anybody.

She climbed to her peak rapidly. His hands slipped under her buttocks and he plunged deep into her body's crevice. She sensed his helplessness in the knotting of his muscles. She didn't feel him climax but she knew he had, because he softened and collapsed next to her, panting.

She smiled through her own breathlessness and toyed with his wet hair. She was accustomed to his movie-star handsomeness and had begun to see more character. His eyes were capable of varied expression, confessing his feelings and opinions. His cheeks puffed to wonderful red apples when he smiled or acted silly. He never trimmed his moustache quite perfectly, and there were always a few little bristles that didn't mesh. The sun had lined his skin, making delicious crinkles at his eyes. She found his body fascinating, not only because it was so well developed, but because it moved with a panther's grace and a little boy's hesitation, all at once. She liked to feel the rough hairs on his inner thighs, and his football-scarred knees. She liked his cologne and the way he plopped down when he was bushed, and the way cigarette smoke wisped from between his lips.

But even now, filled with love, Amanda felt cold and scared. This sleepy, gorgeous man, nestled in the sheets beside her, still kept her locked out. She and Jason weren't complete yet. She stroked his eyebrow and spoke in a soft voice. "It's been very rough for you, hasn't it?"

"Pain in the butt," he murmured.

"I couldn't believe it when I read the stories. Poor Greg. I saw him in the hospital. He's really in pain."

Jason's eyes glowed with rage. "Well, four guys jumped him. They beat on him for about half an hour. Really enjoyed it. He's never going to be right."

She hissed, shuddering closer to Jason. "This is outrageous. And the bombs . . ."

"It's bad news." He sat up very suddenly and passed a hand over his forehead. "You got the lighter?"

She rolled over and tapped with her fingers until she found the Bic on the bedtable. "Here."

He pulled a cigarette from the deflated pack on his own night table and stuck it between his lips. She leaned towards him, raising herself slightly, and lit the cigarette. His face gleamed in the brief orange light, then fell once more into shadow.

"Be careful with that," she admonished.

"Yeah." He smoked silently for a few moments. Then he said, "I'm getting tired of this bullshit, Amanda."

"Which bullshit is that?"

"Pulling guns at meetings, putting on a circus for Helen. The stakes always get bigger, but I'm a parody of myself."

Amanda propped herself against the pillows and ran her fingers down his back, liking the way it gave him chills. "I can understand," she said. "You'd like to spend your time creating, not troubleshooting."

He laughed. "That's it," he said cryptically. "That's the problem all right."

She stopped the back massage and pulled the sheet further up her exposed body, aware of the swollen sensation in her breasts from the pressure of his hands. "What *is* the problem, Jase?"

"Me," he said, and coughed from the smoke. She watched his back muscles bunch with effort, and rubbed his shoulders. She couldn't keep her hands off him.

"Meaning what?"

"No meaning. I've been doing this for twelve years now. I know every corporate exec in the *Fortune 500*. I've played golf with presidents. I do the rubber chicken circuit year after year. It's all crap." He exhaled sharply, then turned his head to caress her with cat's eyes. "The women were getting stale, too. I made it with models, centerfolds, pro cheerleaders. You know how fast that gets boring? Then it had to be wives of business associates or there was no excitement. Then it started to be daughters of business associates, and I got scared. I'm a country boy, Amanda. My Mom and Dad ran a dairy farm. I didn't want to end up a degenerate."

She shivered at the grief and self-loathing that infected him. "I'm glad you didn't."

He sucked on the cigarette and made the ash glow red. "I started drinking to kill the pain. It made me nasty, especially to women. That's why I gave you a hard time when we met. But you had little blowtorches in your eyes and you cut right through my armor. I was back on the farm, Amanda, smelling the goddamn hay."

She laughed. "Wow."

He reached out and touched her chin tenderly. "I got real feelings again. You saved my life."

"Did I?"

"Sure."

"Then why so miserable?"

He gave another secret laugh and withdrew his hand. "You solved the sex problem, not the rest of it."

"Can I try?"

He shook his head and doused the cigarette in a bedside ashtray. "Nope."

"Give me a straight answer, Jase."

That brought another smile. "Let's keep what we've got. Sex was never this great. It's better with love, for sure. I like thinking about you when you're not here, and I like that you think about me."

She felt tears slide down her face. "Jase, I love you so much. I wish I could really know you."

"You'd be disappointed."

"Try me."

"Leave it alone, Amanda." He twisted around and lay beside her. He kissed her lips and stroked her hair.

"What's going to happen with The Pueblo?" she asked.

He shrugged. "Nothing. It goes on."

"Even with all this violence?"

"We're not going to shut down because of some psycho."

"But the police can't do anything . . ."

Jason shushed her with a finger on her lip. "Come on, Amanda. Don't give me a headache over this. I've had it all week."

"Sorry. I was just interested."

"But there's nothing you can do."

She lay back, staring at the opposite wall and the framed prints on it. She was aware of light changing in the streets outside. "I know," she said. "That's been the story of my life."

"Christ, Amanda, don't start pitying yourself." He snuggled next to her, pulling the sheets over his chest. "You're designing the whole project. You're in charge. Don't get bent because you can't bring in the Indian."

Amanda fell silent and she could almost hear the silent hum of the electronic clock. She listened to Jason toss and felt his naked buttocks brush against her. "You know," she said finally, "I was reading what the Indians are saying. About how we're messing up their land."

"Yeah?" he mumbled.

She glanced at him, then back at her spot on the wall. "I do lots of research on any project I design."

"And?"

"They have a lot to say, Jase. I don't pretend to be an ecologist, but this may *not* be the perfect structure for this area. It's like putting up glass office towers in old gingerbread neighborhoods. It looks lousy. And it makes problems. *You* understand that. No sunlight, wind damage, traffic tie-ups, disruption of community. That always hurt me, Jase, to be a part of taking things away from people. Maybe because I was always thrown out with the garbage. But the idea of telling some poor couple to pack up or never see the sun again . . . it makes me miserable."

Jason turned back to her. "We're not putting up glass towers in an old neighborhood, Amanda. We're putting up a hotel in a desert. *Everybody* gets to see the sun."

"You know what I mean, damn it. That was just an analogy. I don't like to think that I'm hurting people."

"You think that's what you're doing?"

She couldn't tell whether his voice was mocking or sympathetic. "I don't know. Look, you're closer to it than I am. You designed the building. You know about the roads and the airstrip and the water and the power lines. Bradley is a boom town, a suburb with no city. Can it take the overload? And Jason, the desert is a beautiful place, and . . . shit, I don't know what I feel. I love this project. I envision this thing rising out of the desert and it's gorgeous. Then I think about the Indians packing up their trucks and driving away. . ."

Jason chuckled and touched her hair. "You're sentimental," he said. "I like that. The chic designing lady is a sap."

Her eyes blurred again. "Yes, I *am* a sap. I cry at Kodak commercials where the families are reunited, and I cry at little puppies in a pet store, and I like stuffed animals and love songs. I kept my teddy bear until I was nineteen . . ." She shook off the memory as too dangerous and smiled. "I used to wear a leather jacket and skintight jeans, but I kept this fuzzy blue mouse pinned to my collar. Yeah, I'm sentimental. And I worry about the Indians."

He shifted under the sheets. "Good. It makes you cuter. Get some sleep, Amanda. We all have to face the bullshit in the morning."

He let his voice trickle off as he burrowed into his pillow. Amanda remained propped up, her chest tight and hurting. She felt movement in her emotional landscape. She was changing. It couldn't go on much longer, being in control of her life and yet losing control over what happened to her. Thrilled about power and money and upset about the Indians. In love with Jason and hating his secrets. Triumphant over Byron Moore but terrified of seeing him again.

She pummeled her pillow and rested her cheek against it. Her body throbbed pleasantly from the lovemaking. Her mind raced wildly. A decision took shape that scared the hell out of her, but made sense.

As the sun rose high in the morning sky, Amanda drove a rented Cutlass sedan across the straw-colored high desert. She wore a lilac ensemble of light jacket over a shirt and sweater, with matching pants. Her feet were cool in sneakers. It was good to shuck business duds for a day and let brushed cotton pamper her skin.

The Indians' land was parched and dusty, with occasional clumps of sage, and long stretches of turkey wire wrapped around wooden fence posts. Against bleached sky and gunmetal clouds, high tension towers marched across the horizon. Amanda drove past a rusting truck body and stone huts. A pack of stray dogs scurried and barked after her car.

She took a deep breath and kept her foot on the gas. This was nuts. At least she should have told Jason or the police. But Mandy Gray often did crazy things. Like talking an armed fat man out of shooting a boy. Or screwing a diplomat in his own embassy. Or trying to find a psychopathic Indian.

She drove into the crumbling business district—a few blocks of stores, mostly boarded up. Some shops had iron gratings across their fronts. Windows were broken. A movie theater displayed an elaborate marquee, but only a few plastic letters remained, spelling nothing. Indian youths hung out in packs on the street. They squinted evilly at her car, and flashed lewd smiles. They smoked cigarettes, and wore leather vests over bare whipcord bodies, or denim jackets over rock concert T-shirts. Elderly people tottered by, their faces like tanned parchment. Behind plate glass windows, merchants looked out bleakly.

Amanda drove with damp hands, searching for a parking space. She waited for a battered pickup truck to back out and rattle down the road. Amanda pulled head-in, stopping the engine and yanking up the brake. She leaned back in the seat as stifling heat replaced air conditioned coolness. Through her sunglasses, she scanned the street. People passed by, shopping. She didn't see any youth gangs here. Just poor people, shuffling through a hot desert morning.

Amanda took a deep breath and got out of the car. The air slapped her like a great hand. She breathed pungent smells of heated asphalt, gasoline, and rotting garbage. She read the signs over the hardware store, the drug store, the liquor store. Filthy windows looked back, hiding faded merchandise. Grime coated every sill. Nobody bothered to sweep or hose down. And yet these weary victims had found a lawyer to fight The Pueblo. Because The Pueblo, *her* Pueblo, would isolate this ramshackle town forever and drive it into total ruin. These Indians and poor whites, deprived of almost everything that gave dignity to life, wanted to cling to their wasted existence.

Amanda shivered. Nothing was that black and white, she told herself. She struck off, walking purposefully down the street and catching stares. Her back tingled from the looks. Her ears reddened as she caught insinuating voices. *Damn, I should have told somebody.*

She stopped in front of Nate's Cafe. Neon beer signs flickered and buzzed in the soiled window. Her body seemed to swell and throb. Angry at her fear, she forced her hand to grip the doorknob and twist it open, and forced her legs to carry her inside.

There was no air conditioning, but a damp coolness washed over her and sucked away the heat of the sun. Fans turned slowly on the molded tin ceiling. Amanda's eyes teared from the smoke that fogged the room. An ancient jukebox played current rock music, at a volume that made her stomach twitch. Amanda noticed shadowy men and women seated at plain wooden tables, and at the long mirrored bar. A pink and green neon sign flashed on and off over the cash register. A dark-haired Indian youth blinked at her from behind the bar. He wore a flannel shirt and jeans and he wiped the bartop with a dirty rag. *Not Happy Hour at the Algonquin,* she thought wryly.

Amanda's nostrils recoiled at the smell of spilled liquor and urine. She took off her sunglasses and tried not to look back into the hostile eyes that stripped and gutted her. She went to the bar and sat stiffly on one of the stools.

The bartender looked at her with open hatred. "Yeah?"

"How about a rum and tonic, lots of ice?"

The bartender grinned. She heard snickers from elsewhere in the room. The music thumped in her head. The bartender made the drink, with exaggerated languor. He placed the filthy glass in front of her. Amanda braved the grime and took a sip. The tonic water was flat but the rum was strong and burned her throat.

"I'm Amanda Gray," she said. "I'm designing the interiors of The Pueblo."

Suddenly, there was only the music. Nobody spoke. The bartender looked around, then back at her. "What are you doing in here?"

She felt perspiration trickle down her ribs and puddle at her waist. Her heart threatened to burst through her clothes. "I've heard that Lone Dog comes here. If he's here now, I'd like to talk to him."

There was some laughter behind her, and a few pornographic comments. The music ended and Amanda heard the swish of fans in the silence. A fly buzzed insistently. She realized that the place was alive with flies, though she hadn't noticed before.

A new song began, a slow country tune. The bartender shook his head. "You better get out of here."

Amanda's fear transmuted into anger, as it often did. "I don't have a gun," she taunted. "And there are no cops outside."

"Hey," the bartender said, "I don't want to talk about it. I want you out."

"Sure," she said. She took money from a sports wallet she carried in her pants. She gave him a five and noticed he charged her three-fifty. She took the change, pointedly leaving nothing on the bar. "Tell Lone Dog I was here. I was willing to listen to what he had to say."

"I don't *give* a shit," the bartender said.

"That's too bad," Amanda snapped back. Her head throbbed and her body was a drawn bowstring. The bartender regarded her with disbelief. Amanda spoke again. "You're really terrific at jumping guys and wrecking stuff that doesn't belong to you. You like to make threats and run. But you don't really want to accomplish anything. I came here to listen, and maybe do something. But what you want is to be bad little boys. Well, forget my sympathy. You can all twist in the wind."

Amanda turned and strode across the room, nearly exploding with terror. She prayed that she had enough time to get the hell out and onto the street where, presumably, there was a cop within shouting range.

Her hand reached for the doorknob when she heard the voice. It felt like a knife blade between her shoulders.

"Stand still."

Amanda stopped, cursing under her breath. Everything drained out of her. She let her hands drop away from the door, and turned around. A fat Indian youth in a Stones T-shirt and faded jeans stood by an open door leading to a back room. "Come on," he said.

Right, Amanda thought wildly. *Now what do I do?*

The fat boy smiled. "Nobody's going to shoot you, baby. Just want to talk to you."

Amanda rationalized that they would not rape or beat her,

knowing who she was. It was a tenuous security, but it got her back across the room and past the fat boy, who stank from body odor.

That fat boy shut the door. The back room was small, dark, and stale. Chairs were piled atop tables, and there were racks of glassware and cartons of soda bottles. A window let in a knifepoint of sunlight. The room stank of beer and mildew.

Three Indians sat around a wooden table; they'd been playing cards, and there was money showing. A fourth Indian sat in a wooden chair tilted up against a back door to the street. A thin sliver of daylight rimmed his face.

"I'm Lone Dog," he said in a surprisingly thin voice.

Amanda struggled to breathe. "How do I know that?" she asked.

She sensed, rather than saw, his smile. "You have to take my word for it. You are crazy, making a scene like that. You know you're crazy?"

"I've been told," she said.

"Yeah. Well, whoever told you was right. What kind of shit is this?"

"I wanted to hear what you had to say."

He snorted. "You *heard* what I had to say. I say don't build the hotel. What's so hard about it?"

She sighed. She'd run with mean kids, and she knew all about bluff, but this boy was a killer. "I've always designed in harmony with the setting," she said. "I don't ignore what the land needs and what people want. I don't come from this part of the country but I've come to love the desert, and I'm not out to take away your land. I think I can suggest ways to meet everyone's needs. I can talk to Helen Tennyson and Jason Turner about changes, before the construction goes too far. *If* you stop throwing tantrums and tell me what your people really need."

Lone Dog was silent. He picked up an open bottle of beer from the floor and tilted it to his lips. He belched. "Okay," he said. "What my people need is white pussy. I mean all we got is Indian pussy."

The other youths in the room cracked up. Amanda felt her face burn. She ran her tongue over her lips. "Cute," she said. "Is this going to be the tone of the conversation?"

The laughter continued. Lone Dog drank more beer. "Let me tell you what the story is. Your liberal bullshit is like all liberal bullshit. What we want is no hotel. No big shots flyin' their choppers in. No golf courses with little Indian boys as caddies. No Indian sisters as whores."

"Don't be ridiculous," Amanda said warmly, "nobody's going to do—"

"Shut up," Lone Dog said. He sat up and slammed his chair's forelegs onto the floor. Suddenly, he was vulpine and deadly. "No hotel. That's the only deal."

"It's unrealistic," Amanda said. "I'm trying to help and you're being a child."

Lone Dog laughed crudely. "Well, I'm really sorry about that. Look, Amanda, sorry you wasted your time. But I'm *glad* we blew up people. We're going to blow up more of them, break their asses right and left. You're finished. Everybody's going to die, baby. I can't be stopped. I am the wolf witch. I am *immortal*."

The laughter became raucous. One of the Indians at the table filled his mouth with beer and spat it on Amanda's legs. She gasped. "You son of a bitch—"

"Get out," Lone Dog warned. "And don't come back. You get one free trip and then you pay."

The fat Indian opened the door. Amanda was trembling convulsively. She bit back her humiliation, knowing there was nothing she could do or say that would make a difference. She walked rapidly out of the room and through the bar. This time she opened the front door and hurried into the street. The light and air smacked her with oven heat. She kept walking, oblivious of stares and comments. Her wet leg felt diseased.

She found a parking summons on her windshield. With vengeful fury, she tore it up and dropped the pieces on the sidewalk. A small crowd began to gather. Amanda slid into her car and shut the door. It took her several tries to insert the ignition key. Deliberately, she sat still and calmed herself, not wanting to have an accident here. She put her sunglasses back on and backed carefully out of the parking space.

Amanda tore up the street and turned the radio to the first beautiful music station she could find. She usually hated that kind of music, but she wanted something, anything, to wash away the snarl of the jukebox rock. She drove out of town and began to feel less shaken out on the desert where the rocks glowed fiery orange in the waning sun and the sky looked clean and endless.

Amanda let the crying come, a necessary release. Lone

Dog had put the fear of God into her. She knew he was truly dangerous. This was not a game. Helen had to be made to see it, and Jason. Amanda's world had abruptly grown more brutal, nearly as brutal as it had once been, and her classy afternoons in designer showrooms seemed faintly absurd.

chapter 14

AMANDA ran into news reporters at the entrance to the office tower that held the Bradley headquarters of The Pueblo. *Of course,* she realized; they were all news right now, and she'd driven straight to Lone Dog's neck of the desert. Shaking from her clash with Lone Dog, Amanda tried to get past the cameras and microphones, but they stoned her with questions.

"Did you try to meet with Lone Dog?"

"Did you find him?"

"What did he tell you?"

Amanda shook her head, fighting back tears. "Please," she murmured, "I didn't see anybody. Let me through."

Two of Helen's flacks emerged from the building and ran interference for her. They said "No comment," and pushed back the reporters so Amanda could get into the building. She sighed with relief as the air conditioning touched her heated skin. As she strode under the steel sculpture that hung suspended from the four-story ceiling, one of the flacks fell into step with her.

"Helen wants to see you right now," he said.

Amanda wasn't surprised. The flack stayed behind to prevent the media from advancing. Amanda pressed the elevator button and took off her sunglasses. She took quick, calming breaths to reassure herself, and watched people crisscrossing the lobby. The elevator door closed and Amanda rode up to the twentieth floor.

She organized her thoughts as she walked down a lavender-carpeted corridor filled with artwork. Helen's secretary smiled sympathetically and buzzed her in.

Helen stood by a custom desk, framed in light from three windows. Her blue ruffled blouse seemed to emit a dark light, hissing with anger. "I think we'd better have this out," she said.

"Maybe we'd better."

"What the fuck were you doing in the Indian quarter?"

Whew, Amanda thought, *you don't mince words.* "What makes you think I was there?"

Helen rolled her eyes heavenward. "Oh, Christ. Is it going to be *that* kind of discussion?" She focused her rapt eyes on Amanda. "Could we not waste time?"

Amanda had learned something about power games from Byron, and a bit more from making it on her own. Deliberately, she picked out a chair far from Helen's desk and sat down, crossing her legs. "Why do you think I was in the Indian quarter?"

Helen glared. Her eyes acknowledged the point scored, but she remained at her desk and spoke in a clenched voice. "You were seen driving there and driving back. You were watched on the streets of South Bradley. I raised heaven and earth to get the police to go after Lone Dog. They have the whole town under surveillance."

Amanda's blood pounded. "Okay, you got me. What's your problem?"

Helen smiled. "So we're going to play hardass. I knew you'd be poison from the beginning. You survived Byron Moore and made a name for yourself. Okay, dear, I have no strength to fight. You don't have to tell me where you went or what you did. But you *do* have to pack your nightie and get the hell out if you're going to sabotage my project."

Amanda needed a shower and a stiff drink. "Actually, Helen, I had every intention of reporting to you. If you weren't so paranoid, I would have come up here on my own. Thanks, by the way, for rescuing me from the media sharks."

"Don't thank me," Helen said. "I didn't want you to say anything dumb."

Amanda smiled. "Do you have anything to quench my thirst?"

"Dear, I'm not here to entertain you. I have work to do. I just want to know what's going on with my own people."

Amanda uncrossed her legs and leaned slightly forward. "Okay. I drove into South Bradley to try to find Lone Dog. I'd read that he hangs out there sometimes."

"Yes. That's why the police have it staked out."

"Well, I don't know how good the police are, but I spoke to Lone Dog."

Helen remained outwardly impassive. "You did."

Amanda nodded. "Or at least some guy who said he was Lone Dog. I couldn't see him clearly."

"God in heaven." Helen looked tragically out the window, magnificent in profile. *She could play Medea,* Amanda thought. Helen turned back and rapped her knuckles on the desk. "What did you talk about, may I ask?"

Amanda briefly repeated the conversation. "He's not going to negotiate," she finished.

Helen sucked on her lower lip. "Neither will we, Amanda. You *did* hear me say that?"

"Yes."

"So what could you offer him?"

"My word."

"To do *what*?"

"To listen, and consider. To make changes."

"On whose authority?"

Amanda battled her mounting anger. "Yours."

"But I said I *wouldn't* make changes."

"I hoped to persuade you."

"Did you?" Helen went behind her desk and sat slowly and ominously. "How *dare* you!" she spat. "How dare you take it upon yourself to suck up to that scum? You're working for *me*."

"No," Amanda said. "I work for myself. You contracted with my firm to have me do the interiors of your hotel. The contract does not limit the people I may talk to, nor does it limit my ideas."

"Ah, well, a declaration of independence." Helen sighed and seemed to study her hands on the desk. "You're intent on some kind of clash of wills. I don't have the time or the patience for it. I didn't like your fresh mouth or your snippy attitude from the start. You're a new kid on the block. You've had some lucky breaks and you have some talent. But you're way out of your league with this job. Jason *begged* me to take you on. Well, *he* can take responsibility for your fucking up. So far I haven't seen any designs that make my blood rise. It all looks ordinary, and I'm beginning to worry about your ability. Let me assure you I have other people on call."

Helen leaned forward, eyes narrowed. "I don't give a damn what our contract says. I am building this hotel. I am taking the risks. I am putting up the money, including the money that pays *you*. I don't let scum stay in my hotels and I don't close down because scum tells me to. Join the Sierra Club in your spare time and talk to the Indians *after* you finish this assignment.

"But right now, stay out of it. You have no authority on this project. You may have cost us more equipment, more injury, God knows what else. You made me look like an ass. Give it up, Amanda. Go back to your desk and draw some designs. For God's sake, you've got Jason humping you, isn't that enough?"

Amanda leaped from her chair. "Shut your filthy mouth."

Helen darkened. "Temper, too. Did I strike a nerve? You aren't pregnant, are you?"

Amanda shook her head, about to explode. "You're some piece of work, Helen. I don't know how you manage to stay in business."

Helen thrust a hand crudely between her legs. "Brass balls," she said. "I strap 'em on every morning. Don't like my language? Don't like my personality? *Good*. Who needs bosom buddies? Just enjoy the money and the opportunity I'm giving you. Be a good little twat and stay out of my way. Meeting is over."

Helen snatched up the phone receiver and punched out a number. Amanda stood in the middle of the office, stunned, as Helen swiveled toward the window and spoke softly into the phone. Amanda felt the blood rush to her head. Beaten and infuriated, she spun, and strode out the door, ignoring the secretary on her way back to the elevator. A terrific bar waited on the mezzanine level.

A half hour later, Amanda nursed her second vodka stinger. The shakes had calmed, but the underlying rage and despair remained, like a throbbing wound. She listened to the rock music, and let her eyes reflect the designer lighting. The plush bar was nearly empty.

She was at a crossroads, for sure. She couldn't continue to design this project under these conditions. Her rational mind reminded her that Helen had been deliberately insulting, just to get Amanda's goat. It didn't matter. The disrespect was there, and the arrogance of Lone Dog, and the threat of Byron Moore, and the mystery of Jason.

Too many phantoms to fight. She was like a kid at the joystick, with aliens zooming in from all sides, and she was out of lives. Amanda took a sip of the cold, clear drink. She smiled as she remembered how she once drank vodka—from the bottle, along with her badassed friends.

The rock beat thumped in her gut. She stared into the glass and cradled it with both palms. She could play back the movie of her life on the blank screen of her memory. Like the clip of T.J.'s Thunderbird, gleaming in the Westchester night, with the radio loud and the top down. She always came back to that night, to her last try at suicide.

Amanda took more of her drink and surrendered herself to the cradle of memory.

Mandy threw back her chiseled head and laughed as the T-Bird roared through curving streets. The scream of the engine, the stink of burned rubber, exhilarated the sixteen-year-old girl. *Man,* T.J. was cruising.

Mandy tightened her grip on the half-empty bottle of vodka in her fist. There wasn't a hell of a lot of sensation left in her hand, and pretty soon she'd drop the bottle. The thought made her giggle. Curt shifted next to her and his hipbone jarred her pelvis. She muttered, "Get outta here."

Curt looked at her with cat's eyes in a lean face. His mane of silky hair gleamed. "Shit, Mandy, you're ripped. Lemme have the bottle."

She jerked it out of his reach, tipped it back, and let the clear liquor flood her mouth and dribble down her chin. She belched. There were loud protests from the other kids in the car. From behind the wheel, T.J. yelled, "Cut the shit, Mandy. You mess up this car, it's your ass."

"Just drive," Mandy slurred, "and leave the drinkin' to us."

Mandy loved being wasted. It felt so good to lose control. The cold wind lifted her shirt, and she felt the wetness of spilled liquor on her jeans. The leather seat punched her spine. She watched the star-parade of lights on the elegant homes set far back on their lawns.

Mandy's heart lifted. The other kids didn't know what she was talking about when she got going on contrast—"the white T-Bird, man, cruising down the black road, and us all grungy against the sharp houses. Like we're puking and cursing and they're serving canapes in tuxedoes. Can't you psych it?"

The other kids just shook their heads and laughed, but she knew what she meant. She drank up colors and shapes the way she drank liquor. Mandy drew pictures of it all, gorgeous doodles on her notebooks. Mr. Franklin had asked her to draw for the school magazine. She'd been flattered, but she never got around to really doing anything.

Woosh! T.J. was pounding it out now, so damned fast that Curt slammed into her and snapped her ribs against the door handle. She clutched the bottle and screamed. "Who-o-o!" she cried, as T.J. flattened out. "Good move!"

The pills were working now, making the sky ripple and the stars grow big and blinding. She could hardly feel her skin. She thought a spider was crawling up her breast, but it was Curt's hand. She shifted and kissed him passionately, tasting stale cigarettes on his breath. The car lurched and T.J. leaned on the horn. She broke the kiss and laughed, falling back against the seat. Her loins burned with sexual itch. Her ass felt like lead.

"I want pizza," she murmured. "Can we stop for pizza?"

"Sure," someone said.

"Anchovies," someone yelled.

"Mushrooms . . . pepperoni . . . extra cheese . . ."

The voices mushed together. The movement sent whirlwinds down her stomach. She rubbed against the car seat, panting. Curt snorted with laughter and plunged a hand under her jeans and panties. She felt herself wet him. She managed another swig of vodka.

She felt the T-Bird leave the road as some creepy homeowner shouted from a window. "Fuck off!" she bellowed. She hoped to God it was her fake parents. Her fake daddy with his nasty words, and his quick hand. *Slap*, and she was off his back. Mom just left lots of cheery notes with little happy faces over the i's while she popped off to meetings. Of course Mandy had the big house to herself a lot, and she and her friends did a job on the liquor and on everything else. Screw it. Daddy had some black woman driven in once a week from Brooklyn just to do the freaking laundry. He could afford breakage. Just like he could afford *her*. She'd learned a couple of years ago that she'd been adopted, when she'd needed some medical records for school. Mom and Dad told her then, and said she'd never find her real parents.

As the T-Bird thumped and bumped up a sandy incline into an abandoned patch of woods, a profound ache cut Mandy's insides open and her soul's blood poured out. Her palms sweated. The T-Bird jolted to a stop and doors chunked open. Cold air swirled into the car. Mandy's sneakers slipped on the mud. She swayed and crashed against the car. She looked up at the icy black void and the stars stabbed her eyes, like silver needles, tipped with her ruby blood. She wanted to sink down onto the earth and be sucked in.

Hallucinations flirted with reality. Mandy rested against the car. Willowy and long-haired, she looked aristocratically beautiful. Her eyes appreciated the tapestry of early spring branches woven against the housetops. She shivered. The blood in her fantasy turned into a hot bath, rushing from her brass faucet at home, steaming as it filled the yellow tub with bright red. She felt herself stepping into the blood, sitting down in it, watching it roll over her flat belly, watching her young woman's breasts bob in the crimson sea.

The kids passed around joints and lit up, making bright spots of orange against the blackness. T.J. bent low and took a deep drag, shutting his eyes and hissing as he retained the smoke. She smelled the pot, and thought of brick fireplaces. A red rose in front of the fire. A wine glass, half filled. A naked man with feathered hair and blue eyes, and herself in a white sweater and nothing else, her bottom naked and throbbing.

A pattering noise snapped her reverie. Joey was pissing next to the car. Curt's breath steamed Mandy's ear. His arm wrapped languorously around her and his tongue parted her lips. He pushed his groin against hers and rotated his hips. Mandy still gripped the vodka bottle in one hand. She draped her free hand around his neck. Her tongue probed his cheek and throat. He unzipped his dungarees and jerked them stiffly down around his legs. He tugged at her snaps and zippers and she wriggled to help. Suddenly, her buttocks were seared by icy metal. Wind rushed between her thighs. His hands dug under her shirt and roughly massaged her breasts. Mandy heard the other kids so clearly it thrilled her.

She shut her eyes and saw shapes in brilliant electric colors. If only she could paint them! Curt couldn't seem to penetrate her, so he bumped and banged into her and she humped back, faster and more rudely. She swooned from dizziness. She felt him convulse and spill all over her belly and down her legs.

A rush of agony tore her skull apart. Depression cracked her ribs and exposed her beating heart. Her bones ached. She was aware of a brittle, tinkling sound. Then she saw her delicate tapered fingers holding a fiery shard of glass. It caught silver flame from the moonlight. She was a dying animal, a bleeding, wounded beast. She felt the monster come spinning from her womb, trailing a bloody umbilical cord, snapping its razor teeth. She needed to kill, now . . .

She brought the shard of glass down into her upturned wrist, cutting deep. It burned and then was cold. She heard herself screaming. She cut again and again and heard all their screams, and for an instant imagined her funeral. She lay so beautiful and pale in an oak casket, her body shrouded in chiffon. . . .

Then she went blind and knew she was staring into headlights. Abruptly, she was lucid, still leaning half undressed against the T-Bird as the cops came to her. She felt embarrassed at her bleeding arm, and she cried piteously. "I'm sorry . . ." she whimpered. "I'm sorry . . ."

Mandy's fake parents didn't bother to visit her in the hospital. The school therapist came to see her as Mandy lay in bed with the stench of chemicals in her nose and one arm flung over her forehead. She listened to the drone of the older woman. At this stage, the depression lay on her like a cold fog.

She was released and driven home by her father, a bony man with a cropped haircut and tortoiseshell glasses. He was a corporate accountant and made more money than God. Mandy sat back and brooded in the Mercedes. She watched the stately houses sweep by, and the acres of green landscaped beauty. The splendid homes were as bleak as gray prison walls for the broken teenager.

Mandy fled to her room, expecting the usual shit. Mom would cry and wonder how she screwed up. Dad would avoid her and be scared because he was losing control.

But this time it was different. Mandy was called downstairs an hour after supper. She rolled off her bed and fluffed back her hair tiredly. Her bandaged wrist ached. Only her drugged condition had prevented her from finishing the job. That, and her friends holding her back. Mandy shook her head. They were all getting pretty sick of her. They liked to horse around, but they didn't like getting busted. Mandy was *too* off the wall.

She grabbed her worn teddy bear and came down. Right away she saw Mr. Moore in the living room. She'd glimpsed him once or twice when he'd visited Dad on business, usually after she was asleep. He was incredibly handsome and hypnotic. As he stood, his slate eyes surveyed the priceless display of paintings and sculpture. This was the one part of her life that Mandy loved. At night sometimes, she'd sneak downstairs and run her fingers over the pre-Columbian masks, the decorated boxes, the urns and figures. She knew her folks couldn't care less. They collected to show off and for tax write-offs.

But Byron Moore knew what the hell he was looking at; Mandy could tell. He wore a natural silk suit that flattered his godlike body. His glistening black hair was shot through with stone gray and his skin was tanned. Mandy felt her thighs warm at the sight of him, and her heart thumped. Her father, who sat on the couch, motioned her to a side chair. Mandy glanced at Moore with veiled eyes and curled into the chair, fondling her teddy. She looked at her folks and at Moore with suspicion and hostility.

"You've seen Byron Moore here a few times," Dad said, as he fiddled with a lighter and a pipe.

Mandy said nothing.

Dad exhaled angrily. Mom sat on the sofa across the room from Dad, twining her hands in her lap. Dad said, "It's time you met him. Byron runs several major art galleries and sits on the boards of two great museums. He's an international collector and dealer and an independent multimillionaire and businessman. He's important and influential."

Mandy stroked the bear's ears and brushed her lips against the matted fur. What the hell was this speech for?

Dad reddened. "Would you like to say hello, Mandy?"

Mandy scrunched deeper into the chair. Byron Moore smiled and his eyes caressed her like loving hands. "That's all right," he said. "Mandy's pretty scared and lonely right now."

"Well, as long as you don't mind her rudeness," Dad said. He finished lighting his pipe and the sweet smoke drifted through the room. Mom sighed painfully and her eyes darted like a trapped bird's. "Can we tell her?" she said. "I don't think this is fair."

Dad clamped his teeth around the pipe stem and shook his head. "Byron, I apologize for both of them."

Mom crimsoned. "Don't apologize for *me*. Who do you think you are?"

Mandy felt a trembling seize her limbs. To her chagrin, tears filled her eyes. "Stop it!" she muttered under her breath.

Byron observed the scene, apparently unembarrassed. He picked up a crouching African fertility sculpture and turned it in his hand, expertly studying it. He put the piece down and casually stuck his hands in his trouser pockets. "Well, I'll come to the point." he said pleasantly. "Mandy, I've made a proposition to your parents. It's kind of an important one and I'd like you to hear it. I know you've been through hell and I won't remind you of the details. Just consider what I say, and don't question my motives. Your parents have done a lot for me, and it's time for me to repay them."

He dropped gracefully into a chair that faced Mandy's. She found herself staring helplessly at him, her nostrils filled with his male scent. "I've watched you grow up, Mandy. Watched you change from a sad, brooding little girl into a wild and troubled teenager. But I'm not interested in your drugs and your drinking and your antisocial behavior. I'm interested in your God-given talent. Your artistic ability."

Mandy's eyes widened. Byron said, "You're gifted. Of course you have no training, and no discipline. You're raw and unformed and you need years of work. But, Mandy, the talent is there, enough talent for you to turn professional. Graphic arts, designing, illustrating, advertising—they're all open to you. I'd say in ten years you could write your own ticket."

He excited her beyond anything she'd known. She'd become tough and cruel and unfeeling, except when she got wasted and fell apart. Now this exquisite man was capturing her heart and it scared her. "You're crazy," she said.

"Mandy!" Dad hissed.

Byron raised a restraining hand, never taking his eyes from her. "No problem. Mandy, I didn't think you wanted to pursue your art studies right now. Right now, you want to be dead. You're in deep trouble. You have a police record. You've been kicked out of three schools. You're suicidal, and may have to be institutionalized. Have you thought about that? Life in a mental institution?"

Mandy shrank back in the chair and her eyes followed his. "You're nuts," she whispered. "You're worse than my shrink."

Byron smiled. "Just more to the point. But I have a better solution, Mandy. A solution that will straighten out your life and help you become an artist."

Mandy looked at her parents. "What is this crap?"

Dad chewed on his pipe and looked annoyed. Mom turned away and Mandy saw that she was weeping, her fist at her mouth. Suddenly Mandy was afraid and her chest tightened. "Hey," she asked, "what's coming down?"

"Listen to me, Mandy," Byron said. "I'd like you to live at my estate for a year. Think of it as a year away from hassles and trouble. During that year, I'll feed and clothe you. You'll live in luxury—designer wardrobe, gourmet food, fast cars, spending money. Private tutors will complete your high school education. Meanwhile, you'll dry out, get drugs and alcohol out of your system. You'll learn how to speak civilly and walk gracefully and how to behave among people. You'll become gracious and sophisticated. I'll have you trained in art, and you'll have your own studio. At the end of the year, you may choose to stay with me, or go back to your parents. But you may *not* leave at any time during the year."

He fell silent. Mandy hugged her bear tightly. "You're crazy," she whispered again.

Byron pursed his lips. He stood up and looked confidently at Mandy's parents. "Is that about the way we discussed it?"

Mom just bowed her head and nodded tightly, profoundly embarrassed. Dad seemed tired. "I told you what she is. I'm sorry you wasted your time."

Byron smiled and glanced at Mandy. "I don't see it that way. I think she's excited about the idea, but confused. We threw her a curve."

Mandy looked coldly at her fake mother. "Am I being sold?" she asked. "How much are you getting for me?"

Mom looked up at her with red-eyed fury. "You ungrateful child. How can you say that?"

Mandy curled up tightly like a flower shivering against a winter blast. "You're all a bunch of freaks."

Dad slammed a hand on the lamp table and shot to his feet. "Okay, enough," he said. "Byron doesn't have to be subjected to her. The man was decent enough to make this incredible offer and she does what she always does. The girl wants to die. Let her do it and give us all a rest."

Mom shook her head wildly. "This is insane. There's got to be something we can do."

Mandy began to sing "All You Need Is Love" in a taunting voice. Mom screamed at her, "Shut up! Shut up! Shut up!" Dad grew redder as he watched, impotent. *Eat your hearts out,* Mandy screamed silently.

Byron's face twitched with distaste and embarrassment. "Okay, listen. Rob, Jenny, why don't you go in the other room? Too much tension in here. The poor girl is terrified. Let me stay with her."

His words restored some order to the battered room. Mom got up and rushed out, and Dad followed, his back straightened in martyred resignation. Mandy sang after them, louder and more angrily. Byron watched her and said very softly, "You'll come to understand, Mandy, that this is a miracle for you. You'll be very very happy."

He smiled, and Mandy stopped singing. Her throat hurt. Her insides congealed, and she hugged her little stuffed bear in panic.

chapter 15

THE memories shifted, like colored pebbles in a kaleidoscope. Amanda remembered the trendy boutiques where Byron bought her wardrobe: jackets, swimsuits, armfuls of bracelets, jeans, dresses, sandals, earrings . . . on and on went the fittings as she swirled in front of mirrors. Mandy had always spurned fashion for grungy dungarees and men's shirts, but now she wore expensive clothing, always appropriate for whatever occasion. Byron wouldn't allow anything else; he had servants lay out her clothes, and fill her closets.

A makeup artist showed her how to bring out her natural beauty. "You need a cover stick to even your skin tone," the woman said cheerfully, "a little blush, but not too much, and only across your cheeks where the sun would put it. . . ." Mandy learned how to choose a fragrance and how to recycle makeup. "Mascara goes in the trash every six months," the woman lectured. "Otherwise you risk bacterial contamination." Mandy liked the challenge of working with color and tone on the planes of her face.

She remembered sitting in a private salon as a hairdresser trimmed her hair to two inches above her shoulders and tapered it toward her face to play up her cheekbones. The new look was sexy and girlish, and gave Mandy a sophistication she'd never known.

A physical therapist created an exercise regimen, with a daily two hour workout at a ballet barre. "Bends, kicks, stretches," the therapist said. "And classical ballet movements, great for your muscle tone." There were to be deep knee bends with five-pound weights, exercise on Nautilus machines, and calisthenics on the beach. But here Mandy drew the line.

"Forget it," she said with a laugh. She stuck her hands on her hips as her hair blew in the salt wind. "He can make me wear what he wants, but I'm not doing any push-ups."

The therapist simply nodded. "Okay, hon. I'll tell the boss."

Mandy watched the therapist jog away and turned back to look at the waves. She shielded her eyes, liking the wind and sun on her skin. A few minutes later, Byron joined her. He wore a polo shirt and slacks and looked magnificent. He held a tall iced drink.

"The exercise routine is vital," he told her. "You're out of shape. Your body is wrecked by alcohol and drugs. You can't skip one day of the regimen."

Mandy grinned. "I'm skipping *all* the days, man. You want to buy me stuff, it's okay, but don't screw around with my time."

Byron sipped his drink. "*You* screwed around, Mandy. Now you have to get to work."

"No dice. You want to take me back home, go ahead."

"No," Byron said softly. "We'll try again tomorrow."

Mandy looked at him, incredulous. "Man, don't you listen?"

"Yes I do."

He turned and walked away. She called out, "When's lunch, Byron? I'm starving."

Byron turned, and regarded her sympathetically. "No meals today."

"Huh. . . ?"

He sipped more of his drink. "You can't be rewarded for being obstinate and rude. You refused to exercise, so I refuse to feed you. Breakfast is at seven tomorrow."

Mandy's jaw dropped. "Hey, man, it's eleven-thirty in the *morning*. I'm not waiting until *breakfast*."

"You have no choice, Mandy. That's what you must begin to realize."

He turned again and continued on. Mandy shook her head, only vaguely worried. "Jesus," she muttered, "the guy's a loony."

Byron wasn't joking. Mandy wandered back to the house at noon and asked the servants about lunch. They repeated Byron's order. Mandy cursed them, but they ignored her. She stormed through a center sitting hall and scooped up a nineteenth century bronze clock from a demilune table. "I'll throw this through the fucking window," she threatened.

Byron appeared at the doorway. "Then you'll pay for it," he said.

"You can't starve me!"

"Yes I can." His eyes were cold. "I can do whatever I want. Now put that down and go amuse yourself. You wanted a day without responsibilities. Enjoy it."

By that time, a manservant had come up behind Mandy and wrestled the clock from her hands. She stood in her beachwear, mocked by the bookcases and Sheraton sofa. She began to cry. "This is stupid," she pleaded. "I'm sorry, okay? I'll do the damn exercises. I gotta have lunch."

"No," Byron said, and left the hall. Mandy looked around in blind panic. She dropped into a Chippendale side chair, and her stomach cramped. She tried to calm down, telling herself that he wouldn't go through with it. She needed a drink, or some hash. She couldn't stay here in this madhouse.

All day, Mandy stalked through the house, up and down the stairs, in and out of rooms. She haunted the kitchen for two hours, screaming, cursing, and begging for food. She watched dishes being set out for supper. She threw a tantrum, kneeling on the carpet and bringing her fists down again and again on a polished drum table until her knuckles split. She ran outside and across the beach as sunset stained the ocean. She splashed wildly into the surf and threw herself into the waves. She let the undertow smash her against the rough sea bottom, but she couldn't drown herself. She swam blindly toward shore and a roller carried her exhausted body far enough for her to stand up, limp and bedraggled. She stumbled onto the beach and collapsed to her knees, as her eyes looked up at the brilliant mansion on the hill.

Finally, she stumbled back to the house as night fell. Her stomach gripped her with pain, and she had the shakes. She staggered through the house, from room to room, looking for Byron. She found him on a private second floor balcony that afforded a panoramic view of the north gardens. Evening light enveloped the stately ionic columns as Byron sat in a wrought iron chair and read a book. Mandy stood in front of him, hugging herself.

"Please . . ." she whimpered. "Help me . . ."

He looked up at her, with quiet disgust. "You've made an ass of yourself all day," he said.

She licked away tears. "I have to have something . . . I'm hungry."

"You can go without food for three or four days before you're really hungry. You're feeling nothing but self-pity now. What you really want is a joint, or a beer."

She nodded. "Yes."

"At least you admit it. Well, Mandy, maybe you've learned a lesson."

"Yes, yes, I've learned. I'll never refuse to do anything again, I promise . . ."

He smiled. "Your promises are worthless. You haven't begun to discipline yourself. Go to bed, Mandy. Tomorrow's a new beginning."

She began to tremble as she cried. "God, Byron, please. Just some supper. Come *on,* man."

"You're foul-smelling and foul-mouthed," he said. "You're spoiling my book and my view. I'm very disappointed in you. Get to bed and try to behave yourself tomorrow."

He went back to his book, ignoring her weeping and convulsions. Mandy wanted to kill him at that moment. She felt the hatred in her hands, but she was consumed by weakness and withdrawal pains. She stumbled from the balcony and a servant guided her to her bedroom. She crawled into the imposing Sheraton bed and clutched the pillow with both hands. She bit down into the sheet and suffered spasms. Outside, she could hear crickets and nightbirds and the rushing of the surf. She felt homesick and lonely. She vowed to slash her wrists tonight, to go to her bathroom and find her razor and do it. But she couldn't get off the bed. She could only weep and retch and feel like a fool.

Somehow, she fell asleep, and woke up when a maid came to rouse her. She was helped into the bathroom where she showered with soap and hot water, and washed her hair. Byron had breakfast brought to her bedroom: orange juice, black coffee, toast and butter, and two poached eggs. She wolfed it all down and ten minutes later vomited it all back. She dressed in a tank top and shorts and shakily poured more coffee. She drank it slowly as she looked out the window and wondered what was happening to her.

That morning, she let the physical therapist show her the exercises. She could barely get through a few repetitions of each, but she bit her lip and didn't complain. She began to like the exercises after a few weeks. She even took pride in her aching body. She enjoyed the quickness in her legs and the sheen of new strength in her skin. She learned how to swim, and to play tennis and occasionally joined Byron and his friends for a game. She had always liked to ride, and Byron owned magnificent horses. She swung open the wrought iron gateway leading to the main alley of his classical gardens, and rode at an easy canter between marble cherubs and down a path lined with geraniums, ferns, and lilies of the Nile. At length she'd break through a hedge of clipped yews to open lawn, and dig her boot heels into the animal's flanks. With her eyes shining and her face blown red, she'd gallop madly down the lawn to the beach and pound along the curling strand.

Sometimes she'd race Byron along the ocean's edge, plunging through banks of cold stinging mist, laughing with the first genuine pleasure she'd known. How her heart would beat then! She desired Byron openly at those moments, her eyes vivid and her heart hungry. She'd break the tension by careening away down the beach.

Byron brought in tutors for english, algebra, science, art, music, and history, and arranged a full school day for Mandy five days a week. She rebelled at her first lesson, lolling on a couch and munching apples. The tutor, previously warned, shut his books and left the room to tell Byron. Mandy flew to her feet, panic-stricken. "Christ, no!" she yelled. She yanked open the door and tried to find the tutor, but it was too late. She suffered another day and night without food. She broke everything she could get her hands on that night, ripping the striped bed canopy and draperies, slashing the custom-made wallcovering. She smashed a lamp and dug scissor blades deep into the bedtable. After her tantrum, she sat on the torn bed and cried convulsively. She went to her knees and ran her fingertips over the angry gashes in the wood, whispering, "I'm sorry, I'm sorry, I'm sorry . . ."

Her punishment was a month of confinement, with meals and lessons in her destroyed room. She had to look at the mess every minute of every day, and was allowed out only to exercise in the gym. "You'll learn to control your emotions," Byron told her.

She did learn, and the confinement had a serendipitous effect. She turned, in boredom, to her books, reading her history text page by page. She began to imagine ancient streets and temples, and to sketch historical figures. She filled notebooks with Caesar and Ptolemy, with Charlemagne and Leif Ericsson. She copied frescoes and sculptures from photographs. She lay on her stomach and read novels and short stories to escape from her prison. She listened to tapes of the works of Shakespeare and Arthur Miller, and recitations of poetry.

She went beyond her math homework and did hundreds of problems, finishing her algebra and geometry texts far ahead of schedule. Byron put her into trigonometry and calculus, and Mandy handled those, too. What Byron suspected proved true: Mandy was intellectually gifted. One she began to read and think, she moved rapidly. She thirsted for more, and Byron slaked her thirst. His private library was extensive and he gave her privileges. The tutors praised her, and after awhile the formal lessons blossomed into intense discussions.

Mandy liked to write, and Byron provided notebooks, typewriter, and paper. She turned out lurid short stories and poems, and a novel about a count and a schoolgirl having an affair on the Riviera. It was terrible, but Byron had a private edition printed and debuted the book with much fanfare at a dinner party. Mandy was pressed to sign autographs by Byron's cronies, and she felt foolish and wonderful.

She found a deep and abiding love for music, listening for hours to the symphonies of Beethoven and Mozart, and the operas of Rossini, Verdi, and Wagner. She learned the piano well enough to get through some Clementi sonatinas and Bach minuets. The Bechstein Grand stood in a huge sitting hall dominated by double arched windows, and Mandy looked winsome playing in her white jeans and rugby shirt, her hair spilling over her eyes, her slender body bowed. Byron watched her from a sofa and sipped tea.

Byron put pressure on Mandy to pursue her art studies. She learned art history, perspective, drawing, painting and sculpture. Expert teachers from the finest art schools trained her in techniques of line and color, in the characteristics of paint, pen and ink, and pencil. That first year was bewildering and exciting for Mandy as she began to discover her talent. She loved best to sit on the beach, with a pad against her knees, and the sun beating on her straw hat as she sketched waves and shells and boats.

One night, Mandy took out her pad and began to sketch her room. She spent hours copying the texture of every fabric and molding. Excitement seized her heart as she sketched, a heightened awareness of her own senses coming to her. It was like getting high and living inside color and shape. She made watercolors of some of the sketches, and, because it seemed natural, she began to toy with the designs. She sketched different curtains, then a different table, then a different bed. She rearranged the room's layout. Her eyes seemed to know what color would work, what shape was needed. She showed some of the paintings to Byron and he studied them for a long time, sitting in a wingchair in his private study.

He told Mandy, "I think this may be your future. You have a flair for design. More than a flair. I'm going to bring in some design people and let you work on this."

Mandy rippled with excitement and clutched the paintings to her chest when she was alone near the sea and the blue sky. Always she had longed to rearrange her world, to make the ugliness beautiful. The drugs and liquor and rebellion had been her only way to alter her landscape. Now there was another way. She could change rooms and even create new ones. God, even the wrecking of her bedroom had been a blind attempt to make it all different.

It was Mandy's seventeenth birthday that fall, and Byron arranged a private dinner for them in his study. A table was set near the fireplace, with a snow white cloth and fine crystal and china. Byron turned the chandelier's dimmer low, and put on tapes of gentle rock music. He wore a dark evening suit with a cream colored vest and silk-figured bowtie. He let Mandy choose her own ensemble and she came downstairs in a wrap sweater frosted with beads and sequined flowers, and a smart skirt. Byron nodded as she came shyly into the study.

"You look beautiful," he said. "Sophisticated and young. I like your hair."

"Thank you," she said softly. She'd had the hairdresser give her an upsweep to accentuate her slender throat. A string of black pearls shimmered against her white skin. She felt proud and sensuous, and wanted very much to have Byron's approval.

"Come on," he said, "time for a birthday toast."

He poured chablis for her from a bottle that lay chilling in an ice bucket. He handed her the glass of wine and held one himself. He lifted his glass and the soft light caught the hard edges of his face. His skin was golden, his hair black and shining, his eyes filled with clouds that floated in a dark sky. "To you," he said. "Happy birthday. And congratulations."

Mandy felt her hand shake as she tipped the glass to her lips. The wine tasted cold and dry and she shut her eyes and felt it cool her throat. Byron held her chair as she sat down, and then summoned the servants. The cook had prepared Chicken Marengo, which he served with heart-shaped bits of toast topped with a chicken-liver spread. Mandy sat with her hands in her lap, her eyes shining as the servant scooped the chicken and mushrooms into her plate. She looked up at Byron for permission to start.

He smiled. "Go ahead."

She ate slowly, as she'd been taught. She drank wine and gradually the hunger in her stomach and the jitters in her chest calmed to a wonderful numbness. Byron talked with her about her studies, about music and art, about his travels. He avoided her past life. It was beautiful to be here with him, a fantasy come true.

"This isn't a normal birthday party for a seventeen year old girl," he said. "You should be having hamburgers or pizza with friends. I've deprived you of that."

Mandy smiled over her wine. "My friends didn't do a lot of burgers and pizza."

"Well, this still isn't very girlish. I'm an aging businessman and you're a kid, and I must be boring you to death."

"Oh no!" She shook her head. "You never bored me. You're incredible."

"So they tell me." His grin betrayed his playfulness. He sat back as the servant put down ice cream with crème de menthe sauce. Two maids brought in a cake with eighteen candles and set it down. Mandy looked at Byron and laughed. Her eyes reflected the candleglow and she giggled and put her hands over her mouth as Byron and the maids sang "Happy Birthday" and applauded.

"Make a wish," Byron said.

Mandy shut her eyes. The wine had made her tipsy. *I wish,* she thought intensely, *that I could stay here forever. I wish I could be a designer. I wish that Byron would fall in love with me. . . .*

Her eyes flew open. She'd surprised herself. She looked quickly at Byron, fearing that somehow he'd read her thoughts. He returned her gaze and she felt her stomach lurch. She leaned over and blew out the candles. The maids retired.

Mandy ate her cake and ice cream, worrying about her half-formed feelings. The music pulsed in her skin, warming her until she felt damp all over. Her sweater itched and she longed to take it off. She felt her face blush and cursed herself for being a stupid kid.

"Byron . . ." she said. But he had risen from the table and he walked toward the door of the study. With a sure motion, he locked the door. Mandy listened to the loud click with terror and desire. He *couldn't* be thinking what she was thinking. He was a man of forty, beautiful and powerful and rich, with the most splendid women in the world eating out of his hand. He certainly wouldn't consider loving *her*.

"Mandy," he said. "You'll graduate from high school this year, but there won't be any cap and gown, and no senior prom."

"I won't miss it," she said. "I never went for that sh—for that stuff."

"You're more gracious than you ought to be," he smiled. "But you'll resent it someday."

"I don't resent anything, Byron."

"You've grown up. Would you dance with me, Mandy? It's not exactly a prom, but it would make me happy."

She trembled and felt her skin flush. "Sure," she said. "If you really want to."

He held out his hands, suavely. She got up and crossed the carpet to where he waited. He'd turned up the volume of the music. Mandy held her breath and felt the blood swell in her veins as he took her in his arms. She stiffened at first, her hand moist in his, her nostrils stinging with the scent of his cologne. Then, at his insistence, she relaxed and let her young breasts crush against his suit. His hands pressed firmly against her lower back, guiding her, and her feet followed his.

He was an expert dancer, smooth and insinuating. They moved slowly around the elegant study and its table, chairs, and desk. The paintings all blurred into streams of warm color. She listened to her heart beating and wondered if he could hear, too.

She became suddenly aware of him bulging against her. She wondered whether to be embarrassed for him, but she was too aroused herself to care. She nuzzled deep into his smooth-shaven throat and listened to his breath hiss rhythmically between his lips. His strength overpowered her. She felt faint and slightly delirious.

They stopped dancing so gradually that Mandy was hardly

aware of it. But she felt his fingers tip her chin up and she glimpsed his eyes for an instant before he kissed her. They were bottomless galaxies of dark sky, pulling her in until she was rushing through space, with stars flung all around. She felt his breath, saw the light glisten on his lips, and then his mouth was on hers, parting her lips. His tongue plunged deeply to taste her youthful honey, and she responded ardently. Her hands interlaced around his neck. He pressed his palms into her shoulder blades and held her as he kissed her again and again. It was wrong and dangerous and perverted but she didn't care.

"Mandy . . ." he said. "I have no right to do this . . ."

"Yes you do," she whispered. "I want you to."

"You're so beautiful."

"You make me feel beautiful."

"It isn't right," he insisted. "I couldn't just kiss you and walk away. I'd want to love you completely."

His words inflamed her skin. "I want that."

"No! You're only a child."

She shook her head vehemently. "I'm not! I don't want to be . . ."

"You need boys your age."

"I don't want a boy, damn it."

"Mandy . . . are you sure . . . ?"

She sought his mouth again, desperately, and thrust hard against him. She hardly remembered his hands undressing her. Her sweater was one moment on her body and the next moment a black, glittering cloud on the carpet. She arched her lean strong body, straining against her bra, and writhed under his exploring fingers. He trailed kisses down her throat, where her perfume had been applied. "So beautiful," he said huskily, looking at her. "So young and sweet."

"Byron . . ." she begged.

She tried to undoe his bowtie and vest, but her fingers were useless. He smiled and grasped both her wrists in his hands. While she sat on the sofa he undressed and it was magic to watch him. With exact, confident movements he removed his jacket, vest, tie, and shirt. She gasped as he exposed a deeply tanned and powerfully muscled torso. Thick hair furred his broad chest and wrists, and muscles bunched and knotted in his back. Mandy had only fantasized about a man's body like this one. He slid his pants off with no self-consciousness, and took down his briefs. He turned to face her, his features a questioning mask, amused and savage. She shivered on the sofa, trying to avert her eyes from his full, desiring manhood.

She sat half-naked, with a man who ruled an empire. He sat next to her, his smell a mingling of cologne and maleness. He unhooked her bra and took it from her. He bent and suckled her breasts, tonguing her young nipples into erection. She threw back her head, moaning. He gently pushed her onto her back and took off her skirt and panties. Cool air rushed between her legs as he parted her knees with his hands and rained kisses down her fluttering belly and into the crease of her thighs.

She heard herself gasp again as the warm motions of his mouth ended her childhood. The rough stroke of his tongue, the suction of his lips, the rush of hot breath in her most secret places, drove her into a frenzy and her head thrashed from side to side. She sobbed raggedly. She lifted her arms helplessly over her head and gripped a throw pillow. He licked and nibbled until she exploded deep inside and felt warm fluid wetting her legs. Then he kissed her belly again, and her ribs and her breasts. She shuddered all over, exhausted with pleasure beyond anything she'd imagined.

"Please . . ." she managed to whisper.

He arched above her, his body like a marauding panther's. She ran her hands over his flanks, marveling at his hardness. He was marble and steel, he was silk wrapped around stone. He was warm and pliant, alive and pulsing. She looked up into his burning eyes, which lit her soul with electric fire. He parted her cleft and she hissed in excruciating pleasure. He raised himself so that his thick organ rubbed against her clitoris, scraping back and forth until she went mad.

"Oh God . . ." she panted. "No more . . ."

Suddenly he plunged deep and hard, and she screamed with the force of it. She had not been a virgin but she had not been a woman either, until now. And yet she felt no joy, no release. She felt a sudden icy terror, slithering with frozen coils through her heart.

Byron filled her to bursting. She rotated her hips to match him, and flung her arms around his neck. She trailed her fingers down his sweating back, feeling the ropes of his muscles as they coiled under his skin. Driven by ecstasy and fear, she wrapped her legs tightly around his clenched buttocks and cried out with each stab of his invading cock. Her climax came in descending waves, red and blue and violet.

Her skin seemed to undulate with the force of it, and his invasion became burning and painful. She bit her lip hard and tasted blood. His eyes had become bright yellow, with tiny diamond points, as if he'd mutated into a primordial beast and understood no language. She became very scared. God, she thought, he was raping her! She was just a kid . . . she hadn't known . . .

She punctured his skin with her nails and panted in fright and pain as he drove on and on, oblivious to her discomfort. How long could he keep it up, how long before he finished. . . ? Ice constricted her pounding heart. She wondered if she would die.

Then his body contracted, and he stopped moving inside her. She could feel him spurt into her torn inner flesh. He collapsed on top of her, shivering and groaning. With wonder and tenderness, Mandy stroked his hair, his back, and his shoulders.

Finally, he lifted his head and looked at her. His eyes had become warm and gray again. "You're a woman, Amanda. Now and forever."

She nodded, voiceless. She held him, rocked him, crooned to him, crying and shaking. He'd torn her apart and put her together, and she'd never be the same again. She only knew that she needed him as she needed air and food, and that tonight marked the beginning of her new life.

chapter 16

ONCE Byron possessed Amanda, he turned her rescued life into a nightmare. After the birthday dinner, he called her "Amanda" and not "Mandy." When he finished making love to her, he dressed and left the study, shutting the door with a soft click. Amanda lay curled on the dampened couch for a long time.

Finally, with an emptiness chilling her soul, she also dressed and walked stiffly to her own bedroom. She remembered lying in the moonlit darkness, her eyes open and staring at shadows as the changed on the wall. Her insides burned. She'd let boys screw her, but not until this night had she let a man possess her.

Byron waited for her at the breakfast table the next morning, something he rarely did. In a white open-collared shirt and white slacks, his tanned skin glowed in the early light. He poured coffee as she sat down. "Good morning, Amanda."

She only nodded with lowered eyes.

He laughed, and his eyes twinkled. "Are you embarrassed?"

Her face heated and she gulped her orange juice. Three walls of glass flooded the breakfast nook with sunlight. "Don't be," he said. "I'm not. I feel absolutely wonderful. Do you?"

She managed to look at him, nearly blinded by his presence. "No, I feel lousy."

He buttered toast. "What hurts?"

"Everything hurts. My head is splitting."

"Too much wine. You can work it off this morning."

"Are you *serious*? You want me to do those damn exercises?"

He nodded. "You bet. No vacations from that."

She sighed and stirred cream into her coffee. "I wish I could be as confident about everything as you."

"Well," he said, "I've got some experience. You're confused and maybe wounded a little. It's not a simple thing for a woman to be loved the first time. You were really marvelous, do you know that?"

She blushed up to her crown. "Please, Byron . . ."

"It's all right to talk about it." His tone became paternal. "You musn't ever think it was dirty, or scandalous, or wrong. I—well, I didn't plan it that way, but what happened was beautiful and natural. I love you, Amanda. I say that without hesitation. I hope that someday you might love me, too."

Amanda took quick, shallow breaths, her heart thundering. She sipped her coffee and burned the tip of her tongue. "I don't know what to say to you."

He smiled charmingly. "You don't have to say clever things. You just have to continue growing and learning. You must become a fine designer and a wonderful woman. That's all I ask. I have to give you the option, soon, of returning home or staying with me. I guess I've complicated that choice."

Amanda lowered her eyes and toyed with her spoon. Her skin felt heated and dry. This man had broken social barriers, had violated her child's body, had committed the crime of rape. She knew that. And he was dangerous when he couldn't control his lust. She knew that, too.

She also knew that she needed him, in some undefined and terrible way. Her body craved him again. More than that, her soul craved his discipline and praise. He was the only adult in the world who had any expectations of her. He had taught her to accept challenges, to challenge herself, to be proud of herself. He was quick and generous with praise for her accomplishments. Byron had been a marvelous teacher, knowing precisely in what measures to give punishment and reward. Amanda couldn't walk away from such a perfect father, even though this "father" had committed incest.

"I don't know," Amanda said. "I don't know what I want to do."

"Fair enough," Byron said. "You have time to decide.

And I have time to prepare myself for your leaving." He gave a little sigh. "*That* won't be easy."

She looked quickly and affectionately at him. "Don't sweat it too much. You're pretty terrific. I'm just kind of mixed up about last night."

"So am I."

He broke into a grin, which made her laugh. She got up and sat on his lap, snuggling close to him. She loved the crisp sting of his aftershave. She looked deeply into his eyes and kissed him. Then she leaned against him. "Byron, this is so weird."

"But nice."

She smiled into his throat. "I must be a real jerk to you," she murmured. "You've been to bed with all kinds of rich, sophisticated ladies."

He squeezed her more tightly. "I'd trade them all for you, Amanda. You're giving, and hesitant, and innocent. I find that refreshing."

"Teach me what to do."

"Oh come now, you're not *that* inexperienced."

"I am, with you."

He held her away from him. "Yes, I *will* teach you, Amanda. I'll teach you every secret of love that I know. But don't assume that's all of it. I think you'll surpass your teacher. Your body is magnificent, if you didn't know."

She sought his mouth again. The morning sun heated her back through the windows. Her desires astonished her as they leaped to life, overcoming fear and bafflement. How could she dream of giving up this magnificent man and all the criminal ecstasies of living with him? Amanda had made her decision.

It was deliciously sweet for a while after that. Byron treated Amanda like a doll princess. He gave her a bigger, more lavish bedroom with an adjoining dressing room. Amanda would sit at the vanity and experiment with cosmetics as the chandelier blazed overhead. She felt sinful as her toes dug into the thick peach carpeting, and sometimes she tossed back her head and laughed delightedly.

Often, Byron would surprise her with a gift of fresh-cut flowers or a box of candy. He'd share wine with her as they sat naked and cross-legged in bed. The wine would spill on her breasts and she'd giggle and brush at the wetness. Byron would watch with amusement and blazing eyes.

With grave gentleness, he instructed her in the ways to please a man. ''Here . . .'' he said, as he guided her fingers to his manhood. ''Hold it . . . don't worry, you won't hurt me . . . it feels wonderful when you move your hand like this, just enough to create friction.''

''Byron. . . ?'' she breathed, as her skin shivered.

His smile reassured her. His own fingers pushed away her hair and his lips brushed her throat, encouraging her to go on. She trusted him fully, until the night he inducted her into terror.

''Try with your mouth,'' he told her that night. Seeing the fear in her eyes, he smiled. ''Go on. It will feel strange at first, but I think you'll be very good at it.'' His eyes darkened then, and his voice thickened. ''You need to be a complete lover, Amanda. Nothing held back.''

She curled at his opened legs. She first touched, then stroked, his erect organ, frightened of the dark veins that roped its length, at its angry red color and its bigness. Like the rest of him, it pulsed with strength. She imagined it deep inside her. Aroused, she cradled the penis between her hands and bent to kiss its taut head. She tasted salt and dampness and felt it spasm at the touch of her lips.

''Use your tongue,'' Byron said. ''Slowly . . . swirl . . .''

Driven by his voice, she touched her tongue to the organ, running his length and circling his thickness. Blood roared into her ears. ''Take it in your mouth,'' he said. His voice was thin and distant.

She barely heard him. Byron's sexual center was her universe. She engulfed him avidly, as his hands massaged her shoulders and neck. His fingers gripped her hair and pushed her head down as she suckled him, the warm motions of her mouth eliciting deep groans. She became terrified at his helplessness and the convulsing thing she sucked. His hands became steely and insistent. He wasn't in control anymore. He was hurting her, forcing her to gag. She wanted to stop now, to hold him and be loved by him.

She sensed his climax an instant before it happened and she tried to wrench away but he held her down. The cock bucked and convulsed in her mouth and she choked on the thick warm syrup. Suddenly, she was thrown over, pushed down into the soft sheets. His face loomed over her, contorted. ''Stupid bitch,'' he growled. ''You spoiled it.''

She could barely breathe. Her stomach heaved at the come

in her mouth, and her skin felt cold and ashamed. She shook her head, her eyes wide.

"Jerk." He slapped her hard, across her cheek. The pain astonished her. Tears welled in her eyes and she stared at him, terrified. "No . . ."

"Never!" He slapped her again. "Never do that, never . . ." His hand struck each side of her face, and Amanda felt her cheeks blow up. Blood filled her mouth, mingling with his come. She whimpered and put up her hands. He straddled her. "You've got a lot to learn, Amanda. You're going to get this right, let me tell you. If it takes a hundred times, you're going to get it right."

He raised his arm and smashed her face with his full strength. She screamed as agony burst like red stars in her brain. He beat her for an eternity, his thighs clamping her in a fleshy prison. She became a heartbeat and nothing more, fluttering near death, beyond fear. At last, he climbed off and got out of bed. He left the room, slamming the door behind him. Amanda curled into a ball and reached blindly for her tattered stuffed bear. She hugged the mute beast as her blood poured onto the pillow.

Byron sent a doctor to see her that night. The doctor asked no questions, but simply treated her with ice packs and pain killers. He suggested she see an oral surgeon. Byron had Amanda driven to a doctor in Smithtown, where the work was done. She had to drink meals through a straw for three weeks while her jaw was wired. Pain woke her up at night, and drugs made her drowsy during the day. Byron insisted that she keep up her exercises.

She didn't see more than a glimpse of Byron for a month after the beating. She sleepwalked through her days, barely caring if she lived. She neglected her studies and sat for long hours on the autumn beach, shivering in a blanket. She swore she'd leave as soon as she recovered, and hitch to California. She'd start a new life there, and forget every bad break she'd had. She could draw now, and she could earn money from it.

The fierce vow kept her going, but as November fled past and fireplaces were lit, Amanda felt a lassitude grip her soul. She sat one bleak afternoon in an upstairs sitting room, leafing through magazines. Her jaw had healed. With her hair brushed over her shoulder, wearing a red sweater and blue jeans, she looked sad and pretty.

Byron walked in. He carried a gaily wrapped box with a

bow on it. He sat in a chair opposite the sofa. Amanda glanced at him and glued her eyes to the magazine page. Her face flushed.

He said, "It's taken me a long time to face you again. I feel pretty ashamed."

She said nothing, and flipped a page.

Byron sighed. "I don't even *want* you to talk to me yet. I don't think I'd respect you if you did. Like all humans, I have a monster inside me. When I lose control, it breaks its leash and hurts people. It devastates me that it hurt you. You are the sweetest, most wonderful thing that's come into my life, and I wounded you. It's unforgivable. I only pray that someday you can accept me again, with this flaw. This . . ." He held up the box. ". . . is for you. An offering. I'll leave it with you. Please think about letting me back into your life, Amanda."

He got up and placed the box softly on a coffee table. Then he left the room. Amanda was crying by this time. She turned her face toward the draped window and touched a hand to her hair. She reached for the box and opened it with shaking fingers. Inside waas a wristwatch of marvelous thinness and exquisite design. She clasped it around her wrist and looked with wonder at its shimmer against her soft, pale skin.

Amanda went to Byron a few days later as he groomed a horse, and said, "Thank you for the watch. It's beautiful."

He looked at her, the brush in his hand, and nodded. "I'm glad you like it, Amanda."

She was shaken with a powerful need to be loved by him. Amanda could not possibly understand, yet, how Byron manipulated her emotions. She was a beautiful, poised young woman in some ways, but still a scared little girl who couldn't survive outside this estate and who lived for the approval of her master.

None of this occurred to Amanda now; she felt only a warm sweep of love and a wash of guilt. She trembled as he caught her up in his arms. He held her tightly and she cried in his embrace. She leaned her tearstained face against his chest and he stroked her hair. "I'll make it up to you, Amanda. I'll give you the world."

"I can't hate you," she said.

"I'm glad, Amanda. It would hurt me beyond imagining to lose you."

Byron did give her the world after that. Servants packed

steamer trunks and they flew to Europe on his private jet. He showed her England and the Scottish highlands. He escorted her down the boulevards of Paris and through the flower-strewn markets of Brussels. He sailed with her on Lake Geneva. They cruised the Greek islands and visited museums in Florence and Rome, where Amanda stood transfixed before matchless art treasures. Byron took her to Morocco and Egypt, on safari through Kenya, and back home via South America, where he tended to business. They arrived back on Long Island breathless and laughing. Amanda leaned back in the limousine, her pulse thready and her mind jammed with images. She looked at Byron in wonder.

The tour was Amanda's debut into the world. She liked being photographed and interviewed. She loved to lie on a hotel bed and read the local reports of her carryings-on. She adored seeing herself on TV. Byron smiled with patient indulgence as he dressed for dinner, while Amanda sat cross-legged in front of a TV screen and squealed at the sight of herself.

After the tour, Byron showed Amanda his own private bedroom. Amanda gaped at the airy vastness of the chamber, with its hand-painted Chinese wallpaper, marble mantel, and opulent crystal chandelier. She sat, a little stunned, as Byron lit a fire. He poked at the sputtering flames and looked intensely at her.

"What do you know about me?" he asked.

She was surprised. "Not much, I guess. Only that you're rich."

He laughed. "Come, Amanda, you're nearly nineteen, and world-traveled. You can't behave like a silly kid."

"Well, you're a big man in the art business."

"Lots of other businesses, too," he said. He seemed satisfied with the fire. He pushed the long brass poker into the flames, thoughtful. "I control many people, Amanda. Does that scare you?"

She shook her head. "No. My stepfather had lots of money, too."

Byron uttered a derisive bark. "Don't compare us. Your adoptive parents are pawns to me. I came out of the slums, did you know that? Bullies beat the crap out of me, until I learned how to use my fists. I found out that I had hard fists. I learned that I could intimidate my enemies." He looked at her. "I liked the power. I *needed* power, after the poverty and hunger I grew up with. And I got it."

He stirred the blaze and it crackled. "I licked my ignorance. I know more than the professors know. I got revenge on everyone who hurt me. Everyone."

Amanda listened raptly, not really understanding. Byron yanked the poker from the fire, and her eyes were held by the glowing white tip. "I like to hear about your life," she said. "It reminds me of my own."

He turned to her with a look of pure revulsion. "Don't ever compare your life to mine. Your life was useless until I found you. What did you ever do for yourself? You polluted your body with drugs and liquor." He shuddered. "Yes, I was poor, Amanda, but I had drive and determination. I kept my body pure, I resisted temptations, I triumphed. You crawled in the gutter. *I* made you. I gave you life."

She shrank from his fury. "I didn't mean to get you upset, Byron. . . ."

"You have to understand, Amanda. I created you. You are my masterpiece. I took your body, your sweetness . . . God, you drive me crazy, do you know that? Your flesh is absolutely perfect, absolutely . . . *NO!*"

The cry was torn from his throat. He brought down the poker sharply and the white-hot tip stabbed through her wrist. Fire raced through her arm and neck and exploded in her brain with shrieking agony. She heard her own scream echo within her, and her chair clattered over backwards. She saw Byron through a film of tears and dimly heard his voice.

"Pain is part of it, too," he said. "Pain purifies." He seized her wrist and twisted her arm to force her to her knees. He touched the poker to her throat and she could hear her flesh bubble as she screamed. Her body spasmed.

"I can't stand for you to be so beautiful," he said despairingly. "Would you beg for me to stop, now? I need you to do that. You must be totally dependent."

The poker touched her cheek. Vessels ruptured in her throat as she screamed. She thrashed in his grip, her knees thumping against the carpet. She smelled her own burned skin. "No more . . ." she whimpered. "No more . . ."

He let her go and she pitched forward.

Byron was breathing hard, his wide chest heaving. His hair

hung damply in his eyes. He jammed the poker back into its stand and reached down for her. His eyes had softened. He pulled her up and searched her agonized face. "I love to look at you," he said. "The curves and planes of your face are marvelous. I can look for hours and always see something new."

She barely comprehended his words. Her burns blistered and she swooned. He carried her soaked body to the bed and gently set her down. With sure fingers, he unbuttoned her blouse and took it off. He finished undressing her and sponged her soiled body down. Then he stripped off his own clothes with urgency. He was already hard and crimson. Amanda's eyes fluttered open at his kisses. She tried to refuse, but his mouth was already between her legs. Amanda could not control her response. She panted as he aroused her.

He arched above her and slipped deep into her with a single motion. He stroked rhythmically and only sighed as he climaxed. She lay silently and numbly as Byron caressed her body. At last, he left. Her wounds hurt murderously, making her gasp and bite her lip. She couldn't sort out her feelings, beyond the physical pain. Later, she felt no anger, only despair.

There was no apology from Byron this time, although there was a gift of beautiful pearl earrings. There was always a gift after he hurt her, for as long as the hurting went on.

It went on for two more years, though not on a regular basis. For long periods of time he'd be loving and solicitous, stopping to listen to her play the piano or to watch her paint. He took her to gallery openings, to museum exhibits, to Hawaii and Australia, Japan and China. They were photographed and interviewed wherever they went, so Amanda became a celebrity. Byron boasted of her designing skills and phone calls came from design firms eager to be affiliated with the influential Byron Moore. He sent Amanda's portfolio to one or two places he trusted. The response was positive, even enthusiastic. She was untrained, but very talented.

Byron talked with Amanda about doing professional work. She was nineteen now, elegant and lean, tanned and stunning. She wore a white jumpsuit and Byron's eyes devoured her.

"Yes, of course," she said. "I'd love to design professionally."

"All right," he said, "but we won't jump into this. You can make a fool of yourself with your lack of experience."

"I won't," she promised.

Byron set up an office for her, with a breathtaking view of the beach and ocean. Amanda had the walls painted and dressed up the room with chintz drapery and upholstery. On one wall she hung a collection of wildflower prints. Magazines came and Amanda began to appear on fashionable color pages across the country.

Amanda never spoke publicly of the times Byron hurt her. Usually he just beat her, savagely but carefully so that no bruises showed. She came to dread and anticipate the beatings. When he was out of control, he'd throw her to the floor and kick her under the ribs. At other times, he'd pin her against a wall and take his time, slapping her breasts and shoulders, punching her low in her belly, pausing between blows to let her recover and await the pain. When she was limp and shaking, he'd gather her in his arms and rock her back and forth. Well-paid doctors stitched the lacerations, reattached retinas, and braced the sprained joints.

Occasionally he did bizarre things that humiliated more than hurt. Once he tied her wrists and ankles to the bedposts with silken cord. He sat for hours, watching her suffering naked form. She pleaded with him to release her when cramps knotted and agonized her body. She voided onto the sheets and after awhile the urine burned her tender skin and she screamed in pain. The itching made her thrash her head from side to side and snap with her teeth at the bonds. Finally, she convulsed and twitched, her teeth chattering, her eyes rolling back in her head. Her wrists and ankles swelled and purpled.

At night, Byron untied her and had servants dump her into a bath. Later, he brought in a supper of lemon chicken and shared it with her. She sat in bed, in her robe, and ate very little. "Understand," he told her, "at times your perfection creeps under my skin. It itches and burns. I need to reduce your beauty. I need to balance your splendor. It's the artist in me. You're really very good about it."

She didn't answer him. She was twenty years old, and she knew he was insane and dangerous. She was an accomplished young woman, trapped in horror and splendor as Byron Moore's mistress. Yet part of her was still a frightened child and she couldn't run from him, not yet. She just gazed at him now as he spoke and forked chicken into his smiling mouth. His nearness drained her of spirit and sense.

One night he took her down into the basement and chained

her to a boiler pipe. He left her there with no explanation and turned out the light. She sat naked on the concrete floor, with the stink of mildew in her nose. It was cold and she shivered. She listened to the bubbling of hot water in the pipes. She felt living things run over her legs, and tap small hairy feet on her skin. She huddled there, making mewing noises and shivering. During the night she was bitten and screamed at the sudden fire in her thigh. Eventually, she curled next to the boiler to feel the dim warmth, and forced herself not to sleep.

Byron took her out in the morning. She could barely walk up the steps. She mumbled and shivered and stared wildly at him, half wild with fright. That afternoon, when she awakened in bed, there was a diamond and gold bracelet on her night table.

Amanda couldn't remember exactly when she changed. It wasn't one blazing moment. She turned twenty-one, then twenty-two, and grew out of her need to be subjugated and hurt. Her designing skill bloomed and she gained a reputation that didn't need Byron's pull. She accepted commissions on her own, for private homes, then for commercial spaces that included a bank and a suburban shopping mall. She began to recognize the talent and beauty that Byron had seen in her. She didn't like herself yet, but her voice and carriage and eyes revealed more confidence and more independence each day. She put on makeup and clothes now for her own pleasure, and she hated and feared Byron's sadism. Her childish terror had turned to adult shame.

Byron seemed to be tiring of her. He visited her bedroom less frequently, and his lovemaking had a tinge of boredom in it. He took a long European trip without her. Amanda felt hurt and frightened at first. She missed him, and wrote long passionate letters to him. But slowly, her emotions subsided. She found she could enjoy horseback riding, sketching, swimming without him. After a few months, she began to look forward to his absences. She felt stifled when he was around, poking into her room and her life.

It was about this time that Byron's sadism stopped. If pressed to choose an exact moment, she would have said a spring night on the balcony, with the fragrance of trees brushed in by the salt wind. Amanda stood with her hands on the white railing, filling her senses with the beauty. Byron emerged through the French doors. She knew by now, from the unevenness of his breath and the tautness in his stance, that he was angry and out of control.

"I don't know you anymore," he said sulkily. "You're out of reach, Amanda. What the hell is wrong between us?"

She tensed, her nerves and muscles dreading the pain. Her heart and mind became sick at the thought and she rebelled at being his victim. She lowered her eyes and shook her head, not knowing what to say. He spun her around, tearing her hands from the railing.

"An answer would be nice, damn it!"

She looked at him, her breasts heaving. His skin was blotched. He looked older. She shivered at the memory of his strength. Then, very suddenly, a black anger swept through her like an abrupt thunderstorm. "Don't hurt me, Byron." she said coldly. It was a command, not a plea. "It isn't becoming anymore. It makes you look ridiculous."

Her cool words stopped him and he looked at her with astonishment and horror. He turned and went back into the house, and Amanda sank into a chair, unnerved. It was a turning point, though she didn't understand why. And it was only a month later that she met Kevin Warner and began to emerge from the dark pit.

chapter 17

KEVIN Warner was not a knight in armor. He was a prosperous business attorney, and his wife was a musician and social snob. They were looking for a decorator to turn a bleak condominium apartment into a sophisticated *pied-à-terre* for occasional nights in town.

By this time, Amanda had opened an office in Manhattan, where the couple came to consult her. She looked at photos of the apartment and said, "Of course, I'll have to see the place myself."

"Of course," Joanne Warner said. She was tall and tailored, with cinnabar lips. Kevin looked well built and put-upon. Amanda discussed the job with them, feeling out their ideas and expectations. "As long as it has a real New York look," Joanne said, "we leave the details up to you."

"That's an ideal situation for a decorator," Amanda smiled. "I can't tell everything from the photos, but I do see a lot of exposed pipes and beams, and a very small kitchen and bathroom. This might be more than a paint and paper job."

"We can spend fifty thousand," Joanne said.

Amanda nodded. "I think I can bring it in for that. I'll check with the contractors." She jotted notes on a pad. "I take a down payment of twenty-five hundred and another twenty-five hundred when the work begins. That goes toward my fee of twenty percent of total expenses."

For the first time, Joanne looked at her husband. "Kevin?"

He nodded tiredly. "It's fine with me."

Joanne looked icily at Amanda. "All right, Miss Gray."

Amanda felt her heart lift at the sale. "Thank you very much. I'm glad you came to me."

Kevin made a sardonic face. "Oh, she's been dying to meet you."

Joanne shot a deadly glance at her husband. Amanda flushed slightly. Sometimes it annoyed her, but she knew that her notorious life as Byron's mistress brought in clients. She had to keep telling herself that her work was good enough to *keep* those clients.

"Do I live up to your expectations?" Amanda asked.

Kevin smiled winningly. "I didn't have any expectations. I make my judgments based on the facts."

"Good for you," Amanda said. Kevin suavely took out his checkbook and wrote out a check for twenty-five hundred dollars. He tore off the check and handed it to Amanda, who handed back a contract form outlining their agreement.

Kevin stuck out his hand as they all stood. "I look forward to our working together," he said.

"So do I," Amanda replied.

Amanda looked out her office window after the Warners left. It was afternoon. Trucks, cabs, and cars clogged the deeply shadowed street. Amanda had come to love the city. She felt a freedom here that was denied to her on Byron's estate.

More and more, Amanda had been reflecting on her life with Byron. She was tired of it. Well, damn it, she had signed no agreement. Why didn't she walk out? Because she couldn't. He'd chained her tightly to him, finding her secret fears and needs. As much as she hated and feared him, as much as her skin crawled at the memory of his sadism, she needed him. Here, in Manhattan, she played the independent, creative woman. But soon she'd go down to the street, where Byron's limo would drive her back to bondage.

Maybe her flare-up of unhappiness would have ended there, but Kevin Warner didn't quit. A week later, Amanda visited the Warner condominium. She shook her hair loose of a misty spring rain as her expert eyes took in the gray ordinariness of the rooms. She opened the door to the bathroom and it banged against a hamper that pressed against the toilet seat. A hot water pipe dominated the tiny cubicle.

"Well," she sighed, "I ought to be able to pull off a miracle for fifty grand."

When she shut the bathroom door, she heard two clicks.

She stopped, her hand wrapped around the doorknob. The door to the apartment shut with a soft slam. "Oh, shit," Amanda whispered.

But Kevin's voice reassured her as it called out, "Hi! Who's here?" Amanda exhaled with relief.

"It's me," she called back. "Kevin?"

He came into view, in a Burberry raincoat over a dark blue suit. He smelled vaguely of rain and cologne. "How are we doing?"

Amanda gestured at the bathroom. "We're contemplating the impossible."

His eyebrows raised. "Want more money?"

"No. It's just a big challenge."

He smiled. "Well, we've seen your work and we like it a lot."

"Thank you," Amanda said. "I'll try my best."

Kevin looked directly at her. "I know it's not Shangri-la," he said, "but Joanne wanted a New York apartment and this is what I could afford right now. We threw a lot of money into the house in Scarsdale—Joanne wanted that, too. This had to be done for pin money."

She caught his bitterness and smiled. "You're not a pretentious man."

"I'm just lucky," he said. His eyes stayed with hers. "I'm getting into corporate law. Maybe mergers, if I play my cards right."

"Very nice," Amanda said.

He smiled self-consciously. "There are other attorneys as talented as I am. I've had opportunities. I've had my moments of self-delusion. Joanne's a gorgeous woman. I dreamed of women like that. Suddenly, she was attainable. Now I pay for my indulgences." He gestured at the surroundings. "But I'm upwardly mobile, so why not?"

"Why not, indeed," Amanda said.

Kevin laughed to himself and touched the wall. "What do you figure you have to do here?"

"Lots," Amanda said. "I want to lower the ceiling to create a sense of flow between rooms, and to cover those awful beams, and I want to redo the bathroom, and maybe turn half the dining area into a music area. Right now I'm still playing with space modules."

"Joanne will love it," Kevin said.

"I hope so."

Kevin checked his watch. "Got to get back to work," he said. Once more, he magnetized her eyes. "Why do you do this?"

"Say again?"

"You don't have to tramp around in old apartments."

"I don't follow you."

"I'm paying hard-earned money to redecorate this dump, to make me look more important. But it's a joke to you."

She began to comprehend. "Why a joke, Kevin?"

"You could buy this building out of your allowance. Why would you work so hard to decorate it for me?"

A ball of anger formed in her throat. "I decorate because I love it. I don't think about whether I have more money than my clients. Any more than an actor thinks about whether he's richer than his audience. But if it bothers you, why did you come to me? There are hundreds of decorators."

Kevin perched on a radiator. 'I wanted to meet you," he said.

"I see." Fear nibbled at her stomach.

He stood up. "What's your status, Amanda?"

"I beg your pardon?"

"And does it matter?"

"Does *what* matter?"

"Anything," he said cryptically. But she knew what he meant. He was not a rapist in attorney's clothes. He just wanted to cheat on his bitch of a wife, and he wanted to do it with a very risky woman, so he'd feel like a man again. He'd come here to sound her out.

How did she tell him that she'd never considered the possibility? It had always been Byron, and nobody else. She'd been introduced to many exciting young men over the past few years, from the United States and abroad: suave Frenchmen, handsome Swedes, elegant Brazilians. She'd played tennis and swum with them, had dinner with them, danced with them. She'd admired their lean bodies and fine manners and quick minds. The woman in her had felt a stirring in her loins, more than once. But it was—well, like being married. These men were to be entertained, but never considered. Byron was her lover, her owner. Byron's magnificent body held exclusive rights to her flesh.

But of course there had been no formal promise of that. Only his mesmerizing strength and vicious cruelty had imprisoned her. Amanda was now a woman in her early twenties, and there was no reason at all why she shouldn't enjoy another man. No real reason, no reason that made sense.

But who said that being possessed made sense?

But right now, in this barren apartment, with this handsome and eager lawyer, Amanda knew that she was tired and angry at being owned. For the first time, she openly resented her status as a plaything. The revelation did not come with thunder and drums, but with a brief stopping of her heart, and a parting of clouds in her mind.

She wanted Kevin Warner. Not because he was irresistible, but because *he* wanted *her*. He saw her as a woman, as a bed partner. She had never been approached as a woman, certainly not by Byron. Byron had first made love to her when she was seventeen. Since then he'd entered her body thousands of times, violated and hurt every inch of her, punished her, twisted her insides, done everything to her but make her feel like a woman. Now he allowed her to play at being a decorator because it pleased him to display her.

But Byron Moore had suddenly become middle-aged and a bore, and Amanda was an embarrassment to herself. All of this comprehension came in a breathtaking rush as she looked at Kevin. "I've lived with Byron Moore for a long time," she said.

"So I've read."

"How long have you been married?"

"Six years."

"Kids?"

"We're too career oriented right now. Correction: Joanne is too career oriented right now. Maybe in a year or so." He smiled. "You don't redecorate condos in the city if you have little kids."

"No, I guess you don't."

He checked his watch again. "Listen, Amanda, why don't we talk about this place later this week? I have a sailboat moored at City Island. We can hit one of the restaurants there, or just sit on the boat and have tuna sandwiches."

So it was happening. "Sure."

His eyes narrowed. "Date?"

"Yes."

"I'll phone your office during the week, to confirm. Say twelve-thirty on Wednesday?"

"Fine."

He looked boldly at her, challenging her. Waiting for her

to demur, for her to realize that she could not do this. Amanda smiled. Kevin pursed his lips and his eyes told her that he thought she was going to stand him up. He said, "Talk to you," and left the apartment.

Amanda felt herself get the shakes. This act of rebellion stirred and paralyzed her. Its very ordinariness astounded her. An attractive married man had asked her out, with the intention of scoring. Not a titan of a man like Byron, not a hypnotic, insane master of her body and soul. Just a guy with a yen. And she'd agreed. She felt caught up in the unexpected eddy of fate.

After three dates with Kevin, she agreed to go sailing with him on a brilliantly sunny afternoon. She wore a cricket cap with a white cotton top and blue canvas shorts. Kevin sailed his boat far out into the Sound, and anchored it under a hot June sun, in a secluded cove. The water was cold and choppy, shattering light into millions of fragments. Amanda watched Kevin stow and secure things, muscular and athletic in his navy sweatshirt and white trunks. He had good legs.

She relaxed in a canvas deck chair. Kevin poured wine into paper cups. She said, "We haven't had tuna sandwiches yet."

"Light lunch," he bantered. "That *is* what I said, isn't it?"

"Seviche of sea scallops and mango is pretty fancy."

"But was it *good*?"

"Wonderful," she said. "But you're not being free and unpretentious. We're supposed to be sneaking around. Isn't an elegant lunch at the clubhouse a little risky?"

He smiled. "You're my decorator. Business meetings are perfectly natural—and deductible."

"We haven't talked business yet."

"I lack self-discipline."

"Uh-huh." She smiled at him. He sat opposite her. His face glowed in the hot light. She tried to make sense of the moment, an unremarkable one for a twenty-two year old career woman in New York, but a stunning one for Amanda Gray. Surely Byron knew. Any moment, he'd fly over in a chopper, or send speedboats roaring up. She shivered the length of her body and felt a cold shadow pass over her.

"What's wrong?" he asked.

"Nothing."

"You're thinking about him, aren't you?"

She shielded her eyes to see him. "You're perceptive."

"You're obvious." He put down his cup of wine. "Hey, Amanda. I'm scared, too."

"Are you?"

"I'm not even sure why I'm doing this. I could have cheated with a safe, quiet girl. My secretary is just waiting for me to ask. But it had to be you." He sang the last sentence and she laughed. He laughed also. "I guess once in our lives we have to be crazy. It wasn't easy to ask you for a date."

"It wasn't easy to accept."

"Come on. You've been with kings. You're a golden girl."

"Do I really intimidate you?"

"You confuse me."

Her heart punched her ribs. It was here and now. They'd waited, decently, for three dates. They couldn't be accused of unbridled lust. But the boat ride wasn't for enjoying the tangy salt wind. It was time. Emancipation. Graduation. Moving on. Passages. This was something Amanda had wanted to be able to do for a long time. It was her transition from an incredible past to God knew what future. But she hadn't been this girlish or excited for many moons. She looked with all her might at Kevin and said, "I don't always like being made of gold."

She put down her cup. He exhaled sharply and stood up, lightly rocking the boat. She heard the cries of birds and the slosh of water against the keel. Kevin took off his sweatshirt and the sun glistened on his smooth skin. He took one step down to the tiny cabin below deck, and held out his hand.

Amanda uncurled from the deck chair and took his hand; it was dry and warm. She followed him down the three steps. He took off her sunglasses gently and laid them aside. He steadied her face as he kissed her. She thrust her tongue hesitantly into his mouth. She trembled at the taste of this new man, the first new man in six years. His kiss had none of Byron's fire or intensity, but it was thrilling.

The rest happened with gratifying ease. He looked at her with boyish astonishment. He seemed to realize that he was using the toy of a very rich and brutal man. Then he kissed her fiercely. She flung her arms around his neck. She felt him bulge between her legs and her excitement spiraled, made intense by the forbidden mood.

Amanda realized that her momentous surrender to another man would be sweet but not wonderful. She as too scared and baffled; he was too tense. And, of course, she didn't love him. But it didn't matter. Amanda played her hands along his shoulders and down his back, liking the way he shivered. She touched her fingertips to his flat stomach and teased the skin just under his trunks. They fell together onto the bunk and Kevin struggled out of his bathing suit.

Amanda quickly removed her top and her shorts and she turned, naked, to him. She smiled at his intake of breath. His hands touched her smoothness with wonder and appreciation. She shuddered at the thought of his eyes on her naked breasts, the first male eyes to see her undressed since she was a kid. She didn't feel like the tough, defiant teenager now, or the pliant, frightened mistress. Kevin's hands moved over her body almost reverently.

She bent down and kissed his chin and his throat, and his hands went around her back, trailing down her spine, molding to her buttocks. She stretched her full length atop him, moistening his hard organ with her vulva. They petted for a while, and slowly he gained confidence. He used his finger to massage her clitoris and soon she was moaning. She felt the rocking of the boat as she encircled his shaft with her hand and made him shiver.

He turned them both over so he could mount her. She looked up at him with excitement and encouragement. She shut her eyes and hissed with pleasure as he penetrated her. Kevin was not inventive, but he had power. He knew how to vary his rhythm and time his strokes. She ran her tongue across her lips at the sensation of his thickness boring in. Christ, would Byron know? Would he be able to see signs of another man's entry? For a moment, Amanda felt vindictive and triumphant, wishing Byron *could* see.

She climaxed quickly and gently, mostly from the daring of the act. Kevin thrust a few more times before he stiffened, and she held him tenderly as he emptied into her They lay side to side afterward, his head cushioned against her hair. The mast creaked. A power boat roared by.

His eyes were dark and deep. "I don't know what to say," he told her.

She touched a finger to his lips. "Shh. Talk isn't necessary."

"I feel like an asshole."

She smiled and toyed with his earlobe. "We're still new lovers, Kevin. It's tough to talk in bed unless you're close."

He grunted and rolled onto his back. "Tough when you *are* close."

"Uh-uh. Don't tell me your wife troubles."

"Don't worry, they bore *me*." He sat up, hugged his knees. She ran a finger up his backbone and he shuddered. "Sorry," he said morosely. "I didn't do much for you, Amanda."

"Don't do this to yourself. You're imagining what kind of lover Byron is, and how you compare. I don't want to think of him when I'm with you."

He turned to look at her. "I don't know whether that's flattering or not."

"It's honest. You're an interesting, good-looking, intelligent man. I like you."

"Thanks." He urged her to get up so he could get out of the bunk. He stood as well as he could in the cramped space, and put his trunks and sweatshirt back on. She watched the gradual covering of his nude body with some regret. It was a treat to look at another man. She put her own clothes back on and followed him up to the deck.

The sun hit her with hard brightness. Kevin unfurled the sail and started the trolling motor. Amanda took the wine bottle from its cooler chest and poured more wine for both of them. She handed a glass to him and they toasted. Her eyes swept the beautiful water and distant land with appreciation. "What do we do now?" she asked.

"We go back."

"And then?"

"What are you getting at?"

"I'd like to see you again." She smiled at his reaction. "If you still want to cheat on your wife, I still want to cheat on Byron."

"You don't dignify it, do you?"

She draped her arms over his shoulders and nuzzled his ear. "I don't want to make it a lie. The truth *is* dignified. I enjoyed today very much."

He grinned into the breeze. "I did, too."

The spray wet her face and she relished the sensation. "It's good to have fun."

She saw Kevin Warner a few times after that. She didn't really like him as much as she said she did, but she needed to make it a real affair if it was going to have meaning. Amanda was also a caring and sensitive woman, and realized it. Her pretense made Kevin feel terrific about himself, and he needed that. But sensitivity aside, the fling began to be dangerous, what with ducking photographers and prying eyes. Joanne was suspicious, even though she had no proof; her voice was pure Antarctica when she phoned Amanda at the office.

They both knew that it had to end quickly, but it didn't matter by then. Kevin had gathered strength to separate from his wife, and Amanda would always remember Kevin fondly, for reasons that had nothing to do with love. She knew, after the day on the sailboat, that she was going to leave Byron.

It wouldn't happen in a week, or a month, but her affair with Kevin had given her something to cling to: an image of herself as a desirable, valuable woman, who could enjoy sex without punishment. She finished the Warner condo and it was written up. She wore a heartstopping dress to a party at the place, and Amanda loved the attention and the new commissions she got that night. She loved Kevin pouring drinks for her and spilling liquor, and she loved Joanne's glacier eyes. Amanda had completed, by herself, the fairy-tale transformation Byron had begun.

She went over accounts with her money manager, opened bankbooks, leased a Manhattan apartment and decorated it. She needed to be totally ready. Leaving could not be done like a scene out of Verdi. She had to be rational with Byron. She had to convince herself. She worked hard that winter, allowing herself a Christmas vacation at Vail, where she skied with Byron. He didn't hurt her anymore. He hadn't hurt her for months; it was almost as if he knew, and wanted to change her mind with kindness. His lovemaking was cold. Fine, she thought. She didn't want to walk out on overpowering passion.

In the spring, she made her final plans. She had clothing sent to the New York apartment, and she spent long evenings in her bedroom, remembering. She looked out at the ocean view she knew so well, her skin tightening at the memory of the beatings and horrors she'd endured here. She wondered how badly she was scarred, how long she'd last on the outside. But she had to try.

When Byron struck, the blow was so cruel that Amanda nearly crumbled. She came back to the house from a shopping trip on a May afternoon, with the sky shrouded in fog and a chill wind sighing from the sea. Almost blithely, she went upstairs, girlish in a flap sweatshirt and striped cords. Maybe this weekend, she thought, she'd sit down with Byron at the wrought iron table overlooking the sea, and talk.

She flung open her bedroom door and felt the breath leap out of her throat. Her bankbooks had been slashed and strewn on the bed. And her clothes—the clothes she'd sent to the city—the blouses and skirts and dresses and suits and slacks and blazers—were cut with pinking shears, sliced by knives, the tatters dumped all over the room.

Amanda stood at the door trembling uncontrollably. The frustration choked her. He'd known. He'd known everything. She was seventeen again, and he was punishing her. She felt the fury and despair gather in her chest and like a howling banshee she let out a terrible scream.

"Shut up," Byron said.

He stood just inside the room, in a white shirt and charcoal slacks, his hair now iron-gray, his face lined by too much sun.

She was hyperventilating and she sat down in a chair to regain her breath. Byron shut the door. "Bitch," he spat. "What the hell were you trying to pull? Were you going to sneak out in the middle of the night?"

"No," she whispered, utterly defeated. "I was going to sit down with you. I was going to tell you I was leaving."

"Going where? To your little love nest?"

She looked up at him, and suddenly, overpoweringly, she loathed him. The accumulated pain and violation rose up in her throat like black bile. "Come off it, Byron. You sound like a jerk."

"Do I?" He seemed to struggle to control his temper. "You want to talk about Kevin Warner, or should I produce all the P.I. reports?"

She couldn't stem her tears. "I wanted it to be dignified. I wanted to part as friends. It was so hard . . . so hard, Byron, to find the courage to go. Why did you have to do this?"

"What I did was put a stop to your bullshit. The bank accounts have all been closed. The apartment lease has been broken. Kevin Warner is already taking care of his divorce; I'll take care of his disbarment. I've burned your stupid little bridges for you. You've been a real idiot, Amanda. And I thought you were growing up."

Her hands gripped the chair's arms convulsively. "You bastard," she snarled. "Who do you think you are? What do you mean, disbarment? Do you own the Bar Association?"

"I own enough people to influence events," Byron said. "You know that by now. I didn't want to do it, Amanda. I didn't even *know* this clown. But you had to prove something. What did you prove, Amanda? That you could be independent? You're not independent, you're just foolish. By the way, I've closed up your little office in midtown. And I'm closing the office here, too. You're not ready to be a professional. We've obviously got a lot of work to do."

Amanda felt the breath heave up from her guts. Every word he spoke was a hot knife opening a new wound. And every spurt of bright blood gave her strength.

She stood up. "No, Byron, *you've* got a lot of work to do. You've got to find out when you lost your grip on reality."

"Shut your mouth," he snapped. "You're going to learn how to speak to me."

"Forget it." Her skin tingled with the expectation of his blows, and she almost yearned for the cleansing pain. "I'm walking out. Now. Today. Just the way I didn't want to go. But I can't sit down with you. I can't talk. You'll *never* release me."

"Keep it up," he said. "It's all going to be dealt with."

"I'll bet." Her eyes filled, but her voice remained steady. "Will there be a beating? Or a day without food? Or the cellar? What's left, Byron? Time's passed, baby. I'm twenty-three. What we had is over. Christ, you'll always be etched in my soul. I've been branded by you. But there's no reason for me to be here anymore. When you finish a painting, Byron, you hang it up or sell it. This . . ." She gestured at the mess. ". . . this is shit. How *dare* you close my bank accounts and invade my apartment?"

He shook his head. "Nothing is yours, Amanda. Surely you understand that. Whatever you are, whatever you have, is mine. I created you."

"No you didn't. You guided me, you taught me, you trained me. You also abused me and tortured me. Which do you want credit for, Byron?"

He made an exasperated noise, but his eyes wavered. He clearly hadn't expected this reaction. "You're raving. You'd better sit here and think for a while. We'll talk in the morning."

"There's not going to be a morning," she said, and never had her determination or courage been so high. "I'm out of your life, Byron. You can't close my business. I'm a designer. I can open an office anywhere. I can open a bank account with the money I earn. I can buy clothes."

"No. You're not nearly ready to be on your own, Amanda. Not when you do stupid things like this. . . ."

"Like what? Screwing another man? We're not married, Byron. We're not engaged. If anything, you functioned as my stepfather, and stepfathers aren't supposed to rape their daughters. Would you like to take your case to court?"

He barked with derision. "Try that, and you'll be fried."

She exhaled. "I wish to hell you hadn't pulled this stunt. What a damned stupid way to part."

"You still think you're going?"

She nodded. "Yes. You can keep the torn clothes. Maybe you want to make my bedroom a shrine."

She strode toward the door. He stood in front of it, his hand on the doorknob. "What a fool you are."

She looked coldly at him. "Byron, you'll have to kill me to keep me here. I swear before God, you'll have to kill me."

He returned her look for a long time. He was too talented a reader of human character to doubt her sincerity. He sighed and he said, "Let's take a ride. I think the sky's clearing."

"All right," she said, knowing she'd won, but not believing it.

They went outside together. She walked silently with him to the stables, and the grooms saddled two horses. She mounted and tried to calm her pounding heart as she and Byron cantered through the gardens, past the yews, onto the drenched sand. Around them, fog swirled, but above, the purple clouds cracked with glowing pink. A stink of fish came strong into Amanda's nostrils. She shivered at the chill that she had come to know so well, a chill that penetrated her bones.

He reined up beside her, looking regal. His hair blew in the wind and his eyes pierced her heart. "You're right," he said. "I can't lock you in your room forever. But I *can* stop you from leaving. I can cut off the phones; I can block the roads. I can prevent you from setting up business, anywhere. I can destroy your reputation. I can follow you wherever you go, and know every move you make. I can have you found and brought back to me whenever I please."

His words gripped her heart and shook it. She saw Byron through a blur. "Then do it," she said. "You knew a time would come when I'd leave. You could have said goodbye gracefully. But you decided to behave like a little boy whose toy is being taken away."

Waves rushed against the beach, hissing on the sand. "Well," he said at last, "you *have* become strong, haven't you, Amanda?"

"I guess so."

He smiled, half to himself. "Then maybe you *ought* to go away for a while. I'll miss you terribly, of course, but you need that freedom. I can't have you cheating on me and doing things behind my back. Then, after you've come to your senses, you can come back."

"I won't come back."

"Yes you will." he gentled his horse. "I'll keep an eye on you, Amanda. I'll watch you, every minute. I'll know when the time is right to have you here again."

"Listen to me!" she said viciously. Her hair tossed wildly and became damp with salt. "If you follow me, or harass me, or interfere with me, I'll expose you. All of it. I'll sue you for rape and sodomy and abuse and everything else I can think of. I'll drag you through mud. I swear to God, Byron."

He hissed. "What a savage you are, Amanda. I couldn't take all of the guttersnipe out of you. Fine. Do what you have to. But you won't be rid of me, not as long as you live. And I'll have you again, and when I do, you'll beg for me. I want you out of here in an hour."

With startling suddenness, he turned his horse and galloped furiously up the beach. Amanda turned away, watching the ocean burst into glittering light as the sun broke through. Her tears spilled hotly down her face. It was wrong, all wrong. She felt more imprisoned than ever, more helpless in his grip. She yearned for the safety of this beach and the security of her room. Then she told herself to get out and to keep running, before she changed her mind.

She kneed her horse and looked away from the sunset that blinded her, and made her see swirls and white stars. Much later, Amanda realized that this was the first sign of her impending blindness. At that emotional moment, she paid it no attention. She rode unseeing along the beach, feeling the thud of her horse's hooves in the sand. She rode out of her old life that day, and into her future.

In Amanda's exhausted mind, the sunset swirled into a blur of amber, and feeling returned to her body. She became slowly aware of sitting in a leather-upholstered booth at the hotel bar, with a vodka stinger in her hand. *God,* she thought, *I didn't mean to relive it all.*

She sensed a presence and looked up. Jason's eyes held deep concern. "Are you okay?" he asked.

She nodded gratefully. "I needed a drink and some time. Things are pretty bad."

"I've heard. Can we talk about your stupid stunt?"

She smiled. "Why not?"

Jason slid into the seat opposite her and covered her hands with his own. Amanda let herself rest in his eyes and cherished the here and now.

chapter 18

IT wasn't any use for Amanda to try to hold back. Jason had found her at the perfect moment; she was more than vulnerable. He took her for a long drive through Bradley and out into the desert. She told him everything she'd relived in the bar. Everything she'd held back even in their most intimate talks. She let him into her life.

"This is just great," she said when she'd finished. She hung her arm in the open window and looked out at grazing land that stretched to meet a streaked sky. "Vomiting out my whole life."

"Feel better?" Jason asked.

"Of course I don't feel better. I feel like a fool. What was the point?"

"To make sense of it," he said. "To get it under control."

Sure, she thought. And once again, he'd been the tender, masterful listener. Ears perked as they drove over white highway and rutted road, through little flyblown towns and past huge ranches. Always listening, never talking. He shared nothing with her, except his body.

But she *had* noticed something happening during her monologue. She used the word *victim* again and again to describe herself, and every time she did, Jason corrected her with the word *fighter*.

"You've got to start believing that," he told her. "A victim takes it. A fighter gives it back."

"What's the difference if I keep losing?" she asked.

Sand made the car fishtail on a sharp turn. Jason twirled the steering wheel and granules spattered the windshield and flared with sunlight. The town around them was dreary and bleached. It was all so white and two-dimensional out here, she thought.

"What the hell are you losing?" he asked. "You own your design agency. You're doing the biggest hotel in the country. You're famous, you're rich, you've got a hell of a man."

She laughed. "Give me a break."

"Give *yourself* a break. You survived. You walked out on a man who eats chairmen for breakfast." He lifted his hands from the wheel and gestured dramatically. "Even now," he continued, "you mouth off to Helen. You go looking for Long Dog and *find* the son of a bitch. Where do you get off being a victim?"

Amanda smiled as her hair blew in the wind. "You sure make me sound exciting."

"What does it sound like to *you*?"

"Like you're selling hard. Why is my happiness as important to you?"

"I don't like mental cases in bed."

"Oh." She enjoyed the swift unwinding of a four-lane highway beneath the tires as they sped beneath blue sky. She could see the hazed glass towers of Bradley in the distance. She'd always liked driving on a long road, approaching a city. The moment held promise, yet was tinged with melancholy.

"It means everything," Jason said quietly. "The way you feel about yourself. That's how everyone judges you. People believe what you tell 'em. It takes balls to win."

"You sound like Helen," Amanda said. "Brass balls, she told me."

"And isn't it true?"

"So what's your point?" she asked. "That powerful people have power? You're not saying anything, Jase. Unless you're telling me that Helen is really shy and insecure."

"How do you know she isn't?" Jason asked. "Want some supper?"

She looked at him, startled. "Which question should I answer first?"

Smiling, he gestured at a roadside restaurant. "I'm in the mood for steak and beer."

Again, Amanda felt a glow of domesticity. She cherished the warmth until it burned out, like a spark from a fireplace. "Sure."

Over expertly seared steaks, with steaming baked potatoes,

Jason relentlessly hammered at his point. "You don't know what Helen really thinks. You just know what she says and does. Everyone's afraid of her because she talks loud. That's what goes, Amanda. Nobody respects anybody for their knowledge."

"Wow," she said. "I never heard you philosophize this much."

He drank a deep draft of beer from a slender glass and his fine cheekbones caught a slash of red sunset through the window. "Who the hell wants to hear philosophy?"

"I kind of like it."

"You're a liar. Listen, Amanda, I can tell you that women don't want intelligent conversation from a man. I don't care what they say in the ladies' magazines."

Amanda bristled, even though she suspected his tongue was in his cheek. "So we're probing the depths of feminine psychology, are we?"

Jason chuckled. "Hell, I'd never say that in public. But it's true. I can feel it when their eyes are stripping me. I can smell them wetting their panties. And over in the corner is some ordinary-looking jerk whose brain can swallow me whole and spit out the pits. But they don't look at *him*. They just want to get into my pants, and into their brutal little fantasies. I can score with any man's wife, Amanda. Or daughter. Or mother."

Amanda shuddered at the depth of his anger. "What brought all this on?" she asked. "Why are you so upset?"

He looked out the window and his eyes, the color of the evening sky, softened. "Makes no difference."

"It makes a *lot* of difference. I never thought of you as bitter."

"No, huh?" He looked at her with a kind of vicious amusement that didn't please her. "I'll bet you didn't think at all about my mind."

"Whoa, now—"

"Come on, babe. You're like all the others. You melt as fast as American cheese. It's an old script, Amanda."

Her dinner lay like bilge in her stomach. Outside, she could hear the *whoosh* of cars going by. The world darkened. She felt on the edge of something momentous. "I don't know why you're trying to tick me off," she said. "If you think I don't care about you . . . about what you think, and feel . . . Jesus Christ, I think about you all the time. I've wanted you to open up to me, to let me know you . . ."

Astonished, she realized she was crying. She felt the tears slide absurdly down her face as she lowered her blurred eyes and stared at the half-finished meal. Jason exhaled in anger and frustration. "I'm sorry," he said.

She shook her head. "Don't apologize."

"I don't know what the hell I'm doing here."

"You're talking like a jackass. Showing absolutely no insight about what I feel."

He assumed a woeful, sheepish expression and looked adorable. Beer foam clung to his moustache. "Well, that was my way of making you feel terrific."

She laughed hopelessly, and dug out a tissue to wipe her eyes. "Damn it, Jase. It was a good conversation. What's the matter, was it coming too close for comfort? What the hell would be wrong with letting go? I love you, in case you forgot."

"I didn't forget." His hand covered hers on the table. "I'm not a good talker. It all made sense to me at the moment. I just took a wrong turn."

Amanda looked piercingly at him. "You don't take a wrong turn unless you want to."

A guarded look came over his eyes. "Let it go," he said. "Let's get some coffee and apple pie. You've had a rough day."

She nodded, biting back her disappointment. "Well, thanks for the pep talk. Some of it helped. If I'm a fighter, I've been sparring with shadows."

He squeezed her hand with more honest feeling than she'd ever felt from him. She wondered if she'd made a breakthrough and how she'd done it. But she didn't care much. She needed him, and it was okay to be confused and okay to accept help. That much she'd learned.

Soon after her heart-to-heart with Jason, it was travel time again for shopping. Now that Amanda was only shopping for The Pueblo, the showrooms and galleries phoned incessantly and dangled goodies before her eyes. Amanda hated to reject or hurt anybody, a result of her years of being battered. But of course she couldn't stop everywhere and she couldn't waste time considering items that had nothing to do with her design concept. So this trip she pegged New York City and Long Island and a few of her old friends. She instructed her people at her New York office to keep San Francisco, Chicago, and other major cities on hold.

Amanda flew first class, not wanting to mingle with real people as she sometimes did. This was going to be a quick in-and-out, not a major visit. She had begun to feel a bonding with the land in Bradley, and at this point she needed to be at the site, to see the girders and beams, to catch the rhythm of the days and nights. That made her smile ruefully as she sipped a vodka stinger from a plastic airline glass. What use could she make of the disgusting bar she'd visited, or the vile men who had made her skin crawl? How could she work poverty and unemployment into her overall motif? God, she was stabbed with guilt.

She shook back her glossy hair; she'd combed it softly in waves over her ears, with feathered bangs in front. She'd worn a white blazer over a royal navy blouse and gingham plaid skirt. Businesslike and ultrafeminine, her mood of the moment. More of a need than a mood, to cleanse the bar from her soul. To reassert her independence. She took a long swallow as the plane lunged into its takeoff run. She shut her eyes; after all this time, even after wild helicopter rides, airplanes still scared her. She held her breath as the ground dropped away, and the earth angled. She looked out the window then, to see the grid of roads and the curve of the planet and to experience that delicious moment of terror as she realized that she was absurdly unsafe in a tiny metal casket in the middle of the sky.

Naturally, she was summoned to a courtesy phone when she arrived at JFK and Joanna Lafferty, from her Manhattan showroom, begged Amanda to come over *before* going anywhere else. Amanda had intended to go there anyway, and accepted, especially since Joanna had arranged for a limo to be waiting.

"There!" Joanna said dramatically, sweeping a black-draped arm. "Dripping in hot."

Yes, indeed, Amanda agreed silently. Joanna was always dripping in something; she was an extravagant, drop-dead designer, which had never been Amanda's style. But over the years, Joanna had given Amanda some neat ideas and some fascinating individual pieces which accented well. Joanna had carrot-red hair which she'd moussed into a petrified tangle. She wore her usual black shirt and pants and velvet boots and a huge hunk of gold jewelry swung around her neck. Joanna always wore bright red lipstick and nail polish and Amanda thought she looked like Vampirella, but prettier. In a sense, Joanna was Amanda's alter ego, the devilish woman who did outrageous things.

Amanda, in her innocent-white blazer, walked amid opulent neo-Victorian settings, admiring the sheer decadent grandeur of it. "Look at this," Joanna bubbled in her Lauren Bacall voice. She showed off a gorgeous etched-glass table surrounded by red-lacquered chairs. Red lacquer appeared to be the dominant theme, along with Chinese red wallpaper and deco chandeliers. "And here," Joanna added, "padded ceilings. I love those. I've got stereo speakers in there, and mood lighting."

"Nice contrast," Amana said with reserve. "The padding and the fussiness of the furniture," Oops. That had come out catty. Amanda ran appreciative fingertips over the chairbacks. Joanna seemed not to notice the sarcasm as she hustled Amanda through other rooms. Amanda grew dizzy at the opulent gray-marble floors and green-and-pink wallpaper. There was a make-you-gasp living room—at least Amanda surmised it was a living room—with striped and floral fabrics and deep red walls, and a revoltingly sumptuous marble and brass bathroom. *My God*, Amanda thought, *I know this is the cutting edge, but it's so awful.*

"Well?" Joanna asked eagerly, her Valiumed eyes glistening. "What about going whole hog out there? Puffy and lavish—make a real statement."

Amanda grew giddy imagining The Pueblo furnished like a Victorian bordello. Probably there'd be guests who'd love it. "Joanna," she said, "this is absolutely eye-popping."

"I know. I'm getting incredible press for it. I've done my own place this way, and I've got three commissions *including* David Garrison, the real estate wunderkind. Can you imagine?"

"Impressive," Amanda said, with a tinge of jealousy. Garrison was building more commercial real estate than anybody else, and Amanda had sort of hoped that she could worm her way into his affections. But if he liked forest green silk moiré and cherry cotton shirring, then he'd never like Amanda Gray Designs. Amanda regretted the surge of envy that pricked her heart. It was part of the business, of course; competition for the big client was fierce.

"Can you use it?" Joanna insisted.

Amanda looked coolly at the flamboyant woman. She was pushing; it took *chutzpah* to sell a rival designer this way.

Joanna Lafferty designs in an Amanda Gray building. "We are definitely using reds and greens," Amanda said, "but not quite this way. We're capturing a desert feeling, a sense of vastness and intimacy if you can imagine that."

"You mean earth tones?" Joanna sniffed.

"To some extent. But not what you're thinking. I'm afraid it won't be Victorian, though."

"Uh-huh," Joanna said. "Well, I'm telling you, this is what is being done. I mean, maybe not in office buildings, but in a *hotel*, this is what they want."

"I'm sure. I can see it in midtown, but not in Bradley, New Mexico."

Joanna smiled wickedly. "Oh, I bet they'd gape over it in Bradley."

Amanda thought about the men at the bar. "They probably would."

Amanda hugged and kissed Joanna goodbye and took deep breaths of gasoline-laden city air when she went outside. The closeness had suffocated her. But Joanna, the bitch, was probably right. With Byron's backing, Amanda had made a solid reputation as an intelligent, sensitive designer who avoided fads and used what was best for a particular job. Today, though, the fads were all that mattered. Tycoons were born every minute: young, voracious money-grubbers with no breeding and no taste who just wanted their lives to look like glossy magazines. They were made to order for the Joanna Laffertys and their ridiculously overdone looks. Stung, Amanda could imagine David Garrison in a silk robe, flopping amid his padding and lacquer. After all, the man didn't give a damn what he did to a skyline or a city neighborhood, or to its water or air, or what wind tunnels he created, or how he blocked out sunlight. Just erect the glass monoliths and rake in the millions and become a tastemaker and a power-broker in the urban jungle. Why not live in a pseudo-Victorian whorehouse? Oddly, it all made Amanda think of Byron. Underneath the acquired savoir faire, Byron was just another grubber, a self-made man who made more than most others.

Byron had charisma, which had taken him further. In another life, he might have been an evangelist preacher or a politician. He was also cunning and smart enough to read and absorb. He had taste, or acquired it as he went along, and when he'd decided to make a fortune in art, he'd immersed himself in the world of art and had become an expert. While other magnates just threw money around and acquired expensive junk, Byron had become a force from within. That was the difference. But Byron's blood wasn't any shade of blue, and his heritage was of the gutter.

And Amanda's heritage? A gardener and an unknown mistress of Byron Moore's. Roots in the earth, all right, and a cold, lifeless upbringing in a sterile suburban house. So where had *she* gotten taste? Here was the joke: from Byron. From the ambiance and expertise of the man who himself had learned it all from scratch. And now Amanda, briskly snobbish and set up in business by her sugar daddy, made rude noises at other designers. It was all a wonderful perversion of renaissance ideals and everything in human history that had spoken of standards and continuation. So Amanda Gray's taste was more subtle than Joanna Lafferty's. Big deal. Amanda Gray was designing a rich man's watering hole that would wreck the ecosystem of the desert and crush thousands of native American lives. And if Amanda did it in cooler colors and softer fabrics, what the hell difference did that make? It would be just another whorehouse, but you wouldn't need sunglasses to look at it.

With such destructive thoughts, Amanda drove out to the Hamptons and paid a visit to her friend Ned Coburn at his gallery. Ned was showing a slew of laminated pieces, which he'd collected from designers in Boston, California, and New England. They were all using the new Colorcore laminates and Amanda marveled at their intricacy and imagination, though she found most of the pieces somewhat grotesque, like surrealistic jukeboxes and tinkertoy sets. Ned, in his standard T-shirt and brightly patterned shorts, showed her whimsical cocktail tables, chairs and highboys. Sometimes the mica-like material was carved and routed to play with two or more colors; sometimes it was layered or highlighted. "Fun," Amanda said. "But is anybody using it?"

"A few," Ned allowed. "Most designers I know still like wood better, and this stuff is playtime. But I've sold a couple."

Amanda shook her head and poked her way around the spacious, airy gallery. Her eyes fell on one piece, which caught her with its soft pink, gray, and almond tones. She ran her hand over the top of the secretary/sideboard, which appeared to imitate or suggest a French marquetry pattern. "I like this," she said. "Who did it?"

"Young man in New Mexico," Ned told her. "George Deal."

Her heart paused and her eyes sought Ned's. "Deal?"

"Know him?"

"Is he a Navajo?"

"Matter of fact, he is. But he doesn't live on the reservation. He has a place out in the desert somewhere. A real loner."

I'll bet, Amanda thought coldly. If he was Peter Deal's brother, or cousin, and he was an artist, he wouldn't want to associate with his family. Amanda's brain was already doing computer images of the piece in various places in The Pueblo. "What does he want for it?" she asked.

"Interested?"

"Obviously."

Ned squinted, and scratched his lightly bearded chin. "That one is priced at twenty-seven fifty."

"What if I wanted a quantity—say ten or twenty?"

"You serious?"

"Never more."

Ned's face grew boyish with delighted surprise. He'd sold Amanda a number of individual pieces over the years, one or two of which she'd used in the embassy in Bahru. But this was bigger business; Ned was a laid-back beachcomber sort of man, but he also understood the importance of The Pueblo. "I'd have to get in touch with him."

"Why don't you give me his number?"

"No phone."

"His address then, or post office box. I'm flying back to Bradley tomorrow, and I can look him up myself."

"And do me out of the commission?"

"Wouldn't dream of it."

Ned went behind his cluttered cherrywood desk and rummaged through seemingly meaningless stacks of receipts, notes, and papers. At last he came up with an index card. "Here."

Amanda took the card. "If he contacts you before I get to him, tell him I want to order a few of these. I'd also like to see his other work."

"Sure," Ned agreed. "Can I put up a sign now?"

She laughed. "Sure. 'This piece used in The Pueblo.' "

She let Ned ply her with a cup of home-brewed coffee and a fairly old piece of crumb cake from a bakery box. Then she left and drove back, with some professional glances at the homes along the dunes. She regretted how crowded and unplanned the Hamptons were becoming. More new money was being thrown at new toys, with no concept of what would happen after immediate gratification. Again it made her think of Byron, who, after all, lived pretty close by. It wasn't all that easy for Amanda to drive here without getting nervous twinges or looking both ways for suspicious looking cars. Byron was the same as the magnates: he wanted immediate gratification, and meted out terrible abuse if he didn't get it. They were all the same. Even Jason Turner belonged to the club. A steak and beer dinner and a pep talk, and Amanda was supposed to rally 'round and smile.

She took in a concert that night, heavy on Mozart, and flew back to Bradley the next day. She had rejected one trendy look and bought another, possibly for reasons that had nothing to do with design and everything to do with guilt. But she was pleased with her trip. She liked being decisive, and there'd be a lot more decisiveness from now on. That much, Jason had accomplished.

Amanda's first positive action was to bring Danny and Terri out west for Danny's birthday. She felt almost girlish arranging a party at the Drover's Inn, in a wealthy suburb of Bradley. She played hostess with a kind of manic flair. Danny stared at her a lot.

"You look like you're havin' a ball out here," he said, waving a double Dewar's and water.

"So I am," she smiled. She flung her arms around Danny's broad back and kissed his damp mouth. "I'm glad you came."

"Yeah," he said, and wriggled free. Amanda laughed and let him go.

"Okay, refuse the boss's advances," she joked. "See where it gets you."

Terri joined them, weaving through the small crowd around the bar. "Hi," she said.

"Hello, sweetheart," Amanda said, and grabbed Terri to kiss her. Terri smelled delicious, and looked like a high school kid on prom night.

"I feel terrible," Terri said. "You didn't have to go to all this trouble for Danny's birthday."

"Sure I did." Amanda cradled her piña colada in both hands. "Danny's my boobie. I missed him. I miss all the folks back home."

Danny scratched his jaw in bemusement. His curly hair glistened in the light and he looked a little oxlike and out of place against a vase of peonies on the bar. This place wasn't the usual cowboy roost, which was why Amanda liked it.

"Missed you too," Danny mumbled. "What the hell goes on with that Indian?"

"Not much, lately," Amanda said. "Since I saw him, he hasn't attacked the building site."

"What did you say to him?" Danny asked.

"I told him to cut it out," Amanda said solemnly, "or I'd get *you* after him."

This brought laughter, and Amanda let the drink swirl in her brain. She felt fiercely strong with her friends around her. Danny and Terri were like family. She needed to have her people by her side now, to remind her that she counted.

Somewhere in the back of her mind, she began to be annoyed that Jason hadn't shown up yet. True, he'd warned her that he might have a business meeting, but damn it, she *missed* him, and it was spoiling the evening a little.

"Well, listen," Amanda said, "I've got the whole Pump Room set aside for us, and you can choose anything on the menu. Try the cheddar cheese soup with sherry, and listen to the waiter, he'll steer you right."

Terri glanced at Danny, a little overwhelmed. She seized Danny's arm and leaned into him, nuzzling softly. Danny smiled at Amanda. "You're nuts, that's all I can say. This is comin' out of the company, I hope?"

"None of your business," Amanda smiled.

"Hey, don't tell me this is out of your pocket! This has to cost—"

"A fortune," Amanda whispered. "I've bankrupted myself. Wait 'til you see the cake."

Danny blushed and Amanda felt wonderful. Of course, she *had* paid for the party out of her own funds. She thought that she *might* begin to enjoy having money if she could do things like this with it.

Her eyes, scanning the room for Jason, found Lacey. Amanda felt her heart dip. She'd avoided talking with Lacey since the awful night in the office, but of course, she'd invited her here. And Lacey had accepted. Maybe that meant a thaw, a chance to renew.

" 'Scuse me," she said to Danny and Terri. "You two go in and eat. Hey, did you see the room I got you at the hotel?"

Danny turned fiery red. Terri lowered her eyes. "Yeah," Danny said. "I'm getting Terri another one just like it."

"You do and I'll fire you. I want you to have a good time here."

Danny took a swig of scotch and shook his head. "Jesus, Amanda, you're nuts. We're not married yet."

Amanda raised her eyebrows. "*No?* Well, don't make it public."

She laughed to herself and left the two kids to whisper about glamorous, crazy Amanda Gray. Amanda decided she wanted to be notorious. She didn't have much choice about it anyway, so she might as well play it up.

Now here was Lacey, a vision in blush pink taffeta trimmed in seed pearls and lace. Her eyes found Amanda and flicked away, panicked. Amanda could almost hear the girl's heart flutter. *Welcome to the club,* she thought.

"Hi," Amanda said. "I'm so happy you came."

Lacey forced herself to look up. Amanda tried to read the topaz eyes. She saw love and hatred, aloofness and desperation, all coming and going like ghostly figures in a fog. "This is a beautiful place," Lacey said.

The breathy, long-missed voice sent chills down Amanda's back. The whole frightening incident rushed back into her memory. "Yes it is. It has a kind of New England charm, which is unusual for New Mexico."

"It's very nice." Lacey pulled at her left index finger with her right hand, and her exquisite head turned on her avian neck.

"Why don't you get yourself a drink?" Amanda urged.

"I will. I just got here, I—I'm looking for people I know."

Amanda fought to breathe evenly. This was awful. "Oh, there are a couple of old buddies around, besides Danny and Terri. Hey, I want you to come see the site tomorrow. We're giving a grand tour for the New York contingent."

"I'd like that," Lacey said coolly.

"Great." *Well, damn it, talk to her. Don't let it end in mutual pain. Say something that will mend the hurt.* Amanda took a breath. "Lace, this is no place to talk. It's too crowded. Why don't we have a quiet lunch later this week? Just you and me? I hate being on the outs."

Amanda could almost hear Lacey's eyes slam shut. The girl stiffened and tossed her hair. "I don't think I want to. What good would it do?"

"Talking always does some good," Amanda said tightly. "I don't want you to hate me."

"You should have worried about that when it counted," Lacey said.

Stung, Amanda recoiled. She felt her cheeks burn and she said, "All right. Clear enough. Consider the invitation rescinded."

Amanda thought she detected a slight shudder of uncertainty in Lacey's cool demeanor, but she might have been hoping. "I—the party was a nice idea," Lacey said.

"I think so, too. Enjoy yourself."

Lacey colored brightly and turned away. Amanda felt bad that Lacey was so embarrassed and confused. She sighed and finished her drink. Suddenly, she wasn't looking forward to the party.

While Amanda presided over steaks and chutney in New Mexico, Helen Tennyson met Byron Moore for dinner in an elegant French country restaurant in Connecticut. Here the mood was quiet and discreet. Helen glittered in a metallic panne velvet dress that bared a smooth shoulder. Byron, his hair whiter than ever, looked stunningly tan in a black evening suit. The chinking of silverware blended with the sibilant sound of conversation.

Both diners paused, smiles frozen politely, as the waiter tenderly opened a steaming dessert soufflé and poured on a rich sauce. He left Helen and Byron beneath the rose-tinged lighting and murals. Helen and Byron sensed the hostility in the air; the blue-blooded, old-money clientele didn't cotton to self-made millionaires.

"How is the construction going?" Byron asked as he sampled his soufflé. "Any problems from those Indians?"

"No, thank God," Helen said. "It's so embarrassing. Everyone asks me about it."

"Don't knock it," Byron said. "You get lots of free publicity,"

"Some publicity." Helen sipped at her wine and checked her watch. She was growing bored with Byron's company. With an agreement to purchase all the art for The Pueblo from Byron's galleries, the evening's commerce was over. "Maybe that idiotic stunt of Amanda's did some good."

Byron's eyes flickered subtly. "She was always a headstrong girl."

Helen feigned embarrassment. "Oh, that's right. I'm sorry, Byron, I forgot that you lived with her."

"Well, she lived with *me*." He smiled. "Are you imagining wild scenes?"

"No. I'd laugh out loud if I did. Tell me, Byron, doesn't it sometimes embarrass you a little, this sexual thing with young girls?"

Byron knew Helen well enough to avoid being taken aback. He calmly ate his soufflé and considered before he answered. "I enjoy controversy. I enjoy being attacked. It gives me a kick to watch fools eat their hearts out."

"Well, *that's* honest."

He gave an eloquent little shrug. "I do nothing to encourage the wild stories, or the rumors. I have enough money and influence to live outside the expectations of society."

"Good for you." Helen finished her dessert and studied Byron. His immense power and personal charisma radiated as far as the red banquette where she sat, but her own potency shielded her. They were evenly matched, and stalked each other warily. "You have another sweet young thing now, don't you?"

Byron flooded his mouth with wine. "You mean Heather." He sighed. "I'm really too old to be educating little girls. She's boring. She's got real singing talent, but no curiosity, no drive, no discipline, no patience. She wants to be tickled and entertained all the time. Video baby. Not worth the work."

"What a shame," Helen consoled. "What will you do with her?"

"I don't know," he said. "Maybe kick her out. I'm an aging man, without a wife or family. It's lonely, Helen. I'll tell you, don't sacrifice it all for the game. It gets cold in the winter."

Helen was struck by his tone. Was the man serious? "Well, Byron, this is a revelation coming from you. Are you growing sentimental?"

"Could be. I miss Amanda, that much I'll tell you. She was a special woman. A remarkable woman. Once in a lifetime find, like the rarest of rare paintings. Once I cleaned her up and restored her luster, she glowed. Hell, *you* must know that."

"Indeed." Helen's mind was coiled now, and alert. "I've found her a little flighty and snippy, to be honest. Talented, of course, but not very respectful."

Byron laughed, drawing stares. "She was never respectful. And why should she respect *you*?"

"Oh, all right," Helen sniffed. "To hell with *this* conversation. I didn't realize you were still gaga over the girl."

"Always," Byron said soulfully, and leaned a little toward Helen. "I'm even a little jealous of her relationship with your architect."

"Oh, Jason." Helen drank more wine and considered her own murderous feelings. "Well, it was inevitable, I suppose. He always goes trotting after a new pair of bra cups."

"Seems serious," Byron said quietly. "From what I can gather."

Helen looked oddly at him, disturbed at her own fury. "Well, hell, Byron, if it really bugs you, why don't you break them up? Take her back to your house. You certainly are obsessed with her, aren't you?"

Byron's eyes stormed for a moment, but his face remained controlled. "Just attached, Helen. You don't forget someone you loved."

"No, I suppose not. Well, feel free to come out and visit her. I think a gathering of her amours would be nice. Lend the proper circus atmosphere to the project."

"Not me. I just don't like losing control. Any more than you do."

"I'll go along with that. But I don't think Amanda would want your assets."

"No, not Amanda." Helen tightened her mouth, careful of permitting any more of her feelings to escape. She worried about Jason, despite her grip on him, and she worried very much about Amanda Gray. The woman had walked out on Byron Moore and prospered, and that took an inner strength and determination that Helen feared. She decided it was necessary to break up Jason and Amanda, and to step on each of them a bit. She also caught the metacommunication in Byron's casual chatter, and wondered if anybody else was aware that the man was deranged.

"Well," she said with a carefree little sigh, "I'm so glad we had this heart-to-heart. Rest assured that Amanda is quite well, except for her failing eyesight, and not missing you at all."

Byron called for the check. "What's wrong with her eyesight?"

"I don't know," Helen sighed, as she fidgeted with an

earring. "She made an appointment with an ophthalmologist at a rather big hospital. She never wore glasses or anything, did she?"

"No," Byron said. He took the check from the waiter and scanned it curiously, then slapped his American Express gold card on the tray. "Must be eyestrain. Designer's occupational hazard."

Helen studied Byron and caught his quickened breathing and rapid blinking. The man was tremendously excited, almost uncontrollably so. What in hell was going on? "No doubt," she said. "This was instructive, Byron. I look forward to our doing business."

"So do I." Byron smiled, his manicured fingers drumming on the tablecloth.

The waiter returned and Byron signed the bill. "Excuse me for a moment," he said to Helen. "I have to make a quick phone call."

"That's all right," Helen said. "I have to be going anyway. Thanks for dinner."

"My pleasure," Byron said, smiling and rising. Helen stood also and smiled back. She gripped her handbag demurely and walked away, aware of Byron's eyes between her shoulder blades. It annoyed her that she couldn't figure out his motives. Amanda was of crucial importance to him, which gave the girl an aura of mystery. Helen detested mystery.

Byron went quickly to the phone and dialed a close and powerful friend who sat on the boards of several major hospitals. From this friend, Byron got the name of the hospital and the ophthalmologist that Amanda was probably seeing. Byron asked his friend to get a copy of whatever records there were on Amanda's checkup, and to send that information on.

Byron's friend bridled at this breach of ethics, but he owed Byron heavily and it wouldn't be a difficult favor. Byron hung up, excited at the prospect of taking control of events. So, the blindness was hereditary, or at least it might be. At the very least, it would be terrifying. If Amanda was really going blind, she'd need him again, he felt sure of it. He'd have to keep a close watch, prevent her from getting too much hope. This was a brilliant opportunity, and Byron knew how to take advantage of opportunities. Aroused, he slung his topcoat over his arm and left the restaurant.

chapter 19

JASON sat on a rock overlooking the highway. He was dressed for a party, but his linen suit jacket was in the Maserati. The setting sun made blinding white arcs of his shirt-sleeves against his black cardigan vest. He'd driven here at reckless speed.

He pushed a hand through his blowing hair and looked at the flaming mountain ridges. The black two-lane road cut boldly through the rock, its white center line phosphorescent. Jason didn't know where the hell he was, but he swore he could see the dull blink of lights from the construction site, just beyond the wall of rock on the horizon.

He lifted his head to look aimlessly at the setting. What next, he wondered? Keep driving until he flipped the car? Go back and mingle with Bradley's social elite? Amanda was there, and he'd pointedly ignored her the whole evening.

Not pointedly. Cruelly. And she knew it.

He rolled up his sleeves and felt the cold wind ruffle the fine hair on his wrists. Rum on the rocks had made him dizzy and fried squid and mangoes heaved in his belly. His trousers itched. It was going to get inhumanly cold in about half an hour. Already the sky glowed blue, cooling to dusk.

God, he loved Amanda. He kept conjuring her face, and her eyes burned into his heart. She'd worn a black pleated chemise tonight, with a pearl and diamond necklace. He imagined the softness of her fawn's skin.

He uttered a curse and turned his head. His muscles pounded and he felt flabby. He'd neglected workouts. His shoulders and chest were no longer cut cleanly, and his stomach had softened.

Wind scoured the rocks, and the remaining sun lit them softly. Jason fought for breath, and buried his head in his hands. An anxiety attack shook his body.

Headlights searched the growing darkness and a car turned off the highway and parked behind the Maserati. Jason heard the spit of tires on sand and the squeak of brakes. He heard a door slam, and footsteps on the treacherous stones. They were woman's footsteps, but not Amanda's.

Helen's voice said, "Jason?"

He felt almost relieved. He looked up at her with tear-stained eyes, and felt embarrassed. "Why did you follow me?"

"I was worried," she said. "Couldn't you just take a walk in the garden?"

Jason felt soiled and stupid. He shook his head in wonderment. There Helen stood, in her six thousand dollar white silk-organdy dress, utterly contemptuous of the desert. She looked pissed off about having to climb rocks in her evening wear.

"I needed to take a ride," he said.

"You didn't throw up, did you? I'm not standing in puke?"

He smiled. "No."

"You're doing this too often, Jason. You fell apart at that banquet in Atlanta, and now this. If you can't handle your liquor, drink less."

"Don't sweat it," he said.

"I'm not sweating. Are you coming back?"

"In a while."

"And what will you do then?"

"Huh?"

"When you come *back*. Will you get more polluted? Say something stupid? I need to know."

"Why?"

"Because you're my superstar. I parade you in front of important people to dazzle them. If you make them uncomfortable, you're a floperoo."

The rock faces became glass, shot with orange and green and turquoise. Jason felt crushing power in his hands. "I'm sorry if I embarrass you."

"Apologies won't help. I'll drive you back."

"I can't leave my car here."

"I'll have it picked up."

"It won't be here."

"Then you'll buy a new one. What *is* all this bullshit?"

Jason sighed. "Helen, you were a fool to drive out here alone."

He stood up as red fingers of sunlight slipped from the rock and the sky purpled. The wind turned icy. Jason could sense a scuttling of hairy legs and a slither of scales as the desert awakened. "I want to stay here for a while," he said.

"You'll die."

"It's a clean suicide."

Helen exhaled with exasperation. She walked closer to him. "Is this because of Amanda?"

"Get lost."

"*Is* it? All of this romantic posturing? Are you agonizing over what to *do,* Jason?"

He turned sharply to her. "Why don't you give it a break?"

Surprisingly, Helen did not retort. Her eyes drove deep into Jason's, stabbing his brain. "It's never been quite like this, has it?" she asked. "None of your sentimental attachments went this deep."

"It's what you wanted, isn't it?"

"No." Helen reached out, and her cool, marble fingers touched Jason's cheek. "I wanted you to keep her in line, that's all. Why did you fall in love with her?"

"What do you want, Helen? Drop the other shoe."

She smiled through glistening lips and shook her head. Her finger traced a path of ice down his jawline. "If I ordered you to leave the little twat, would you?"

"Try it and see."

"I've made you ditch your lady friends before."

"I remember."

"And resent it." Helen's eyes shifted. She should have been freezing in the desert night, but she remained poised and elegant. The flash of her rose-milk skin aroused Jason.

"What the hell does it matter?" he asked. "I might marry her."

Helen's mouth dropped open. "*Marry* her? You couldn't stay married."

"The words don't hurt anymore," he said. "Why do you waste them?"

Her hands imprisoned his face with an urgency he hadn't

felt from her in years. "I hope I don't waste them. I hate it when you're a jerk."

"You made me one."

"And what have you gotten that isn't good for you? There would have been nothing, Jason. Why do you keep forgetting that?"

He seized her wrists and pried her hands away. "I've never seen you this worried."

Helen moistened her lips and now she showed the effects of the cold. Her skin paled to bluish white, and her eyes teared. "Because you're the best. If you fall for this cunt, you'll drive her out in half a year, and you'll slash your wrists. You sold your soul to me, and without me you'll turn to dust. I don't want to see that."

Jason folded his hands over her smooth shoulders. "You really think I can't find a life for myself now? Or do you *know* I can?"

Her smile showed glistening teeth. "How will she manage to train you in what you don't know? Or save you from execution?"

Jason felt the wind saw through him like a cold blade. Bile rose in his mouth at what Helen said. His hands squeezed her arms, tightly enough to force a gasp from her lips. "I can be a flack for somebody else," he said. "I can charm customers in any line."

"You know I won't allow it."

"Bitch."

"Slime." She was flushed, and her breasts rose and fell raggedly beneath her dress. "Nobody wanted me in the board room. Nobody wanted me to be the boss. They hurt me to my bones, trying to stop me. I didn't become kind from the experience. Don't begin to believe that I've fallen in love with my creation. I'll throw you away."

"It might not matter anymore."

Tense, she leaned toward him. "Could you be that romantic, Jason? Throw your life away for love?"

"You couldn't understand that."

"Of course not. It's asinine."

Jason wrenched away from her and walked into the shadowed blackness. The air rattled with wind. He wished some god would infuse him with the guts to defy Helen. *He* couldn't do it. Because after a brief victory, he would hit the skids and Amanda would walk out of his life.

"Jason?" Helen called. "Are you all right?"

"Yeah."

She laughed, low and sinuous in the frigid darkness. "You are so beautiful," she said. "Nobody can resist you."

"Fuck off." He dug a cigarette from a pack in his shirt pocket, and cupped his hand over the lighter. He filled his lungs with rich, toxic smoke and felt his chest constrict.

"This has to stop," she said.

"Sure."

"You can't run out of parties anymore. If you become useless to me, I won't forgive you."

"I'll bet." He inhaled, making the tip of the cigarette glow orange. The steep, jagged rocks made bulky shadows against the vault of night. The moon was a copper shield on the horizon.

"I'm driving you back," she told him. "Clean yourself up."

"Okay."

"And clean that woman out of your system."

He spat smoke and turned to glare at her.

"Do it," Helen said. Her eyes were silver shackles that bound him. "I'm sorry I threw you both together."

"Leave it alone, Helen."

"Never." Her expensive perfume infused the night. She embraced him lightly and he felt her breasts touch his shirt. He shut his eyes. "I'll never leave you alone," she hissed. "Don't you remember when you first came to me? When you were an unbearable beautiful boy and I was young, and I had your beauty for my own? I lost that, Jason. Why?"

He opened his eyes. "We're all losers, Helen."

Her nostrils flared. "I took away your teenage floozy, Jason. I made you stay with me. Remember?"

"Yes, damn you."

"But you withheld your magic. I couldn't get off on the motions. So I lived without your stud services and just used you. But no other lady can have you, not for real. You'll die lonely, heartbreaker."

Jason stamped out the cigarette. "Are you going to keep this up for long? I'll grab a nap."

Her smile flashed again. "Don't feel too rotten. Consider the alternative."

She turned, showing a slash of alabaster spine. Jason raged

with the desire to kill her. He knew he was capable, and the bitch knew it too. And bet that he wouldn't.

Not this civilized stud with his silk tie knotted perfectly. Not drunk and depressed as he was, not dying inside of hopeless love. Without Helen, there *was* no Jason Turner.

As Jason lay naked in the channel-quilted bed, Amanda had the shakes for a cigarette or a Valium, but with stupid pride, she resisted. Her lean body gave alluring point to her panne-velvet robe as she held a telephone receiver to her ear and punched numbers. She looked hungrily at Jason's tanned skin against the light gray bedclothes. Blankets covered his hips, which was just as well. She didn't want to be sexually worked up now. She was too annoyed by his attitude. He lit up a cigarette without hesitation, and he *had* to know it bugged her.

The phone rang at the other end, and after a moment, Amanda snapped, "Adam, it's Amanda Gray. Did you ship the carpet samples?"

Adam gave a hurried excuse and Amanda said, "No time for games. If you can't deliver by tomorrow, I'll have to go somewhere else. This is your number one priority."

Adam apologized again, and Amanda hung up. She shut her eyes and massaged her forehead. Jason said, "Take a break."

"That's *your* specialty," Amanda said. She took a deep breath. "I'm sorry."

"No problem."

She turned to face him fully. The spotlighted Noah mask on the wall seemed to chuckle. "I think there *is* a problem."

"We can talk."

"No. We haven't talked in a long time." She went to the big double windows and looked out at the desert. From this townhouse apartment, she could see yuccas, mimosa, and distant white buildings. The sky was achingly blue, dotted with white cloud puffs.

"We're tired," he said.

"Why? You lie around all day. You get drunk and disappear. You missed Danny's party, you made a jackass out of me when you didn't show up, you smoke yourself blind . . ." She stopped the momentum.

"Finished?"

"No."

"What do you want me to say? I do a lot of PR, Amanda. I'm a celebrity."

"And an architect. When do you draw? When do you take your blueprints down to the site? I've been there fifty times. I've been thinking about what the Navajos are saying. Do you know this hotel is going to take away water from the reservation? These people have had a court claim on this acreage for years and they're going to lose everything now."

Jason looked quizzically at her. "Water rights? Who've you been talking to?"

"Richard Juan," she said, feeling righteous and angry. "I mean, I haven't spent much of my life fighting for causes, but I'd hate to be part of a project that takes away water from the Navajo to fill a lake for millionaires."

Jason studied her. "You can quit."

She shook her head. "I don't want to quit, Jason. I just think we ought to talk about this. Maybe there's a way to let the Indians keep most of the water, maybe lease it from them."

"What?"

Her face grew hot. "That's right! My God, this thing is going to make millions. Why not give the Navajo some of the profit? We're going to dam their river and divert their water. Doesn't it bother you?"

He put out the cigarette and stretched his arms behind his head. "These big construction projects usually hurt *somebody*."

"And you just go along with it?"

"As opposed to doing what?"

Amanda sat on the edge of the bed. She could smell his dried sweat and the stale odor of their lovemaking. "I don't know. I'm asking you. You're a master architect. You designed The Pueblo. You had computers and a staff of geniuses. Couldn't you find a way to let the Indians keep their water? I don't know much about it, Jason. I look to you for those kinds of ideas."

Jason reached out impulsively and tangled his hand in her hair. She recoiled at the anguish in his eyes and the puffy, dissipated wreck of his face. "What ideas, babe? You want to sit down and work out a better plan?"

She nodded. "Yes, I guess that's what I want. Maybe it's stupid and romantic, but I kind of envisioned the two of us being brilliant together. We could pull it off and score a lot of points with everybody. I mean, love is supposed to be inspiring, isn't it?''

He laughed at that and moved so he could pull her close. She rested her cheek in the damp hollow of his neck and pressed her hand to his chest. She could feel his heart beat. ''Amanda, you want to make everything bright and lovely. You're Rainbow Bright.''

''Yes. That's exactly who I am, and I'm starting to like it.''

He breathed evenly into her hair and she could feel him slipping away, even as he petted her. ''Don't look for trouble, Amanda. Take it light.''

''I can't take it light. I'm learning who I am, Jase. At first, I just wanted to get free. That was enough then. Not now. I need more, and not just more money. I lived with a man who did nothing but destroy. I need to build. I need to make the world better than I found it.''

He said nothing, but simply held her for a long time. She let their breathing and heartbeats mingle and she writhed gratefully under the stroking of his hand. She floated in this limbo of comfort, not wanting to leave it. But the insistent sunlight stabbed into the room and made the mess look shameful. The city honked and clashed, and Amanda had to go to work.

She got up with an effort and slipped out of her robe, letting it drop in an azalea cloud to the floor. Her aching body strained against her bra and panties, and for an instant she lusted to be thrown on her back and ravished. The need passed.

''What *are* you doing today?'' she asked.

''Sleeping. Catching a flight to New York later. I have to confer with some attorneys about a convention center in Dallas. Of course, we confer in Manhattan. Makes sense, right?''

She hadn't known about this. ''When will you come back?''

He half shut his eyes, choosing his words with precision. ''Can't say. I'll call you.''

She stood in her underwear and felt her life drain out of her. Her heart pounded wildly. ''Are you coming back at all?''

He folded his hands over his chest. ''I never stay in one place too long, Amanda.''

She sucked in her breath and stood absurdly in the middle

of the bedroom. "What is this, Jason? The kiss-off? What the hell is coming down?"

His eyes opened, unreadable. "It's not the kiss-off, Amanda. I'm not walking out on you. I'm just flying to New York. Let it go."

"Is this Helen's idea?"

He shook his head in weary anger. "No."

"I love you," Amanda said viciously. "I found out I *could* love. I gave you my life. I believed you were part of making the world more beautiful. But you're a total cynic, aren't you? Commitment scares you to death, and your secrets have you paralyzed. I guess we have irreconcilable differences."

"I guess so," he said. "You'd better go to work."

He burrowed under the blankets and pretended to sleep. Amanda decided that she ought to get dressed and get out of here before she made a screaming spectacle of herself. Later she would face the devastation of losing him. She turned her graceful back to him and went to the closet to choose her outfit for the day.

chapter 20

AMANDA floated in the doctor's reclining chair as tears ran down her face. Her closed eyes felt the cold sting of drops. Ten minutes, Dr. Mitchell had told her. In a way, this forced relaxation was nice. Her body seemed to levitate, and sleep flirted with her.

The office was dark and air-conditioned, entombed in a downtown medical building. Dr. Mitchell was soothing. Only once, when he'd touched her eyeball for a glaucoma test, had she flinched. Otherwise, the experience had been pleasant.

Not pleasant was the mounting terror that crawled over her chest. The doctor had said nothing one way or the other. She prayed now, as hard as she'd ever prayed, that it was nerves, or fluid that could be drained, or a muscle that could be relaxed. She'd happily go through surgery; she'd go through anything to save her sight.

She exhaled and tightened her lips. This was no good. Jason had flown out of Bradley yesterday afternoon and she'd wandered around like Bambi without a mother. The poor guy just couldn't handle Amanda's control and new sense of mission. He'd snapped on a flashlight to guide her to where she needed to go, and then he'd shut off the light and left.

She dared to open her eyes, and saw only a film of water. The blinds were drawn, and slices of sunlight slid in. Amanda felt like a fool for allowing herself to love so deeply. She'd known what Jason was. She just hadn't known herself.

The air conditioning whispered as Amanda's vision cleared. She glanced at the machines and trays and charts, feeling scared. She was tempted to play with the instruments, but didn't dare. She had a full day of work ahead. Without Jason, there was no reason to have long lunches. Lacey was back in New York, and so was Danny, preparing for his wedding. There was nobody here.

She looked up at the acoustic-tiled ceiling. Even the construction site was quiet. The police feared that Lone Dog was cooking up something really bad. Amanda wondered how she really felt about the Indians. She'd been reading like mad at the local library, and talking to Richard Juan. Her intellect felt wretched about the exploitation the Indians had taken from the government and private industry. But what did she *feel*? Amanda had always been self-centered; she knew that. Was she suddenly, sincerely bleeding for others?

She didn't know the answers. She knew she was going through changes. She was mutating again, like some Andromeda strain, and she had no more appetite for The Pueblo. She worked with effort, finding ways to avoid picking up a pencil. Goldbricking had never been her style.

The office door clicked open. The nurse said, "How are your eyes?"

"Fine."

"Would you like to wait in the doctor's office? He'll talk to you in a moment."

Amanda's heart flip-flopped and she nodded. "All right."

Like a little girl dreading an injection, Amanda followed the nurse through the office suite to a private consultation room. She sat in a stuffed leather chair facing a massive desk. Behind the desk, a picture window looked out on gardens and a blazing parking lot beyond. Spires of cactus protected the room from sunlight.

Amanda let her eyes wander over the framed medical school degrees on the wall. She wrung her hands in the lap of her polka-dotted dress and tried to return to her thoughts. It was no good. They just swirled around like colored pebbles in a kaleidoscope.

Her pulse stopped when Dr. Mitchell walked in and flashed a meaningless smile at her. She tried to read his face as he sat behind the desk.

"Amanda," he said, in his syrupy voice, "your eyes look okay—no obvious problem there."

She wasn't fooled. Her mouth dried, and she fumbled in her purse, wanting tissues.

"I've looked at the records that were sent from your doctor in New York."

"Dr. Fabiano."

Another meaningless smile. "Right." He brought his fingers together over his desk. His eyes were brown and sincere. "I think I have a good idea of what's happening. You know what the retina is?"

"It's the optic nerve, isn't it?"

His smile froze. "It works *with* the optic nerve." He drew on a pad with a pencil. She noticed that the pad bore the logo of an eyedrop manufacturer.

He pointed with the eraser. "The retina is back here. It's made up of nerve cells and fibers and blood vessels. Actually, it's part of your brain. It grows out of the cranial cavity and is the part of your eye that really 'sees.' Follow?"

Amanda nodded. Her eyeballs felt taut, about to explode.

"Well," Mitchell said, "the retina takes impressions of the world and the optic nerve carries them back to the brain. By the way, when I examined the retina, I noticed a papillodema, a slight swelling of the optic disc. That usually indicates a tumor of the brain. . . ."

Amanda swallowed, but couldn't get the saliva down. "Are you sure?"

"No," he said. "You'd need further tests, maybe even a C.A.T. scan. But that's only one possible cause for episodes of blindness. A sudden loss of vision like yours may also indicate a closing of the main artery of the retina caused by an injury to the optic nerve, or by a nervous disease. It says here you stopped seeing Dr. Fabiano a while ago."

Amanda became aware of the sunlight in the parking lot. She also noticed the too-long hairs jutting from Mitchell's nostrils. "Yes, I did."

"Why?"

"I guess I was afraid to hear this. I make my living by designing interiors. If I can't see, I can't design."

Mitchell nodded. "I understand." He put down the pad and regarded her with a kind of imperious pity. "You might be suffering from a nervous disease that's affecting your retina. The burning pain and the blindness would come from the artery shutting off. This kind of disease can be progressive and irreversible."

"Then I'm going blind."

Dr. Mitchell sighed softly. "A disease such as this can stop of its own accord. It can proceed slowly or quickly. I can't tell you definitely that you'll be blind in a day or a month or a year, or ten years. Or even a lifetime."

"What can I do?" Amanda asked.

Dr. Mitchell pursed his lips. "I'd suggest you make an appointment with Dr. Fabiano again. Since I'm not your regular ophthalmologist, I hate to make long-range recommendations."

"That's all right. I trust your judgment."

He smiled. "I won't make a final judgment. You should go to more sophisticated medical units for more tests and consultations. Meanwhile, you can live normally, to a point. I would advise against driving alone, and to stop whatever you're doing if you have another episode. Don't try to cross the street or cook food if you're undergoing an episode and expect it to clear up."

Amanda fumbled for words. Her brain slammed against her skull, utterly out of control. She had to look calm, stay civilized. "What . . . I mean . . . should I go to a center for the blind, to learn braille, to . . ."

"Whoa," Mitchell said. "You're panicking. That might all become necessary. But right now the prudent course is further testing, further consultation. I'll give you some names and phone numbers."

"Should I be observed in a hospital?"

He shook his head. "It's not an emergency. You can go home, do whatever you want. Feel free to call me if there's any pain or discomfort."

He stood up, ending the interview. Amanda stood also, though how she stayed on her feet was a mystery. Knowing was supposed to bring relief. It brought only wild confusion and a pitching and rolling of her stomach.

She thanked the doctor again. Why did you always thank the doctor for news of your impairment or death? After the receptionist processed the check she handed Amanda an appointment card for six months hence. Amanda crushed the card into her purse and left through a waiting room crowded with sullen people. In the corridor, she bent to drink cold water from a steel fountain and then took the elevator downstairs.

Driving back to the townhouse, Amanda nursed a whopping headache. She'd indulge herself this afternoon. Take two extra-strength Tylenols and a glass of grapefruit juice. Lie down with the air conditioner going full blast, and listen to

Mozart. No work. Hey, she'd just learned that she was going *blind*.

She'd supposed that she would strain to drink in every color and shape once she knew she'd never see again. It didn't happen. She drove as she always did, selecting things to notice, ignoring everything else. The enormity of how her world would change when the darkness enwrapped her did not penetrate. It was her mind's defense against insanity.

People go blind, she thought hysterically. *They learn braille, they get wonderful dogs, and they do everything they did before. Write symphonies, run offices. No designing, of course.* What was she complaining about? She had plenty of money, invested well. She wouldn't go hungry. And she could hear. That meant music, talk, birdcalls. Her body could feel cold water and sun and she could taste food and wine.

And then, for an instant, her creative mind imagined endless darkness, pressing in like a wet blindfold, never peeling away. She imagined flicking millions of light switches and no light ever going on. She imagined her world the size of a broom closet. The vision made her heart race. Sweat popped out on her forehead and her hands grew numb on the steering wheel. She pulled over, through two lanes of traffic.

She let the car idle by the curb as she sat back and cried with great, heaving sobs. *Jason,* she pleaded while tears coursed down her face. *Oh, Jason, please help me . . . help me . . .*

Jason emerged from the glass-fronted lobby of his office building and walked down white stone steps to a marble courtyard, where he spotted a girl he thought he knew.

He carried a suede underarm case and felt good about conning those smart lawyers into a zoning variance. He'd pushed Amanda into a back corner of his mind and he breathed the spice of the city in summer.

Who *was* that fox, anyway? She was tall, with endless legs, but there was a touching vulnerability about her. She dipped her head to spoon yogurt into her mouth as she perched on a marble planter. Jason looked openly at her, reaching for names.

The girl looked up, sensing him. She reminded him of a doe, surprised while grazing.

"Yes?" she asked, her plastic spoon poised. She wore a vanilla two-piece dress with delicate stripes. Her body arched cleanly. Was she a dancer?

"You look familiar," Jason said.

Her eyes widened, amused. "Sorry. I don't recognize you."

"Do you work in this building?" he asked.

She shook her head. "Two blocks down. But I like to eat here."

Jason's eyes scanned the shimmering street, where traffic wavered in the heat. A tugboat hooted in the river. "What firm?"

"Look, could you leave me alone?"

He smiled. "Sorry. I'm not coming on to you. I really think I know you, and it's bothering me."

She considered. "I work at Amanda Gray Designs."

"You're Lacey."

She gave him a searching glance.

"I'm Jason Turner," he said. "I stopped by once or twice to pick up Amanda."

Lacey looked confused for a moment. Then her chiseled features relaxed and she allowed a brief, shy smile. "Oh. Yes, of course. How are you?"

"Hot," he said. "I'll leave you to your lunch now. I feel better."

He repositioned the case and turned to walk away. She said, "Wait a minute."

He turned back. Lacey lowered her eyes. "How is Amanda?" she asked.

"Busy," he said. "I guess you're pretty busy *here*."

She nodded. "Yes. Work is piling up. You have a beautiful suntan from being out west."

"Thanks." He wondered what she was up to. He thought she was the most sensuous girl he'd ever seen, a vision glimpsed in a forest. But she impressed him as painfully timid.

Lacey averted her face, ashamed and blushing. "I'm acting dumb," she said. "Forgive me."

He shrugged. "Making conversation isn't dumb."

She looked up at him with a sudden direct gaze that took his breath away. "I'm being a jerk. You're standing there waiting to go somewhere and you can't figure out what I want."

"I'll confess to that."

She exhaled sharply. "I'm kind of glad you came along. It's lonely and frustrating, working on this project alone—well, of course we've got other people. You understand. . . ?"

She made a tiny fist and berated herself for babbling. Jason laughed. "You wanted to go out to the job site?"

"Or have Amanda work back here for a while. It's selfish, but I feel left out. This is the most exciting thing I've ever been involved with—and I stare at the same office walls everyday. It doesn't *feel* different."

Jason began to like the girl. "You want me to smuggle you into Bradley?"

"Could you do that?"

"Sure. We'd disguise you as a squaw."

Lacey pushed back her glossy hair and chucked the empty yogurt container into a paper bag. "This is all stupid. I mean, I'm working in the *big city,* right?" She exaggerated the words and made a funny face. "But the city is a bore. I like to be on the move. I want to be there, on the desert. This must be jabberwocky to you."

"No," Jason said. "You're fun to listen to."

She snorted. "Yeah, right. I don't know why you're wasting your time."

Jason sat next to her. She gave off a soft, summery smell. A stirring animated Jason's chest, and a deep foreboding. Ugly memories tightened his stomach, like alien worms chewing their way out.

"It's my time to waste," he said. "Obviously, you want to talk to someone."

"Yeah. I do."

"So do I."

"You? I wouldn't have thought so, Mr. Turner."

"Mister?"

She responded to his grin with an abashed smile of her own. "Well, I don't know . . . I mean, what do I call you?"

"Jason."

"It feels funny."

"Why? Are my gray hairs that noticeable?"

She shook her head and touched his jacket sleeve. "I didn't mean it that way. You're a celebrity."

"True. Notice the crowds straining to touch me."

She laughed again. "Well, you know what I mean. As an *architect.*"

Truthfully, Jason wasn't sure why he was being so successful in beguiling this exquisite young creature, who'd seemed to him far more sullen and reserved than she was acting now.

But it felt fine. "I'm not really terrible," he said. "I like listening to you. I listen to sons of bitches most of the time."

She stopped laughing and her lips pressed into an appreciative smile. "Thanks. You're awfully nice."

"Don't say that. It makes me sound harmless."

She took an apple from her bag and bit into it. Jason watched a piece break off cleanly with a snap and watched her tongue flick it into her mouth. He had a wild urge to kiss her. "Okay," she said through a mouthful of apple. "I don't think you're harmless anyway. I've read about you."

"And you're not frightened?"

"I have tear gas in my purse."

It was his turn to laugh. "I'll tell you the truth, Lacey. It's pretty lonely for me, too, in the big bad city."

"Well, without Amanda."

That stopped him. *Amanda. Remember her?*

"I'm without Amanda more than you think," he lied. "We don't cross paths that often. It's so damned hectic out there—not very romantic or exciting by the way, so don't think you're missing anything."

Lacey ate her apple thoughtfully. "Mandy is crazy about you."

Well, what did he do? What did he *want* to do? Shit, he knew what he wanted to do. He wanted to make love to this nymph, to slake old hungers, to shake off the straightjacket of his love for Amanda. A love that seemed far away and cold and dangerous at this distance. He wanted to appease Helen and keep his lifestyle, and to hell with his manhood. It was much easier when he lived without thinking. Amanda complicated his life.

"We've had some good times," Jason said carefully. "But, like they say in the gossip columns, we're just good friends."

"Wow," Lacey said. "Is this a scoop?"

"You can take it to the composing room."

She finished the apple and dropped the core into the bag. "I don't know what to say."

"No comments necessary. These things get blown up by the media. You learn to ignore it after awhile. Fortunately, Amanda's levelheaded and we have no problem with loose talk."

Lacey listened with fervent eyes and Jason felt like a slime bucket. He was bailing out, and Amanda would have to land the plane by herself. *Crummy bastard,* he thought.

Lacey sat quietly as a cloud passed over the sun and shadows drifted across her face. "I think—God, don't call me a bitch for this—I think it's not totally like you say. Is it?"

He felt relief. "You're perceptive."

She smiled. "I read people pretty well. You're more hurt than anything else. Did she stick it to you?"

"Amanda? Not a cruel bone in her body."

"So what *did* happen?"

"Hurts are complicated, Lacey. It's not one person or one remark. You get into situations and they screw you up. I don't want to make you my shrink and—no, don't protest—you're sweet as hell, but you don't really want to get your head junked with my problems."

She sighed. "I think you're wrong, but okay. I see a lot of things, though, Jason. Things they don't write about you."

"Well, they never captured my essence."

"No, they didn't."

He checked his watch and he was honestly late for his next meeting. He stood up. The clouds played hide-and-seek and his hair blew in a sudden wind that whooshed around a corner. "Lacey, would you let me treat you to dinner?"

"Yes."

"Meet you at five, in front of your building. We can have drinks first."

"You're on."

"I promise not to turn bestial."

She crossed her legs fetchingly. "I wouldn't mind," she said shyly.

Damn, his heart was doing rumba rhythms. "See you later," he said, and moved away into the stream of pedestrian traffic. He was in a sweat, not sure what was going on. He knew he was playing fast and loose with two hearts, knew he was the best at the game, and hated his own guts.

Lacey watched Jason get swallowed by the crowd. Her head pounded from effort, but her throat pulsed with triumph. Helen had been right. It had been easy. She wouldn't have thought so, not with a man like Jason Turner. She worried about how she would perform, when it came time to pretend passion for him. But she'd manage it. It was worth what she had to endure. Worth it to win, and win big.

chapter 21

AMANDA channeled her terror into activity. She worked on her designs, eating lunch at her desk. She met with her financial advisor and updated her investments. She made appointments with ophthalmic specialists. She relentlessly drove Jason from her mind whenever she thought of him. Only now and then, in the darkness of her bedroom, did she cry.

She also booked a flight to Italy. She had a business reason: to shop in Florence and Rome for accessories. She put the flight and her accommodations on Helen's expense account. But her real reason for going was personal.

Her adoptive parents lived in a restored villa in the hills of Tuscany. Amanda had known this for some time, and felt relief at their distance. Now she wanted to see them, and to ask about her real mother. She was scared to death; the memories hurt. But she was not a kid anymore.

The sky over the Florentine hills was blue enough to hurt as Amanda took a cab to the villa. She looked out at olive groves, and she smelled hot Italian sunshine. The villa stood splendidly on a hill, white on a broad green lawn, framed by cypresses. The air was perfumed with grapes. How alive her senses were! She thought of her real father; were these gardens bought with Tom's daughter?

Amanda paid the driver to wait. She stood aristocratically in a belted linen flax dress, her hair pulled back and braided over her shoulder. The Grays were expecting her; she'd phoned from her hotel in Florence.

Were they frightened, too? Amanda wondered. She hoped so.

* * *

She was led under a classic archway to gardens in the back. Five cypresses stood guard over a riotous rose garden. Here, on the terrazzo, the Grays waited for her at a small table set with fruit, coffee, and wine. Amanda stopped at the end of the stone walk and looked at them through her sunglasses.

"It's been a long time," she said.

"Yes," Jenny agreed. Amanda was depressed by their appearance. Jenny was swathed in a loose white dress with a hood. Her face had leathered from sunbathing and her lips were white. Rob just looked foolish. A white fedora shadowed his bony face, and he sported a deep-navy jacket with white polka-dots. God, Amanda thought with revulsion, these were Westchester nouveau snobs, Babbits who'd bought a fifteenth century house and debased it with their trendy clothes and ignorance. Who do you think you are? she cried silently. The Renaissance began in Florence.

"Sit down, Mandy," Rob said. "How about some wine?"

"That would be nice," Amanda said. She sat in a wrought iron chair.

They surveyed each other, warily and with masked emotion. "Well," Jenny said at length, "you've done a lot with your life."

"I've tried," Amanda said. A servant poured the wine. She sipped it: a chilled white, stronger than she liked.

"What brings you here?" Rob asked.

"I'm shopping."

Jenny smiled, her eyes glittering in her sunburned skull. "You've come to Italy before to shop. You never visited us."

"No," Amanda confessed. "I made it a point not to."

Jenny's gnarled hand tightened on her coffee cup. Rob snorted. "This is going to be ugly, right?"

Amanda took a breath, and her nostrils stung with the odor of flowers. "I don't mean it to be."

"Why *did* you come?" Jenny asked. "We've been trying to figure it out since you called."

"I have some questions," Amanda said. "Loose ends that need tying up."

"I see," Jenny said.

Amanda sipped more wine. It made her drowsy and warm. Her eyes darted from rose to cypress to cloud-brushed sky. "This is magnificent."

"Thank you," Jenny said. "It was a wreck when we found it. The courtyard was a mudhole, and the roof leaked. Remember, Rob?"

Rob grunted. "We got in touch with the *Belle Arti,* the Italian arts commission, and got a local architect to direct the restoration. Took four years to finish it."

"We restored some of the frescoes," Jenny added smugly. "And we gutted the tower to make guest rooms. Would you like to see it all?"

"Later," Amanda said.

Jenny's face turned dreamy. "We're so happy here. It's what we dreamed of."

"Is it?" Amanda asked.

Rob said, "I always wanted a villa in Italy. You can keep your overpriced real estate in New York. Just gives you ulcers. This is real, you know? It's the *earth.* And when you think of what you can get here, and how cheap it is, you've got to be crazy to throw your money into an acre in Westchester. I'm living like a prince here. Servants and cooks. I go into Rome every couple of weeks on business, then come back and sit in the garden . . . you'd appreciate it, Mandy."

"I'm glad you found a place for yourselves," Amanda said.

Jenny and Rob exchanged glances. Jenny said, "Well, you didn't show up to wish us luck."

Amanda smiled. "No. I came for information."

"Such as?"

"Who my real mother was."

Jenny paled beneath her tan and breathed in sharply. "What brought that up?"

"You know I've been looking for my real parents."

"We can't help you," Rob said.

"Sure you can. You took me when I was a baby. You knew who they were."

"*Excuse* me," Rob said testily. "Don't tell us what we know. It was black market. . . ."

"Forget the bull," Amanda said. "I believed it long enough. I know that my father was Tom Crawford. Byron Moore's gardener, and that Byron wouldn't let him keep me. I know that Byron directed the search for adoptive parents and found you. How am I doing so far?"

Rob flung an arm over his chair, flustered. Jenny clasped

her hands together on the table. Rob said, "What did you do, hire a P.I.?"

"Yes, I did."

Jenny shook her head slowly, and tears welled in her eyes. "I always knew it would come back to us."

"Shut up," Rob snapped. He looked at Amanda with utter hatred. "Are you enjoying this? What'd you do, wait thirteen years to show what a big shot you've become?"

"Okay," Amanda said. "I admit I'm enjoying it, but you know what? I really don't have any appetite for revenge. That's the irony. A decent person doesn't get a kick out of hurting people, not even people who should be hurt."

"Who made *you* our judge?" Jenny demanded.

"You did," Amanda shot back. "With every little slap in the face, every cold shoulder. I could feel your hatred, like ice in my skin. You deprived me of love, you starved my heart. It made no sense. . . ."

"Stop it!" Jenny hissed. "What do you want from us?"

"I'll settle for answers. I need to find my mother, and soon. I need to know why you adopted me when you hated me."

"Personal reasons," Rob said.

Amanda turned to him. "You're not going to play games, are you, Dad? Look at me. I'm not the little girl you ignored. I'm not helpless anymore. Your friend Byron did a great deal for me."

"I'm glad you appreciate something," Rob said.

Amanda laughed bitterly and shook her head. "You're a piece of work."

"This is boring," Jenny said. "Can't we stop?"

"I don't think so," Amanda said. "Do you know what it's like growing up without any love at all? No hugs, no bedtime stories, no dollies? Nothing close, nothing warm. Just your cold eyes telling me how I was screwing up your life."

Damn. She hadn't wanted this to come spilling out. The villa seemed to scowl in disgust at the mean little people who lived here.

"Are you finished?" Jenny whispered.

"No," Amanda said. "Why did you take me? What did you get for it?"

Rob had been holding back his defensive rage. Now he stood up and jerked a thumb toward the archway. "Get out of here."

"Now that's sharp," Amanda said. "Really in keeping with the house. You've gotten so polished."

"I mean it. I don't have to take this, not from you. Don't come flying out here to dump on me."

"Why not?"

Jenny pleaded, "Amanda, just go."

"Why not?" Amanda repeated to Rob. "Don't you deserve to be dumped on? You used me. And in return for keeping me on ice for Byron Moore, you live in a villa. That doesn't seem fair."

Jenny wept now, unable to withstand this barrage. Rob's face, beneath the absurd white hat, was dark with rage. "How about if I get the police up here?"

"How about if you do? And how about if I mention Byron's name and get reporters to ask *him* the same questions I'm asking you?"

Jenny looked up so sharply it took Amanda by surprise. "Don't get upset, Mother," Amanda said. "How many secrets do you think you have left?"

Rob turned and looked out at his estate, his aging shoulders slumping. The high-fashion outfit hung ludicrously on him. He yanked out his chair and sat down roughly. "I don't know who your mother was, Mandy. I didn't want to know. I didn't want *you*, that's for sure."

"Then why did you adopt me?"

Jenny sipped coffee with desperation. "What's the purpose of this, Amanda? Just to hurt us back? You've done that. Why don't you leave us alone?"

"Because I want information. When you give me the information, I'll go."

"We don't *know*," Jenny insisted. "Rob just told you that. It was all arranged through attorneys."

"Did you want a baby?" Amanda asked.

Jenny sighed, exhausted. "No."

Rob snarled, "Shut up, Jen."

"No," Jenny said, and looked at her husband with red eyes. "I don't want this scene to go on. I don't want to sit here and be hurt by this girl. She was always hateful to me, always. I wanted her dead. I wished for it everyday. I didn't want to hold out for sixteen years, and I had to. It was living hell for me."

Rob flung himself sideways. "Christ."

Amanda had to clamp down hard on her emotions. ''What are you talking about, Jenny?''

Jenny looked bleakly at Amanda. The white hood gave her a ghostly mien. ''Do you really want to know? I never wanted children. Rob was going to be a successful accountant, a big man in business, and that's what I wanted. I grew up poor. I had to work and give my wages to my mother. I watched other girls with wardrobes and cars. All that mattered to me was having money. I know you don't think much of that.''

''There are worse sins,'' Amanda said.

''So I married Rob, because not many sharp guys wanted me. And Rob wasn't making it. We lived in an apartment in Kew Gardens with the Long Island Railroad in the backyard and iron bars on the window. I had nothing.''

Amanda poured wine and drank it slowly. Jenny's eyes were hate-filled as she spoke. ''Then Rob lost his job, and he was picked up by Charlie—I forget his last name—''

''Hughes,'' Rob said.

''That's right, Charlie Hughes. A millionaire. Big estate in Putnam County. Millions in debts. He was a high roller, Amanda. He liked Rob. Gave him a charge card with a two grand limit, just for discretionary spending, plus a top salary. Rob and I bought a house on Long Island and sunk a pool and we started to live.''

''What's the point, Jenny?'' Amanda asked.

Jenny looked bravely at Amanda. ''Charlie went crazy and lost the company to Byron Moore. Byron made Rob executive V.P. Remember, Rob?''

''No,'' Rob griped.

Jenny blinked coldly. ''You know what happened for us, Amanda. Rob became rich, and we had everything we wanted. Byron did it all for us. He could have dumped Rob when he took over Charlie's company. He could have put us on the street. But he made us rich. And then he came for his repayment.'' Her voice turned bitter. ''It wasn't Rob's potential that made Byron take the risk. It was *quid pro quo*. It was all planned. And we were greedy enough to fall for it.''

Amanda's mind leaped ahead and she understood. The shock was less than she would have imagined. Maybe she'd already grasped the design of it. Surely nothing the man did would surprise her. ''It was an arrangement,'' Amanda said. ''He needed adoptive parents and you were available.''

Rob cracked the wine bottle down on the table. "Are you having a good time with this?"

Amanda reeled with a sense of deadly violence. These people had been laid flat on a surgeon's table and had their self-respect removed. How could she want revenge when the Grays suffered damnation every day of their lives?

"You owed him," Amanda said. "He didn't know how he could use Rob when he elevated him, but he saw a weak, grasping man, and he knew you'd be perfect someday, for something."

Jenny shivered, despite the heat. "And we hated you. From the first day you came, to the day he took you."

"Yes," Amanda said. "And that was his plan, wasn't it? To keep me with you until he was ready. Until I was sixteen and going to hell with myself. He wouldn't want to play God with a sweet, obedient girl. So he gave me to you, knowing you'd resent me and hurt me. Byron likes to arrange life. He likes to make it happen his way."

Rob drank more wine. "That's right, Jen. Don't give me credit for doing a thing with my life. I did pretty well, with you on my neck. We're here, right? You've got it all. You never asked what it would cost."

Amanda felt sick. Her anger had changed into wrenching pain. These people were too dreary to hate. She saw them now with a new mind and new heart. She saw them with eyes that were going blind.

She swallowed hard and swiped at her tears under her sunglasses. It was too awful. How much was she supposed to take?

Jenny struggled to control her own passions. In a dark voice, she asked, "What else do you want to know?"

"My mother's name," Amanda said.

"We don't know it," Jenny told her. "We knew your father was the gardener, but Byron didn't reveal your mother's name. She must have been important to him."

Amanda believed her. The mystery went unsolved, and Amanda would go blind and never see her mother. There was no way to exact revenge for what Rob and Jenny had done to her.

Amanda stood up. The memories flooded back: nights in the T-Bird, roaring through the elegant streets; afternoons locked in her room, hugging her teddy bear and writing love poems to TV actors; mornings in front of the color TV, watching hour after hour of cartoons. Waiting to be hurt, wanting to be held.

Amanda cherished the memories angrily as she glared at the fashionable, aging couple on their terrazzo. Time seemed precious to her now. She ached to see the sky and the roses and the vibrant white clouds. She needed to find her mother. She needed to be rid of Jason, rid of Byron, rid of every barbed hook that ripped into the flesh of her life.

No. She couldn't be rid of Byron. She'd have to see him, because he knew who her mother was. She dreaded it, but her disease gave her strength. Who could hurt her now, when God was hurting her so brutally?

"I'm so damned sorry about this day," she said.

"So am I," Jenny said.

"And I'm sorry for both of you. I truly am. I don't think any of us deserved what happened."

Rob said, "You deserved whatever you got."

Amanda swallowed down her anger. "I guess there won't be forgiveness and reconciliation," she said cruelly. "I'm glad you have to live with your stupidity. I won't see you again while you're alive."

"Go away, Amanda," Jenny whispered.

Amanda looked at them one last time, the sun-poisoned woman in the white hood and the crude peacock in the navy polka-dotted jacket. Then she turned and walked briskly out of the rose garden toward her waiting cab.

chapter 22

BYRON Moore didn't like hotel nightclubs, not even his own, but Heather was singing here tonight. The room was packed with glittering women and silver-haired men. Smoke hung in a colored fogbank over the tables, and waiters in plum jackets hustled trays of drinks. The room buzzed with talking.

Byron sipped a bourbon and water as sensuous lighting picked out the glistening planes of his face. He associated nightclubs with sweat. Everyone sweated, even the women in their off-the-shoulder dresses and ropes of diamonds. Sweat popped out on their upper lips and the napes of their necks. They were gorgeous women, laughing arrogantly. Byron watched them with bored disdain. Any one of them would desert her investment banker or real estate developer for a weekend with Byron Moore.

He tasted bile in his throat. More and more, he was suffocated by people. He craved solitude, and Amanda.

How *had* he made it through the years without her? The thought simultaneously amused and infuriated him. It irked Byron to think that, with all of his power, he needed one dominant love in his life. Was he seeking his mother? He'd considered and discarded a number of psychological answers. Early in his adult life, Byron knew what he needed from women, and had taken it. Mary, Amanda, and Heather had satisfied his bodily lust, his artistic need for feminine excellence, and his overpowering obsession to control. These women had also slaked his feral thirst for inflicting pain, the pain he had never inflicted on his father. But romantic love? That had never been part of the equation.

Whatever Byron had done, wherever he'd conquered, it had been deliberate and cold-blooded. The thrill had always come from the artistry involved and the amount of ownership gained. With patience and creativity, he had learned to appreciate food and wine, and to wear clothing well. At first, he used his money to buy good clothing at good stores. He wore the Brooks Brothers look because other businessmen wore it, and thus gained entry into their world. He didn't wear his expensive suits or accessories with pride.

Later, when years of experience had given him time to observe—he was always the consummate critical observer—Byron put together a wardrobe that mirrored his own personality and style. Whether he chose a chalk stripe suit, a pair of cap-toe shoes, a bright pocket square, or a pair of braces, and whatever the expensive fabric or style of handstitching, the clothing always proclaimed Byron Moore's fashion. He became amused to see wealthy businessmen signal each other with dropped Oxford lapels or Brooks Brothers buttonholes. Byron knew all the signs, and he could discern the genuine leather attaché cases that bespoke status. But no businessman could signal Byron Moore, because Byron had his clothing designed exclusively for him. Once again, in one more realm, he had gained control.

Why, then, the breakdown over Amanda? He had *not* crumbled when she left. He hadn't brooded about his estate, tumbler in hand, staring wild-eyed at the sea. He'd kept on with his work, managing his empire. He'd enjoyed a rather neat rise in his real estate fortune as he became more involved in commercial properties. As always, Byron had observed and sensed the trends. He saw that in the heartland the glut of office space and the decline of energy-based economy had choked off further construction, and he saw that in New York tenants filled office space as quickly as it was built. He gathered investment groups to finance office towers, he co-oped mortgages, and he became a silent power in gentrifying barrios and slums. Byron's artistic nature caused him to be fascinated with new commercial architecture, and he commissioned leading designers to develop properties. He adored using new computer technology to create realistic photos and maps, and to plan entire downtown areas. He became responsible for vast projects involving square miles of malls and offices. He bought hotels. His fortune boomed.

Yet somewhere in the back of his deteriorating mind, it

became clear to Byron that the frenzy of business activity was only a smokescreen. He had known from the first days of his success, when he used his mother's money to buy potato farms, that he was not whole. He knew, in lucid moments, that nothing he accomplished would ever quell the frustration that burned like angina in his chest. He knew that no matter who he owned, what he built, or who he hurt, that he would carry the emptiness in him until his death. Only Amanda had come close to filling that emptiness. Only in fashioning the beautiful, successful, whole woman out of the bitter ragamuffin had Byron felt the thrill of artistic fulfillment.

Maybe it was because she was so like him in some ways. She'd been frustrated and deeply wounded, as he had, and her artistic drive had kept her sane. Like Byron, she'd learned how to control and manipulate her world. She mirrored his triumphs, and mocked his failures. In his darkest moments, he knew he wanted her back so he could destroy her, to find relief from the pain that clutched his heart.

Byron had made the world fall to its knees. But only the fall of Amanda Gray would bring him peace.

The band blared into life. Colored spotlights whizzed back and forth across the stage curtain. From speakers, the emcee's voice shouted: "LADIES AND GENTLEMEN, THE FOUR WINDS PROUDLY PRESENTS THE SONG STYLES OF HEATHER LAINE!"

Byron's neck veins throbbed. He drank harder as he looked past the silhouetted heads and shoulders of the crowd. The band thumped into an up-tempo arrangement of "For Once in My Life," and Heather strode onstage to generous applause. She smiled professionally, her skin vibrant against a ruffle-back taffeta dress. Leggy and curvaceous, she showed plenty of skin for the middle-aged men.

She plucked the mike from its stand and acknowledged the applause gracefully, then pumped her body into rhythmic motion and sang. Byron turned away. Her voice was smoky and smooth. She sounded terrific; disciplined and polished. She had talent and presence, and he'd torn it out of her, one bleeding day at a time. But there was no surge of triumph, no kick. His need for Amanda had spread like a carcinoma through his bones and his blood.

He finished the bourbon and put the glass on a tray. Tiredness pulsed in his limbs. He'd read over the reports on Amanda's condition. Results were inconclusive, but frightening. He'd have to follow up, and stay close. It definitely looked serious, and he sensed triumph. He felt braced by the feelings of risk and hopefulness.

With a practiced scrape of a match, Byron lit a cigarette. Heather sang a ballad now, and it depressed him. At odd moments, he saw what he was, and he was appalled. He inhaled painfully. The music hammered in his skull. He was buffeted by unwanted thoughts, and that showed lack of control. He needed to have Amanda locked in her room, whimpering. He needed to hear her play the piano while he closed his eyes.

With a snarl, Byron crushed the cigarette in an ashtray. Purple light played over his face as Heather sang. A woman approached him, a shadow at first, fetchingly elegant. He caught a hint of subtle perfume. He watched her come into the halflight, alluring in a side-draped silk dress. She looked at him out of jeweled eyes. He stared at her bare flesh, unbroken from throat to breasts but for a shoulder panel. When she breathed, her sculpted collarbone protruded.

"What brings you here, Amanda?" he asked.

She stopped a few feet from him. "I wanted to see Heather. She's fantastic."

"Thanks."

"You're miraculous, Byron. I mean that sincerely."

"I know you do."

Amanda gazed over the crowd, to the child who performed on stage. "I feel like a graduate, coming back to school to see an old teacher. And now you have new kids. I've been replaced."

"Are you jealous?"

She smiled. "Of course. I want to be a kid again, performing my heart out for you."

He lit a second cigarette, put off guard by Amanda's unexpected appearance. She didn't seem shaken by her impending blindness. Things were going wrong. "Would you like a drink?"

She shook her head. "I've had one. I'm here with some friends. You own this place, don't you?"

"I'm partners with Helen Tennyson."

"That's right. You and Helen know each other.'

"For many years."

Amanda turned to Byron. She wore flashing diamond earrings, and her skin glowed. *He'd* made her look like that. Amanda was his triumph, not Heather. Not even Mary.

"Byron," Amanda said. "I've learned about my real father. Did you know that?"

"How would I know? I don't watch your every move."

She flushed. "I won't tell you the whole story now. Too little time, and too much distraction."

"We could go somewhere."

"I'd rather not. What's important is that I know how you planted me with the Grays, knowing you'd come back for me. But I'm still missing one piece of information: my mother's name. Could you tell me?"

Byron spent some time smoking and studying her. He had to admit he'd been surprised by this revelation. He'd kept an eye on Amanda, but didn't know she'd been so resourceful. In a way, he was proud of her.

"Your father was a healthy man," Byron said. "He went to bed with more than one woman."

"No bullshit, Byron. You know who my mother was. She was someone important, someone who shouldn't have been screwing with the gardener. She's meaningless to you now, but she means a lot to me. I need to see her."

"Why?" Byron asked.

"My own reasons."

"Is there something wrong?"

Amanda looked suddenly pale. "The usual day to day troubles, Byron. But it's not your affair. Will you tell me her name?"

Byron glanced at Heather as she soaked up applause. He realized that Amanda was afraid. She wanted to see her mother before she went blind. He said, "How much is it worth to you?"

"What?"

"I've never given a favor without a favor," he said. "What favor are you willing to give?"

The band played again and Heather began a second set. The audience was becoming bored. They swirled ice and whispered to each other. Heather had appeal, but not staying power. He made a note to shorten her act.

Amanda said, "No deals, Byron. I thought you might be ready to tell me. Not out of decency, just out of mutual pain."

Byron smiled to himself. He moved a step closer to Amanda

and nobly fought an urge to touch her shoulder and press his lips to her fragrant throat. "I can't tell you about your mother, Amanda. There are reasons."

"You have reasons for everything, but I'll find her."

"Good luck," Byron said. "Are you really angry?"

"Yes," Amanda said. Her voice was a razor. "You took an infant from her parents and arranged for her to be misused just so you could save her. You always wanted your life to be art, Byron. You rearranged events and people. But you went too far. You had no right to do that to me."

Byron let his cigarette glow red. "There are different ways to look at it, Amanda. You would have been a poor, undernourished child. Tom couldn't have raised you alone. Your mother would have abandoned you in any case. I had you placed with the Grays because they were stable and reliable. You would have failed without me."

Amanda shook her head and sighed. "You have no sense of reality. Why should you? Enjoy Heather. She'll be a star if you want her to be. But treat her gently."

"I'll treat her as she asks to be treated," he said.

"Good night, Byron."

"Good night."

She turned, and left the nightclub. Byron cursed under his breath. Sometimes he hated Amanda for being so strong. But if she weren't that strong, she wouldn't be the only conquest he wanted.

Heather finished her act and the audience applauded tepidly. The band played loudly to cover the lukewarm reception and Byron's temples grew hot with embarrassment. She'd made him look bad and he couldn't allow that.

A spotlight found Byron and he grinned and clapped his hands in a fury, as others strained to see him.

The trip to Florence and the confrontation with Byron were harrowing for Amanda, but the next event in her life was welcome: the wedding of Danny and Terri. Amanda flew to New York and drove a rented car to the church in Merrick, Long Island. It was a hot and dry summer afternoon, with a bright blue sky and streaks of white cloud.

Light streamed in golden shafts through the stained glass windows as Amanda sat silently. She wore a light, breezy summer dress with a big bow at her throat. People turned to stare at her, and she enjoyed the attention. The priest was a white-haired man with glasses and a pink face. Amanda watched with fascination as he performed the mass, attended by white-robed altar boys. Danny was charmingly uncomfortable in his wedding suit, but Terri glowed in her gown.

The hymns were soothing for Amanda, who had grown up without religion. Here, she felt a sense of family and continuity. Friends and relatives crowded the pews: cousins and aunts, fidgeting children, nodding grandmothers. Amanda yearned for it so deeply that it tore her heart. Never to gather with people you had always known; never to feel protected from blindness and pain—it hurt too much. Amanda wiped her streaming eyes with tissues, feeling like a fool.

The priest celebrated the Eucharist as the organ played a broad and uplifting hymn. Parishioners and visitors flowed from pew to altar in quiet streams to receive communion. Amanda kept her eyes on Danny and Terri, loving them very much right now. Lacey wasn't here either, though she'd been invited. What a stupid waste. All the lonely people, loving uselessly.

When the ceremony ended, Amanda drove to the Sunset Inn for the reception. The evening brought cooling breezes. The darkening sky streaked with blue and scarlet. Amanda needed a drink.

Lights burned in the rustic catering hall, set on acres of landscaped grounds. Headlights, glowing against the dusk, formed a procession down the entrance road. Amanda let the valet take her car and stood for a moment in the fresh wind, smelling pine and lilac. Sunset streaked her face and shoulders with red.

She was infused with the love of ceremony tonight. She let herself be swept up in the perfumed crowd as she went inside. Chandeliers glittered in the ballroom, and the band played thumpingly. Some guests gathered in knots, talking and sipping drinks. Others queued up for the smorgasbord of ravioli, meatballs, roast beef, turkey, fruit, and caviar.

Amanda found other friends of Danny and Terri at her table, where she left her purse to go to the bar. She heard whispers as she passed. People knew who she was and pointed her out. But she didn't belong to anyone.

Finally, the bridal party was announced, and Amanda stood and clapped lustily as Danny came in, waving like Rocky after a title bout. Terri smiled shyly, awed at being the center of attention. Amanda felt lightheaded by now and she applauded the bridesmaids and ushers, the maid of honor, and the best man. Her eyes filled as Terri danced with her father to "Daddy's Little Girl." She clasped her hands at her lips and let the tears flow. *Please, God, make them happy,* she prayed.

Danny found her first as the festivities got underway. "It wouldn't be nothin' without you here," he effused. She let him crush her in his bear hug, and she smelled sweat and cologne on his skin, and the damp fragrance of his hair. She gripped his big hands and gazed into his face.

"I'm so happy for you," she said. "You're a terrific guy."

He grinned sheepishly. "It's great that you came. I mean, this isn't exactly the elite of society. . . ."

"Oh shut up!" she admonished. "I'd rather be with real people like these than the phonies I meet at banquets."

Danny laughed. "Maybe I can send you to Aunt Lucia in Red Hook, and she can tell you about her heart surgery, huh? Or my cousin Joe, who's big in garbage."

She playfully swatted him. "You're a snob."

Terri came up and clutched Amanda in a tight, grateful hug. She felt birdlike, as if she had hollow bones. Her suntan was beautiful and made her eyes even darker. "Thanks for everything," she said breathlessly.

"You're welcome for everything," Amanda smiled.

Terri's eyes grew serious. "I hope you're having a good time . . . I mean, this isn't your crowd . . ."

Amanda rolled her eyes. "Will you both stop? I *have* no crowd. *You're* my crowd. I'm having a ball."

Danny looked proudly at Terri and touched her laced shoulder. "Come on, hon. We gotta say hello to some uncles."

Terri hung on to Amanda's hands. "Listen—be happy here, okay?"

"If you say so." Amanda looked at Danny. "Where to on the honeymoon?"

"St. Thomas," Danny said.

"Terrific. Soak up the sun and don't think about anything."

Danny and Terri both smiled like kids, caught up in their own happiness. Danny threw his big arms around Terri's waist from behind and she snuggled to him, lifting her face to be kissed. Amanda felt her heart tear open, but liquor kept the pain away for now.

* * *

Outside, night had settled dark and cool. The parking valets lounged on a fieldstone wall, smoking pot and cracking jokes. A dusty blue Regal pulled to a stop just at the entrance to the Inn. One of the valets jumped down from the wall and walked over to the car.

The car doors opened and four dark-suited young men got out; they were swarthy and sullen, and one of them was fat. The valet said, "You're a little late, guys."

"Can't stay," the fat youth said. "We just want to deliver a present."

The valet's eyes narrowed. These guys looked weird, like orientals or something. But he was kind of mellow, and anyway there were four of them and a driver, and the valet didn't feel like getting the shit kicked out of him. "Well, there's three parties tonight. Which one did you want?"

"Rosetti wedding," the fat boy said. "We'll find it."

"Up to you," the valet said, and wandered back to the wall. The breathing of the four men mingled with the chirruping of crickets. The fat boy nodded, and the other three reached into the car and brought out weapons: a 9mm Browning automatic pistol, a 12 gauge pump shotgun, and two 9mm Uzi semi-automatic rifles. The fat boy kept his eyes on the valets, who couldn't see clearly from their wall.

"Let's go around the back," he said, indicating the dark path to their right. "Those assholes won't follow us."

The others nodded. The four men melted into the darkness as the driver remained behind the wheel, smoking a cigarette.

Inside, the band played rollicking tarantella, and two loose circles of guests joined hands and swept around the floor, shouting. Danny and Terri danced in the center of one circle, their eyes bright and their faces streaming. Terri's father clapped his hands and bounced up and down next to his wife. Another young couple whirled barefoot in the center of a second circle. Grandmothers in dark dresses, white-haired and tiny, sat in chairs and nodded their approval.

Amanda stood at the perimeter of one circle, her hands clapping rhythmically. The pulse of the music bubbled in her blood and she felt her mouth smiling. She tossed her hair and enjoyed the warmth of the room on her damp skin. Drinks swirled in her brain; food lurched in her stomach. Bitterly, she knew that she'd have to leave soon, and catch a red-eye special back to Bradley. She didn't like facing her blindness and her loneliness together. She wanted to grab on to this moment.

She kept her eyes on Danny and Terri. *Dance,* she urged them. *And hold tightly to each other, because you're all you have . . .*

And then all hell broke loose. Explosions roared through the music. For a frozen instant, there was no sound at all, and then shouts turned to screams. Chandeliers swayed and shattered. Windows broke. Shards of wood and metal flew through the smoky room. The lights blinked off and on again. Bodies thudded to the floor.

Violence hit the room like a freak storm. People jerked in blind reaction. Amanda spun confusedly, trying to see. She heard a sharp chattering noise, like a string of firecrackers. More screams. A tornado of dread spiraled up from Amanda's heart.

She rushed through the banquet room, past terrified guests. She heard the chattering again, and somewhere in her dazed mind she realized she was hearing weapon fire. Now she saw that some of the guests were slumped on the floor, or over chairs, and there was blood.

"Oh my God," Amanda whispered.

Her body refused to function. The double doors of the banquet room had been flung open and were chopped with holes. Who were they? Where . . . ?

They appeared so suddenly that Amanda could only scream and freeze where she stood. She saw four of them, and at once she recognized two. From where? God in heaven, from *where?* She saw their dark suits, their cold faces and black eyes, and their guns. They looked insane here, among the floral centerpieces and bowls of soup.

Someone slammed into Amanda's legs and she was thrown across the room. There was a momentary sensation of weightlessness. Then she felt the carpet burn her face. The concussion jarred her teeth. She saw table legs, fallen forks, a cigarette still smoldering. She couldn't breathe.

The guns opened fire again. They targeted the chandeliers now. Shards of crystal flew across the room. The killers prowled, spraying bullets into tables, curtains, and chairs. Amanda tried to crawl for cover as they stalked relentlessly. Bullets swept the floor nearby, spewing out wood chips. She buried her head, biting down so hard on her lip that she tasted blood.

The gunfire went on and on, its hideous rhythm sinking into Amanda's brain. Her skin crawled, expecting to be ripped by bullets. Then, abruptly, it was over. Shoes clicked on the floor as the killers fled. Amanda lay sobbing on the carpet, and her heart slammed against her bones.

She pushed herself to her knees. Numbly, she grasped the table and pulled herself up, and in doing so yanked plates and glassware onto the carpet. Each thud made her gasp. She stumbled toward the doors. From the lobby, she saw the red taillights of a car recede into the night. She stood trembling, unable to comprehend her emotions.

Behind her, the ballroom lay in darkness. Wind blew through shattered windows and ruffled shredded curtains. Stunned guests poured out of the room. Amanda heard weeping and petrified chatter.

She hugged herself, ice cold. She didn't hear her name at first, only a long, terrible wail of inexpressible grief and rage. Then it became clear that the wail cried "*Amanda!*" and that it demanded her soul and her crucifixion. She turned, half knowing the horror that awaited. She could not bear to witness it, and knew she could not avoid witnessing it.

Danny stood in the hellish doorway, and he held the dead body of his bride. Terri's veil brushed the floor as it dangled from her long, dark hair. Her face was turned toward Danny's scarlet chest. Oh yes, the white shirt was scarlet; it wasn't the light. Terri's arm hung limply.

Danny walked toward her and stopped a few feet away. Amanda saw the blood now. It was impossible not to see the blood. It drenched Terri's white gown. It pattered to the floor like rain, ran in tributaries down her arm, across her palm, to the tips of her dead fingers.

Danny stared at Amanda. His tears ran helplessly, but his eyes held no grief, only inhuman agony. Her blood smeared his face and hands like warpaint.

Warpaint.

Amanda's eyes squeezed shut and she felt her entire body clench like a great fist. Lone Dog. And she'd bargained with him.

"Oh, Danny . . ." Amanda wept.

"She's dead," he told her, his voice coming from the grave. "I never knew her. How are you going to make that all right, Amanda? You went to them. You brought them here."

Amanda shook her head as dizziness swept her and grief roared like a crushing tidal wave through her chest. "No, Danny. No . . ."

"Don't tell me no!" Danny cried. His voice broke, and crumbled into heaving sobs. "DON'T TALK TO ME!" Nobody dared approach him. Many turned away, or saw to their own dead. In the distance, sirens wailed.

Danny knelt, as somberly as he had knelt at the altar to take his vows. He laid Terri's shattered body on the carpet and with shaking, clumsy hands, arranged her veil to cover her obscene wounds. If the blood could be ignored, her face seemed angelic and asleep.

Danny stood, radiating power so vehement that it crackled light into the black room. "They're dead meat," he growled. And then he screamed it, so wrenchingly that it made Amanda shut her eyes and cry. "THEY'RE DEAD MEAT!" The last word was drawn out like a dying shriek, and Danny raced toward the lobby doors, slamming through rubble. Amanda saw him stand on the portico, his arms pumping as he screamed impotently. Then his face was illuminated by the red lights of squad cars.

Amanda kept her eyes closed now, feeling the cool, wet relief of her tears against her hot skin. She brought her fists to her mouth, pressing hard with her knuckles to keep back the vomit. She tasted blood on her tongue. She heard herself scream them, and the sound was distant, ripping out her soul. She prayed to be blind when her eyes opened again.

chapter 23

HELEN stood behind her desk, almost afraid of Amanda. Her eyes blazed with determination. "Listen to me," she said. "I understand your feelings."

"You understand nothing," Amanda said.

"Woman, I am not made of stone."

"Bullshit."

"*Goddamn* it! All I'm asking is that you stay here and get your head together."

"My head's together," Amanda said. "It's the only part of me that is."

"Then make sense. Don't make things worse than they are."

"For who?" Amanda said harshly. She stood exhausted on the custom carpeting. Her striped skirt and blouse were the first comfortable clothes she'd worn all week. A white bracelet set off one tanned arm.

"For all of us," Helen said, attempting to sound reasonable.

Amanda kept her gaze level. "You don't care about anyone but yourself, Helen. You want to bury this thing. Get on with the work. Bank your money. I don't care about any of that now."

"Then what *do* you care about?"

"Danny. Terri's family. Me. I've got to know what's happening to us."

"And seeking out those . . . *vermin* . . . That's going to give you some kind of wisdom?"

"I don't know. But I have to talk to them. Not the killers; they won't be waiting around. But the men in that bar, the men who hated me so much."

"How noble." Helen sat down, furious.

"No, it isn't noble," Amanda said. "It's selfish. But I'm going to learn why Terri was butchered. I'm going to learn why I'm designing your lobbies, and who's going to use them, and who's going to be shut out. And when I find out, I'll make new decisions."

"Like what?" Helen asked. "Whether to quit? Whether to go away and sulk because your stud walked out on you? Isn't that what it's really about? All this talk about truth and your inner self?

"You can't be getting any joy from this, Helen."

"Am I right or wrong, honey?"

Yes, she was right, partially. Amanda *was* enraged and hurt over Jason, but it was more than that. There was the part of her anguish that Helen could never understand, the part about grief, and shock, and a hole in your life that could never be closed.

Amanda said, "It doesn't matter what you think about my motives. I'm going."

"Don't do this."

"And don't act pathetic!" Amanda cried. "It happened *because* of you. If you hadn't silenced all the opposition, if you had *listened* . . . But you never listen. You and Byron are cut from the same block of stone. You roll right over everybody. And you get penthouses and villas and everything you want. And when your victims get sliced up, you tell someone to hose down the blood. Accept some blame, Helen. Terri is *dead*. Don't you feel anything at all?"

Helen was silent. If the woman harbored contrition or uncertainty, she didn't display it. But for an instant her eyes turned inward. "Being hurt wastes time," she said wearily. "You can't waste time and win."

"You've wasted your life, then," Amanda said.

"Don't make moral judgments for me. I ask you for the last time not to embarrass me or jeopardize the project."

"I'd like to embarrass you," Amanda said. "I'd like to see you crawl."

She was ready to crack like a dropped vase and fall into fragments on the carpet. She turned and walked out. She thought she heard Helen punch numbers on the phone. Fine. Let Helen send out the police. Amanda would race them across the desert.

* * *

She drove in a cold fury down the stark two-lane highway, through harshly beautiful desert. This time she could sense ghosts on the land, and she crushed the gas pedal to the floor. She roared past a lumbering mining truck, carrying coal from the reservation. She saw soaring buttes on the horizon.

Her hands stayed firmly on the wheel and the shoulder belt cleaved her swelling breasts. How in God's name was she still functioning? She'd stayed at the Sunset Inn while the police questioned witnesses. She'd held on to Danny while he shook. She'd stayed while they stuffed Terri into a plastic body bag and strapped her to a gurney. She didn't remember sleeping that night, though somebody checked her into a nearby motel. She'd stayed for the three days of the wake, as mourners screamed and fainted before the casket. It was unbearable to see Terri so serenely beautiful. Amanda vividly remembered the suffocating sweetness of the flowers, and the muffled weeping. She remembered the choking haze of cigarette smoke in the outer rooms, and the haunted faces of relatives and friends who milled around with no hold on reality.

They thanked Amanda for her help. What had she done? She didn't recall. She remembered sitting next to Danny's big red chair in the first row of mourners, and letting him cling to her like a little boy afraid of the dark. Again and again he broke into guttural sobs as she crushed his head to her chest and cradled him. She made him take meals back at his mother's apartment, and she helped the women serve. She was, for those few days, a member of the family.

She went to the funeral, horribly aware of the irony of being in church again for Danny and Terri. Overcome, the priest had to stop and be helped by altar boys to a seat, where he remained with his head in his hands. Terri's brother tried to deliver a eulogy, but only sobs came through the mike. Amanda watched the coffin rolled down the center aisle by employees of the funeral home, each man with his hand on his heart. She watched the priest slowly swing the censer and bless the remains. Ritual. Ritual to hold lives together until they could begin to heal.

She held an umbrella at the cemetery where earth lay heaped next to a gaping grave. She looked at Danny's slumped form and heaving shoulders as the priest made his remarks. Then the family members and friends hurried to their cars and turned on windshield wipers and headlights. Machinery lowered the rain-spattered coffin into the shadows. Amanda tried to grapple with meaning at that moment, and couldn't. At least Danny had stopped blaming her. If only she could stop blaming herself.

She slept for nearly sixteen hours after that, and awakened with brutal determination. She sipped black coffee and read newspaper accounts of the ghastly slaughter. She even smiled with bitter amusement as Indian spokesmen and politicians elbowed each other aside to make exculpatory statements. Genuinely concerned tribal leaders had been made to look bad by the terrorism of one sociopath. The situation looked uglier each minute Lone Dog stayed free. Nassau County police were cooperating with New Mexico authorities in a massive manhunt.

Amanda drove past an Indian family at the side of the road. She outran a trundling pickup truck crowded with another family. The sky raced her, bright blue and cloud-streaked. She drove through deep canyons, awash in blue shadow, past grazing sheep and Indian hogans. When she reached high ground again she passed bleak concrete housing. With each mile, her throat tightened more painfully and her mind focused more clearly. She needed to confront the horror, and turn it into something good.

Once again she drove into the border town and once again she parked on the grim main street. She almost courted the stares this time, as she walked along the sidewalk. Her hair blew in the hot wind.

The bar was more crowded than it had been the first time. She heard a burst of talking when she opened the door and stepped in. The talking stopped when they saw who she was. By now, Amanda's face was known. She ran her eyes over the sweating Indians at the little tables, and at the bar. She smelled an overwhelming stink of body odor. *Are you sympathetic?* she mocked herself. *These are not pretty, homeless children or abandoned puppies. Can you care for them, Amanda?*

"Where is Lone Dog?" she asked.

They continued to stare at her, with amazement and loathing. They slipped their drinks and shuffled their feet. The bartender set up drinks on the bar. One kid lit a cigarette. The jukebox played. Amanda felt damp and her skin crawled.

"Are you going to protect him?" she demanded. She heard her voice break with emotion. "He murdered a young bride and killed four others. Helpless, unarmed people. People who had nothing to do with The Pueblo.''

A voice called out, ''He was after *you,* bitch.''

Her face flamed. ''But he didn't wait to find me. He just killed. He's made you all look like murderers. He's set you back a century. Is he still your hero?''

Eyes flickered. The silence grew oppressive and tense. The air turned heavy, like a sac of diseased fluids about to burst. One customer got up and brushed past Amanda as he walked to the door.

''You were warned,'' another voice said.

Amanda made a fist. ''They're going to hunt down Lone Dog and put him away, and The Pueblo will rise in all its glory. Maybe it could have been different, but you just want blood.''

There was low laughter. They jostled each other and made rude comments. Amanda took a deep breath, wondering where this would lead. They were utterly ignorant of what this all meant. They enjoyed what Lone Dog had done. It made these impotent men feel *macho*. They could forget that they lived in stinkholes without electricity, and that they took welfare. She should have understood that before she came. They wouldn't bow their heads or join hands with her to build a better world.

The door clicked shut.

Amanda gasped softly at the sound. The man who'd gotten up now pulled down the torn shade. She felt her skin grow clammy under her thin dress. Her nipples thrust against the soft rayon of her bra.

''You can't murder people,'' she said passionately. ''You can't justify what he did. I came here alone, but the cops will follow.''

''They've been here,'' somebody said.

Two lanky boys got up and opened the door to the back room. Amanda blinked nervously. She heard the breath of the man behind her. She crossed her arms over her breasts. ''Okay,'' she said. ''I get the message. I tried, and I don't owe you anything else.''

That brought loud laughter from some of the men. The fat boy came out of the back room and Amanda's scalp crawled. He smiled at her. ''You better come in here,'' he said.

She saw glistening eyes and wet lips turned toward her. She shook her head. ''Don't do this. Not after what's happened.''

The man behind her grabbed her arm and twisted it. She screamed as the pain raced like brush fire into her shoulder. She writhed against his grip but he pushed her inexorably toward the back room. Terror rose up in her throat like thick syrup. "You're crazy. . . ." she said.

She was shoved into the room and the door was slammed closed. Her memory picked out the stacked tables and chairs, and her senses again recoiled from mildew and the taste of dust. She tried to count how many boys were in the room. She saw five. Would they let in all the others, one by one?

The fat boy stood a few inches from her and his breath stank of whiskey. "You came back," he said with disbelief.

"Your friend murdered five people," Amanda hissed. "Don't you understand what's going on?"

"Yeah," the fat boy said. "I was there, remember?"

Oh Christ. Her mind raced, creating and rejecting ways to escape. *Please,* she prayed, *please make Helen send the police*. "I don't remember," she said.

He laughed. "Stupid cunt." He unknotted the white sash around her waist, and with thick, stained fingers, flicked open the buttons of her blouse. He looked with filthy eyes at her breasts. He jerked her head up with his thumb and forefinger. "This is gonna take all afternoon, baby."

Her blood nearly deafened her as it thumped in her ears. With the last remaining courage she could muster, she worked up saliva and spit hard in his face. His cheek glistened with it. He slapped her. She turned her head. Then she was thrown onto the floor by many hands. She heard a scorpion scuttle past as wet lips closed over her throat.

In the darkness of her pale pink bedroom, Lacey averted her head to one side and panted as Jason fucked her. She focused on the tailored draperies and the glow of streetlight through the windows. She didn't want to look into his eyes.

He grunted with effort as he plunged deep inside her, using a hard rhythm. She dug her fingers into his knotted back and her palms became moist with his sweat. She bit away tears as pain burned her tender canal, but she gasped for him and let his chest sway against her breasts. He was heavy and hard like a tiger. In her imagination, the tiger became real, and she felt cat's fangs tear open her throat and claws rake her sides. Her imaginary blood welled onto her bed and dripped to her sculptured carpet.

He thrust deep and high into her recesses, as cold as a doctor's exploratory tube. He shuddered and moaned and then lay spent beside her, stroking and nuzzling. It was over. Lacey stared at her molded ceiling. Her throat felt raw. Her skin throbbed. She forced herself to look at him. Surprisingly, his eyes gleamed with tenderness and his lips curved into a gentle smile. "Are you okay?" he asked.

She wet her lips and tested her throat. "Uh-huh."

His fingers traced the jut of her chin and nose. She shivered at his touch. "Why did you go to bed with me, Lacey?"

The question caught her off guard. "I wanted to."

"You suffered."

Oh my God, she thought. Men were supposed to be oblivious to such things. "Don't be silly . . ."

"Shh," he said. He shifted closer to her and half raised himself on one muscular arm. A comma of dark hair drooped over his eye. "You didn't owe me this."

Her tears scalded her cheeks. Traffic whooshed by outside. Thunder rolled ominously in the distance. "Jason, I wanted to make love to you. I really did. I . . . maybe I was tired. . . ."

He touched his forefinger to her lips. "There's nothing to apologize for. I was selfish. You're a very arousing lady and I didn't feel like being frustrated. So you have a right to bash me one."

That made her smile. "I'm not into sadism."

"What *are* you into?"

He heart raced. "Huh?"

He laughed. "I meant in your head." He tapped her forehead. "What are you feeling about me?"

She lifted her arms seductively and folded them around his neck. "Well, I'm feeling relaxation, and safety, and warmth, and companionship, and curiosity, and a wonderful sweetness. How's that?"

"I like it," he said. He kissed her cheekbones and her eyelids. "I'm feeling a desire to touch every part of your body."

"I like *that*."

"If only I had sex appeal."

"Silly."

He kissed her throat and then lay back down beside her. She snuggled under the blanket, drawing her knees up to her stomach. She could feel his come fizzing inside her, like some vile, warm potion. He puzzled her. He was genuinely attractive, and he treated her gallantly. He was a witty dinner companion, a hell of a dancer, and a gentleman. And he hadn't really hurt her tonight, or at least he hadn't tried to.

For a moment, she felt rotten about tricking him. But then she remembered that he was two-timing Amanda. And she remembered that she was being paid lots of yummy money for making love with this man. With lots of money in store, and a chance to supplant Amanda.

Lacey recoiled from her naked ambition, but she justified her feelings. She was gifted, bright, and worthy. But Amanda had been the prisoner and mistress of a famous man, so *she* started at the top. Lacey had to yes ma'am and no ma'am and miss the glory. And Amanda had slapped Lacey in the face by rejecting her honest love after giving off lots of signals. Amanda trotted off to New Mexico to party and get interviewed while Lacey provided the designs. Amanda threw herself at Jason while Lacey slept alone. But now Helen had seen through the cheating and lies, and offered Lacey a shot at power and success. Lacey decided she'd do anything to get it.

And she wouldn't apologize, either. She would learn to enjoy sex with Jason, or at least to pretend expertly enough to convince him. She could get off on taking him away from Amanda. She would ace this assignment, and then she'd make it on her own talent.

She looked down at Jason, and his eyes had fluttered closed. He looked helpless as he slept. "Good night, heartbreaker," she whispered, and kissed his lips. She drew the blanket to her bare shoulder and smiled.

In her townhouse suite near Bradley, Helen propped herself on silk pillows and read the morning newspaper while she drank hot tea. A bed tray held the teapot, and some croissants and apricot jam. Helen wore stylish glasses and her hair was disarrayed from sleep. Her bed jacket was of lace-trimmed red silk, to match the vivid chintz wallcoverings.

Helen savored the tea as she read about Amanda Gray being gang-raped. Helen explored her body for symptoms of emotion. She felt only an incipient headache. The stupid woman. What did she think would happen?

Helen couldn't resist a slight smile. She *had* thought of calling the police and having them intercept Amanda, but then she'd had the clever idea to let the woman take her lumps. Amanda still trusted people, still searched for innate goodness. Helen knew better: scum was scum.

She grimaced as she read, and she carefully spread jam on a croissant. They'd found her in an alley behind the bar. The medics got her to the hospital and lots of icepacks and sutures did the trick.

With a shiver, Helen realized she was not enjoying this. The girl was a pimple on Helen's butt, and needed to be put in her place, but Helen generally preferred civilized revenge. This was disgusting and common. She dropped the paper on the bed, leaned back, and cradled the teacup in both hands. It looked as if she could turn Lone Dog's butchery to her advantage. Certainly Richard Juan couldn't make much of a case for his tribesmen after this. The savages weren't ready for legal rights. And as long as Lone Dog kept eluding the police, the wounds would fester.

The door chimes rang. Helen smiled. "Come in."

The door opened and Lacey came in, clearly surprised to see Helen in bed. "Oh God, I'm sorry . . ."

"Close the door," Helen smiled. Lacey complied. "I knew you were coming this morning. I like to laze around and have breakfast in bed. God, if I haven't earned *that*, what *have* I earned?"

"Nothing," Lacey said.

"Come here," Helen told her. The girl wore a clingy yellow summer dress that showed off her slender shoulders and her stunning legs. Her eyes looked out with jeweled brilliance. Helen's blood thrilled.

Lacey approached the bed. Helen patted the moiré silk. "Sit."

Lacey perched uncertainly. Helen put the breakfast tray aside and took off her glasses. She moistened her lips and fluffed her hair. "Well, how's Jason?"

"Fine."

"Is he satisfied? Happy?"

"I think so."

"Oh, I'd bet on it." Helen reached up and touched the girl's hair, noticing the startled intake of breath. "You are truly a work of art. The man must think he's died and gone to heaven. Tell me, does he get off on kinky stuff?"

Lacey blushed deeply under her tan. "He's pretty straight, Miss Tennyson."

She laughed. "Oh, come now. Please call me Helen."

"All right."

"I'm sorry if I'm being crude and nosy. I find this all delightfully funny. I don't generally arrange for women to seduce Jason on purpose—usually it's the other way around. This just sort of evolved. He and Amanda are splitsville, I take it."

"Well, he doesn't talk about her."

"I'll bet he doesn't." Helen hooted. "You're wonderful to put up with this sleazy stuff. I haven't seen this kind of commitment in a long time. You're special."

Lacey's eyes burned. "Thank you. I hoped you'd notice."

"Oh, I notice. You can bank on it." She folded her hands in her lap. "I'm inclined to pay you more than I promised. I feel ridiculously generous with you. You're worth a fortune. Would you like more money? As much money as you could ever spend?"

"Yes."

"God, you're direct. What's hurt you so deeply? What's made you so enraged?"

"That's my business."

"Whoops." Helen saw the girl's sudden fright, and she cupped Lacey's face with her palm. "Don't fret. You had a right to tell me off. I'm a hard-nosed old bitch, and I talk this way to everybody. You don't hate me, do you?"

"No," Lacey said. "I like you very much."

Holy shit, Helen thought. "Well, what other rewards can I give you? Besides money, and Jason, of course."

Lacey laughed.

Helen cocked her head. "What's funny?"

Lacey shook her head, smiling as she directed her eyes to the antique Persian rug. "Nothing."

"Oh, come on."

Lacey looked at her. "Jason isn't much of a reward for me."

Helen's eyebrows knit. "Huh?" she said stupidly, and then it dawned on her. Her heart did somersaults. She had fantasized this, but hadn't really expected it. She was too hard-bitten and realistic to expect even small miracles. She *had* considered seduction, as an exercise in will, but she'd envisioned a tedious process.

"I'm sorry," Helen said. "I probably should have sensed it. I just picked up on your jealousy over Jason and Amanda."

"I *was* jealous," Lacey said.

Helen threw her head back with laughter, then looked with delicious eyes at Lacey. "Yes, you were, weren't you? Well. My Lord. You *are* working your buns off for me, aren't you? It must be living hell."

"It's not as awful as I thought. Jason is sweet."

Helen couldn't stop laughing. "And doesn't catch on that he exerts absolutely no attraction at all. God. What a gorgeous joke. What a gorgeous joke on everyone. My dear, dear girl, you are a treasure beyond anything I've known. Are you going to make another play for Amanda?"

Lacey went rigid. "No. I've gotten over her."

"Oh no you haven't," Helen chided. "But it doesn't matter. I respect your spunk, and your decision makes me happy. I also find you very beautiful and very sexy and very exciting. Would you like to make love to me, Lacey?"

Lacey's eyes went wide. "I . . ."

". . . didn't expect it?" Helen smiled and drew Lacey close. The girl stiffened against Helen's embrace for a moment, then yielded cautiously and allowed herself to be cuddled. "I always shock people. But I don't want to shock you, darling girl. I just want to love you."

Helen's lips nuzzled Lacey's throat and downy shoulder. Lacey hissed gratefully. She shifted and turned her child's face up to Helen. They kissed passionately. Helen's tongue found the recesses of Lacey's mouth and her hands worked down the straps of the girl's dress and folded over pigeon-soft breasts. She'd read Lacey's arousal correctly, and now Helen could explode with the pleasure of loving the woman who commanded Jason's body. Helen moaned with pleasure, and with a glad cry of triumph, Lacey lifted her body to be taken.

chapter 24

JASON took two weeks off with Lacey. They went to shows and nightclubs and gambled in Atlantic City. They spent whorish days and nights in Lacey's bed, or in Jason's, ordering gourmet breakfasts. To Jason's delight, Lacey became a more fervent lover. Rarely had Jason felt as strong or in control.

That was one reason why he put Lacey on hold and came back to the site of The Pueblo; why he stood now on a rise overlooking the great gash in the desert and studied the water mains and power lines that gridlocked the earth. A powerful wind blew his hair awry. The sky overhead glowed dark blue, but dark clouds piled in heaps on the horizon.

The way Lacey had serviced him made Jason bolt. Too many ugly memories flooded back. The morning after, he hadn't liked his domination over Lacey. He needed to be alone, to be sure. So he emerged from the decadent twilight of tumbling with her, back into the real world.

And that's when he picked up a newspaper and read about Amanda: his second, and more powerful reason for coming here.

Jason wore a blue chambray shirt and faded dungarees stuffed into leather boots. His chin was black with unshaven beard. He picked his way among rubble and rock, and kicked a shattered beer bottle. He smiled. The workmen were not awed by the power of nature.

He tried to make sense of his emotions. He'd felt shock when he read the gruesome story. Numbness protected him on the flight to Bradley, and the drive out here. Now he stood lonely and shaken, not knowing what the hell he felt.

He tried to light a cigarette, turning away from the wind and cupping his hands around the match. It didn't work. He tossed away the match and dropped the unsmoked cigarette onto the ground. His eyes scanned the mighty excavation, the tracery of scaffolding, and the dozing yellow earthmovers. He could envision the finished structure, and the new roads sweeping away. The potential beauty caught his throat.

But The Pueblo would alter the desert flower. Jason remembered what Amanda had said about designing in harmony with an area. This project was not in harmony with anything. It was Helen Tennyson's Great Pyramid, and so far its construction went on at fearful human cost. He hadn't been party to murder for a long time. The old wounds throbbed painfully.

Thunderheads swelled and marched across the sky. Eerie light irradiated the earth. It seemed to flicker on the metal conduits and great tunnels of PVC pipe that sprang from the excavation like the black roots of some carnivorous plant. Jason turned to go back to his car, and then he stopped. He hadn't seen the other human figure, so quietly did she sit on a foundation wall. He recognized Amanda and a cold wind sighed in his veins. She seemed small and frail against the massive pipes and thick electrical cables. She seemed in danger of being devoured by the grazing machines. Above her, the heavens turned ominously green.

He skidded on loose sand as he walked down the hill. If she heard his approach, she didn't signal it. He stopped within a few yards of her. She hugged herself, cold in a hooded top and warm-up pants. Her body looked thinner than he remembered.

"Amanda," he called.

She turned, and didn't seem shocked to see him. "Jason."

He swallowed like a tongue-tied fool. Her face was discolored and still slightly swollen, but she looked okay. He didn't focus on the delicate scars or the black bruises. He looked instead at her eyes. "I was busy," he said. "I didn't hear about what happened until now."

"And you came right away."

He flushed. "I came to look at the construction. I'm not going to lie to you."

"Good."

She turned back to look at the horizon and he felt his body clench. "It's going to rain pretty hard."

"I guess it is."

"Why don't you come back with me? We can have dinner."

"No, thanks."

He battled unreasonable anger. "Amanda, I've got some explaining to do. I know that. I don't want you to hate me."

She smiled. "I don't hate you, Jason."

"Why in hell did you go to that bar? Didn't you know what they'd do to you?"

She stood up, pale with pain. She looked at him and crossed her arms over her breasts. "No, I didn't. Everyone asks me that. I wasn't looking to be raped."

"I didn't think so."

She kicked at the dust with one violet sneaker, and stared at the ground. "I needed—I thought I needed—to make contact with those men. I couldn't accept Terri's murder as senseless. I could never accept the horrible things that happen as senseless. I'm a designer. And I'm a fool."

"And now?"

Her eyes filled. "I'm still a designer, and still a fool. I want to make things make sense and have order."

"I'm glad." It seemed crazy to know that he'd caressed her broken body just a few weeks ago. "I care about you. I'm going to help the police find those animals. . . ."

She half smiled at his frustration. "You *are* upset, aren't you?"

"Is that so hard to believe?"

Her hair riffled over her eyes and she pushed it away. "No. I know that you can't bear to see me hurt. At least not by others."

"That was a cheap shot."

"I don't feel terribly expensive."

He moved closer to her. "Damn it, Amanda, don't throw stones at me. I never wanted you to be hurt like that. I didn't want your friend's wife to be killed. Stop blaming bystanders for your pain."

"Very insightful." She spun away from him. "I don't blame you for anything. I only blame you for walking out on me like a coward with no explanation."

The wind howled now, as if it spun down a long tunnel. The earth darkened. Lightning played at the edges of the world. Amanda looked up, controlling tears.

"I didn't walk out," Jason said. "I went away. I had to do that."

"Who were you with?" she asked.

"What kind of question is that?"

She searched his face. "You weren't alone all this time, not if you were so tied up that you didn't see the news. I know what keeps a man out of touch like that."

"Is it important that you know? Usually, a woman doesn't want to lacerate herself."

"I guess not. She just accepts the inevitability of the departure. Wakes up one day to an empty bed and thanks God for having loved."

"This is bullshit," he said testily. "I didn't walk out on a wife and two kids. I needed air. Jesus, Amanda, you're no beginner."

"No, I'm not," she said. "Not in being hurt and abused. But I'm a beginner in loving and caring, and I need a lot of guidance in that area. Did you mean anything you said? Was it all lies?"

He glanced up at the towering thunderheads, dizzying in their height and closeness. A crack of thunder pealed across the desert and reverberated against the hills. "No," Jason said. "It wasn't lies. You're a hell of a woman, Amanda. But I had to move on."

"Why?"

"Don't be an ass."

"I *feel* like an ass. I felt like an ass in the hospital the last two weeks. I've gotten used to feeling like an ass, so what's one more time? Why did you go away, Jason? Was I boring?"

He couldn't deal with genuine grief and pain. Away from Amanda, he could pretend she was another hot lay, and nothing more. Not here; not at the mouth of a man-made canyon, not with a desert storm crashing over their heads. Not when he could drown in the green seas of her eyes or touch her honeyed skin, or taste the curve of her mouth. Not when he could remember the salt of her nipples or the musk between her thighs. He'd nearly defied Helen over this woman.

Nearly.

"It's not going to work" he said to her. "Not standing here and talking about how we hurt each other. Absolve yourself, Amanda. It's my fault."

"I don't know you," she said. "You never gave me a chance."

"Come on, Amanda. Let's get to my car before we get blown away."

Amanda shook her head. There was a wildness in her eyes now. "I don't want to go with you."

"Amanda, you'll be hurt."

"Not a new experience, Jason. And not one you'd ever comprehend."

"Knock it off. Nobody likes a martyr."

"I'm no martyr. I've made no sacrifice. But I might, I just might. I'm going to take on your boss. I'm going to fight Helen Tennyson. She had me raped, and she had Terri murdered, as surely as anybody did. She's everything that's mean and destructive in the world. She and Byron—the power seekers. Power is good, isn't it, Jason? The penthouse suite, the limo, the jet. It's worth slicing throats for and breaking hearts. Is that why you flew the coop, baby? Did Helen have a job for you?"

Her words beat against his head like hurled stones. "No," he said. "I didn't do it for Helen."

"Not for power? Not for the big orgasm of calling the shots and making people cry in front of you?"

"It wasn't calculated, Amanda. Just a chance meeting."

"With who, goddamn it?"

He dug in his heels at a gust of wind. "Lacey Coleridge."

She seemed momentarily stunned. Her eyes lost their grip and swam desperately for shore. "Lacey?"

"We ran into each other in New York. It just happened."

"Very good, Jason. That certainly stabs me in the heart."

"I told you it wasn't planned."

"No, huh?" She flattened her mouth and dug her fingernails into her palms, as if fighting a terrific battle inside. She shook her head, baffled. "The bitch."

Jason exhaled, fatigued. "Christ, I didn't want a scene like this. I wanted to make peace with you."

"Smokeum peacepipe, eh?" She uttered a short, derisive laugh. "Hey, Jase, I don't fault you for it. And it really doesn't matter. I'll get over you. My time's going to be at a premium. I'm going to the State Senate, to the Navajo chiefs, to anybody I have to see. I wanted this commission. I wanted it the way I wanted breath. But a lot of things are different now."

"I guess so," Jason said sadly. "What happened to you in that bar . . . ?"

"Was incidental. Everyday violence in a violent world." Her bitterness was turning hysterical.

"Amanda, have you talked with a doctor since you were attacked? Have you had counseling?"

"A shrink? I don't need shrinks. I cure myself. It's kind of mystical, but very effective. The laying off of hands. Everybody's hands. Yours. Helen's. Byron's. Hands off my mind."

"You're crazy, Amanda."

"Getting there. Slowly but surely." She swept an arm to indicate the excavation. "This has to be different. It can't be built according to your plans. This place is cursed. You don't build hotels on desecrated ground."

A thunderclap split the skies and lightning sizzled. "You're raving," he said.

"It's about time somebody raved. About time *I* raved. There are ghosts here. Don't you see them?" Her eyes were shut. "Terri's ghost. And my ghost."

Jason grabbed her, and roughly turned her around. Her eyes flew open. "Cut this shit," he said. "Don't do this to yourself."

"Don't worry, darling," she said. "I'm not over the brink yet."

He gripped her shoulders. "Look. Forget all the crap. Let me drive you to the hotel. I'll leave you there. I'll drive away. Don't stay out here."

"I want to be here. I want to feel the rain."

"Then I'm staying."

She smiled at him, but her body stiffened at his touch. "I don't want you to stay."

He released her, shaking with anger. "What the hell is driving you, Amanda? What's the grandstand play for? Sympathy?"

"Not that," she said, and looked away.

"Have you really become moral?" he challenged. "Is this the humble Amanda Gray? Or are you just trying to make a name for yourself, huh? Build your own reputation at Helen's expense? Who made you a saint, Amanda?"

She braced against the wind. "Are you being cynical for me?"

"Yeah, I'm cynical. I think saints look nice on calendars. I don't think they really exist. I think you're a sharp woman with a God-given talent and a fire in your belly. I think you fought your way out of hell because you wanted to make something of your life. I don't believe you've turned into a Salvation Army girl."

She took his hands and held them tightly. "And I think *you're* a lousy coward. I think you dug a hole you can't get out of but you're too scared to ask for help. I think you're so weak and useless that you'd rather dump a woman you care about than work at it. I think you're a lazy shit who won't give up your dish of cream. How am I doing?"

Jason wrenched his hands free. "This isn't where it's at."

"Too chicken to fight?"

"Shut up, Amanda."

"Make me."

He growled, and turned away.

"Come on back!" she yelled. "Act like a man."

He dared not look at her. He could feel the love creeping back into his vital organs, carried by reluctant blood. Her taunts ripped through him like armor-plated bullets, but taunts wouldn't make him spill his guts. He knew that he didn't deserve her and couldn't keep her. And Lacey was sweet compensation.

He looked back at her anyway, and fought off her wild beauty as she stood defiantly on the foundation wall. "I'm getting the hell out of here," he said. "Are you coming?"

"No."

"Do you have a car?"

"Of course I do."

"I'd suggest you get into it. I don't want you dead."

"Blow away, Jason."

Briefly, the rage and love stormed to the surface. "Christ in heaven, Amanda, can't I reach you?"

"Never."

"I don't understand you," he said hollowly.

"Give it up. Get out of my life."

He scraped his brain for something to say and came up empty. He wanted the last word, but no last words were there. He kept the twisting pain in his chest, where it squeezed his heart. He strode away from the excavation, childishly hoping that Amanda would get her legs broken in the storm. Never had Jason felt like such a failure, not even when Helen rescued him from personal hell. He was walking out on Amanda for real. And not five hundred Laceys would make up for this one loss.

* * *

Amanda would not watch Jason walk away. She turned her face to the west. What a damned fool she'd been, to cry to him and plead with him. For what? She didn't dare love him, when she didn't know if blindness would blot out her sun forever.

Thunder cracked. Amanda began to walk aimlessly, away from the grotesque pit in the earth, away from the cables and pipes, the scaffolds and earth movers. She walked out where there was only grassy sand and jagged teeth of rock. The desert glowed with a hellish tinge.

Her body groaned with pain. It hadn't gone away, not for a minute since the rape. God, how the word dignified what had been done to her. She could relive it at any moment, in every cell of her skin. The images were branded on her retina. The questing lips, like bloodworms, festered in her flesh. Not that she'd seen very much. Mostly she'd kept her eyes shut, or fastened to the beamed ceiling. She counted the seconds for each spiral of pain. First she felt the weight on her half-naked body. Then the sting of fire between her legs, and the thrusts, battering her canal. She panted as the seconds passed, and then, at last, the cramp would subside and there would be a hot ache deep inside. Then a few blessed seconds of relief, and the next assault.

Soon she lost count, and stopped pretending. Nausea racked her, and dizziness made her lose consciousness. Pain became the center of her being, the totality of her life. The fire burned fiercely and when each new cock rubbed her raw flesh, she screamed.

They beat her up when they were through fucking her. By then, she was insensitive to pain. Her mind had layered oblivion between her senses and her understanding. She perceived most of the blows as dull thuds, echoing deep inside her body.

Amanda realized that she was running. She stopped, short of breath, and dropped down on a smooth boulder. Perspiration drenched her back. Her side stitched agonizingly where the ribs had been cracked. Ironically, she'd been saved from mental breakdown by her years with Byron. She'd learned to steel her mind against physical assault, at least.

Lightning exploded in searing brightness. She cupped her hand over her eyes. *It's not working,* she thought. Her mental shields were down. Her armor was broken, pierced by too many lances. She shouldn't have talked to Jason. She shouldn't have learned it was Lacey he loved.

Lacey. Swinging both ways, taking her man.

Yes, he was, Amanda despaired. *He was mine, and I lost him. I keep losing, over and over again.*

Amanda saw the vivid image of Terri's mutilated body in Danny's arms. She blinked hard to clear her vision. She was on the desert, unprotected. She shook her head. No, Terri couldn't be dead. Jason couldn't be gone. Those *things* in the bar couldn't have forced her down on the floor and rammed into her bleeding body again and again.

She stood up, and the lightning struck once more. The sky exploded in white light. Thunder crashed down in shock waves, rolling over the shaking earth. Rocks flared in garish illumination, slick with rain. A horned owl stood out in deathly silhouette. Amanda spun, as the rain burst loose from the sky and swept in howling sheets over her. Where was the excavation?

Drenched, Amanda cried out, "*Jason . . . !*"

She took three steps, and felt her legs stiffen up. She looked hard through the rain, mortally afraid. Lightning ripped the sky again, and this time the burst was so bright it smashed against her eyeballs with blasting agony. She screamed and clapped her hands over her face. Hammer blows struck her skull. Dizzy, she swooned, but kept herself upright.

She kept her hands tight against her face, staring into blackness. It was velvety and complete; no swirls, no helixes, no spots. She heard the pounding of thunder against the rocks, and the hiss of rain. The downpour battered her, knocking breath from her lungs. The wind howled like wild coyotes in the cliffs.

Amanda took her hands away and blinked open her eyes. The blackness remained. It pressed her cheeks and forehead like a cloth mask. She blinked rapidly, forcing tears. Her fingernails clawed at her skin. She stumbled, trying to find the way back, but in total blindness she could barely stand. Torrents of rain beat her down. Vaguely, she thought about her hood, and how she ought to put it up. But she had no strength to act on the thought. Her hands played idiotically at the air, and water dripped from her fingers.

She took a step, and stumbled. She cried out as she fell, and scrambled to her knees. Pain stabbed her palms. She'd cut herself. She held up her hands but saw nothing. Now the darkness pulsated, like an alien bloodsucker draped over her face. It sucked her eyes from their sockets and sipped the blood from her brain.

She began to run, panting with exertion. Her sneaker struck a rock and she pitched to the ground. She sprawled there, pummeled by rain. Thunder banged over her head. But there was no more lightning.

Half an hour later, Amanda sat huddled in the desert, rocking back and forth and moaning. The rain had stopped. She shivered like a puppy. Fresh wind cleansed her face and chilled her skin beneath her soaked clothes. Her stomach cramped violently, and her teeth chattered. She felt the evening sun warm the nape of her neck. But she hadn't seen the sun break open the clouds. She hadn't seen the colors of the desert sparkle and blaze as the storm passed. The blackness stayed.

She was lost, and knew it. If nobody found her, she would die of exposure tonight, or of sunstroke tomorrow. In her mind, colors flowed and melted into one another. She tried to remember all the colors so that she would still know what color looked like. The memory would fade as her eyes failed to renew their perception. And soon there would be no color, not even in her mind.

Ozone stung her nostrils. A drone pressed her skull from inside. For a terrible, mocking instant, she thought that the world lightened, that there were shapes . . .

Please, God . . . please . . .

The blackness rushed back, slamming windows shut. She raised up her hands, making talons of her fingers, and she screamed to the heavens like a wild creature. Her howl of despair spun on the wind.

And at that moment, a vision came bright and whole into Amanda's mind. In colors so bright that they hurt, she saw what The Pueblo had to be. She saw a desert unspoiled and eternal; she saw pipelines and cables stretching like shimmering light bridges from desert rills to Navajo houses; she saw diamond-bright water flowing through lucite webs. The vision sang to her with electric voices, and resonated deep inside. At that moment, she understood.

Dizziness swept her like a hurricane and she sank to her knees. She bowed her head, swaying back and forth as her eyes burned with pain. The vision faded and the blackness pushed in harder. The drone came louder now. She shook her head to get rid of the humming noise. She looked up, and the sky spun, but it was a sky of her imagination.

Byron Moore shielded his aviator sunglasses as he peered down from the passenger seat on his chopper. He had no doubt at all now that Amanda was blind. He'd watched her scuttle like a crab across the desert, only yards from The Pueblo construction site. Now she knelt and cried. No doubt at all. "Take her down," he told his pilot.

A different, sharper drone awakened Amanda and she pressed a hand to her forehead to still it. She felt drowsy and she couldn't see. She blinked, and her eyelids scraped cloth. Her eyes were bandaged.

A strong hand pressed her shoulder, urging her to lie flat. Now she felt strong vibration the length of her body. "There's a nurse on board," Byron's voice said. "You've been sedated. That's why you feel woozy."

This made no sense to Amanda. She'd been on the desert. There'd been a storm.

She remembered, but the memories were held back. She'd gone blind. She'd gotten lost. Now Byron was talking to her and her eyes were bandaged. And still she heard the drone.

"Where am I?" she asked.

"My jet. I found you in the desert."

"That noise I heard . . ."

"My helicopter." His fingers stroked her feverish forehead, and lingered on her tear-burned cheeks. "We're flying back to my estate. I've already gotten in touch with the best doctors in the business."

"What doctors?" she murmured.

Byron sighed. He seemed distressed. Her heart sank at the sound of his unhappiness. Damn that sedative. It was too powerful. She wanted to rip the bandage away and *see* him.

"Amanda," Byron said with infinite tenderness, "the disease progressed very rapidly. It took your sight."

Amanda shook her head. She felt a pillow at her neck. "No. It's temporary. . . ."

"It's not temporary. Amanda, listen to me. I can tell you now. Your mother had the same disease. She went blind also. That's why I never wanted you to know. I hoped you'd have more years, more time."

"That's not true," she wept.

"Yes, it's true," he said, with exquisite gentleness. "You are blind, Amanda. Forever blind."

She shook her head again. "No," she whispered. "No, it's a lie." She found strength to rip at the bandage, and pulled it down from her eyes. Blazing light seared her, and then the cold, eternal blackness. She was restrained by other hands, and the sting of an injection pierced her arm. "No," she barely breathed. "No . . ."

Byron gripped her hand. "I'll care for you, Amanda."

She wanted to fight him, but the drug swirled into her exhausted brain, and she sank into unconsciousness.

PART THREE

chapter 25

LUXURY, Jason thought, had different meanings. The pink Caribbean hotel behind him was luxurious, and so was the pool before him. The buffet set out on the deck was luxurious. Jason had been trained to appreciate such luxury, to demand and expect it wherever he went.

But there were luxuries that cost nothing. The sky, blue as dyed silk, was luxurious, as was the hot sun that lulled him on his chaise. The island wind was a luxury to his burning face. And Lacey was luxurious, as she dove fluidly into the pool.

Jason watched her as she fished through the water with long, easy strokes. In her black maillot with daring cutouts, she achieved a motion that struck Jason as poetic. He enjoyed the thrill of ownership. He liked showing her off.

Lacey swam back the other way. She could do fifty laps when she was in the mood. Her strength and litheness translated into astonishing agility in bed. She'd become a hungry and eager lover, who adored surrendering to his pleasure. Amanda had asked for equal time; Lacey was a slave, with quick intelligence and feral passion. *It's what I want,* Jason insisted. Yet something remained wrong with the setup, something undefined that tickled the back of his mind.

He allowed champagne to be poured by a brown-skinned boy in a white uniform. He sipped the sparkling wine and dribbled some on his chest. With idle fingers, he brushed away the cold drops. These weekenders had become more frequent since Amanda disappeared, and Lacey had taken over the designing of The Pueblo. Jason wondered where Amanda was, but he buried his curiosity in liquor and sex.

Lacey lifted herself out of the pool and daubed her face with a towel. She posed unself-consciously with the sun at her back. Jason laughed to himself. Helen had given him an unlimited credit line as a present for the weekend. She was so ridiculously obvious sometimes. "Blow her to a good time," Helen had cracked, and hooted like a half-wit. Jason only shook his head and packed his overnight bag.

Lacey walked with mischievous grace to where Jason lay and splashed water on him. He flinched and raised his glass to protect the champagne. "Watch it," he said.

She smiled down at him and brushed her wet hair. He loved to watch the changing light on her skin. "Aren't you coming in?" she asked.

"Later."

"You're a lazy slob."

"True. Want some bubbly?"

She made a face. "I'd rather have a rum and coke."

"Sure." He snapped his fingers to catch the attention of a roving waiter. The brown boy nodded. Lacey dropped prettily onto the chaise next to Jason and creamed her arms with suntan lotion. "I'd like to sunbathe nude," she said. "My tan is terrible. Strap marks all over."

"There's a nude beach nearby," Jason said. "We can go there later."

"Good." She snuggled and writhed until she found a comfortable position on the chaise. She adjusted her sunglasses and put her arms at her sides. Jason watched the slow, even rise and fall of her breasts.

The waiter attended him and Jason ordered Lacey's drink. He sat up on his chaise and wrapped his arms around his knees. He half listened to music from radios. The palm trees shivered seductively in the island wind. "Try the buffet," he said. "It's pretty good."

"Okay." She turned her head toward him. "Want to go shopping later?"

"No. But you go ahead."

"I think I will. I want to buy some silks and some jewelry."

"Buy whatever you want."

She lifted herself on one arm. "Something wrong, Jason?"

"No."

"You sound tense."

"Just bored."

"Uh oh." She sat up and put a cool hand on his shoulder. "My fault?"

"Of course not."

"I've just felt so lazy and piggish here. I've been working so hard . . ."

"Lacey, chill out," he said pleasantly. "You're not boring. You may be hazardous to my health, but you're not boring."

She smiled and squeezed his hand. "Then what?"

Languor spread through his body like slow-acting venom. "I envy you, Lacey. You're just discovering this kind of life. This kind of world. I've known it for years. It's not fun anymore."

She looked sympathetic. "I suppose that can happen. One poolside is pretty much like another."

"It's not the setting. It's the people. I wish sometimes I could cultivate the shallow, greedy approach to life that upscale people have. I wish I could get off on gourmet foods and trendy cars and my investment portfolio. But I can't."

"You're way above the others."

"I'm no better than anybody. I just don't get along with people. I'm a loner—but I hate being alone. Now figure that out."

"It's not so hard to figure." She toyed with his hair. "You're better looking than most guys, and more talented. Ordinary people don't like feeling ordinary."

"Guys in my financial bracket aren't ordinary," he argued. "They're the best and the brightest. I just don't fit in. I never did."

She leaned over to kiss him. Her lips were cold from the pool. "Well, you fit in with me, darling."

The waiter brought the rum and coke and Lacey took it with a smile. She sipped at it, then lay back again, thrusting her body toward the sun. Jason looked at her and became shocked at himself. He'd bared his heart to her, something he had never done with a woman. Amanda had taught him to let go. But Amanda would have understood his agony. She would have drawn him out, shared his pain. Lacey just pacified him.

He finished his champagne, which had become warm and flat, and stood up. His trunks clung to his tight hips. Helen was working overtime to keep Jason amused, to keep him from brooding about Amanda. But Amanda had invaded his heart and brain in ways he never expected. She'd changed his direction. And soon there might not be enough credit cards to stop from reclaiming his life.

He sighed. Not just yet. There was still luxury, and luxury assuaged a lot of pain. With a growl of anger, he shook himself. He strode to the pool and dove cleanly into the irridescent water.

On another beach, Byron Moore opened a bottle of white wine and poured two glasses. He wore a cotton jacket over his trunks, and sunglasses set off his rugged face. The sun was warm, and the ocean wind brought the promise of a storm far out at sea.

Behind him stretched the lawns and gardens of his estate. The great manor house rose majestically against a pale blue sky. Byron walked from the portable bar set up in the sand to Amanda's lounge chair. She also wore sunglasses, to protect her face from the heat. Her shimmering blue bathing suit molded to her curved body. Byron paused to admire the artistry of her form, and to remember, with vivid joy, his stewardship of that form.

"Here," he said, holding out a glass. She reached for it with her right hand, and he gently guided her fingers to the stem.

"Thank you." She sipped at the wine.

"How is it? It's from a vineyard on the East End."

"Not bad."

"I want to promote Long Island wine. I think we can compete in the marketplace. Do you agree?"

"If you like."

He stood behind her, looking out to the ocean. Amanda had asked to face the sea. She wanted to imagine it. She wanted to hear the hiss and wash of breakers, and the distant crash of surf against the jetties.

He placed his wine glass on the bar and almost reverently folded his strong hands over her shoulders. She didn't resist. He shut his eyes as he let the heat of her skin penetrate his palms. He longed to see her naked once more, but his strength lay in his patience.

He said, "There are many sensations left to you. Music. The taste of wine. A touch." He bent and his lips grazed the back of her neck.

"Don't."

He stood erect again. His eyes scanned the ocean. It was going to take a long time to make her love him again. But he *had* the time now.

"Byron, when am I going to see the doctor?"

"Next week," he said. "He thought it would be a good idea for you to rest before undergoing stressful exams. You suffered severe physical trauma. It's a good thing I'd flown out to Bradley to see Helen. When she told me you'd driven out to the site and hadn't come back, I took my chopper up right away. You could have killed yourself out there."

"I'm grateful to you for picking me up."

She drank more wine, and cradled the glass in her hands. He looked down at the smooth, dark mounds of her breasts in the bathing suit. The sun glinted from the light coating of oil she'd put on. "Why can't I see Dr. Fabiano?" she asked.

"I called him," Byron said. "He agreed that it was best to bypass him and go right to the specialists."

"Does he think it's permanent?"

"I'm sorry, Amanda. I wish I could encourage you, but it doesn't look promising."

She shook back her hair. She'd spent a few days under sedation, fed intravenously. Slowly, she was weaned from the drug. She seemed to accept her blindness. She'd had no more tantrums and she behaved obediently. But there was a coldness about her that worried Byron. She was still fighting, even with all the tar knocked out of her.

"Why am I seeing specialists if there's no hope?"

He gently massaged her shoulders. "A nerve disease can progress beyond the eyes," he said. "We want to be sure it doesn't spread further."

"How could they prevent that?"

"I don't know for sure. In a severe case, they might remove the eyes or cut the nerves. Interrupt the disease."

He watched her for a reaction. She stroked the rim of her glass with a forefinger. Whatever she felt, she was keeping it inside. "I appreciate what you're doing for me," she said, "but I can't stay here forever. I need to get back to my own apartment, to make arrangements, to be on my own."

He'd feared this. He'd struck too soon. The blindness itself was not enough. She'd been tempered by pain, strengthened by adversity. His labor would be much more difficult than he'd thought. He felt tired and annoyed.

"Amanda, believe me, I'll help you do whatever you need to do. I love you. I told you that."

"I know. And I don't think I hate you anymore."

"That's . . . important to me, Amanda."

She finished her wine, and reached out with the glass, trying to feel where the sand was. Byron took the glass from her and added it to his own on the bar.

"Thank you," she said, "but I have to learn to do things on my own."

"Of course you do. I'm being overprotective."

The tide came in, and the waves broke higher up the beach, leaving rings of crushed shells and garlands of seaweed. Amanda said, "My mother is blind?"

"Yes."

"Is she dead?"

He considered a moment. "No."

He heard her inhalation and marked its emotional intensity. "Can you tell me what her name is?"

"Mary."

"Tom and Mary," Amanda repeated, softly. "What was her last name?"

"No more information, Amanda. You have to understand. There were agreements made. The records have been sealed. She didn't want her child to know her, or to find her. She was adamant about it."

"Back then. What about now? Have you seen her? Have you told her I'm blind? Maybe she's changed the way she feels."

"You're getting worked up," he said. "I don't want this."

"Well, you're not cooperating, damn it. Why can't you tell me about her now? What does it matter?"

His hands pressed masterfully into her shoulders. "You're losing control of your feelings. You've been through hell. Let me get you well again."

He felt her muscles relax, and he cupped his palms over her face and kissed the top of her head. Her hair smelled burnt from the sun. "You're right," she said. "I was getting hysterical."

"Your bravery is incredible," he said. "I *will* tell you more about your mother. Whatever I'm permitted to tell. There's time, though, Amanda."

He left her and paced the sand, the soles of his feet stung

by sharp debris. Ramrod straight, his body defied the ocean. He felt powerful. He'd won the first round. He would win the others. He would even test his mastery over her; he would give her the opportunity to escape, and she would not go. He felt sure of it. She might resist, but she'd stay. This would be the most important achievement of his life. More crucial, even, than the creation of Amanda would be the restoration of Amanda.

Amanda's reason told her that too many questions remained unanswered. Why had Byron been in Bradley? Why wasn't she permitted to see her own doctor? And why had nobody tried to see *her?* Byron had whisked her back to his estate, and here she stayed. No reporters, no friends. Nobody knew where she was, except Byron Moore.

Amanda could not let grief and terror plow her under. She didn't know if she could survive without her sight, but before she could try, she had to leave the estate and find her way home. If it meant staggering along the highway and thumbing rides, she would do it.

It was good, in a way, that Byron had brought her back. She had a goal now: to learn the truth. It helped her live through the first weeks of blindness without caving in. She kept reliving the vision she'd seen in the desert. It still played in her mind, in brilliant colors. She tried to turn the mystical hallucination into actual design, recasting The Pueblo again and again. It occupied her dark hours and pumped strength into her heart.

The wind blew harder and she lay back, soaking up the sun that burned beyond the blackness. She knew Byron waited for her to give up. *You can wait till hell freezes over,* she vowed.

Danny Rosetti slumped in a metal chair in the Bradley police station and tried to focus on the photographs in front of him. The photo room was situated in a secluded wing of the sprawling station house. Hundreds of photos were filed in drawers according to sex, color, height, and crime committed.

"Finished?" a sympathetic detective asked. Danny looked up, barely seeing the man.

"I guess so."

The cop hefted the drawer from the metal table and replaced it in its filing cabinet. He lifted out the next drawer and brought it over. "I know it's tiring," he said. "Take your time with it. No pressure."

The cop was a big, sweaty man, in a wilted suit. He had the dark coloring and the facial construction of a full-blooded Navajo. Danny pushed a shaking hand through his uncombed hair. Pale and unshaven, he still looked stricken.

"I can't hack this anymore," he said. "Man, I don't know where I am."

The cop set down the drawer with a thud and straddled a chair across from Danny. "I know it's tough."

"You know shit." Danny threw back his head and pressed the heels of his hands against his eyes. He sat quietly for a long time. The air conditioner hummed and rattled. The desert sun bleached the color out of the walls.

The cop lit a cigarette and offered the pack to Danny. He shook his head. The cop exhaled smoke and said, "Look. I can't put you back together again. All I can do is go after the guys who killed your wife. And I can do that with positive I.D.'s and information."

Danny looked at him with emotionless eyes. "You have information. You know who did it. You just can't find him."

"No," the cop admitted. "Not yet. But if we can finger the others, maybe we can break one of them."

"I don't recognize the faces." Danny let his hands drop into his lap, where they lay, motionless. The unbearable pain of losing Terri had eaten a fiery hole in his heart. He had not returned to work since the horror of his wedding night. He'd survived a three-day drunken rage, during which he smashed up his apartment and his car. He'd lost weight, suffered cramps and diarrhea. He'd gone without food and sleep, wanting only to die. Finally, he went to the police.

It hadn't helped. The despair, like a chronic disease, kept eating at his bones. He kept reliving the reception. She was so alive to him that he couldn't accept her death. He expected to see her every time he turned a corner. He expected her voice every time he picked up the phone. The pain was not lessening. It murdered him, day by day.

Cooperating with the police had given Danny something to fill the desolate hours. Plagued with insomnia, he faced an eternity of time, with no relief. Yesterday he was in New York; today he was in New Mexico. There was no difference.

He looked at the world with lifeless eyes, and he felt the chill of death in his throat.

"Rosetti," the cop said. "I'm a Navajo. I know what my people go through, and I know what happens to them. I'm ashamed of Peter Deal. It makes us all look bad to have psychos out there killing people. I want the bastard."

Danny looked at the clock on the wall. "I bleed for you."

"No you don't." The cop put out his cigarette in an already full ashtray, and got up. He went to the window and separated the slats of the blinds with his fingers. The sunlight striped his face. "He knows that desert. It swallows him up. You can't search the whole desert, Rosetti, not all at once. He can keep moving, keep running. And his friends hide him. I'm really sorry for you, son. More than you'll ever believe."

Danny stood, burdened with profound weariness. "Thanks."

The cop gave him a compassionate smile. Danny just stared back, as he felt the texture of Terri's smooth skin, the taste of her mouth, the cadence of her voice. He nearly cried out. And in that moment of bottomless grief, Danny made a decision.

It wasn't momentous, or uplifting. It just made sense, and there was no rational fear left to stop him. He would need a four-wheel drive vehicle, and a couple of guns with ammo. Camping gear. Dried foods and canned foods. "Where's a good rowdy bar?" he asked.

"Eagle Inn. Back in town. Why?"

"I want to get drunk."

"Why not?" the cop said with a shrug. "You *ought* to get drunk. You ought to start a brawl and break heads. Everyone wants to bury this thing. Go ahead and make noise."

"I'll make noise," Danny said. He left the photo room. The cop watched him go and thought hard. How far gone *was* the man? It might pay to keep an eye on him and find out. Sometimes a madness unrestrained by law could do what the system could not do. The cop knew that, and he sensed such a moment of madness right now. It might be his only break.

It would take an hour or so in a couple of bars, Danny figured. Some drinks, and loose talk. Danny framed the scene in his mind as he drove back to Bradley. He'd tell the barflies that he was coming to kill Lone Dog. And that, along the way, he'd shoot down every Indian he found. Man, woman, or child. The story would reach Lone Dog pretty quickly. He'd be waiting.

Danny figured he could cause some damage before he was stopped by the police, or gunned down by Lone Dog. It was worth trying. It was the only thing worth trying. Civilization had failed Danny Rosetti. He had no loyalty to it. He wanted to feel better for a little while.

chapter 26

HEATHER guided her horse along the beach, as cold mist glided past. Her hair hung loosely, framing her tender face, and her body was casually dressed in a Boston U. sweatshirt and jeans. Her bare feet felt cold in the stirrups. She kept her eyes on Amanda Gray, who walked fifty yards ahead.

The sea and the sky merged in a heavy rolling fog. The mare snorted white breath and champed her bit. Long fingers of foam from the waves breaking on the shore curled around the animal's hooves. Heather's heart felt leaden, and a sick jealousy ate at her. This was the worst thing that Byron had ever done. He'd beaten her after the club opening. He'd made her spend double hours at her singing lessons. He'd taken away all her treats: no ice cream, no records, no TV. He'd scolded her for two hours while she rocked and shivered on a chair in her bedroom.

But none of those punishments hurt as much as this. Why did he have to bring back Amanda? Heather knew that Byron really loved Amanda. He always talked about her. He always had her pictures around. Heather tried so hard to make Byron happy, but it didn't matter what she did. Amanda was always on his mind. Heather knew she could never replace the beautiful, sophisticated, intelligent Amanda Gray.

Heather quieted the horse as it whickered. "Shhh," she whispered. "No noise, Cupcake." She bent over and nuzzled the horse's mane, but kept her eyes firmly on her prey. Amanda walked slowly, at the edge of the water. She was barefoot, dressed in grape-colored sweats.

Hatred washed through Heather. "I wish you were dead,"

she murmured. Then she thought, with a shock of excitement, that Amanda couldn't see her. If she spurred Cupcake into a gallop and rode hard . . .

Heather's mouth went dry and her heart pounded. It was so foggy. Heather could say that she just didn't see Amanda, that Cupcake got spooked in the fog. Byron couldn't blame Heather for it, and Amanda would be dead, or crippled. Heather nursed the fantasy. It would be so easy. Amanda would finally be gone.

Waves thundered behind the white wall of fog. The dampness penetrated Heather's sweatshirt and beaded on her skin. She swallowed hard. She leaned across Cupcake's neck.

"*Run!*" she hissed into Cupcake's ear, and her naked heels thumped into the horse's belly. Cupcake whinnied and broke into a gallop.

Amanda let the coldness and fog ice her bones. She felt water lap her ankles, and the mist injected needles into her skin. She knew this beach. Her feet walked unerringly, never straying into the water. She knew without seeing that the sun was absent today, that it was a ghost world. The smells and sounds pressed against the blackness that smothered her.

She felt strong. Jogging and a renewed exercise routine had firmed up her battered muscles and stretched out her limbs. She felt leaner and lighter. She kept to a severe diet, to restore energy and to cleanse her blood. The horror of Terri's death, the trauma of the gang-rape, the loss of Jason, and the shock of blindness had drained her system. She could actually feel the vitamins run out. She'd been shot full of drugs and stitched from stem to stern. No wonder she'd fallen apart. Not even years of steeling her body against pain had prepared her for the drubbing she'd taken.

Which Byron had counted on; she was sure of it. The man who'd designed Amanda's entire life had designed her return to him. He'd expected her to be helpless, traumatized by blindness, and finally ready to be enslaved again. Amanda knew she'd come damned close to it.

But his design had gone awry. It happened often enough. A color came through wrong. A bibelot worth hundreds of dollars clashed with a room. You planned everything, brought the elements together, and screwed up with a detail. Sometimes you had to start from scratch. It was the nature of designing.

What Byron had not respected was a will to live that pulsed in Amanda's genes. *Amanda* hadn't respected it until recently. But it was there. It made her miss the vein in her suicide attempts. It made her survive Byron's manic rages. It gave her courage to leave Byron, the bravado to confront Helen Tennyson, the impulse to love Jason. Now, that will refused to let blindness pitch her into despair.

Amanda smiled to herself as she shivered. It was good to find this force within her, but she wasn't sure what it could do now. She still had to face a barren life, without the man she loved, without the eyesight that meant her career. What was the point of surviving and being alone? Her stupid life force never asked those questions. It just kept her going.

She stopped and bent her knees, pressing her hands against her thighs. She wasn't getting younger, for sure. She fantasized a hot bath and lunch, and then some heavy thinking about getting out of here. Byron was not going to let her go. She'd have to sneak off the grounds and find her way home. Amanda sighed. Another challenge. One more hill to climb.

She pushed her hands through her hair. Foam tickled her feet. She heard a low drumming that vibrated in the sand. She paused, holding her breath.

Hoofbeats.

She turned, disoriented. Was Byron riding out to meet her?

The hoofbeats came louder. The horse was running. She felt a catch in her heart. She stared into blackness and tried to hear the direction of the sound. It seemed to be all around her.

"Byron?" she called.

She smelled the horse. The animal was on top of her! She flung herself sideways, slapped into the water, and skidded on the shell-covered sea bottom. Waves broke around her, and spray showered her face.

She lay panting in the water, her fingers digging for purchase in the soft mud. "What the hell is going on?" she demanded.

She could hear the snort and pant of the horse. It was standing still. And she could sense the breathing of the rider. It wasn't Byron.

"Who's there?" she asked. She cautiously pulled herself upright and stood soaked and shuddering, ankle deep in the surf.

"Why didn't you stand still?" a girl's voice said. "Now I have to do it again."

"What are you talking about?"

"You might as well stay there," the girl said. "You can't see me coming, and I can see you, so you can't get away."

Suddenly, Amanda realized whose voice it was. "Heather?"

"Yeah. Now you know."

"What's the problem?"

Heather laughed. "Don't be a total jerk, Amanda. I'm going to run you down."

"What?" Amanda cried. "Heather—!"

But the horse trotted away, up the beach. Amanda tried to control her thinking. The girl was out of it. That didn't help. She could work at this all afternoon, and sooner or later, Amanda wouldn't be able to gauge her approach.

Amanda sloshed to the beach. She could scream, but no one would hear at the house, and on a day like this, nobody would be outside. She had to bring the girl off the horse.

Terrific. Execute a stunt play without eyesight. But there was no time to think it out, because here came Heather again. Amanda strained to catch the direction of the hoofbeats. She was scared to death, but she couldn't panic. She couldn't!

From her left. They were coming from her left. Amanda turned and stood her ground, though her legs begged her to run. She forced herself to visualize the horse. She saw the phantom animal pounding through the surf. She saw the horse's broad, lathered chest, flaring nostrils, bulging eyes. She pictured a white blaze on its forehead. She saw Heather in the saddle, in a white dress for some insane reason, hair streaming out behind her.

Coldly, Amanda calculated the distance. She'd ridden this beach with Byron, raced him often enough to know pretty well how far away the horse was. The heavy fog and booming surf complicated things, but she thought she had a fair notion.

Pound, pound, pound, pound, here she came. *Run!* Amanda's legs begged her. But she wouldn't run. She faced the horse and watched it come closer in her mind. Thank God for her training. Her visual imagination was keen and practiced. She had developed marvelous spatial perception.

The hoofbeats filled her brain. She pushed aside images of hooves flying at her face. She concentrated only on the horse approaching. She correlated the image with the sound. It was very close now. Maybe ten yards.

Okay, she decided. *Go with ten yards. Count down. Nine yards, eight . . .*

Her breath stopped. Her throat shut down. Her sightless eyes pushed against her sockets. For a millisecond, she fantasized Jason, naked and gorgeous in the sunshine.

Three yards, two . . .

She lunged and clawed with both hands. Her fingers raked knotted mane, metal bit, bridle . . .

She grabbed hard and yanked down. Her feet were dragged from beneath her and she was pulled through the wet sand. The horse screamed in surprise and reared up. Amanda let go of the bridle and hurled herself aside, twisting and rolling in midair. She hit the sand hard, and felt the bite of broken shells against her skin. She heard a tremendous thud nearby and an explosion of agonized breath. Then she heard hoofbeats receding down the beach.

She lay for a moment, out of breath and bursting with pain. She slowly pushed herself to her knees. Water slammed her back as a wave broke, and she cursed.

She heard whimpering. "Heather?"

"I'm hurt . . ."

Amanda shut her eyes and felt relief wash over her. She wiped her eyes and mouth with her wet sweatshirt sleeve. She carefully stood up, and cried out softly at the stings and stabs of her open wounds. She felt a warm stickiness in her side. Fresh blood.

"Where are you?" Amanda called.

"Here . . ."

"Keep talking," Amanda said. "I'll find you."

"Please . . ." Heather said. Her voice was faint.

Amanda followed the pleading voice, wondering if the girl was going to grab her leg and try to drown her. She reached Heather and knelt down, waving her hands in the air. Heather seized her hand and held onto it.

"Are you hurt badly?" Amanda asked.

"I don't think I can move my leg."

"You probably sprained it. Just lie still. You can make it worse by moving."

The girl began to cry. "I wanted to kill you."

"I gathered that. What the hell got into you?"

Heather didn't answer.

Amanda was hurting pretty badly herself, but her anger had blossomed. "Listen, honey. Right now, I'm the only one between you and death. I'm banged up but I can walk. Maybe I can even get your horse and ride. But you have to talk to me first."

Between sobs, Heather said, "Why did he bring you back? He keeps thinking about you. If you were dead, he'd forget."

Amanda tried to process this. It sounded so absurd at first that she was inclined to laugh. But she remembered being sixteen, and utterly mesmerized by Byron Moore. She remembered her total, absolute dependence on the man, and the sick love that was born out of torture. Byron was a master at breaking down defenses in young girls. He used tenderness and brutality in perfect measure to create a need for him. Many times Amanda had wanted to kill women she perceived as rivals. She could understand Heather's pain and envy. Byron had enslaved Heather, and now had brought Amanda back to the house. No doubt Byron tormented the girl deliberately. Amanda knew he was dissatisfied with Heather and maybe intended to rid himself of her as an artist would shred a failed canvas.

Amanda pushed down the gall in her throat. She explored with her fingers and found the girl's forehead and limp hair. She stroked softly, and her fingertips came away wet with blood. Heather was really hurt.

"How did Byron find you?" Amanda asked.

Heather seemed surprised by the question. "What does it matter to you?"

"It matters," Amanda said. "I don't want to take him away from you. Can you believe that?"

"So why did you come back?"

"He brought me back, when I went blind. But I'm going to leave. I don't love Byron anymore. I don't really think he loves me either. Not really. I think he truly loves you, but I think he's confused. Sometimes men get confused when they get a little older."

Amanda could feel the thready pulse in Heather's hand. Heat crawled up Amanda's drenched back; the sun must be breaking through. She could almost sense the lightening of the sky.

"You're lying," Heather said.

"I'm not lying. I'm in love with another man. I want to go

back to him very much. Look, sweetheart, let me get some help for you."

There was a long silence, broken by Heather's gasps of pain and the muffled crash of the waves. Amanda's own injuries throbbed insistently. "I didn't mean it," Heather said suddenly. "I didn't mean to kill you. . . ."

"Well, you sure put on a good show."

Heather began to cry more steadily. "Oh shit. I'm sorry, Amanda."

"Yes, well I'm in pretty bad shape now from trying to avoid your runaway horse, so I'm not too thrilled with you, either. But I don't think it was premeditated. I think living in this magic kingdom with Byron can distort your reality."

"I hated you so much . . ."

"I know," Amanda soothed. "I know what you feel. How *did* he find you?"

"My parents knew him. My Mom and Dad were divorced. Dad was really good with electronics—computers and stuff. Byron bought the company he worked for. That's how my Dad knew him. Mom was a drunk, and Dad walked out on her. I remember when I was five years old I used to come home from school and she was in bed, puking, and I picked up the beer bottles . . ."

Amanda's chest tightened. She could see the pattern. "Didn't your father take you?"

"No," Heather said. "My Mom wouldn't let him. Once he came for me in his car, in the middle of a rainstorm, and he dragged me out of the house. My Mom just staggered around, throwing kitchen knives. She was too wasted to do anything. He took me to McDonald's and stuff, but the cops came and took me back."

"Poor baby. It must have been hell."

The sun was definitely out; it beat down on Amanda's back and pressed against her skull. She could smell fish and hear gulls crying. "I had two brothers," Heather said distantly. "They used to rape me. They did it first when I was nine. I got this boyfriend when I was twelve. He was twenty-two, but I told him I was eighteen. He beat me up all the time. I tried to shoot myself with his gun once, when he wasn't there, but I only shot my foot." She actually laughed. "That's when Byron took me. When I woke up in the hospital, he was sitting by my bed and he said I wasn't ever going back to that guy or my brothers or my Mom. He said he'd handled all the legal stuff and nobody would ever hurt me again."

The waves gentled now, rolling in a murmuring rhythm. "And Byron taught you to sing, and to read, and to be a lady."

"Yes," she said. "I can't believe how great he was. And I've been a total snot. I mean, I fight him all the time. He cares so much about me. And when he hurts me, I deserve it. I know I deserve it. I'm such a scuz, I really am. That's why I took a hairy when you came back. I mean, you're such a lady, you're so beautiful . . ."

Amanda kept smoothing the girl's hair, which was now sticky from blood. "I think Byron is dedicated to you, Heather. I think he won't give up on you until you're just what he wants you to be."

Amanda stood up, dizzy but stable. It was rough seeing herself mirrored and reliving her abasement. Heather was a much better slave for Byron. She lacked the life force that had animated Amanda. Heather truly loathed herself.

But Byron wasn't happy. He wanted Amanda, the woman he couldn't ever possess. Well, Amanda was going to spoil the man's fantasy. "I'll come back as quickly as I can," she said to Heather. "Lie very still, and be calm. I know my way back to the house."

"Hurry," Heather said. "It hurts bad."

Amanda walked cautiously, almost sniffing out her direction. Heather called, "Amanda."

She stopped. "Yes?"

"I could get you out of here if you want to go."

Amanda's heart lurched. In the back of her mind, she'd thought of this, but she didn't know how to broach it. "What do you mean?"

"Well, Byron won't let me roam around too much, but I could take a horseback ride or something with *you*."

Amanda smiled. The girl was excited; this was an easier way to get rid of the competition. "We can talk about it."

"And I can even tell you about a place where they can look after you—with your blindness and all."

"Oh?"

"Yeah. Byron took me there once. There was this blind lady there that he went to see. I think it was a kind of hospital."

Amanda stood poised on an imaginary precipice, buffeted by emotional winds. "A blind woman?"

"He watched her and talked to some doctor and then came back. He was all hot about the place, how it was historical and all that shit."

Amanda moved toward Heather. "Did he ever mention the blind woman's name?"

"No."

Amanda clenched her fists. Dear God. Byron was mad, beyond hope. To take the child there, to let her see . . . but Byron would do that. "Heather," she said, "I'd like to go to that place. Could you tell me where it is?"

"Sure," Heather said. "I can't go with you . . ."

"No, of course not. Just give me the address. And get me off the estate. I swear, Heather, on my life, that I won't come back, and I won't see Byron again."

"You mean that?"

"Oh yes, Heather. I mean it."

"Okay."

"Sit tight," Amanda said. "I'll be back in a jiffy."

She scrambled up the beach, moving by memory in the direction of the house. Everything was focused now; everything had a purpose. Amanda would send Cupcake an apple. Cupcake and Heather had given Amanda the key to unlock all her doors. If she could just elude Byron, just for a short time.

chapter 27

DRESSED in a light cotton top and skirt, Amanda carried a small valise to the waiting limo. She was tense and weary from waiting at this deli, but she knew that calling a car to the estate would have landed her in her room. She and Heather had waited until Byron left on business. Amanda packed her bag and Heather led her, both of them on horseback, far down the beach. At every moment, Amanda expected to hear the drone of a dune buggy. But Byron must have descended further into unreality, because they were able to leave the estate unpursued.

Heather took Amanda to the next estate and up to the road. They'd walked their mounts then, as Amanda tried to remember what this terrain was like. She wore big, dark sunglasses, and she'd tied her hair into braids to make herself look as different as possible from her pictures. Nobody knew that Amanda Gray was blind, so that would help.

Heather guided Amanda to the roadside deli, where Amanda called a limousine company she'd used in the past. She hugged Heather then, and said goodbye. "You're young, and you're beautiful, and you're valuable," she'd said. "Try to believe that you matter. That you can succeed on your own."

"Maybe that's okay for you," Heather said. "But I'm not like you are."

"Maybe not," Amanda said. "Thank you for what you've done."

"Forget it," the girl said. "I owed you something. I was a real asshole."

"We all are, once in a while," Amanda said. She listened

to Heather ride away, leading the second horse. Then she waited, anxiously, sweating in the heat of the afternoon, always expecting the slam of the car door that meant her recapture. She knew she'd started a deadly countdown when she left.

The limo was cool and comfortable. Amanda gave the driver the name of the West Hills Sanitarium in Westchester and settled back for the long ride. It was good to cushion her battered bones and to feel the rocking motion of the car. She listened to traffic rushing past, and to horns blaring. She wondered where she would go after she saw the woman she believed was her mother. Who would be able to help her once Byron knew? Maybe she would help herself, or at least try.

The car was not hijacked by Byron's forces, and finally, Amanda arrived. The overpowering fragrance of flowers assaulted her senses as she stepped out of the limo and told the driver to wait. She had asked the driver to help her find her American Express Gold Card, the one in the name of Helen Tennyson Associates. It was a terrible risk; the driver could have snatched her bag and run, stolen her card, or called Helen. But Amanda had no cash and the driver would not squire her around on sympathy.

It hardly mattered. Her time would run out soon, no matter what evasive maneuvers she took. Byron would swoop down on her and snatch her up again. She nearly fell over steps in her reverie, and had to feel her way up to the entrance. Her body passed from blazing sun to cool shade. She searched for a door, found it, and pushed it open. Inside, a musty smell greeted her, and silence, punctuated by soft murmurs.

Hands were suddenly at her elbow. "Can we help you?" a male voice asked.

"Yes," she said. "I want to see somebody."

"Who?"

She hesitated. She didn't know who this man was: clerk, orderly, doctor, or administrator. If Byron had put Amanda's mother here, he had clout. A word from Amanda's lips and the phone call would go out. Amanda would be detained while Byron flew up in his helicopter. He would come in and say, "Hello, Amanda. This was very stupid of you."

"Ma'am?" the voice said. "Are you all right?"

"Yes." To hell with it. She could scream. She could create publicity. There was no subtle way. "I want to see Mary."

"We have several Marys here."

I must be impressing this man as a raving lunatic. They're probably readying an injection right now. She took a deep breath. "I . . . don't know what last name she goes under now. It might be . . ." She had a flash of inspiration. "Crawford. She's blind, like I am."

"Oh, Mary Crawford," the man said. Amanda smirked triumphantly. It would be typical of Byron to register the woman under the name of her lover.

"Yes, that's her."

"And how are you related?"

"She's my mother."

"Ah. Yes, I do see a resemblance."

Amanda shut her eyes. All the exhaustion and tension swept over her. "Oh, dear," the man said, and hustled her to a seat. It was a lobby sofa by the feel of it. "Thank you," she managed to say. "I'm sorry for behaving so badly."

"Don't worry about it," the man said. "I gather you haven't seen your mother for a long time."

"No, not for a long time."

"Dr. Fielding is your mother's attending physician here, Miss Crawford. Is it Miss Crawford still?"

"Yes."

"I'll get Dr. Fielding for you. Do you need some water?"

"No."

Dr. Fielding arrived about fifteen minutes later by Amanda's reckoning. She felt him sit down beside her, and his hand covered hers. "Miss Crawford," he said, "this is unexpected, to say the least."

His voice was firm and doctorly. "I know," she said. "I didn't really know I'd be up here until I came."

"Let's walk out back. The gardens are beautiful. I'll describe them for you."

"Fine."

He guided her through what she supposed was the lobby of the building, and through a door. She felt the air again, fresh and warm on her face. Her feet touched wood; a portico? The briskness of the breeze and the open sensation around her made her believe that she stood high above a vista. "I think it's probably very beautiful," she said

"Yes it is. Byron says I don't appreciate the beauty. Do you know him?"

"Byron . . . ?"

She could almost hear him smile. "Byron Moore. The art magnate. He's the one who pays your mother's bills, Miss Crawford. Certainly you knew that."

"No, I didn't. I knew she had a benefactor, but . . . well, I've been out of touch for a long time."

The man knew. He'd called Byron, and the game was up before it had begun. "Where *have* you been?" he asked.

"Around the world," she said.

"You haven't been blind very long, have you?"

"It's that obvious?"

"To a doctor, it is. What happened?"

"A nerve disease."

"I see. You do know that your mother is terminally ill?"

Amanda's hands reached out, and, thankfully, found a railing to clutch onto. She felt as if she were falling over the portico into a chasm below. "No. I didn't know."

Fielding paused. "Sorry to shock you. I somehow thought you would be aware. She has a brain tumor. Inoperable. She suspects, but doesn't know everything. Be careful."

"Then you'll let me see her?"

"Of course. Why wouldn't I?"

She held tightly to the railing. "No reason. I . . . it's just been so long, I'd given up hope."

"No, I don't think you've given up hope. I think you had some reason for not coming sooner, and for not claiming to be related to the woman."

"What are you talking about?"

Amanda heard other footsteps now, slow, hesitant footsteps, and the tapping of what sounded like a cane. "I'm not a stupid man, Miss Gray. I know who you are. Only a hermit wouldn't know who you are. Even the chauffeur knew."

Amanda let out a long breath. "I guess it was dumb to pretend."

"Can you tell me what in hell is going on? Byron Moore installs a blind woman in West Hills, oh, twenty-five years ago or so. The talk said she was his mistress, but Byron wasn't famous yet, and nobody knew for sure. He's come back four times a year since, to check on her, to make sure her care is excellent. He guided her publishing career. But he never spoke to her. And now, *you* show up claiming the woman is your mother. *Another* ex-mistress of Byron Moore. And also mysteriously blind. I'm fascinated."

Byron's first mistress. God in heaven. Of course. It all made sense, finally. She knew her macabre lineage.

Amanda tried to read the doctor's voice. She believed—and it was a terrible gamble to believe this—that he was *not* loyal to Byron. "Dr. Fielding, I don't know much more than you do. But I promise that I'll tell you what I know if you won't tell Byron where I am and if you'll let me talk to this woman."

He chuckled. "You're not in a position to strike bargains. But I'm not going to betray you. The woman is standing here now, Miss Gray. I deliberately let her hear. I want to make trouble. I've waited a long time to annoy that pompous son of a bitch. No, I won't put him on your tail. I might even help you cover your tracks. I'll come back for you in a little while, and get you some coffee."

"All right. Thank you."

Fielding left. She heard his precise footsteps and the slam of a door. Amanda stood utterly still, clinging to the railing. "Mary . . . ?"

She heard the woman's breath. "That was a very stupid thing Dr. Fielding did," the woman said.

"I'm sorry. I didn't think he would do that."

"It's all right," the voice said. "What makes you think you're my daughter?"

Amanda struggled for rational speech. The moment overwhelmed her. Her eyes strained madly to break through the blackness. "My father was Tom Crawford," she said. "A gardener for Byron Moore. He made love to a woman and she became pregnant. Byron took the baby away, and placed it with Rob and Jenny Gray. He took the child back at sixteen. He told me that my mother's name was Mary, and that she was blind."

Amanda choked on her tears. Mary said, "Let's walk, Amanda. I know these gardens by now. The blind *can* lead the blind, just this once."

Mary led Amanda through the circuitous gardens. Amanda felt flower heads brush her ankles. She heard the drone of bees and the lap of water against a nearby shore. "I was an artist," Mary said as they walked. "I did abstracts, but mostly romantic stuff. They said I combined complex mathematical variations with a juicy and free-running style." She laughed a gossamer laugh. "The critics liked it, and buyers liked it, which was pretty amazing since I was thirteen at the time."

"Thirteen . . . !"

"A prodigy. You have exciting chromosomes, dear." She took a breath. "My parents died when I was eight, and I was raised by an aunt and uncle—your great-aunt and great-uncle, I guess, but you wouldn't want to know them. They were vicious to me, but Uncle Paul recognized the dollar potential in my work. It's wonderful how I recall this. There are times when I forget everything, Amanda. And times when the headaches are so bad that I cry."

"My God."

"Well," Mary said, and sighed. "I had some local showings, and got some coverage, and a young gallery owner named Byron Moore got to know my work. He was daring enough to give me an exhibit. Byron was already making his name as a dealer and a business genius. He just took what he wanted. But you know that."

"Yes."

"So," Mary said. Amanda heard treetops rustling in the wind. "I was on my way. Meanwhile, I was being molested regularly by Uncle Paul. Aunt Doris wouldn't believe me. Nobody would. Uncle Paul used to hit me with a wrench when he thought I'd told on him. He broke my arms three times, my legs twice. He gave me several concussions, and doctors think my brain tumor came from one of them."

"You know . . ."

"Well, I know right now. Maybe I won't know this evening. It comes and goes, Amanda."

Amanda shivered. She could hear hysteria in the woman's voice. But right now, that didn't matter. Right now, Mary was saying what Amanda had waited to hear.

"Go on."

Mary laughed. "Before I lose my grip again, huh? Well, I ran away from Uncle Paul. I wound up on the streets of Chicago. I slept in an abandoned apartment. I begged for food and worked odd jobs. I barely escaped prostitution. But I did become a rather legendary graffiti artist—which got me excited about doing site art. Later on, I did whole walls and frescoes." She sighed again. "But not then. Then I got addicted to heroin and I caught hepatitis and wound up in a hospital, dying. That's when Byron came for me."

"Yes, of course," Amanda said bitterly. "I'm sure he watched you all the time."

"I think he must have," Mary said reflectively. "Anyway, Uncle Paul was arrested for molesting a neighbor's child, and Byron urged me to tell everything in court. He got Uncle Paul sent away and he became my legal guardian. It happened very quickly. I was sixteen then, and a wreck . . ."

"Stop it." Amanda said. "I can't listen to it."

"I'm sorry." Mary's hands found Amanda's arm and held tight. "I wasn't thinking. It isn't right for me to speak that way to you. Because it's true, Amanda. What you think."

"Yes. I know."

Mary seemed to be gathering her thoughts. "That was when Byron built his estate on Long Island. He brought me back to life. He taught me how to dress and speak and walk and write and read . . ."

"And play the piano and ride horseback," Amanda murmured.

"Yes, yes, all of that. He made me draw and paint, of course, and got me shows in the best galleries, and seduced me. Which wasn't too difficult since I was desperately in love with him. He was my healer, he was my god. I gladly became his possession."

"The first one," Amanda said.

"Was I? Yes, I suppose so." She stopped. "My head's pounding like blazes."

"Please," Amanda begged. "Please finish."

Mary caught her breath. "I'll try, for your sake. He became overbearing. He supervised every move, chose my wardrobe, selected my books. Then he turned sadistic. I don't think *he* knew it was in him. He whipped me one night, with a horsewhip he'd brought home from an antique auction. I remember cringing naked in a corner. He kept coming after me, screaming and lashing me. I can still feel the pain of it, like no pain I'd ever experienced. I fainted, thank God. I woke up in a hospital and he came in with a diamond brooch and I forgave him. And of course he did it again, and worse things, and I took it, and still loved him. . . ."

"No more," Amanda said. "I can't stand hearing you talk about it."

"Forgive me. It's hard to think of you as mine. I found Tom, and he was gentle and sweet and strong, and I needed that. I relished the danger of loving him. I wasn't very careful about taking the birth control pills Byron got me. I'd forget them in my excitement. And I became pregnant."

"I know the rest of the story," Amanda said. She found Mary's hand and held it.

"That's right," Mary said. "You do. Byron never hurt me while I carried you. You should know that. I had the best doctors. I was put to sleep during delivery, so I wouldn't see the baby, and I never did see you. You were gone when I woke up. I cried for days and days. I felt so empty."

"So did I," Amanda said.

Mary's voice broke. "I started to go blind soon after that. Byron took me to lots of doctors, but they couldn't help. When I went totally blind, he brought me here, to this place. And here I've stayed, forever, it seems—unable to see, to paint, to live. I needed to be creative, so I wrote novels, and Byron had them published. But no, he never did speak to me. I was so surprised to hear Dr. Fielding say he kept coming out. I suppose he just didn't know what to say. But it was sweet of him to come. Romantic."

"Romantic!" Amanda echoed bitterly. "God in heaven. I . . . don't even know how to speak to you. I know my artistry comes from both parents, and I'm happy about that. But I don't know how to talk to you."

"It's going to take time," Mary said.

Amanda's spirits leaped. "Yes, it sure is. And whatever time we both have, I'll be here, even if I have to live here. We'll know each other, I swear that. I won't lose you now."

Mary held both her hands. "I hope not. I know I don't sound very motherly, but I've had no practice. I'll learn, Amanda. I certainly will learn."

Amanda wiped away the tears that pooled at the corners of her mouth. "Maybe it was worth it to inherit your blindness. It brought me to you."

Mary said, "Inherit?"

"Oh, please, don't even begin to blame yourself. You couldn't have known."

"But you told Dr. Fielding you had a nerve disease."

"Yes, the same one. It destroyed the retina."

Mary seemed to be thinking. "That's odd. I'm sure I went blind from glaucoma. We ignored the symptoms for too long and it was irreversible by the time we found out. Can you inherit glaucoma?"

Amanda felt her heart stop. "Glaucoma?"

"Yes. But even if it *can* be inherited, you said you had a nerve disease."

"That's what the doctor said—at least he said it *might* be a nerve disease. And Byron confirmed it, and said you had the same disease. That I inherited it. That there's no hope."

"No," Mary said. "You didn't inherit my disease. My disease was glaucoma."

Amanda turned, wild with emotion. He'd lied. Why had he lied? What difference would it make whether it was inherited or not?

Unless it wasn't irreversible. Unless it was not a nerve disease; she'd never had the chance to have further tests—Byron had swooped her up and insulated her from the world.

Amanda fought the crazed hope that smashed against her chest. "I have to see Dr. Fielding," she said. "Will you come?"

"No," Mary said. "My headache is worsening. But please come and see me before you go home."

"Oh yes," Amanda promised. "I'll come to see you." She breathed deeply to remain in control. There was no reason to hope, none—but Byron had lied.

Amanda held her mother's hands, and by God, if there was a way, she'd see her mother's face, and she'd see Byron fry in hell.

chapter 28

THE intercom buzzed and Lacey said, "Yes, Maggie?"

Maggie's voice sounded terrified. "Lacey, it's Amanda. What should I do?"

"Amanda . . . ?" Lacey looked around in horror. This was Amanda's desk, in Amanda's office. Only the bright yellow flowers on the cocktail table were Lacey's. "Send her in."

Lacey sat back, and absentmindedly snapped open the top button of her dress. The office door opened and Amanda walked in, slowly and cautiously. Lacey hadn't realized how affected she was going to be. She still loved this woman, as much as she hated her. And she hated her even more for her strength.

"Amanda," Lacey said breathlessly. "I . . . we didn't know where you were. What happened?"

"Lots," Amanda said. Her designer sunglasses set off her white sleeveless sweater and midcalf skirt. She looked rested and serene, not at all like a woman who'd been put through purgatory.

"I'm using your office because Helen put me in charge of The Pueblo," Lacey explained. "Nobody knew where you were, or why you abandoned the project. I hope you'll understand."

Amanda smiled. "You hope I won't kick you out of that chair. But it's all right. What you did makes perfect sense."

With a sharp exhalation, Lacey sat back and felt her face become taut. "Well, I've been doing a pretty decent job,

Amanda, considering that I wasn't prepared for it. Helen's very excited."

"Good for her," Amanda said dryly. "Lacey, I need you to do some things for me."

"Of course."

Amanda ticked off items on her fingers. "I need a plane reservation for New Mexico, for today. Have them bump anybody they can. Tell them I'm blind and need assistance."

Lacey's heart jumped into her throat. *"What?"*

"Yes. I made it here from memory."

Lacey stood up, shaky. She studied Amanda fiercely. "When did it happen? My God . . ."

"Recently. Don't get hysterical."

"Not the beating . . . ?"

"No," Amanda said. "I knew it was coming for a long time. I just didn't think it would be this soon. So you'll very likely continue to handle The Pueblo. I just need to meet with Helen in Bradley."

"Sure," Lacey said. "Do you need some help now? I mean, whatever I can do . . ."

Amanda groped for a chair, found one, and sat. "Don't be so obvious, Lacey. I just need the plane reservation, and a limo to the airport. I need it quickly, too. I don't have a lot of time."

"You're not dying . . . ?"

Amanda laughed. "No, I'm not dying. I just have a tight schedule. Would you make the calls for me?"

Lacey sat down again, thinking furiously. "Yes. Right now."

Lacey jotted *Call Helen* on her desk pad. She picked up the phone and told Maggie to make the reservations. She tried to still her volcanic emotions. Amanda was blind. This was so unexpected. It meant the company was Lacey's, and everything she'd sacrificed her body for—*if* Amanda didn't find out from Jason what was going on.

"Tell me what happened to you," Lacey said.

"No," Amanda demurred. "I'd rather not. I don't think we have very much to say to each other."

"What's that supposed to mean?"

Amanda seemed to look right at Lacey, which gave Lacey the creeps. "It's not a crime that you're making it with Jason. I never owned him. It's the sneaky, greedy way you went after him. And after my job. You're an immoral little snake."

Thunder pounded Lacey's head. She smoothed her long hair back with both hands. "I'm sorry you found out from someone else," she said. "You're so wrong about everything."

"I don't think so," Amanda said coldly. "But this isn't the time to discuss it. If Jason wants you, he can have you. If you want this company, I can't stop you from taking it. God knows, I can't contribute very much. But to do it all out of petty vengefulness, because I didn't want to swing your way . . ."

"Shut up, Amanda."

"Hit a nerve?" Amanda taunted. "I really dislike myself for being petty, but I get very few satisfactions these days."

"Get out," Lacey said. "Wait in the outer office."

Amanda laughed. "This is still my office. Helen doesn't own the building yet, does she?"

"All right, then stay," Lacey said.

"Fine with me," Amanda agreed. "Want a mint?" She took a roll of mints from her purse, and popped one in her mouth.

"No," Lacey replied, and resumed her work. Amanda smiled.

Helen moved swiftly when she hung up the phone. She ordered Lacey to fly out to Bradley in Helen's private jet. Jason would pick her up for a jaunt to Hawaii. It was cursed bad luck that Jason happened to be in Bradley just now; he would be more than suspicious of this junket. Too bad. He would go.

Helen waited for Amanda in her office, and stood up when Amanda came in. The woman looked stunning, Helen decided. Even blind, she carried herself with assurance and sophistication—maybe even more than she'd shown before.

"You're absolutely remarkable," Helen opened.

"Thank you," Amanda said. She didn't know this office as well as her own, and stumbled as she tried to find her way.

"To your right," Helen guided. "The tub chairs. Almost there . . . now."

Amanda sat down and took a long breath. If one looked for it closely, Amanda's exhaustion showed in the tense line of her mouth and the tightness around her eyes. She slipped off the sunglasses and put them in a case in her purse. Helen flinched, half expecting to see grotesquely scarred eye sockets. But Amanda's eyes looked as beautiful and penetrating as ever, except that they flicked helplessly, seeking vision and finding none. It made Helen shiver.

"I'm sorry for abandoning the project," Amanda said. "Whatever I may have been going through, it was unprofessional and inexcusable."

"I don't think you can be held accountable under these circumstances."

"My going blind was not your fault," Amanda insisted. "It was my job to find a replacement. . . ."

"I put Lacey in charge."

"I know, and it was a super choice. I probably would have done the same myself."

"Would you?"

Amanda smiled. "Yes. Even though Lacey stole my guy. I don't let things like that cloud my professional judgment."

Helen touched her fingertips together as she slowly swiveled in her chair. "Have you . . . made up with Jason?"

"No. We spoke before I went away. It wasn't nice."

"I'm sorry. You and Jason seemed to be a promising pair."

"I know." Amanda seemed desperate to see Helen. The lack of eye contact must be driving the girl crazy, Helen thought. "But life goes on."

"Indeed. So now you've come back to apologize."

"And to resume my involvement with The Pueblo."

Helen tensed. "How do you propose to do that?"

"I'm going to court to have construction stopped. I think I can get a restraining order."

"Well, now," Helen said sweetly. "You've come back feisty."

"Then I intend to submit a new design, once I can touch base with an architect. I have the concept and I can think out the interiors, but I need help with the shell."

"What sort of design?"

Amanda shifted forward in the chair. "No fair giving previews. It's going to be different from the one you've got now. It's going to harmonize with the desert aesthetically and ecologically. And it's going to boost the economy of the reservation, not wipe it out."

"I see. Tepees on the grounds? Little Indian bellboys?"

"You're so gross, Helen."

Helen stood up with an electrifying intensity, and pushed aside the swivel chair. "What do you want out of this, Amanda? How much compensation?"

"Compensation for what, Helen? Do you have something to hide?"

"Bitch." Helen came around her desk. She let a vindictive smile touch her lips as she watched Amanda try to find her. "You're just bright enough to cost me money. I think you're also bright enough to take a lump sum for your troubles instead of wasting all that time."

"I don't want to be paid off," Amanda said. "I'm not going to sue you for making me blind, or for my rape. That's what's on your paranoid little mind. I'm serious about stopping you. I know myself a little better now. God knows, I've had the chance to look inside. I still want to design, and I still want to make money at it. That hasn't changed. But I want to do some good with it, too. I've been a victim all my life. And I think I ought to devote some of my energies to other victims, who aren't in a position to fight back. You would never understand that."

"Oh, you're wrong," Helen said. "But I'm doing more good for people by creating jobs and business than any bleeding heart can do by ladling out soup."

Amanda stood up. "Well, I appreciate your capitalist approach, and you're probably right. But power corrupts, Helen, and that's always the end of the line. It may be trendy to want power, and chic to go after it like a barracuda, but I was never trendy. When you get power you go crazy with it, and you stop seeing whatever it was you dreamed in the first place."

"Very stirring," Helen said. "Clap clap clap. But I think you're full of illusions. I think you want to win. I think you're jealous of me, and of Lacey, because she's got Jason and she's got eyes. I think you're a bitter, vindictive loser with no more morals than I have."

"Think whatever you want," Amanda said. "I don't care very much. Lone Dog couldn't stop you by murdering innocent people, but I'm going to stop you by jailing guilty ones."

"Oh, are we ever rolling with oratory," Helen snarled.

She went to her desk and disconnected the phone, rolling up the connecting wires and putting them into her dress pocket. "Amanda," she said, "you've gotten me very upset. I have to think about what to do with you."

"You can't do anything with me."

"Of course I can. I can't let you go to court and the media. I've got a business to run. I have to put you out of commission."

"You can try."

Helen paused by the door. "Listen to me," she said. "The windows in this office, if you'll recall, are sealed and shatterproof. The drop is twenty-two stories."

Amanda gasped. "What . . . ?"

"Be quiet," Helen snapped. "The phone is out. The door is equipped with a computer-coded lock. I'm sending my secretary downstairs, and the office is soundproofed. There is a bathroom and a conference room off the main office, and a refrigerator in the wall opposite my desk. Someone will come back for you once I've arranged for your . . . deportation, or whatever. I won't be seeing you again. You've been the most irritating person in my entire life. Relax, and wait."

"Helen . . . !"

Helen shut the office door behind her. Amanda sank into the leather chair behind the desk and slammed her fist on the wood.

The jeep was a shimmering insect scuttling along a serpentine highway, against miles of snakeweed and juniper and rock. On a flat-topped ridge overlooking the road, three Indian youths watched the jeep. They were lean and dark, dressed in faded clothes. One of the boys held a walkie-talkie to this lips.

"He's all alone," the youth said.

A squawk of static was followed by a muffled voice. "No sign of cops?"

"Nothin'."

"You sure?"

"Shit, man, I can *see*. He's alone."

Another burst of static. "Okay. We're gonna get him."

The youth put down the walkie-talkie and squinted. He saw the jeep kick up plumes of dun-colored dust. "Real fuckup," he said.

"Time for a white sacrifice," another youth said.

The three of them laughed.

Danny blinked to keep his eyes open. Fatigue hung over him like a wheeling buzzard. His face was a brush of whiskers. The endless road shimmered and danced before him. Thirst drove him mad; his canteens had run out miles ago and he had no idea how far it was to the next town. Hunger pincered his belly. The jeep's air conditioning was giving out; a wet, cool wind oozed from the vents, and the belts shrieked under the hood.

None of this frightened him. He courted death. He hadn't found innocent Indians to kill, nor would he have killed any. He knew that now. He'd kill Lone Dog if he saw him. He'd use the .22 gauge shotgun or the small-bore rifle stuffed in the back seat. But he didn't think he'd see Lone Dog.

Danny took the undulating curves with almost dreamlike smoothness. Somewhere beyond the white horizon was a dark tunnel which would take him to some kind of rest. He prayed that he would die. Soon, maybe, he'd have the courage to stop the jeep, get out, and lie down beside it.

A light blue sedan came charging down a slope to the side of the road. It spewed rocks and debris and thumped hard on its springs. A shred of lucidity in Danny's brain told him that this wasn't a mirage, but a real car.

The sedan stopped across the road, blocking it. Danny jammed his foot hard on the brake and the sudden deceleration jolted his mind into focus. He saw two armed men standing beside the sedan. They were Indians, and they aimed rifles at his jeep.

Lone Dog.

A punishing emptiness yawned in Danny's heart as he realized that he'd blown it. Lone Dog had come for him, all right, but Danny would never have a chance for revenge. Briefly, he thought that he would reach for a rifle in the back seat, aim, and take down the Indians. But the jeep was already rolling to a stop and the Indians ran to either side of it. Rifle barrels banged up against the filthy windows.

"Get out," one of them shouted. The voice came muffled through the door.

Danny sat trembling in the driver's seat. The exhausting miles of driving, the accumulated grief and rage, overtook him. Paralyzed, he blinked out slow tears and waited to be shot.

The door was jerked open and oven-hot air slammed into Danny's face. A hand seized his wrist and pulled him from the jeep. He grunted as he was spun around and pushed hard against the fender. "Spread!" a voice barked.

Danny rested his cheek and arms on the scalding metal skin of the jeep. Hands roughly searched him, chopping his legs apart. "He's clean."

Another of the Indians had searched the jeep and came out with the guns. "Looks like this is all he was packing."

"Who were you going to shoot with that?"

Danny said nothing. A cruel, merciless face leered into his and its foul breath sickened him. "I said who were you going to shoot?"

Danny shook his head as his heart raced. He longed to get his fists on these animals, but he had no strength. The Indian hit him low in the stomach and Danny saw blazing lights as he doubled over.

"Get him in the car," a voice said. "He's gone."

The Indians didn't speak as they drove Danny, blindfolded, to Lone Dog's hideout. Danny felt the gut-wrenching harshness of the terrain through the bottom of the car. His eyelids scraped against a filthy red bandana, and now and then sunlight created scarlet brightness against his eyes.

The sedan stopped with a squeal of brakes. Danny was hustled outside and marched across unyielding ground, a rifle barrel pressing his spine. He heard a wooden door open, and he was pushed through. Abruptly, the blazing heat switched off and became cool dimness. He heard a fan whirring. The stench overpowered him.

Fingers yanked at the knots in the bandana and pulled it off. Danny blinked at the sudden light. He was in a wooden shack. Three small windows, covered with torn paper shades, let in pale light. Before him, at a battered bridge table, sat a young Indian, a leather vest over his naked skin, a bottle of whiskey in front of him. Some liquor had spilled on the man's chest, and glistened there. Other Indians sat on a junked sofa, or chairs, or on the floor. Danny saw a few girls. They lounged sluttishly against the walls.

The Indian at the table sipped from a glass of the whiskey. Danny watched a long, irridescent beetle crawl across the table. "You feel the guns in your back?"

Danny's guards shoved the rifle barrels hard into his spine. He had the shakes so badly he could barely stand.

"That's so you'll keep cool while I talk. I'm Lone Dog."

Danny's tired heart surged at the name. So drained was his spirit and so spent was his body that he couldn't summon the rage to leap over the table and strangle the man who had ordered his wife shot. A sense of unreality distorted the moment.

Lone Dog laughed. "You're pretty calm, man. How come you didn't bring any cops with you? You crazy?"

Danny heaved a big, shuddering breath. His blood began to pump now, slowly and steadily. He began to deal with the presence of his wife's killer. "I didn't want cops," he said. "You wouldn't've showed yourself."

Lone Dog glanced at his friends and drank more whiskey. "No, man, that's true. So you got to see me. Not many white men get the chance. I'm a wolf witch, baby. I go into the desert and nobody can find me."

Danny choked on futility and madness. The mocking face in front of him seemed to melt and swirl. He worked saliva into his arid mouth and spat at Lone Dog. Very little moisture came out. Lone Dog snarled and swiped at his face. The Indians behind Danny clubbed him with rifle butts. Danny felt the heavy blows crack open his skull. White lights crashed in front of his eyes and flame shot through his neck. He moaned and fell.

He was dragged to his feet. "Hey, don't take it personally," Lone Dog said. "We didn't care which one of you white scum we killed. It was a message. And nobody listened. So we do it again."

"She was my *wife*," Danny mumbled, half-crazed with pain. He wept silently, blinded by tears. "Oh God, I want her back. . . ."

Lone Dog shook his head. "What a shit. Hey, *bravos*, do a good job on him. Kill him slow. We'll ship him back in little pieces."

He swallowed the last of his whiskey. His face flushed with anticipation, and his pants bulged with an erection at the thought of the bestial murder to come. Danny felt his chest ice at the realization; for the first time since he began his odyssey, he knew fear. The will to live stirred in the pit of his soul, and he shook his head and pleaded. "No . . . don't kill me . . ."

Lone Dog glared at Danny, and his eyes were cold and deadly. "Do it."

Danny was struck again in the head, and went down. He felt as if he were falling through a tunnel. His side exploded in red agony and he knew he'd been kicked. His failing eyes saw weirdly distorted images of the others in the room laughing and drinking. He scrabbled with bloodied hands, trying to grab a leg, a rifle, anything.

He heard a sudden, deafening whine and for a moment he thought it was damage from the blows to his head. But he recognized the whistling drone. His beating stopped.

"Son of a bitch!" Lone Dog screamed. His eyes blazed and his gray lips curled back. He yanked a pistol from his pants. Other gang members cocked their rifles.

Danny lay still. The helicopters outside hovered overhead. Then, like a shocking voice inside his head, words penetrated the shack: "ATTENTION! THIS IS THE POLICE! MAKE IT EASY ON YOURSELVES! COME OUT WITH YOUR HANDS ON YOUR HEADS, ONE AT A TIME!"

Lone Dog stood by the table, enraged. He looked at Danny with loathing. "How did you get them here?"

Danny lay in a warm slick of his blood. "I didn't . . ."

"Get away from him!" Lone Dog screamed. "He's mine!"

Lone Dog stretched out his skinny arm and aimed the pistol. Danny looked into the black hole of the muzzle. At the same time, he heard the splintering crack of the door being kicked in. *"Drop it!"* a voice commanded.

Lone Dog drew back his lips and hissed like a rattler. An earsplitting shot made Danny wince. Lone Dog's arm seemed to leap with a life of its own and a red blossom spread in his shoulder. Danny watched the pistol tumble from his hand and clatter onto the table. Lone Dog groaned and touched fingers to his wound.

Danny twisted his head. He saw a fat Indian boy take aim at the cops. In the next instant, Danny was half-blinded by a spit of fire, and a second explosion clapped against his ears. The fat Indian careened backwards and slammed hard against the wooden wall.

The other Indians dropped their rifles and slapped their hands on their heads. More S.W.A.T. sharpshooters swarmed in; they wore camouflage caps and flak jackets. They hurled the Indians against the cabin walls and cuffed them. Danny found strength to drag himself upright, using the table as a support. Dazed and hurting, he stared at Lone Dog.

Later, Danny couldn't recall the instant he went mad. He felt his body lunge across the table. In a frenzy, he threw his arms around Lone Dog and tackled him to the floor. Lone Dog fell on his wounded shoulder and screamed with pain. Danny straddled the Indian and cannonaded his fists into the frightened face. He thought he saw a grinning death's head for a moment, and then he saw the Indian's skin split open and spew blood. Lone Dog's arms clawed at Danny's shoulders, but Danny felt nothing. He let every poisonous ounce of grief and outrage pour into his hands, and he let his awful sense of loss find expression in the brutality of his blows. He got off Lone Dog when there was no more face to see, and he dragged the Indian to a standing position against a wall. Now Danny pistoned vicious punches to Lone Dog's ribs and chest and stomach, grunting with each blow. He heard ribs crack and organs crush, and the sounds flooded Danny with relief.

The police detective who had helped Danny look through photos motioned the S.W.A.T. captain to hold off. The cops herded the other Indians outside and the S.W.A.T. captain cleared his throat and looked away. The detective adjusted his sunglasses and watched the beating go on.

Finally, the detective and two other cops wrestled Danny away from the horrid mass of gore that was Lone Dog. The Indian toppled over and sprawled on the floor. The cops picked him up and carried him out. The detective lit a cigarette as he surveyed the blood-sprayed cabin.

"He'll be a hurting for a long time," he said.

Danny let himself be led outside, too. The blazing sunlight seared his eyes and he put up broken fingers to shield them. He began to feel the swollen agony in his hands, but it didn't matter.

Danny watched as the Indians were prodded aboard three police choppers, while three more circled overhead. Lone Dog was strapped to a gurney, and EMT's started an I.V. and gave him oxygen. "How did you know where I was?" Danny asked.

The detective allowed a rare smile. "I figured you were ready to do something crazy. I had you tailed. When you left the Eagle Inn, I had a homing device planted under the hood of the jeep. When the jeep stopped in the middle of the desert, we figured you'd been picked up, so we moved in. From the sky, starting with the jeep's position, we found this place easily."

Danny watched the end of the nightmare and sweated in the sun. It made no difference, really. Nothing mattered without Terri, and nothing would make sense of her stupid, cruel death. But for the first time, as the choppers lifted off in clouds of red dust, Danny felt the possibility of life.

chapter 29

JASON and Lacey walked barefoot on pink sand, along a secluded island beach. When they came to a curved strand that jutted into the water, they stopped. Jason unfurled a beach towel and dropped onto it, stomach down. Lacey sat next to him and took a bottle of suntan oil from a straw bag. She unzipped her shiny maillot to expose most of her tanned breasts, and whipped off her straw hat.

Jason peered at the Pacific, and the sails that punctuated the horizon. Further down the beach, the surf rose majestically and curled down watery alleys. Jason was getting a headache from the roar of it, and from the blast of rock music on nearby radios. He was glad when Lacey came back from taking a phone call and suggested this walk.

He folded his arms and rested his cheek on them. Lacey massaged fragrant oil into his back. "Like that?" she asked.

"Mmm."

She laughed. "Not talkative."

"I don't talk when I'm in ecstasy."

She laughed again, falsely. Though the afternoon was bright and calm, and though ginger and plumeria filled the air with their exotic odors, Jason was stormy inside. The false note in Lacey's voice sounded more dissonant each day. He'd heard it first—hell, he didn't remember when he'd heard it first, but he heard it now. Jason knew he was not the same man he'd been before Amanda. More and more coldly, he saw what he'd allowed himself to become. More and more brokenly, he realized that Amanda's love for him was the first good thing that had ever happened. Her strength, her humor, her special quality of life had nearly made him a man. Courage began to grow in him as his ache for Amanda grew more urgent.

Lacey's fingers worked perfunctorily, the way her body worked in bed. Why hadn't he noticed that, too? She performed like a paid whore, and she faked her orgasms. He smiled ruefully. He'd been so busy gratifying his ego that he hadn't paid attention.

"What are you thinking about?" she asked.

"Me."

"What about you?"

"What the hell I'm doing here."

Her fingers moved up to his creased neck and touched the tips of his ears. "You're on vacation."

"My whole life is a vacation. Why another R&R right now? Does Helen want us to get married?"

Lacey's fingers spidered down his ribs and dug below the waistband of his trunks. "Would you hate that a lot?"

Jason turned over, forcing Lacey to lift her hands. He propped himself on one elbow. "Wouldn't *you* hate it?"

"I care a lot for you, Jason. I didn't think it would get this serious."

"I didn't know you *were* this serious."

She toyed with a comma of his hair. "And you're not?"

He tried to fathom this. "I haven't thought about it a lot. I've only been serious twice in my life. Once I won't talk about, and once was Amanda."

"Oh."

"Don't be upset. I heal slowly."

"I'm just impatient."

"*Do* you love me?"

She rested her hands in her lap, and nodded tightly. "Uh-huh."

He sat up all the way and draped an arm around her hunched shoulders. "I don't know how to respond to that."

She shook her head, her eyes lowered. "You don't have to respond. You didn't make any promises."

There it was, the false note. Jason knew something was off key, though every one of her words and gestures was right. He'd been with too many women to miss the signals. As sure as he knew that Amanda was for real, he knew that Lacey was phony. Or maybe it was his own twisted fear. Maybe the kid was hurting and he was being cynical.

"I'm a few years older than you, Lacey."

She looked up at him. "So what? Oh, Jason, couldn't we just go away for a while? Not one of Helen's little trips, but you and me, together, where *we* want to go? We could get ourselves straight and know for sure."

Her words stroked him like magic hands. She knew what he longed for. "Helen would be pissed. You're her wonder girl."

"The designs are done," Lacey said. "Construction is way behind and it's going to be months before interior work. I'm serious, Jason. I know it's a whim, but we're not working out. You feel the tension too much, and I don't blame you."

"True." He framed her face between his hands and she leaned forward to be kissed. He caressed her mouth and her tongue sipped at his inner cheeks. Her hands slipped over his hot shoulders and her body arched against him like willow against steel. She teased him with the softness of her naked skin.

Her breath was warm. "You don't think you can ever love, Jason. But I know a good thing when I find it, and I haven't had a lot of good things. All I want with you is some time."

Christ, why was he throwing roadblocks in his path? Amanda had loved him, but Amanda was gone. Nothing was going to change. Now Lacey offered surrender and devotion and he needed that. He was scraping forty and pretty soon he'd be too old to be a gigolo for Helen. And somehow, he cared now about living. Amanda had done that for him, too.

He released Lacey and sprang to his feet, agitated. He was torn between the memory of the one woman and the promise of another. Lacey remained seated on the towel. "What's wrong, Jason?"

"*I'm* wrong," he growled. He looked out at the silver ocean, studded with sun-diamonds. "I throw away beautiful things."

"You haven't thrown *me* away."

"I'm working on it."

She stood up and stopped behind him. He could feel the warm puffs of her breath on his back. "I know you're afraid of things, Jason. I know you have secrets. But it doesn't matter. Whatever is hurting your heart, I can heal. Haven't I proved my feelings for you?"

The question rankled him. Lord, he was suspicious. Maybe it was Helen's outlandish sponsorship of Jason and Lacey, compared to her pathological fear of Jason and Amanda.

"You have nothing to prove," he said. He turned to her. "I need some space. I need to listen to my own voice."

"I know," she said. "And that's why I think we should go away . . . where we can both listen, to ourselves and to each other. That's what we both need."

He shook his head, baffled. Lacey was looking so sincerely at him; how in hell could he doubt her?

A chill ran down his back as he suddenly realized something about her, but he couldn't verbalize what he'd seen. The comprehension came and went in a flash and left him worried. "It would be good," he admitted. "God knows it would ease my load to get away. If Helen agrees."

"I think she will," Lacey said enthusiastically. "She likes me a lot. I think I'm like a daughter she never had."

He laughed. "Helen never had ovaries, let alone a child. She's all brass inside."

"Oh, I think she has some kindness and warmth in her. But I'm kind of a marshmallow anyway. I always look for the good side in people."

He listened to the hiss of the breakers. "I'd like to see Amanda once more," he said.

"Do you have to?"

"We never ended it, Lacey. I can't live that way."

She sighed angrily. "Forgive me for being so obviously jealous."

"No, it's endearing." He smiled. "I've got to lay the ghosts to rest, before I can be free for you."

Lacey snickered. "You don't want to see the ghosts, babe."

She caught herself the instant she let the words escape, but it was an instant too late. Jason saw her face color and watched her turn away, infuriated. "Why do you say that?" he asked.

Lacey shook her head. "No reason. I'm a genuine nerd."

"Don't be so hard on yourself."

"I *should* be. If I have any confidence in you, I can wait and you'll come back to me."

"Assuming I can find Amanda at all. Do you know where she is?"

Lacey shook back her hair, which was blowing in the breeze. "Why would I?"

"Just now, it sort of sounded like you knew something."

"Not me."

He walked closer to the shore, until wavelets broke over

his feet. He felt very close to some kind of truth. "She might be in New York. Has she checked into the office?"

"No," Lacey said. "She must still be devastated over Danny."

"That's right." He glanced at Lacey. "Aren't you?"

"Oh, Jason. Don't probe for my inadequacies; there are so many. I was never very close with Danny. Of *course* I'm broken up about that horrible murder. Who wouldn't be?"

He put up his hands. "Okay, drop it. I was being a louse."

Lacey smiled bravely. "Thanks. Sometimes I try too hard."

"Lighten up," he said. He locked his fingers around her neck and she bent down to touch foreheads with him. He kissed her hair. "I guess I ought to feel worse about the murder," he said. "I probably would if I stopped strutting on center stage."

"Don't do that to yourself!"

"Oh, let me enjoy whipping myself." He grunted. "That's what they ought to do to that Indian bastard. Whip him to death. If they ever find him."

"They *did* find him," Lacey said, "didn't you read . . ."

Her face went dead pale. Jason stepped away from her. "They found who? Lone Dog?"

She seemed paralyzed.

"Lacey, what's the matter? For Christ's sake, is it Amanda?"

He realized in that moment that Amanda's death would be intolerable. Lacey waved her hand distractedly. "No . . . no, nothing . . ."

"Who did they find?" Jason demanded.

She took a breath. "They found Lone Dog."

"Who found him?"

"The cops."

Jason stemmed his rising impatience. "Look. Something bad has happened. When did you hear all this?"

She averted her eyes and twisted her hands together. "It was on the radio . . ."

"When?"

"Just before."

"Okay," Jason said. "Tell me the whole story."

Lacey had turned completely around and faced the wildly blooming foliage. A bird flashed in the trees. "Lone Dog was in a shack. Danny Rosetti went out hunting him, and Lone Dog grabbed him."

"Danny?"

"Yeah. But the cops put a homing device in Danny's jeep and they came in with choppers and got the whole gang."

She seemed drained of spirit. Jason knew he'd pressured her into saying what she hadn't wanted to say. Now he needed to break her down, coolly and methodically. "Okay, that's good news. That's fantastic news."

"Yes, it is."

"Then what's eating you? Why didn't you want to tell me?"

She lifted her head. "I don't know. I just didn't want to talk about other things. I didn't want to get off the subject again. Damn it, Jason, why are you putting me through this? All I said was that I want to be with you and you're tormenting me."

She was crying. Jason looked harshly at her. "I'm not doing that, Lacey. Not by asking you what you heard on the radio."

"I'm sorry. I'm being a jerk."

He sighed. "Hey look, let's go back. I want to see the papers. I want to see Danny if I can. In fact—Jesus! If Lone Dog is under arrest and Danny's responsible, Amanda's probably in Bradley right now. Or at least she's phoned in. Listen, here's my chance to have it over with. Then we can catch Helen and announce our getaway plans."

Lacey turned back. "Why? What's the rush?"

"No rush. It's just a good opportunity."

"You're really hot for her."

"Get off it, Lacey. You're beating this too hard."

"*You're* the one carrying the torch."

Jason bristled at her tone. "Hey, Lacey, I can't deal with this kind of fishwife jealousy."

"You want her? Go to her."

"I want to say *goodbye*, damn it."

"Yeah, you go say goodbye. You'd better not wave though, because she sure as hell won't see you."

"What does *that* mean?"

Lacey stood with her legs apart, glaring at him. She was in deep emotional trouble right now, falling apart. "None of your business."

Jason stepped toward her, anger building. "Okay, baby. I think it's time we talked. Something's going on."

"Just your attitude, man."

"Talk to me, Lacey."

"Suck ice."

Anger swept over Jason like a refreshing hot shower, tearing him loose from his torpor. He moved to Lacey in three lithe steps, and pinned her arm behind her back. She arched against him, a bow poised to shoot deadly arrows. She writhed, and hissed with pain.

"Let go," she gasped.

"What do you know about Amanda?"

"Nothing."

He tightened his grip and she groaned. "Let's go swimming, baby."

She shook her head and screamed. He clamped a hand over her warm mouth and dragged her down the beach as she twisted and fought. His ankles felt the cold swirl of salt water. He backed further into the surf until waves broke at their chests. She tried to cry out beneath his hand. The water frothed at her chin.

"Talk," he said.

She shook her head.

He took his hand from her mouth and shoved her head underwater. He held her there as sweat broke out on his back. He let her up. She gagged, water dribbling from the sides of her mouth. "You'll die out here," he warned.

She heaved for air, limp now in his grasp. The water foamed around them. Jason clawed his toes into the mud. "You're crazy," she choked.

"What's wrong with Amanda?"

Lacey took more gulps of air. "She's blind."

The words struck Jason like a swung baseball bat. "How?"

"I don't know."

"How?"

She thrashed her head wildly. "A nerve disease," she spat. "That's all I know. She came back to New York and then she flew out to Bradley."

"Is that where she is now?"

"Yes."

"Is that why you wanted to go away with me?"

"Yes."

Jason struggled to stay upright as waves buffeted him. "You don't love me, right?"

"I never loved you."

"What kind of crazy act was it? Why?"

"Figure it out."

"You bitch." He pressed both palms on top of her forehead and ducked her again. He let her up and she gasped piteously. He kept one arm firmly around her bowed back, one hand wrapped in her wet hair. "No more games, Lacey."

She cried now, broken at last.

"Why did you pretend to love me?" he asked.

"Helen wanted me to."

"Helen?" Jason paused while his wounded pride generated rage. "Why?"

"She wanted you and Amanda to be apart."

"Why?"

"I don't know," Lacey wept. "Goddamn it, I don't know everything."

"You sure don't. I can take a good guess, though. Is that why you happened to be eating lunch in front of my building?"

"That's right."

"And all those nights and days . . . you're good. You're very good. But there was always something unreal about it. I should have trusted my instinct."

"Well, you didn't."

"No, I didn't. What's Helen paying you?"

"Lots."

"And you get to design The Pueblo, too. Did Helen make Amanda blind?"

"No. I don't think so. Amanda didn't say she did."

"But Helen took advantage of the situation, as she always does. So we were going to take a long vacation, where I wouldn't be near Amanda. And Amanda would go away forever and not challenge Helen. What would happen then, Lacey? Would you have married me?"

She looked at him with loathing. "No."

"I guess you would have waited for more instructions. Is that why we took a walk? Because you heard about Lone Dog and didn't want me to hear?"

"Yes. Helen phoned me and told me. There were too many radios on the beach."

Jason shook his head and laughed. "My God. What a pair. No morals at all."

"They don't do much good, do they?"

"Well, they can make you whole. But who cares about that in Yuppieland, huh? Just go for the BMW and the condo and the sushi and the Calvins, and to hell with being human. You're a real case."

"Sorry you don't like me."

"Hey, I'm a senior member of this club. I sold my soul a long time ago. I'm tanned from the flames of hell, baby. But you're young and you've got it all . . . and you wasted it. Damn. Didn't you get a rise out of me at all?"

"No."

Jason's eyes narrowed as the realization he'd had earlier popped into his mind. "Right," he whispered, getting it. "*That's* what I noticed. Whenever you looked at me, you always looked at my face, always at my eyes."

"It's more sincere."

"It also means you're gay. One thing I've got—shit, the only damn thing I've got—is my body. Women cream over it."

"Modest, huh?"

"Just realistic. But you never let your eyes touch my body. It never turned you on."

"It made me sick."

He looked sad. "And you screwed me anyway, against your nature. . . . God, you're a little cobra, to go through all of that just to ace out Amanda. Why? It's got to be more than money. It's got to be personal."

"That's right," she said. "It's personal."

His legs and torso shivered in the water, as the sun began to dry his hair. The water reflected harshly in her face. "Why would you want to take me away from Amanda so badly?" The answer presented itself almost immediately. "It's Amanda, isn't it? You wanted Amanda, and she didn't want you. It was stupid, infantile jealousy, and you couldn't take the rejection. You couldn't shrug it off and find another lover like a mature human being. You had to get *revenge* because your whim wasn't gratified."

He cracked his hand across her mouth and she squealed in pain. He held her wet, trembling form tightly. "Video kids . . . bang bang bang, turn it on, grab it, feel it . . . don't wait for anything, don't work at anything, just scratch your itch or hit back, because it's all coming to you. Women have played me for a sucker before, but you're pathetic. You've got beauty and brains and talent and you throw them away. Forget your fame and fortune, little girl. You're getting a good spanking and going to bed without supper."

He spun her and shoved her rudely ahead of him. She managed to stagger through the waves until finally she collapsed on the mud, soaked and freezing. Jason stood over her, his chest heaving with exertion. "We're catching a plane back," he said. "You'll stay with me. You won't get near a phone to warn Helen." He scooped up the beach towel, her hat, and the straw bag, and nudged her with his toe. "Get up."

Lacey painfully struggled to her feet and avoided looking at Jason. She limped on the pink sand, with Jason following. Jason tasted a sour disgust with himself for callously hurting Amanda and for embracing cowardice as a lifestyle. He also felt a renewed, blazing love for Amanda, and whispered a desperate prayer that she'd be there, blind or not, whole or not, to talk to him again and help him drag himself out of the stinking swamp of his life.

Amanda paced Helen's office with the coiled rage of a lioness. She knew every foot of the 35′ by 20′ room. Her palms had memorized the plushness of the upholstery velvet and the smoothness of the linen wallcovering. She could draw the space from memory, but she couldn't get out of it.

She cursed. Her clothes felt grimy. Her brain raced but she couldn't think of any way out. Her hands throbbed from pounding on the glass doors. Nobody had heard.

She stood now by the draped window, unable to look out. Her heart filled with memories of Jason, and with terrible sadness. But she nursed her fury, determined to stay sane until she was released.

The door clicked open. She turned. "Who is it?"

There was no answer. Amanda punctured the air with her hands.

A soft laugh identified the intruder as Helen. "You look ridiculous," she said. "Who did you think it would be?"

"I thought you weren't coming back," Amanda said. "Can I leave now?"

"No, you can't leave," Helen said. "My plans have changed. Until I finalize everything, you can sit tight."

Despair drove through Amanda's chest like a bullet. "You can't lock me in here. This isn't the goddamn Middle Ages, Helen."

"It's whatever I want it to be."

"How will you stop me from going after you? Are you going to kill me?"

"If I have to."

Amanda exhaled in disgust and gripped the drape cord. "I'm disappointed. This isn't the way a top businesswoman operates."

"Shut up," Helen snapped. Amanda heard her walking around in the office. "And get the hell away from my desk."

"Let me go and I'll keep off your property," Amanda shot back.

Helen seized Amanda's shoulder and hurled her aside. Amanda lost her balance and crashed into the wall before righting herself. She stood gasping and biting back tears. Helen said, "Don't play tit for tat with me. I meant it about killing you. I play hardball. You will not mess up my life."

"So fight me in court," Amanda said. "I'm a blind woman. Play fair."

"Not on your life," Helen said. "*Shit!*"

The last word came at the sound of the intercom. Helen snapped "What is it?"

The thin voice said, "Helen, Jason Turner is on his way up."

Amanda drew a quick breath and couldn't believe how fast her heart raced. God, she hadn't imagined how much she'd missed him.

Helen said, "You're going into the conference room, Amanda. It's soundproofed, so don't bother screaming."

"Can't you see the nonsense is over?"

"Yes, I *can* see—but you can't."

Amanda heard Helen opening a door. She tried to locate the sound and move away from it. But Helen's hands were suddenly at Amanda's back, shoving. Amanda stumbled. It was not possible to fight; she couldn't balance herself. The breath whooshed out of Amanda as she was shoved again, hard. She felt herself fall, and hit the carpeting. She lay prone, catching her breath, as the door clicked shut.

"Damn," she cursed. She got to her feet, felt for the wall and the door. With both fists, she banged on the wood, and cried out Jason's name. But she heard nothing through the walls and she knew that nobody heard her.

Helen sat at her desk and arranged her hair with her fingers. She knew her face was flushed with exertion. When the intercom buzzed again, she punched the button and said, "If it's Jason, send him in."

She sat back, and watched Jason come into the office.

God, the man was beautiful. His suntan would win prizes, and his white linen suit showed it off spectacularly. But something was wrong with this picture. His walk was too determined, his sun-crinkled eyes too ferocious. He was bloodthirsty. And why the hell was he back from Hawaii anyway?

"Good afternoon," she said. "Nothing to do in the islands?"

"Not much," Jason said evenly. "After awhile, one beach gets to look like another."

"Where's Lacey?"

"Back at my place."

Helen drummed with her fingers on the desk. "So what's up, doc? I have loads to do."

"Really?" he said. "Your desk looks clear."

"Sign of a good executive."

"The thing is," Jason said, "Lacey and I want to go away for a few months. Be with each other. We're deeply in love."

Helen wondered how to react. He was parroting the script she'd given Lacey. And he sure didn't sound lovelorn. "This is something of a surprise, Jason. What do you mean by a few months?"

"Well, hell, make it forty years."

"What's coming down, Jason? Don't waste my time."

"Why not? You wasted mine."

"Ho-kay. Masturbate in private, little boy; it's nicer that way. I'll be back tomorrow morning."

She stood up and came around the desk. Jason stepped into her path.

"No more horseshit," Jason said in a low voice. "I want to see Amanda."

"So do a lot of other people."

"Cut it. I almost drowned Lacey in Hawaii. She's locked up in my apartment right now, tied to a chair. I gave her a fat lip. Now you know I'm capable of killing, Helen, and I'm as close as I ever was. Do you read me?"

Helen was not used to being outmaneuvered, but this was an effective, if crude, check. "Jason, I can read your anger. But I can't respond to physical threats. . . ."

He laughed. "You just don't quit, do you? Helen, I know it all. About the setup with Lacey, about Amanda's blindness. What did you do, dump her down a sewer? Just how desperate are you?"

"Pretty desperate," she replied. "Maybe you'd better not mess with me."

"Helen, my patience is—"

A terrific thump made Helen wince. It was a heavily muffled sound, but it made the room shake. Jason's eyes darted to the conference room door. "What the hell was that?"

"Big mice," Helen said. "Let's talk somewhere else."

Jason brushed her aside and strode to the door. He turned back to Helen. "If she's in there, I think you ought to have the grace to get your ass out of the office. If not, we'll go find her together."

Helen could not stop trembling. "Have your good times, Jason. You're finished."

"Anything's better than what I had."

Helen composed her face, and walked stiffly from the office. Jason waited until Helen was gone, then pushed open the door. He saw Amanda standing wildly near the custom-made circular table, half leaning against the rear wall. One of the orange-upholstered chairs lay rocking on its side, and the linen on another wall was ripped. Amanda breathed heavily, a little stunned, but absolutely beautiful.

"You threw the chair," he marveled.

"Jason . . ."

He could barely contain the soaring of his heart. "Let me get you to a doctor," he said.

"I'm blind, Jason," she said.

"I know."

"Then why the hell are you here? Get out. You don't need a blind lady."

"Why not?" he said, and his voice gave out. "I've been a blind man."

And then he forgot words, and swept her into his embrace.

chapter 30

DR. Klein turned his palms downward on his desk. ''I think we've focused on it,'' he said to Jason and Amanda.

''Go on,'' Jason said tautly.

Behind his designer glasses, Dr. Klein was a small, frail looking man with ginger hair. He was a renowned ophthalmic specialist, recommended both by Dr. Mitchell and Dr. Fabiano. He'd put Amanda through a series of tests, on the latest equipment, and now he had results. Amanda held her breath.

''I don't see confirming evidence of the nervous disease Dr. Mitchell suspected,'' Dr. Klein said. ''Though the symptoms *do* suggest it, and with your mother's case history, you had reason to worry.''

Amanda's breath rushed out of her and she felt herself trembling. Jason pressed strong, reassuring fingers into her knotted shoulder. ''Is that good news?'' he asked.

''To the extent that a nervous disease would not be curable, yes,'' Dr. Klein said. ''There seems to be no permanent damage to the retina. But—'' As he paused, the tension gathered again, like a coiled predator. ''The tests *do* confirm a growth pressing on your optic nerve.''

Amanda nodded, biting her lip. ''Dr. Mitchell said he'd found a tumor.''

Jason said, ''So what's the bottom line?''

''The growth seems to have been there for some time,'' Dr. Klein said. ''It's either shifted position or grown, and shut off Miss Gray's sight permanently.''

'Is the growth malignant?'' Amanda asked.

"I can't tell you that," Klein answered. "We'd have to remove it and take a biopsy."

"All right."

Klein leaned back, stroking a pencil. "Not so fast. This is high-risk surgery. The tumor is in a dangerous position. Even with it out, there might be irreparable damage to the optic nerve and you might remain blind. You might suffer brain damage. The mass might have metastasized too far to be helped. You might die as a result of the surgery. Please don't assume that your problems have gone away."

Amanda sat thoughtfully. "If I don't have the surgery, I'll never see again?"

"That's a reasonable prognosis," Dr. Klein said.

"And if it's a tumor, and *is* malignant, I'll die."

"Yes."

Amanda exhaled softly, shouldering the burden. "Then there's no choice, is there?"

"Yeah, there's a choice," Jason said hotly. "There's the choice of staying alive—"

"Forget it," Amanda said. "You know me better than that. I don't sit around waiting for death. I *could* learn to live blind, if I had to. But if there's a chance, any chance, then that's the way I have to go."

Jason slumped in his chair, angry. Amanda smiled and covered his hand with hers. "Don't be upset. It's the first hope I've had in a long time. And you're here." She lifted her head and spoke to the doctor. "When can the operation be scheduled?"

"We could have you in the medical center in Albuquerque in two days if you wanted. I'd want Jack Levine to do the surgery; he's the best in the country."

Amanda tightened her hand on Jason's. "Let's go for it."

Jason looked at Amanda, flooded with love. He wanted to fold her into his arms and protect her—as he'd failed to protect her from the cockroaches who'd raped her. But Amanda didn't want protection. He tried to imagine losing her again, losing her forever. He grew sick with the thought. But then, he hadn't told her the truth yet.

And after everything that had happened, she was asking for his strength.

"Sure," he said. "I'm scared but we have to try."

She smiled radiantly. "Good." To Dr. Klein she said, "Let's set it up."

Dr. Klein's eyes flickered with admiration. "I'll have to make some calls, and you'll have to see Dr. Levine for an exam and a consultation."

"Of course."

Jason stood. "Amanda, why didn't you get the second opinion right away, as Dr. Mitchell told you to?"

Amanda said, "I *wanted* to accept that first diagnosis. Maybe it was the best way to finally stop fighting." She sighed. "And Byron was right there when I went out of control, and he made me believe the lie I told myself."

Amanda grew thoughtfully silent as she mulled this over in perspective. Jason glanced at her. "What's on your mind?"

Amanda shook her head. "Silly thoughts. About a man who creates situations and moves people around like chess pieces. Who would have wanted me to think I'd inherited my blindness and that it was hopeless."

"Byron . . ."

Amanda let Jason help her up. "Maybe." She gripped both of Jason's hands. "I'm going to need you very much, darling. The Pueblo is reaching the point of no return. The walls are going up, and soon it will be prohibitive to redesign. We've got to act fast. Submit our design and sell it."

"I know," Jason said.

"You may have to carry the ball alone while I'm in the hospital. Will you?"

"Sure."

"Jason, don't pacify me."

"I said I'd do it." His head throbbed. Christ, he didn't know if he could spill his soul to Amanda, or join her in a quixotic fight against Helen. And when Amanda knew the truth, would she have any fight left?

It didn't matter now. Amanda's face shone with hope and love, and her slender body tautened with determination. Jason would take any chance to hold on to her, even if it ended in a few days, even if she died.

"Thank you, doctor," Amanda said. "Please call me as soon as everything is set up. I need to move quickly."

"Will do," Dr. Klein said. He smiled reassuringly, but his eyes showed grave doubt. Only Jason saw the doctor's eyes and he said nothing to Amanda.

Heather curled, naked, on her imposing Sheraton bed. Her clear-skinned body seemed out of place under the carved and painted cornice, and the striped canopy. This formal bedroom was no sleeping place for a sixteen-year-old girl. But Heather didn't miss the flounces of girlhood; she knew only this elegant chamber, and loved it.

She waited for Byron. He'd said nothing when he learned that Amanda was gone. Heather heard him make a lot of phone calls and watched him spend hours on the portico, just looking out at the ocean. She became frightened when he lapsed into brooding silence; she didn't understand his moods.

But today he'd had lunch with her. He'd smiled and joked, and ordered wine to be served. He bought her a beautiful jade charm on a gold rope. He talked about her singing, and about bringing in professional writers to shape up her act. Heather had soaked up his attention and trembled with joy.

This afternoon, he'd asked if he could come to her room. "I need to be with you," he'd said.

"Yes!" she'd cried. "I've missed you so much."

He'd only smiled, a very sad smile. "Wait for me."

Now she waited, and her skin buzzed. She lay on her side, flipping the pages of a magazine, but not reading. Her hair fell loosely to the sheet, and draped her bare shoulder. Her breasts were hard-peaked with desire, the nipples swollen and painful. God, why was she so hyper? She could feel herself getting wet.

Her door opened with a soft unlatching sound, and Byron came in. He wore a dark blue robe that looked very handsome on him, but for the first time, he looked old. Maybe it was the way the light struck his granite face. The lines stood out, deeply etched, and his neck hung in folds. His gray hair was uncombed.

"You should be painted like that," he said to Heather. "In this light, on that bed."

She felt herself grow warm. "Thank you."

He went to the window and arranged the draperies to diffuse the late afternoon light. The sky outside was white with late summer haze. Byron looked out for a moment, as if caught by some activity. Then he turned to Heather. With a barely audible sigh, he sat on the edge of the bed and drew his fingers along her flank. She shut her eyes and her lips parted in pleasure. "That's so good . . ." she murmured.

"How did Amanda get off the grounds?" he asked.

Heather's eyes flew open. She turned, making the bed squeak. "What?"

"I never did ask you. How did she find her way out?"

Heather's heart thumped beneath her breasts. "She rode down the beach, I guess. I know she went riding . . ."

"Yes," he said. "I remember you telling me something about that. Amanda always was resourceful."

Heather stretched and yearned toward Byron, her naked body a question mark. "Do we have to talk about her? I'm glad she's gone."

"You should never be jealous, Heather. What you can't hold on to is not yours."

"I'm sorry."

He gathered her close and she nestled her face in his shoulder and threw her arms around him. "How did Amanda find the way by herself?"

Heather clung to Byron, terrified. "I don't know."

"How did she return the horse? They were all stabled when I came home."

Heather said nothing.

"And why did Amanda take two horses? There were two sets of hoofprints on the beach, going and coming back. But coming back, there was only one rider."

Heather pulled away from Byron and flung herself sullenly on the sheets. "You just want to hound me."

"I *would* appreciate the truth."

Heather buried her face in the pillow. She blinked out tears and looked idly at the mezzotint hanging on the wall. "Okay, I helped her. I didn't want her around. But *she* asked *me*. I swear it."

"I believe you," Byron said. His hand cupped her rear end and messaged the mounds tenderly. His fingers strayed to her upturned vagina and sank in, making her gasp. With sure motions, he made her flow. The tip of his forefinger rubbed her throbbing clitoris. She felt her organ swell and ache.

"Byron . . ." she groaned.

"I misjudged Amanda," he said, almost dreamily. "But I don't want to misjudge you, Heather. Don't lie to me again."

"No . . ."

"And don't take actions like this on yourself."

"I won't."

"You've been a terrible disappointment."

His fingers never stopped. Heather wept helplessly and bit down on her finger as she climaxed. He withdrew and stood up. She sobbed on the bed, feeling wet and cold. She heard

Byron take off his robe. He slipped into bed with her and the heat of his body pressed against her. She closed her eyes and kissed him, thrusting her tongue deep into his mouth. He returned the kiss coldly but expertly. He pried her head back with his hands. She felt the stickiness of her orgasm on his fingers. He licked her lips and touched his tongue to her teeth.

"Do you love me, Heather?"

"Yes."

"Completely?"

"Yes."

"For always?"

"Yes."

"*You* won't leave me, will you?"

She shook her head, drenched in her tears. "No."

"You'll never betray me?"

"No."

"I need to believe in your love, Heather. I'm very hurt."

She flung her arms around his neck and tried to tell him with her eyes. "Believe me, Byron. I need you."

"I think you do. I think you really do."

"I swear to you."

"I think you depend utterly on me."

"Yes."

He sighed. "That's so good to hear."

He urged her onto her back and she wriggled in anticipation. He dropped soft kisses on her pulsing throat and on each of her shadowed breasts, moving across the mounds and tonguing the nipples into glistening peaks. He pressed his lips to her flat, smooth stomach and tongued her navel. She panted with excitement. He rained kisses at the crease of her thighs. He nuzzled the fur between her legs and lazily draped his tongue inside, lapping the pink folds of her inner lips. She felt herself contract and swell. He tongued her clitoris to red fullness again. She clawed his back with her fingers. Her head thrashed from side to side. She felt perspiration break out the length of her body.

Byron mounted her. She looked up into his aroused face and her hands wildly rubbed the steel musculature of his body. She traced his flanks and belly and chest, then drew her palms along his turgid organ. Her heart nearly burst.

Byron descended and the tip of his manhood split her. She drew back her lips in a rictus of ecstasy and closed her eyes.

He plunged deeper than he'd ever been before; he was so huge this afternoon, thick and hard as marble. She let her fingers race up and down his damp back as he stroked with deliberate ferocity. She tucked her legs up against his hips and moved with him, sucking him deeper inside, milking him. This was the only time she could be sure that she made him happy.

He went rigid so suddenly and fiercely that she stopped breathing. His eyes became twin red suns. He gouted into her, pumping like a severed artery. Then he was done. But he stayed poised above her, looking down half in pity, half in rage. She reached up and touched his hair. He put a finger to her wet face.

"You have absolutely no regard for yourself," he said. "You never will."

She didn't understand him. "I love you . . ."

"You don't know what love is. Loves takes will, and spirit, and life. You're not alive. You died years ago."

"What's wrong, Byron?"

"Everything's wrong, Heather. Amanda was my masterpiece. I can't accept hack work in my life. And you helped her get away. I could have brought her back. I could have made her mine again, and you ruined it."

The fear broke over Heather like a sudden attack of chills. Byron's weight felt heavy and oppressive. "I didn't mean to hurt you, Byron. . . ."

"You don't mean anything," he said disgustedly. "Couldn't you see there were no guards, no alarms? Couldn't you see I was testing her? She wouldn't have gone if you hadn't encouraged it. She'd never leave me . . ."

"Byron, she asked. I swear to God she asked—"

"I've failed with you," he said hollowly. "Totally failed."

"No . . ."

He sat up, still astride her. She looked up at the white tower of his body, bulging with muscle. His hands came to her throat like great fangs. His fingers closed on her child's neck, finding arteries and nerves. Heather's brain screamed and her eyes begged him, but his face was a stone mask. Only the eyes lived, and they burned with hate. Byron applied pressure expertly, and Heather's head became separated from her body. All her life she had despised herself, and asked to be hurt and punished. Now she wanted to live, but she felt the death of her heart, the teenager's heart that did not expect its young blood to be cut off. Then everything burst and blackness rushed in like crashing waters through a broken dam.

Byron watched dispassionately as the girl's eyes popped from their sockets like painted white balls. Her gray tongue rolled out like an escaping slug. At last she stopped jerking and thumping, and her limbs were quiet. He waited with his hands around her throat, to be sure.

Then he dismounted from the corpse and stood beside the bed. He looked down with artistic appreciation at the still warm arms and breasts and belly, and the downy pubis, still youthfully taut, and glittering with drops of his semen.

He lifted her dead wrist and checked for pulse. He let the arm drop back. He took a deep breath and put on his robe. He covered Heather with the top sheet and blanket and turned her face aside. He studied the effect, rearranging her arms and repositioning her until the effect pleased him.

He opened the drapes to let in the afternoon sun. He knew Amanda was back in New Mexico and he would go there, to complete his quest. Byron Moore never had need of constraints. Money and power brought freedom from conventions. Now his brain had found freedom from reason. He was finally, luxuriously insane, and at last he could indulge his artistry as he'd always wanted.

chapter 31

JASON and Amanda drove to the Red Creek Motel, fifty miles out of Bradley. The motel was clean, but peeling and weed-infested. Ironically, it had been built with EDA funds in the early 1970's, when the government tried to bolster the faltering Indian economy. Lacking foresight, the planners dumped the motel off the main roads, where it slowly went broke.

The bitter joke was not lost on Jason as he carried his overnight bag into the room. He knew that if he and Amanda failed the lighted bays of The Pueblo would be visible from here. He shrugged off the thought and helped Amanda take her bag inside. Their stay was going to be brief—one or two nights at most.

Jason washed up in the bathroom, approving the wrapped glass and fresh towels. The cold water felt good on his face. He returned to the room to find Amanda seated in a vinyl chair. In crisp pink blouse and striped jeans, she looked girlish and alluring.

"What's been done?" she asked.

Jason smiled at her no-nonsense attitude. "I think we've got the construction stopped for the moment," he said. "Richard Juan helped me get an injunction."

"Good," Amanda said. "On what grounds?"

"The usual. Evidence of rigged bids and faulty materials. Bradley's shopping mall had an aerial walkway collapse two years ago and twenty people died. They're skittish, and that helps."

Amanda nodded. "What else?"

Jason sat at the plastic writing desk and unclasped his

attaché case. "I've called a meeting for Tuesday. The mayor, Senator Halsey, Dan Ledda, Richard Juan, the whole group. That's when I sell them whatever we come up with."

"Then we'd better get to work."

He took out paper, drafting pencils, and tools he'd borrowed from a local architectural firm. He looked at the compasses and protractors with dull despair. It had been easy to come this far; his forte was arranging meetings and charming judges. Now was the moment of . . . of what? Truth?

"Jason?"

"I'm here."

"You're so quiet."

Outside the window, a red neon sign flashed at the raised roadbed. Cars and trucks whooshed past. Muffled noises came from other rooms. Struck by the innate loneliness of a motel room, Jason brooded. He'd painted himself into this corner deliberately, to provide no escape.

"I'm just thinking," he said.

"About what?"

He looked at her face. "About how good it is to be with you again."

She smiled. "That's nice. But we can fool around later."

'There is no later, Amanda."

Her brows knit in puzzlement. "Huh?"

He got up, unable to sit still. "When I found out that you were blind, that Lacey was suckering me, I had a choice. I could have run out on the whole stinking mess. But I came back to you."

"I approve of your choice."

"Good. Because it committed me to this."

"To what?"

"Locking the door with nowhere to run."

She stiffened, her breasts swelling under the blouse. "Is this going to be momentous?"

"You've spent your whole life fighting. Telling the truth. Taking every kind of shit and picking yourself out of the mud. You never ran away from anything."

"I never had the choice, Jason. And you forget my suicide attempts and my drug dependency. I wasn't exactly Supergirl."

"It doesn't matter," he said. "You stayed alive. When you fell down, you got back in the race. That's why I went for you. Because you *did* try to make ugliness into beauty, to make it better."

She laughed. "Jason, why are you giving me a testimonial? Is this another kiss-off?"

"No way." He sat on the bed and grabbed her. He kissed her with ferocious passion. He tried to make her feel it in her feet. Her arms went around him and clung tightly, and he filled his exhausted senses with the fullness of her breasts and the smell of her hair. This woman was his life, and he finally knew it.

She kept her hands on his shoulders. "What brought this on?"

"Remember in Montauk, when I badgered you about your life with Byron Moore?"

A tight smile tugged at her mouth. "How could I forget? I thought you were pond scum."

"I was," he agreed. "But you have to understand, babe—I'd found a mirror that showed an ugly face, and I went a little crazy."

"You're not making sense."

"I will," he promised. "Just hang on and hear me."

"Sure."

"You had—you *have*—what I'm missing. I never fought. Not for the eighteen years I've been Helen's slave. You hear me say the words?"

"It's not a shocking admission," she said.

"I know. But I pretended I couldn't do anything about it. I pretended there was no other way, because I was too scared to try."

"I can dig that."

"No you can't. You can't comprehend my kind of cowardice."

"Help me."

He let her hands go and stood up. His hands were shaking. Hastily, almost pathetically, he lit a cigarette and smoked himself calm. He went to the window and pushed aside the cheap draperies. Moist air rushed upward from the air conditioning unit. He felt light-headed. He tried to be aware of what he was giving up tonight, of what he was losing. He couldn't grasp it. That was good, because he thought if he really understood, he couldn't go on.

"I'm not going to recite the whole autobiography," he said. "If I bored you to death, you'd never have a shot at the surgery."

"I'd like to think we have lots of time."

"So would I." He felt his eyes grow weary as he inhaled and looked out the window.

Amanda had tried to get Jason to open up since she'd met him, and had sensed the other man inside the gorgeous phony. Now he was ready, but still, his sudden, emotional outpouring stunned her. For an instant, she wanted to shut him up, to put a finger on his lips and whisper that it was all right. Somehow she knew that everything would be different once he talked, and she so wanted everything to be like it was. His kiss just now had spread warm summer through her wintry soul, and her throat caught with love for him. It was enough to be together again after the mistrust and the mistakes.

But it was too late for choosing. Jason had created this moment for confession, and she needed to listen. Her nostrils contracted at the sting of his cigarette smoke, and his voice drifted from across the room.

"I told you once I was raised on a dairy farm; it was in Webster, Ohio. My folks weren't rubes. My father graduated from agricultural school and my mother taught business administration at the local community college. They weren't rich, but they got along. Mom was selfish about her space, and her time, and her work, and Dad was too burned out to play ball out on the north forty." She could tell that he smiled. "You know, we really *did* have a north forty."

"It sounds wonderful."

"Decent," he said. "No reason for me to turn out a loser."

"Easy, Jason."

"No. It's time to be hard. *I* was the screw-up. Everything that happened to me was my own work. I jerked around in school. I found out pretty early that I was gorgeous and I could charm snakes out of trees. Maybe I needed attention, I don't know. I remember I liked to draw. I could spend hours out by the barn, sketching—usually machines and buildings. My folks and my teachers thought I was pretty good. It was the only thing that held my concentration. Usually, I got bored and clowned around, and got into fights."

"Doesn't surprise me," she said.

"I came home with bloody noses and cracked teeth. Hell, maybe I wanted to disfigure myself. Who knows? Lots of dark places in the mind."

"For sure."

He paused. "I'm giving you chapter and verse. I said I wouldn't."

"I don't mind."

"I do. I'm good at talking, Amanda. I'm a riverboat man. You know that."

"I got a few doses of the Turner charm."

She heard him move around. "I grew into a hunk—a hunk of nothing. I traded on my looks. I conned teachers, broke hearts. I stole all kinds of stuff from stores and just smiled my way out the door. I got girls to do my homework. Are you still here?"

She felt her heart fill. "Is that the big secret? If I ruled out guys who'd been rotten kids, I'd have to die single."

"No, that's not the big secret. It was the beginning. I got into pumping iron—you did it in your basement, then, with mail-order stuff. And I kept drawing, but I'd begun designing houses now. I got pretty good at it. I had talent, Amanda. I swear to God I did."

Amanda's rump hurt from sitting at the edge of the bed, but she didn't dare move now. "I have no reason to think otherwise, Jason."

"Nobody else does, either. It's one hell of a scam on the world." He sighed; there was a sudden stink of smoke. Maybe he'd put out the cigarette. "My mother called me a waste, and a few other things,. Dad just didn't notice. By that time, I'd knocked up one of the local sluts, and I had to work at the garage for six months to pay for her abortion. The good news was I graduated from high school and left to go to UCLA."

"Why there?"

"Because they had beaches, and I had the body. Listen to my words, Amanda. I'm talking about a conceited son of a bitch. I got my eyes opened in L.A. Lots of pretty boys out there. I had to hustle in a car wash and play lifeguard at kiddie pools to earn food money. But I wasn't going to come back a loser."

"So you *did* have some spirit."

"Ego."

"So what? Ego drives important men."

"Nice try," he said. He sat at the desk again; she heard the chair rub against the cheap carpeting. "I did the beach scene, and used my sales talent to deal drugs. Meet me behind the concession stand, man. Want some hits? Fifty bucks for twenty-one purple hits on clear plastic—windowpane LSD.

Bags of powder, weed and pills. Acid, pot, and toot. You writing this down, babe?"

"I know the scene," Amanda said tightly. "I've been there."

He let out a breath. "Yeah, I know. My scene was lusher. Lots of the kids were rich, so I scored at good parties. I got through a few courses by making it with the teachers. Turned off yet?"

"Turned *on,*" she said dryly.

He laughed. "Keep it going for me, Amanda."

"Gladly," she said. "I wouldn't award you any medals for your youth, but I've heard worse."

"Like yours," he said genuinely. "That's why I hate my own guts. You had an excuse. I didn't. I just liked good times. Fast cars, wild parties, liquor, and foxes who went all the way. My tastes grew expensive. I met important people and I partied at estates in Beverly Hills and Marin County. Made some contacts I used later on. Spent a lot of time in redwood hot tubs with rich naked ladies. Thought I was hot shit.

"I graduated—it ain't hard in American universities, let me tell you—and I was a bum with a diploma. I bulled my way into Cooper Union in New York and jetted to the east coast. Get the picture, Amanda? I was a superstar, nowhere to go but up."

"You needed someone to guide you," she said.

To her shock, she heard tears in his voice. "Christ, Amanda, don't you see? I had all the chances, all the breaks, and I did nothing. I had no morals, no ambition, no insides. I was a plastic man. I was born without a soul."

"No!" she cried. "That isn't true. You have a soul, and a beautiful soul. I saw it and felt it the first time I met you. I didn't fall in love with a circus barker, Jason."

When he spoke, his voice was drained. "You're more than I ever deserved."

"Don't pity yourself."

"Someone's got to have pity."

"For what?"

He took a breath. "New York was a bucket of ice water. Cooper Union was for real. The teachers wanted me to be an architect. The town was heartless. Good-looking hustlers were like pigeon droppings, all over the place. I wasn't ready to wake up."

She smiled, despite her concern. "I could have told you about New York."

"Yeah, well where were you? I screwed up. I started to flunk out, and I had a hard time earning a buck. I saw a cold winter and a shameful train ride back home. I *had* to be an architect. I didn't matter that I couldn't measure up. I needed the degree. It became an obsession."

She sensed what was coming. "And you cheated for it?"

"I stole it," he said. "I got in tight with a couple of other students—brilliant, creative, innovative people. I used all my charm, and *that* was bankable. There was a competition for a building design. Ten thousand dollars and a staff position in a big development firm. One of my buddies, Eddie Randall, produced a winner. The man was inspired. I copied the design. Then I broke into the college office where the submitted designs were being kept, and I took out Eddie's entry and burned it. Then I went to Eddie's apartment—I had a key, because we were really close friends. I took all his notes and burned *them,* too. You see, Amanda? I wasn't thinking ten minutes ahead. I figured if I could win and get that job, I could disappear in the city and Eddie wouldn't have as leg to stand on. I was an addict stealing for a fix. I didn't care about reality, just about winning."

"I'm sorry for you."

"You can keep it."

She clenched her fists and tightened with emotion. "Did Eddie find out and raise the roof?"

"I was worried about that," Jason said. "I knew I had very little time before the shit hit the fan. So I took my design—the stolen one—and I went up to the chairman of that development firm the next day. I threw everything I had into it. I razzle-dazzled my way past the secretaries. The office suite was like a Roman villa. I got buzzed into the chairman's office. She looked me over hard. *Nobody* got to her without an appointment, but I'd done it."

"Her . . . ?"

"That's right."

"It was Helen," Amanda guessed.

"It sure was. Well, she saw my potential, Amanda. And when she saw the design, she freaked out. I could see the wheels spinning in her head. She picked up the phone and canceled the competition. She said she'd found her design, and her new architect."

Amanda's heart leaped with absurd pride. "Well, Jason, you were resourceful, committed, and talented. You had some positive qualities."

"Yeah," he said. "And positive stupidity. A few days later, Helen called me back and sat me down. She told me Eddie Randall had stopped by. He kept copies of his notes in a safety deposit box. So Helen knew what had happened. Eddie was threatening to blow the lid off."

"I love it," Amanda said. "How did you wriggle out?"

"I didn't," Jason said. "I sat there like a dumb ape and figured the scam was up. But Helen kept her eyes on me—hell, she undressed me with those eyes. She said she'd paid off Eddie Randall, with enough money to make his eyes fall out. She'd staked him to his own office. And she promised him commissions. She kept that promise, too. She also made sure his draft board knew he was out of school and trying to con Helen into lying for him. That got Eddie to Vietnam, where he stepped on a mine and blew up in 1970."

Amanda's spine shivered. "My God. How can anyone manipulate . . . ?"

"She had luck on that one," Jason said. "But it wouldn't have mattered either way. She would have kept Eddie out of circulation somehow if the draft thing didn't work. Eventually, she would've gotten him under her thumb where he couldn't blab. As it turned out, she got rid of him fast. It doesn't make a difference to Helen. Quick or slow, she wins. The fun is in the game."

"I know," Amanda said.

She heard Jason stand again and light another cigarette. She wished to God she could see him. "Helen knew I was a fraud, but that was okay. She didn't need an architect as much as she needed a front man. She needed a stud who could cut through secretaries." He paused. "She seduced me right there, right in her office. No love. No feeling. Just a rush of pure excitement like I've never known. She sucked out my soul and she still owns it."

Amanda found her breath coming hard. "So she imprisoned you all these years. Threatening to expose you if you didn't do her bidding."

"Yes," Jason said. "But she had more luck. One of my first assignments was to win over a city councilman in White Plains, where she wanted to put up an office tower. He was a stubborn, honest son of a bitch. I wined and dined him. I also got to know his daughter. She was nineteen, with a dancer's legs and glossy black hair."

"She sounds like Lacey," Amanda said.

Jason let out a burst of laughter. "You don't quit for a minute, do you?"

"I didn't mean . . ."

"You don't *have* to. You see plenty for a blind lady." She sat rigidly while Jason stunk up the room with smoke. "Yeah, Lacey reminded me of Pam. Demons. Always exorcising demons."

"What happened with Pam?"

There was a long pause now, and Amanda heard the hum of tires on the road, and the hiss of air conditioning. "We hit it off. I was riding high then. I'd won. I'd beat the goddamn world. So we dated, Pam and I, and we made it together. And God help me, I fell in love with her. She was so damned eager, so trusting, so beautiful—I'll spare you the details."

"That would be nice," Amanda said dryly.

Now his words came rushing. "Helen told me to cut it out. If her father caught on, we'd be dead. I felt the leash and collar for the first time, then. I got angry. *I* was the Greek god, man, *I* was the salesman. Who the hell was she? I dated Pam again, and Helen showed me the front page story she was going to put in the papers. About Eddie's design, and the end of my life.

"Well, Amanda, I didn't have the balls to tell her to print the story. I didn't choose Pam over Helen. No heroics. I backed down. I said I'd quit seeing Pam. Hey, Amanda, I wasn't a teenager who'd got taken in by Svengali. I was a grown man. I knew where I was. And I chose the Big Lie."

"I see."

"Do you? Do you see how it burned my gut? I drove around in my MG and got wasted. Had two fights in bars. I drove to Pam's school and honked the horn. Security cops chased me away. I came back. Bulled my way past the housemother. Went upstairs and banged on Pam's door until she opened up. She was all alone, in her lace-trimmed nightdress. So damned beautiful, Amanda. So young and real and loving. And she couldn't be mine because I belonged to Helen.

"It burned until I couldn't breathe. I came in and shut the door. I tried to get it on with her. Pam started to yell. I was scared. I didn't want to be found like this. I started shaking her. She screamed, so I shook her harder and then I slammed her against the wall. . . ."

"*Jason!*" Amanda held her hands to her face.

"Too bad, Amanda," Jason said. "You wanted it. Don't shut it off now, babe. I woke up the next morning in Helen's bed. Helen came in and put a wet compress on my head. I couldn't see straight from the pain. Helen sat down and told me very calmly that Pam was dead. She'd been killed the night before by an intruder. . . ."

"Oh dear God."

"Shut up, Amanda. Listen to it. Killed by an intruder, you see? Nobody had identified the man. So Helen suggested I forget this girl because she was dead and I might as well get on with my work." Jason was crying now, audibly. "And I got on with it. I knew what I was, then. I was a murderous drunken animal. So I got a fashion wardrobe, and a fifty thousand dollar car, and a boat, and a jet, and my own company. But I'm not an architect, Amanda. I'm a clown. I'm a killer. And if Helen says the word, I'll be in prison, and I don't even have the guts to let it happen."

She heard him sit down. She could not weep; she was too tightly twisted inside. It was worse than she'd imagined. She understood everything. And God help her, she still loved him. And she saw why there was no use in that, either.

"You see," he said, "why I probed you. To learn how you got free, how you busted loose. Because I never knew how to do that. I never knew how to fight, or take risks. Loving you was the only risk I ever took. And I was ready to walk out on that."

"And now?"

"Now I'll spit on Satan himself before I give you up. I let you get hurt, so badly hurt that I ought to fry for it. I can't get it back for you, but I can start from today. I've told Helen to screw herself."

Amanda's heart overflowed. "Way to go, Jason."

His voice became sober. "It's a lot of hot air, and you know it. I know I can't have you, because Helen's going to lower the guillotine. And you're not going to spend your life, blind or not, waiting for me to do time."

"Says who?"

"Don't even dream of it," he said. "But I wanted to love you for a few weeks, a few months. I wanted that much."

"I'm glad."

He laughed. "Time doesn't matter. You got me clean and that feels good. It's like getting out of an iron lung."

She managed a smile. "I can imagine."

He stood again. "And having done it, I've reached the end of my line."

"What does *that* mean?"

"It means I'm packing up these drafting tools because I had no business bringing them. And I'm taking you back to Bradley. I want to see you through surgery before I go."

"Where are you going?"

"Back home, first. Make some psychic connection with my beginnings. Then to New York, to wait for Helen to stick me."

"And still not fight?"

She heard him turn. "Fight what? It's done, babe. I wanted it to be done."

Her love for Jason throbbed in her limbs and her throat, and strengthened her fatigued heart. Already, she blamed Helen for everything and forgave Jason, like a good loyal wife. But something was not right about the story; something tickled her brain, something not defined but terribly important. To hell with scruples. She'd waited too long for Jason to come into her life. She wouldn't let him go, not for anything.

"I'm glad I made you do this," she said. "But it was pretty damn worthless if it ends now. What do you have to lose?"

"I don't follow."

"We're here to redesign The Pueblo. Let's do it."

His hands were suddenly on her shoulders. "Amanda, pay attention. I just told you I'm a fraud. And you're blind. Who in this room is going to redesign the country's biggest convention complex so that all the brass at that meeting will get their socks knocked off?"

"We will," Amanda said.

"I can't design buildings, babe. Want me to spell it out?"

"You're lying," she said. "You told me you designed buildings. You said you were good at it."

"I never studied. I never applied any of it."

"But you've been around it for eighteen years. The gift is in you. The ability is there."

"Ability. Not genius, Amanda."

"All right, I'll supply the ideas for now. You've got the

eyes. We just have to sell something, and Goddamn it, Jason, who on earth can sell better than you?''

She heard his breath quicken. ''You sit here, and listen to what I tell you, and you still want to try this insanity?''

''Insanity is what we need. If you're going to prison and I'm going to die on an operating table, let's not be scared to shake the coconut tree.''

He gripped her arms so tightly it hurt, but she didn't care. ''How? Where in hell do we start?''

''With me. I swear to you, Jason, as I was going blind, I saw what The Pueblo should be. In harmony with the land, beautiful enough to attract millionaires, but tied to the reservation—ecologically and economically. It can be done. I guess it was cooking on my creative back burner since the project started, but it took a trauma to make it surface.''

''Okay,'' he said. ''You describe your vision and I'll draw pictures.''

''I saw colors and shapes. You need to make floor plans. Christ, I hope I remember my colors.''

He kept holding onto her. ''Amanda, this is madness. I killed a girl. Do you comprehend that I killed a girl?''

''Accidentally,'' she said. ''In a drunken stupor. It doesn't make it admirable, Jason, and you should pay for it, but horrible things happen to good people. I love you, whatever you've done. I'll help you get through it, because I want to keep you for the rest of my life.''

Her tears ran freely and his lips kissed them as they fell. ''I love you,'' he whispered hoarsely.

''I know,'' she said. Her hands gripped his hair and her mouth searched for his. ''I know.''

chapter 32

MORNING sunlight streamed into Heather's bedroom as a maid pushed open the door. The maid was a small woman in her mid-fifties. She smelled an unpleasant odor, which was not unusual in Heather's room after Byron had slept there. The maid was hardened to the sexual practices of her employer. She was paid well to keep quiet and clean up.

The maid passed the rumpled Sheraton bed, glancing at the young girl under the sheets. Even though Byron had left for a trip, he wouldn't want the kid sleeping late. Humming a song, the maid pulled the drapes and threw open the window. Fresh sea air blew in. The maid turned and called softly, "Heather. Get up. It's late."

The girl didn't move. The maid sighed tiredly. Probably drunk again. Byron liked to get his young girls drunk. The maid moved closer to the bed and shook the girl's shoulder. "Come on, Heather. Byron won't like it. Get up."

Nothing. The maid shook her head. The girl was certainly lovely, lying there naked and only half-covered by the sheet. The maid cautiously pushed aside the limp strands of blonde hair that obscured Heather's face.

When she first saw the swollen, bloated mask, the maid thought that the sun was throwing odd shadows. *"Heather!"* she called out.

She shut her eyes and opened them again. She bit back the rising wave of nausea in her throat and rudely turned the girl onto her back. The maid screamed and fell back against the window, gagging.

She tried to make some sense of it. Who had done this?

Surely not Mr. Moore. He hurt his mistresses; the maid was used to finding blood on the sheets. She expected bizarre, disgusting sights when she came in to clean. But not this. Not murder.

The maid swallowed her illness and made a decision. Mr. Moore was away, and she was not going to take responsibility. She left the bedroom, shutting the door firmly. She marched to Mr. Moore's room, which had a phone. The maid intended to call the police and report this. She had no thought of betraying Mr. Moore; obviously, he wasn't involved in this horrible crime.

The maid could not have known that Byron Moore had slipped the traces of sanity and had fully intended the body to be found.

Amanda sat on a sofa—"glazed chintz" she declared correctly after running her fingers over the fabric—in a high-rise apartment two miles from Bradley. The apartment belonged to a partner in a local architectural firm whose members had been dragooned by Jason to help with the new designs.

"Is it a beautiful place?" Amanda asked.

"Not my taste. Pale colors, Chinese rug, lots of fragile grace."

Amanda smiled. "No mirrors or chrome? Poor baby."

Her hair fell loosely over her shoulders. Thank God they didn't have to shave her head or drill her skull. They were able to go in through the eye socket, carefully removing the eyeball first ("No, we don't *remove* it," the doctor had explained patiently. "We pop it out of the socket, but it's still attached." Amanda had gotten sick to her stomach anyway). The tumor they removed was walnut-sized.

And it was benign.

Amanda nearly wept, thinking about how close she'd come. "It could have shifted any time," Dr. Levine had said.

Thank you, mother, Amanda murmured silently.

She shuddered. Her soft lavender blouse and print skirt flattered her thinned-down figure, making her look feminine and determined at once. She insisted on being dressed. "I don't want to rattle around in nightgowns," she told Jason. "I'll *feel* sick." Only the bandages wrapped tightly around her eyes told of her hours under the knife.

"And my sight . . . ?" Amanda had asked. She remembered Jason holding her hand tightly as she sat up in the hospital bed.

She'd heard the doctor pause, considering his words. "I see no reason why your eyesight shouldn't return. But it's impossible to know if there's permanent damage. We'll have to wait and see. Five days at least before we try. Let it heal, and meanwhile you should get total rest."

Well, obviously he didn't know Amanda Gray. She sat down then, because Jason threatened to club her over the head if she didn't. But her heart pumped adrenalin and she was crazy to get out of the hospital.

"I don't know why I can't just *sit* there," she said. "I'll listen."

"Sure you will," he said. He shot the cuffs of his dark gray barrister suit and adjusted his striped tie.

"Please, Jason. I can't stay here alone while you fight this thing. I got you into it. It's my battle . . ."

"And you've done a hell of a job." He went to the sofa, bent down, and firmly kissed her mouth. Her hands reached for him, but he stood up again. "I *want* to face Helen by myself. This is the rematch, you dig? The same conference room as last time, but last time Helen dominated the meeting and I played the clown. This time we face off." He exhaled. "I've got to do it myself, Amanda. You understand that."

She nodded. "Yes I do. You're pretty terrific, you know that?"

"One shining moment does not redeem my sins."

"Hey, the first time the Mets won in '69, it didn't look significant. But they got to be World Champs."

He laughed. "Sports metaphors she gives me. And anyway, they hit the cellar again." He checked his watch. "Well, it's time for me to go. Wish me luck, babe."

"No," she said. "Luck has nothing to do with it. I believe in you, Jason. I believe that you can whip Helen Tennyson. She's not immortal."

"That helps. How in hell I could ever let you go . . ."

"Shh," she said, putting a finger to her lips. "Stop regretting. It weakens you. Go slay the gorgon."

Jason squeezed her hand and kissed her again. "Stay right here," he husked. "Win or lose, I want you."

"Win or lose, you got me," she promised.

Jason tucked his flexible case under his arm as he walked—jauntily, he hoped—through the polished lobby of the apartment building. He smiled as he passed a man reading a newspaper, and two middle-aged women chatting. Did they know that he was Jason Turner, and that he had renounced his perks and luxuries in favor of a suicide run against an invincible enemy? And that when it was over, he'd be splashed across headlines as he went to prison? He laughed as he stepped into the sunlight. A limo awaited him at the curb.

In the lobby, the man put down the newspaper and watched Jason ride away. In Byron Moore's eyes there was a deadly gleam. He stood up lithely and discarded the newspaper on the lobby sofa. He put his hand in his pocket and fingered a soft leather case. He pushed the elevator button and waited.

This time, *all* of the chairs around the conference table were occupied, and the occupants were noisy. Cigarette smoke formed a blue-white umbrella over the table. The water carafe was passed. Pens scribbled on yellow pads. The press was barred, and waited in a bloodthirsty pack outside the closed doors.

Reflected in the bronze mirror glass was Helen Tennyson, her hair swept to one side, her face so tense with fury that it threatened to crack. In a navy pinstriped suit and ruffled blouse, she sternly announced her mood. She was here to dispose of Jason and assert her queenship.

The men at the table were growing testy over the delay; they didn't like being summoned again, like teachers to a faculty meeting. These were important, powerful boys who liked to be unavailable when called. They waited for Jason, now in a foul mood. Helen barely spoke, and was infuriated that Jason was holding her up. She was not used to losing power plays. She'd gambled that Jason, unused to being defiant, would show up early and wet his pants in his eagerness. She nearly smiled to herself; she'd taught him too well.

As soon as Jason walked in, pursued by flashbulbs and video cameras, and slapped his case on the table, the room was plugged in. Jason sat opposite Helen and the other men seemed to fade. He stood for a moment, looking at her. She looked back and their eyes dueled silently. Then he began to speak.

He used a ringing, persuasive voice. It was the voice he'd trained and polished over the years. He showed them elevations and floor plans. "This is not finished," he said. Already, perspiration shimmered on his temples. His eyes picked out the snowy hair of Dan Ledda, the hunched lankiness of the mayor of Bradley, the sweating bulk of Senator Halsey, the hawklike concentration of Richard Juan, and the worried faces of politicians, bankers, and Indian representatives whose fortunes resided with The Pueblo.

"The design, the concept, the details, need work," Jason said. "But what matters is all here. I worked with some very talented people from Kantor Associates right here in Bradley, and with my own people. And of course, with Amanda Gray, who, as you know, has had surgery to cure her temporary blindness."

This produced a small sensation. Some of the men in the room knew about the operation and some didn't. A current of gossip ran electrically around the room. Helen looked disgusted. "Is this what I have to look forward to?" she asked. "Cheap dramatic effects?"

Jason waited for the outburst to quiet, and said, "Now understand that Helen has put Lacey Coleridge, of Gray Associates, in charge of the Pueblo interiors. Lacey is a talented girl, but she's not Amanda. Amanda has joined *me* in creating this new design."

"But she's blind!" the mayor said.

"But she *won't* be!" Senator Halsey shot back.

"We don't know that—he didn't say it."

"Oh, Christ," Halsey growled.

"Please," Jason said. The men around the table shifted tiredly and grumbled. "Our proposal has a few purposes. One: to build a hotel and resort that is *not* a monolithic structure and does not physically disrupt the natural landscape of the desert. Two: to provide access roads and airstrips that will not disrupt the ecosystem of the desert. Three: to lure important guests, but to make sure we don't further abase the life of the reservation. And I think, gentlemen, that you'll see we've planned for all three goals."

Helen said, "Jason, who decided on these goals? I never heard anybody but *you* mention them."

"*I* like them," Juan said quietly.

Helen glanced at him with deadly amusement. "Well, that doesn't stun me." She looked around the table. "What about the rest of you? Did *you* go running to Jason with demands for assistance to the reservation, or non-disruptive architecture? When did you form a committee? Why wasn't I told?"

"It never happened," Dan Ledda said. "Jason Turner and

Amanda Gray thought it up on their own, without consulting anybody. It's a power play."

There were murmurs of assent. The mayor said, "Why this big to-do all of a sudden, Turner? We were all pretty happy with the *first* hotel."

"And why," Halsey challenged, "didn't *you* think of all this before you submitted a design? What the hell *is* going on?"

"Learning," Jason said reasonably. "I've had my eyes opened and my mind changed, just the way I'm trying to open your eyes and change your minds. You know I've won awards, but I've never been pronounced infallible. I designed a gorgeous structure—I might even use it somewhere else."

"Talk to my lawyer first," Helen interjected.

Laughter followed. Jason nodded. "Good point. Anyway, the structure I designed is not the right one for this place and time. I know that now. Lone Dog did not convince me of that. Observation turned me around. Amanda Gray's observations, and my own. If The Pueblo is built according to the original design, it will be a paradise for wealthy businessmen, and maybe even for Presidents. For about six months. Why? It's going to clash with the surroundings, blight the area by rerouting traffic and bisecting neighborhoods. New slums will be born, people will be dispossessed, depression will crush the reservation, and the court battles will make headlines. That's going to *discourage* your high-rolling tourists."

"That's pretty speculative," Ledda suggested. "Do you have some numbers on that?"

"Yes I do," Jason said. "We've run this all through the computers and we have a few scenarios that should interest you. One for investors, one for politicians, even one for attorneys, Dan." Now the laughter was for Jason, and Ledda fidgeted. "But now isn't the time to recite columns of statistics. I want to give you a concept. I want to show you what can be done to attract these same businessmen and prevent the other problems."

Jason held up a watercolor rendering that evoked some appreciative noises. This was Amanda's vision, translated to color and line. "I think this is even prettier than the first design, and it can make use of most of the foundation that's already been laid. We're proposing a long, low structure with five levels, dug right into this hillside, so that from the rear there are only three levels above grade. We'll put the manmade lake here, and inside we'll use skylit atria for openness and access to the view. We'll have sculpture gardens, reflecting pools, lots of unifying structures."

Ledda bent over to talk worriedly to Helen, who nodded and tapped a pencil against her lips. The other men consulted with each other, sounding positive. Jason let them react before speaking again. He sipped water to soothe his hot throat. "Now," he said, knowing this was the hard part. "We've also proposed rerouting the access roads. Instead of cutting a highway through virgin desert to join with the major east-west routes, we can put a road through this series of canyons, right by the reservation. The trip to The Pueblo will be two and a half miles longer from the main highway, and you've have to come fifty miles further west—but fifty miles *closer* if you're traveling east. The main benefit would be revitalization. For years, the reservations were treated like Third World countries, but the Indians weren't given the resources or mechanisms for development. There's been no on-reservation private enterprise, no VA loans, no FHA loans, no conventional loans. Inter-departmental energy leases have cheated the tribes of fair prices for their minerals. Commerce Department foul-ups have sunk them with debts. Health services are nowhere. The crime rate is fifty percent higher than in rural America. You've got the highest unemployment in the country—well, hell, *you* know the situation."

"Yeah, we know," Halsey said ominously. "And we don't appreciate big city boys giving us lectures on it."

"Hey," Helen piped up. "Did you just lose a friend?"

"No, I don't think so," Jason said emotionally. "I'm not here pitching federal welfare programs. I'm talking about a moneymaker. And if Senator Halsey and Mayor White and you investment boys will think about it, you'll see that you have a hot item here. We involve the reservation. We route traffic *through* it. Indians get to set up concessions on the main road. They build real towns with full services. They become part of the economy, not a drain on it. My structural engineers have come up with a way to route water from the reservation so it doesn't cut off the tribe's supply. We'd pay the tribe for water use and avoid lawsuits. Crime falls, unemployment drops. You can point to a model Indian community in Bradley. You get the glory and the profit."

A burst of cross-conversation filled the room when Jason

paused. "Shit," the mayor grumbled. "This looks like a lot of crap to me."

"What's the problem?" Jason said. "You don't like Indians?" The mayor colored. "So what? Who asked you to like them? You don't have to marry one. You have to see past your bigotry and get selfish. This plan will work. It needs some vision and imagination from you."

Richard Juan said, "I don't like all of it, but details can be hammered out. Generally, the plan recognizes our problems and proposes a way to deal with them and give you what you want. I think it's worth considering."

A banker, bespectacled and graceful in a dark suit, said, "I personally am tired of the publicity and wrangling over this. The Pueblo is proceeding at a crawl. We're all losing out. If Turner is going to throw himself into this, and Amanda Gray will do the designs—assuming she has her eyesight—and the tribes will not throw monkey wrenches into the works—damn it, I'll okay it just to get *moving*."

There was a crack of applause and a lot of assent. Helen spoke quickly with Ledda and then put down her pencil. The gesture produced silence. "I think the design is ordinary," she said. "I think the cost will be indefensible. I see overruns that you can't see. Remember, I know something about putting up buildings and Jason is giving you *part* of the story."

"Damn it, Helen," Halsey said, "don't make waves just to be a pain."

Helen smiled. "I can understand your eagerness to desert me and rush to Jason's side. I'm mean and he's nice. And you're all licking the red man's moccasins because Lone Dog is in jail and the politicians want to make hay."

Jason jumped to his feet. "And what the hell is wrong with that? Lone Dog bloodied everyone's reputation. Nothing on earth can justify what he did. But people respond to symbols, not words. People are going to see rich bastards stepping on poor red babies. If you polarize your community, you'll chase away the executives and politicians who might use The Pueblo. Those boys are not going to stay at a resort that makes negative headlines. But we can raise a new Pueblo on the ashes of tragedy."

"Oh get off it," Helen cried back, as some of the men applauded. "And cut out the stupid-ass clapping. This isn't a high school assembly. This is reality. 'Executives won't stay there . . .' Suck ice, Jason. Of *course* they'll stay there! Do you gentlemen truly see America roused into moral indignation over the treatment of Indians? People see the Indians for what they are—lazy, drunk, murderous bums who wait for government handouts in repayment for Custer's sins."

Richard Juan was on his feet, trembling. "This woman must be thrown out. She cannot be permitted to run anything!"

Halsey groaned. Mayor White said, "For chrissake, sit down, Juan. You know this lady isn't tactful."

"She is an *enemy,*" Juan cried out. "And since you listen to her and do not repudiate what she says, you make your own position absolutely clear."

"Stop it!" Ledda shouted. He banged the table and leaned forward. "Behave like an attorney, Richard. You know she's right—not about what you *are,* but about what people *think* you are. And that image has bearing on this."

"Let it go," Jason said. "It isn't worth it. Everyone knows my plan is workable. Let Helen spew her poison."

"Oh, God help us," Helen said. "Spewing poison. Enemies. Boys, I am talking about the real world. It is time to stop the bullshit. Now listen to me. If you want to give permits and loans to Jason and Amanda for their low-slung wigwam, and if you want to pay engineers to build little Indian trails, you do it. Hell, I do not beg for anyone's business. I am up to my titties in commissions. But I will not be dictated to by gutless politicians or lovesick architects. I will pull out of Bradley, taking my operation with me, and I will leave a half-built white elephant. Now you will have Jason's design, but Jason doesn't represent any architectural firm, since *I* own Turner Associates, and Jason is hereby canned. If you want to trust—what is it, Asshole Associates? —here in Bradley to build this multimillion dollar resort under Jason's inspiring guidance, fine. You'll also have Amanda Gray, who is still blind, pending miracles." She spread open her hands. "I admire such idealism. To back Jason and Amanda under those conditions! And where will you find a developer to come in and complete the project at such a risk? But don't let *me* sway you. Do what you want. I have never seen such incompetence in my life."

A dread, black silence hung over the conference table. The bankers lowered their heads and tapped pencils. The mayor looked at the raised ceiling. Halsey shut his eyes and rested his double chin on his chest. She had them by the balls and they knew it.

The bespectacled banker said, "Well, of course this alters the picture. Without Helen and her track record, we'd certainly find it difficult to support the project." He looked apologetically at Jason. "No comment on your design, of course."

"Of course," Jason said. He felt Helen watching him. She had not exposed him; not because she was a lady, but because Helen used only the weapons she needed for the battle. If Jason escalated now, so would Helen.

Jason envisioned Amanda, sitting on the chintz sofa two miles away, waiting for him. His heart filled with incredible energy. He said, "Helen is great at scaring you. First of all, ask Dan Ledda how easy it will be to fire me from my own company. Secondly, even if Helen does get me out, I have the loyalty of top architects, engineers, and draftsmen. I can set up another company in a week. It's the designs that count. And maybe you gentlemen are willing to accept her disparagement of your local architects, but I'm not. No, what Helen is really threatening to take away is her investment.

"But what *is* her investment? *Me*. Amanda." Jason studied the faces, and saw the confusion and uncertainty. "Even the bulldozers don't belong to Helen. She subcontracted for them. So can you. Her track record is *my* track record. The Pueblo can be built independently. Your only decision is whether to stick with the design that has proved unworkable and dangerous, or to go with my new design, which is going to do it all for you."

The door opened behind Jason. Halsey said, "Helen, I got to say you're losing the debate."

"Am I?" she said. "Then let's end it quickly. I've tried hard to fight fair, but this has gotten too ridiculous. You may as well stop wasting time, because nobody's going to use that design, and nobody's going to pay Jason a penny to build a thing. I regret destroying a man in front of you, but he's asked to have his pants taken down and his heinie spanked."

The men were galvanized. Their eyes flicked from Jason to Helen. Jason's hands remained, white-knuckled, on the table. He was ready for it. With luck, with charm, he could keep them off balance long enough to sell the design. He'd introduced the concept, gotten them to hear it. Now he had to overcome their horror to make them stay with it.

"Boys, let me tell you about Jason Turner . . ." Helen began, but her eyes went from the table to the man who had walked in. Anger crossed her face. "Danny, what in hell do you want?"

Heads turned. They all recognized Danny Rosetti from the media coverage. He had remained in Bradley, seeing a therapist at the nearby medical center. He wore a blazer and slacks for work, and he looked trimmed-down.

"Sorry to interrupt," he said. "I got them to let me in because I heard something and . . . well, I wanted to see you or Jason right away."

Helen sighed with impatience. "That's all right, Danny. We know you're still a little traumatized, so we'll be kind."

Helen ignored the hiss of shocked breath around the table. Jason said, "What's up, Danny?"

The men around the table paid attention to the kid. They were all deeply indebted to him for finding Lone Dog and kicking his ass, and nobody was going to throw Danny out.

"Well, there was a story on the news a few minutes ago. You know Byron Moore, right?"

"Yes, we do," Helen said.

"That girl he was living with—that singer—"

"Heather Laine," Jason prompted.

"Yeah. Well, they found her dead, in her bedroom. She was strangled."

There were gasps and whispers around the table. Helen's eyes clouded for a moment as she recalled Moore's manic behavior during their dinner. "Why is this bulletin so vital right now?"

Danny took a breath. "Well, they think Moore did it. They found his prints all over and they . . ." He turned deep red. ". . . they know he made love to her the night before."

Helen withered him with her eyes. "What are you saying?"

Danny looked at Jason. "Wasn't Amanda Byron's girlfriend once?"

"That's right," Jason said.

"Well, if he's crazy enough to kill this Heather, maybe he'll go after Amanda, too."

"After Amanda?" Jason's throat tightened. "You mean they didn't arrest him?"

"No," Danny said worriedly. "The thing is, the airport says his private jet landed here today."

"Jesus Christ," Jason said. He saw Amanda vividly: alone in the apartment. Blind.

He ignored the loud murmuring around the table and turned

to Helen. "You know Moore. You've done business with him."

"So what?" Helen said.

"You can talk to him, if he's really off the wall. Maybe long enough to keep him busy until the cops get there."

Mayor White was on his feet. "I'm on the horn right now."

Jason nodded. "Helen, come with me. Help me out."

"Be real," Helen said. "Why would I lift a finger for you?"

Jason's reason clicked off at that moment. With an animal cry, he stormed around the table and, with a lunge, he seized Helen around her throat and crushed her to his chest.

"What the hell are you doing?" Ledda screamed.

With his elbow, Jason cut off Helen's windpipe. "Feel like changing your mind?"

"He's *killing* her," Ledda pleaded.

Halsey wiped his mouth with a handkerchief. "Just shutting her up."

Jason's nostrils stung with her perfume. "How about it?" he said. "Help me or I break your neck. You'll send me up the river anyway. What the hell is the difference? One murder or two?"

Helen's face twitched with terror. She managed a weak, rueful smile. "Well," she croaked, "Let's avoid violence, by all means."

Jason released her and she nearly collapsed. Ledda went to her. Jason turned to Danny. "My limo's outside. Tell the driver to start the motor."

Danny nodded, and left the conference room. Jason flung Ledda aside, and seized Helen's arm.

"Let's go," he said grimly.

For the moment, Helen said nothing. Fighting back humiliating tears, she submitted to his strength. In the pit of her soul, she feared that she would never overcome that strength again.

chapter 33

AMANDA stood near the recessed bookshelves, running her fingers over the hubbed spines of books, and wondering if she really sensed light through her bandages or whether she was just hoping too hard. A knock came at the door and startled her.

"Jason?" she said. Hadn't he taken a key? Mildly apprehensive, she turned and called out, "Who is it?"

"Me," a muffled voice came back.

Amanda scowled. Back so soon? Something had gone wrong. Well, they'd expected a rough time from Helen. She must have unloaded with all guns blazing.

"One minute," she said. "It's going to take me awhile to get to the door."

She tried to remember the layout of the apartment. She took a few tentative steps across the Chinese rug, and bumped her knees against a chair. She stopped and sighed. "Jason, what happened to your key?" she said. "This is not amusing."

"Hurry," came the voice outside the door.

Oh shit, Amanda thought. She forced her body to control its movements. She skirted the chair and had clear sailing to the entrance hallway. Her hands found the chain lock and the doorknob. "Okay," she said. "I made it."

She unlatched the door and opened it. As she did so, an ice-tinged thought stopped her. *What if it isn't Jason?* But nobody else knew she was staying here. Of course, a rapist would just choose apartments at random, wouldn't he?

It was too late for second thoughts. The door was open.

She smelled a subtle cologne and sensed a presence. The man at the door walked in.

It wasn't Jason.

Idiot, she scolded herself. He'd been very good, this stranger. He'd spoken only two words, words that made her assume it was Jason. "Who are you?" she asked.

"Hello, Amanda."

It was as if a plug had been yanked out and all of her hope, energy and spirit ran out like used bathwater. "Byron."

He shut the apartment door and chain-locked it. Amanda stood with her hands clenched at her sides. "How did you track me down?"

"It wasn't easy. You moved quickly, and covered your tracks. It took me a few days to realize that Dr. Fielding was protecting you. I'll have his shingle, too, the clown. But it was a matter of being persistent, after all. I wondered if you'd let me in."

"I didn't think it was you."

He chuckled. "Well, that's honest. Amanda, you look beautiful. Weakened and more pale than I like, but truly radiant. I imagine the bandages have a story behind them?"

"Byron," she said levelly. "I don't want to talk to you right now. We can have lunch in a few days and have our last conversation then."

"Oh, I don't want to wait a few days, Amanda. I've really done enough waiting. Why don't *you* sit down, and *I'll* sit down, and we can have our talk right now? You're not going anywhere."

She went cold to her bones. She wondered how long Jason would be at the meeting. Right now, she knew the futility of arguing or trying to dismiss him. The old nightmares rose up and suffocated her heart.

"All right," she said.

She felt his hand touch her arm and guide her to a chair. Her skin crawled at the contact. She sat down, every nerve on edge. She heard him sit opposite her and she was filled with despair.

Byron unbuttoned the jacket of his glen plaid suit as he sat down. He pushed back his white-gray hair with one hand and studied Amanda. He tried to quell his nervousness. "You ran away from me."

"That's right."

"Why?"

"Come on, Byron. It's a little late to be coy."

He sighed. She looked so fragile and vulnerable sitting there. Exactly as he'd envisioned her—but in *his* house, at *his* command. It maddened him to see her as he'd dreamed of seeing her, but somewhere else. It was as if a rival collector had bought, framed, and displayed a painting Byron himself had prized.

"I ordered the security relaxed," he told her as he rubbed a sore on his lip. "That's how you were able to get away."

"I thought it was too easy," Amanda said.

"I wanted to test you. I wanted to see if you would go. I hoped—you can't imagine how I hoped—that finally you had come back to me, accepted me, forgiven me."

Amanda shook her head. "Why did you follow me, Byron? Can't you accept that I don't love you? Why is it impossible for you to give up one woman?"

"Because I *made* you!" He flung himself from the chair, trembling. Amanda cowered at his vehemence. "You little slut. You're nothing. Nothing but my creation. And you persist in crowing about your talent and your strength and your independence. You forget pretty quickly, don't you?"

"We've been over this," she said tiredly. "It's not worth it anymore. You possess miraculous powers, Byron. You can change people. It's breathtaking, the power you have."

Byron turned, under an archway. "So you do understand that."

"I'd be a fool not to," she said. "But you perverted your power. It wasn't enough to resurrect three women. That alone would have made you heroic. *If* you had found those women at random, *if* you had rescued them out of kindness, *if* you had trained them to be independent and creative and then freed them. *If* you had shown them real love. If you had done that, Byron, no prize, no monument would have been too grand."

To his horror, he felt tears sting his eyes. For an instant, he was painfully aware of an immortality that had once lain within his reach. "You're too idealistic, Amanda."

"Am I? I've been told that. But you're worse than cynical. You didn't destroy people for money. You really believed in your godhood. You couldn't *find* a young girl who needed to be saved. You had to *create* the girl. You had to take an innocent, helpless infant and design her life, making sure she suffered pain and degradation. Then you lifted her out of her pit and washed away her sins.'' Amanda began to cry as she spoke. ''You and your sick designs. A mother and a daughter—how symmetrical! Did you know about my mother and Tom? I'll bet you did. Knew it, and waited for her to get knocked up so you could take the child from the womb. That's why *I'm* your masterpiece, isn't it? Because you created me from the womb.''

Byron blinked rapidly, unable to accept Amanda's shrewd insight. He dug another antacid mint from his breast pocket and chewed it. Already demented, Byron sank lower into black insanity with each accusation. He fingered the leather case in his jacket once more.

''And then,'' Amanda said, ''even when you'd played God, you couldn't let it be. Maybe you hated yourself so completely that you couldn't accept the beauty of what you'd made. I don't know; I can't begin to fathom you. But I know you hurt the women you saved—hurt my mother beyond help. You let her go blind, Byron. You knew she had glaucoma but you didn't have it treated in time. Because once she went blind, she'd be totally yours. So you put her into West Hills, displayed like a picture in a museum for you to look at.

''But *I* was trouble for you. Too smart, too strong. So you indulged your sadism, which is really your own self-hatred, and you tried to break me. But I wouldn't be broken, and that destroyed your pride. I left your museum of horrors and it burns your guts that one human being exists who does not need you and who doesn't fear you and who won't be owned by you.''

Amanda took a calming breath. ''You tried again, with Heather. The same pattern, the sick games. But it wasn't the same. You were older. Heather wasn't top-drawer material. And you couldn't get me out of your head, because I was still free. So you kidnapped me, you threatened me, you behaved like a madman, and it didn't work. Then my blindness—you used that, changing the facts to accommodate the situation. And *that* didn't work. Yes, I left. I would have gone to sea in a raft to get away from you. You're a very ill man, Byron. Get help. No matter how many times you chase me and hound me and invade my life, I'll leave. You've lost. Accept it.''

Silence rung in the room. ''I'm sorry,'' she murmured. ''I didn't mean to do that. But you anger me so much . . .''

Byron paced slowly. His fingertips touched a lampshade here, a sconce there. "You don't really understand what commitment is. I'm committed to having you. Yes, I went to great pains to mold my women. I did some awful things, and I begged your forgiveness. That's as much as I can do."

"All right," Amanda said. "I can forgive you for the beatings. Is that what you want?"

He paused a few feet from her. "You don't understand yet. I did everything to make you mine. Everything."

"Meaning what?"

He sighed, rubbing the case in his pocket. "I had Mary put away so you would never know the truth, never become confused by it. And when your father initiated proceedings to get you back, I hired someone to go to California and cut the brake linings in his truck. . . ."

Amanda was on her feet. "Oh my God . . . !"

"Shocked?" Byron spat. "You really *don't* know what commitment is. I had the man killed. That's how much I intend to keep you, Amanda. I risked everything. What have *you* risked?"

"My father . . ." she wept. "You bastard. You scum. . ."

"Oh, come off it. You never met the man. *I'm* your father. Father and brother and lover. The only man who gave meaning to your life. No lovemaking ever touched you as deeply as mine. No music. No tour of Europe. No swim. No meal. Never in your life did your senses know the stimulation they knew in my home. I gave you life. You can't take it away from me."

Amanda searched blindly for Byron. "Get out. I don't want you in the same room with me."

With a sad smile, Byron drew the leather case from his pocket. "That kind of churlishness can't help now," he said. He opened the case. The lamplight sparkled off a polished surgical scalpel. Byron carefully drew the scalpel from the case and replaced the case in his pocket. "I hoped—honestly, deeply hoped—that you'd think about it, understand, give me the chance to be your companion. But you really have it in you to hurt me and show me how tough you are. Fine. But you see, my problem is that I can't function without you."

"That's not *my* problem," Amanda said.

"Yes it is." He stepped closer to the couch, where Amanda stood. "I've made a total commitment. You know, I've broken off with Heather."

"I never asked you to do that."

"No, no, you didn't ask me. I might have done it for you though, if you had. I think I'd do almost anything for you."

"Then leave me alone," she said.

"Amanda," he said sharply. "Stop talking. I made it very definite that Heather is not part of my life. I killed her, Amanda."

Amanda shook her head. "No . . ."

"I made love to her one last time, one very beautiful time. Then I choked her to death. I imagine the police will find me, but that doesn't matter, either. I feel very old and very useless, and ten or twenty more years of old age seems like a silly way to spend my time. What's most important is having you, *knowing* I have you, knowing you need me and depend on me. I *will* win."

"Byron, for God's sake . . ."

"No tears, Amanda." Byron held the scalpel up to the light, watching it flash. He felt himself grow erect, and perspiration wet his skin beneath his suit.

"Please."

"I've burned all my bridges. I've bet the house. Everything for you. Do you realize, Amanda, that I've sacrificed my empire? My possessions, my power, my future? All for you. No man will ever offer you as much. Can you feel it, Amanda? Can you understand? Give me back what's mine. Give me the love I gave my life for."

He blinked back his tears, and moved closer.

Amanda tried to guess where Byron was. His footsteps made no sound on the carpet. She could barely hear over the rushing of blood in her ears. She didn't know if he was armed. Her only chance was to keep talking, to soothe him, to pray that Jason would come back.

"Byron," she said, "I think I'm just confused. It's been so hard, not seeing. Maybe we can work something out . . ."

"No," his voice said. She tried to take a fix on the direction. "We don't work anything out. I'm not going to kill you, by the way, if that's what you're thinking. I don't want a corpse. You've had some surgery, I see, to fix your eyes."

Oh dear God, she thought. "They don't know if it worked."

"Well, I won't take the chance. I'm going to make certain that your eyes never see again." There was a sudden, sharp *ting* of metal against metal, and Amanda gasped. What in God's name was it?

She cautiously backed up, one step at a time. Where was the sofa? She'd been standing in front of it, but now she was disoriented. Her hands clawed the air, trying to find a lamp, a doorknob, a wall . . . anything to give her a clue as to where she was.

She backed up another step. As soon as she felt the pressure of wood against her shoe heel, she knew she was sunk. She tried to move her body forward, but she lost her balance. Her eyes throbbed with pain. She cried out softly and for an instant felt weightless. She dropped into a chair, banging her tailbone on the arm.

His hand closed around her throat. He straddled her body. Her head was pressed into the stuffed cushion. She could smell his warm breath and feel the weave of his suit jacket. She gasped for breath.

"Okay," he said, a little out of breath himself. "Now sit still. I have a scalpel in my hand."

She tried to scream, but he didn't let her have air. She thrashed wildly, feeling her eyelids scrape the bandage. Her heart raced. Now she felt pressure on the bandage, and heard a scratching sound.

"I'm cutting the bandage slightly," he said. "Just enough to get in. Try to hold very still."

Please, Jason. Please . . .

She heard his breath grow ragged. "Now," he said. "Don't move . . ." As horror invaded her mind, she felt a cold stab just under her left eye. She kept her eyes closed, not daring to test her sight. The bandage still covered her, slit enough for Byron to probe beneath. "I've nicked you just under the eye," he said. "Let me just draw my line . . ." She felt the blade trace an arc under her left eye. Immediately, it burned and pulsated and she knew it bled.

"I'm going to take out your eyes," he said. "Leaving only the sockets. Nobody will want to look at you, then, Amanda. Nobody will want to love you. Except for me. I'll love you. I'll keep you safe. I'll see your true beauty."

Her body was immersed in liquid nitrogen, frozen beyond any thaw. Only the steady drumming of her pulse, somewhere in her head, proved that she was alive.

And then her will to live shot current to her dead limbs. Her hands jerked out, seeking Byron's face. Her nails touched flesh and dug into his skin. Byron screamed and drew back.

Amanda thrust forward. She pushed Byron off balance, and

sensed him falling away. She flung herself out of the chair, and pitched forward. She fell, hard, her head striking the frame of a chair. Arrows of pain lanced her eyes. She cried out. She stretched out her arms and dragged herself along the floor.

He pounced on her. She gagged. He wrestled her onto her back. She found his wrists.

A heavy knocking tattooed the door. "*Jason!*" she screamed. From beyond the door came his voice, yelling her name.

She heard a key rattling in the lock. But Byron had chain-locked the door from inside. Amanda fought for breath. She felt a nick on her cheek and then a burning pain. She whipped her head from side to side. Where was the scalpel? Where?

Then, suddenly, without warning, light pierced her darkness. What she saw was barely an image; it was like some ghostly fluorescence. But she saw an upraised hand and a glint of silver. Reacting from instinct, she let both of her hands flash toward the silver and the pink fingers holding it. Her brain focused on his index finger . . . what she thought was his index finger . . . prayed was his index finger. She knew, in that snapshot of time, that Byron didn't know she could see. She worked her hands around his finger and, before he realized what she was doing, she threw every shred of her strength into her hands and pulled the finger back, like the lever of a slot machine.

She heard a loud crack and then Byron's agonized shriek. She thought she saw the silver falling. Then his other hand closed like a bear trap around her throat and blackness rushed in.

Somewhere in the dying recesses of her brain, she heard a terrific bang, and a splintering sound. Red light exploded around her and suddenly the weight was lifted away and she was floating through eternity.

Jason's shoulder detonated with pain as he sailed through the broken doorway and bounced against a wall. He snarled and shook off the agony as his eyes scanned the room. He saw Amanda sprawled on the Chinese rug, and Byron straddling her.

He sprinted two steps and lifted Byron to his feet. Insane with rage, Jason drove his knee hard into Byron's balls. Byron doubled over, gurgling. Jason spun, and, clasping his hands together, chopped down at Byron's neck. Byron folded up and dropped to his knees. The man rocked there, barely conscious. Jason rubbed his knuckles and spotted Helen, who stood by the door. "See to Amanda," he snapped. "Make sure she's okay."

Helen nodded like a frightened child. Jason looked around, then ripped a lamp plug out of the wall. He grabbed the lamp, and tore the cord from its base. Grunting with effort, he knelt behind Byron, yanked the man's arms behind his back, and trussed him tightly enough to cause pain. As he worked, he heard the screaming of sirens in the distance.

Jason pushed Byron onto his side and bound his ankles, then stood up, sweating. Helen had helped Amanda to her feet and stood near her, obviously uncomfortable.

Jason tried to comprehend what had happened. He tried to explain in his mind the torn bandage over her eyes and the blood that streamed down her face and stained her lavender blouse. In one step, he was at Amanda's side and she threw herself into his arms, weeping uncontrollably.

"Shh," Jason soothed as he hung on tightly enough to break her ribs. His hand, shaking, smoothed her tousled hair and his lips found her face and kissed away the blood.

Helen uttered a cry of horror, and knelt down to pick up the scalpel. She held it up as if it were a revolting insect. "The man was off the wall. Incredible. A mind like that."

Jason felt nausea rise in his gut. "My God!" he whispered. "Amanda . . ."

She shook her head even as she held onto him like a drowning dog. "No," she managed to gasp. "He didn't do it . . . he just nicked me. . . ."

Jason shut his eyes. He took a breath and pushed Amanda away slightly so he could examine her. He traced the razor-thin welt under her eye and cursed. "That bastard."

He let Amanda go and whirled to look down at Byron, who had thrown up on the carpet. "You piece of shit!" Jason screamed.

Amanda's voice stopped him. "Jason, no. Please. No more hurting. No more . . ."

Jason clenched his fists and his big chest heaved under his suit. He turned back and scooped up Amanda once more. "Thank God you're all right."

She turned her bloodied face up to him. "Jason, I think I was able to see for a moment. I think I can see light right now."

"Don't move the bandage," Jason warned.

She nodded meekly. "I won't."

"Damn," Jason whispered. "What does that to a guy?"

"Too much power," Amanda murmured, her own head a carousel. "Too much . . ."

Helen sighed audibly. She had dropped the scalpel back on the carpet. "This is awfully sweet," she said. "But you'll pardon me if I go. I guess you don't need me to chat with him, Jason."

He looked at Helen. "Thanks for coming."

Helen made a nasty noise. "Don't be asinine. I'll allow you this reunion. But you realize this was just a diversion. The meeting will reconvene and what I began to say will be said. And then all of your puerile bullshit will be worthless because your plan will be abandoned and you'll be in custody and you can spend your years figuring out why you felt it necessary to pull a stunt like this."

Amanda's hands tightened on Jason's arms. "She didn't say anything . . . ?"

"She was about to," Jason said. "But Danny came in to tell us about that creep."

Amanda smiled. "Danny! So Danny saved my life. Nobody could help *him*, but he thought about me. You see, Helen, that's what makes someone a big man. Caring about people."

"Spare the violins," Helen said. "You can enjoy taking credit for making Jason lose his senses. I hope you two will be very happy. I understand that most prisons do have a spouse visitation program."

"It doesn't matter if I go to jail," Jason said. "If they'll accept our plan, other architects can do it."

"Are you totally nuts?" Helen asked. "First of all, they'll know it's not your plan, because you can't *do* a plan. Secondly, they'll want to fumigate their clothes from being near you."

"It *was* his plan," Amanda said, leaning into Jason. "He has more talent than you think."

"I know exactly what he has," Helen said nastily. "I was there from the start, bimbo."

Amanda stiffened as a thought kicked in; the thought that had been simmering in her mind since Jason told his story. She trembled with realization, with the truth that was so obvious that Jason had never suspected it. She had no proof, but she was alive and with Jason and in the mood to gamble.

"You *were* there, weren't you?" she said to Helen. "In fact, your bodyguards went after Jason the night Pam died, and found him in her dorm."

Helen glanced with astonishment at Jason. "You told her everything?"

"Yes," Jason said. "It wasn't that hard. It won't be that hard to tell the TV cameras, either."

"Big talk," Helen said. "And she still loves you?"

Amanda said, "Maybe I just can't believe that Jason would kill a girl. Even when he's drunk. Even when he's desperate."

"Well," Helen said. "It shows you're not a great judge of character."

"I think I *am* a good judge of character," Amanda said. Jason looked oddly at her.

"What are you talking about?" he asked.

"Yes," Helen said. "I'm fascinated."

Amanda moistened her lips, knowing she only had a moment or two before weakness and aftershock did her in. "I think Helen is the kind of person who *would* have you tailed to the dorm, and who would cover up for you so she could blackmail you for the rest of your life."

"Charming testimonial," Helen said dryly.

"I also think," Amanda said, "that she would think very fast when the bodyguards phoned her and said you were out cold, and the girl was lying there, critically hurt."

"She was *dead,*" Jason said.

"Do you *know* that?" Amanda challenged. "You'd passed out. What if she *wasn't* dead, Jason? What if Helen's boys called up and asked what to do and Helen implied, oh so subtly, that the girl should not be medically treated right away. Or maybe even smashed against the wall a couple more times. To make *sure* she was dead by morning."

"You bitch," Helen snarled. "You're out of your mind."

"Am I? It would be a gamble, of course. Like getting Eddie Randall drafted and sent to Vietnam. Maybe the girl would live, and you'd have to buy her off. But if she died . . . if she *died* . . . you'd own Jason, body and soul."

Jason loosened his hold on Amanda and stared at Helen. "She wasn't dead, was she, Helen? *Was* she?"

Helen visibly quivered, but her eyes stayed firm. "Of course she was dead. The girl is feeding you a fairy tale."

"No, Amanda is right. I don't think you had the boys kill her. I don't think even you would do that. But I think you *let* her die . . . delayed getting help and *hoped* she'd die. Oh Christ, Helen, I loved her. She didn't deserve that . . ."

Helen brushed her cuff. "Enjoy your fantasies."

Amanda said, "Oh we'll do more than that. We'll have the case reopened. The body exhumed. The medical records subpoenaed. Time of death must have been established. If there was a payoff to the medical examiner, we'll know about it. This is going to be an embarrassing time for you, Helen."

"Go right ahead," Helen said, as she lost her composure. "Play games. I don't have time . . ."

"I do," Jason said. "I have a lot of time. Maybe my hands *did* cause her death. Maybe not. Maybe no examiner can truly ever tell. But I will make it hot for you, Helen."

Helen snarled. "Ungrateful . . . if not for me, you bastard . . . if not for me . . ."

"That's Byron's refrain," Amanda said. "You're all the same. Nobody can succeed or fail without you. This isn't your Earth, Helen. It belongs to all of us, and some of us are going to take it back."

"Try," Helen said tightly. "Go ahead and try. You don't have the guts or the will . . ."

"Sure we do," Amanda said.

"Let's go back to that meeting," Jason said. "I want to hear you tell them about me. Because if you do, I'll accuse you of murder and we'll fight it out in court and in the headlines. And I'll add a lot more in the way of kickbacks, rigged bids, payoffs, political bribes . . . Jesus, Helen, I've got tons of stuff in my files. I'll get nailed for it too, but you'll go down in flames. You'll lose it all. Can you risk that, Helen?"

Helen stood silently, almost palpably smaller. Amanda said, "She can't risk it. All she and Byron ever had was their power, their ownership. There was never anything strong and real inside. Only by hurting can they feel alive. You know, I don't feel angry anymore. Just tired."

There was a loud pounding at the door. "POLICE!" came the shout. "OPEN UP!"

Jason held Amanda tightly and looked toward the door. "Let them in, Helen," he said, as exhaustion swept over him.

* * *

Jason and Amanda stood high on an ocher ridge as the skull-cracker pulverized a partly-erected Pueblo wall. Again and again the black ball swung hard. Concrete crumbled in curtains of dust and rubble spewed the ground. The desert sun flamed down from a deep blue sky.

Jason kept his arm around Amanda's shoulders as they watched. They both wore dungarees, but Jason wore a blue shirt and Amanda wore a white sleeveless top. Jason surveyed, through sunglasses, the small army of workmen scurrying to do his will. He'd convinced a number of bright architects from Turner Associates—well, what *used* to be Turner Associates—to defect and join him. The new plan had sold, and Jason was taking a tiny salary as he struggled to get his new firm underway.

Amanda looked up at Jason, shamelessly drinking in the blue of his eyes, the crisp black of his hair, the ragged brush of his moustache, the pores of his beautiful face. She couldn't stop looking at him. She couldn't stop looking at *anything*. "It's going to be beautiful," she said. "I'm more excited about this than I've ever been about anything. Except you."

He smiled. "Keep boosting me. I need it. I don't love taking architectural lessons from kids. I was never much of a grind."

"I know," she said, kissing his cheek. "You were a conceited, opportunistic bum."

"Exactly."

"Well, tough. You've got to earn a living in your middle years. I'm bored with your good looks. You've got to impress me with other stuff."

He smiled. "How's it going on your end?"

"Busy," she said. "Lacey stayed with Helen, of course. The new protégée—and Helen's lover, too, so the gossip goes."

"They deserve each other," Jason said.

'Don't be petty. Lacey is a lovely girl and a talented designer. She's just cast from the new mold. Instant gratification, no patience, no self-examination. I refused her, so therefore I'm a louse and she's owed revenge. Money and power are where it's at, so she sells herself to Helen. It's heady wine."

"With a big hangover," he said ruefully. "Helen's not taking all of this lying down."

"Not with you, anyway," Amanda cracked. She grinned

and Jason pinched her neck. "Helen's going to hound our asses for a long time. She's going to try every trick she knows to crush our little enterprise. And she knows a lot of tricks."

"So do I," Jason said. "And she'll play fair, or I'll blow her out of the water. Filth against filth."

Amanda sighed contentedly and nestled close. "Good. Glad to hear you talk that way, finally."

He turned and studied her, hands on her shoulders. "Which reminds me, how *are* you doing? Your mind, and the stuff I can't see. You came close to going under."

She hooked her hands over his wrists. "I'll recover. I've seen my mother a few times. She'll slip into the final coma pretty soon, but we've had some good talks, and I've seen how beautiful she is. It's going to have to serve."

"I'm sorry."

She shook her head. "Don't be. There'd be too much to be sorry for once you start. Feel sorry for Byron."

"Get off it."

"Really," she said. Only a hairline scar under her eye gave tribute to her brush with mutilation. "He's in a little rubber room, stripped of everything except notoriety. He's the hottest item in the media but he has no power. Worse than death. There's a mini-series in the works, you know. But I'm getting my book in first."

He grinned. "Are you really writing it?"

"I'd better, before the jackals print their lies. *Life With Byron Moore*. Nothing left out. I can hack the talk show circuit. Can you see me and Joan Rivers?" She grew serious as her heart swelled. "And besides getting loads of bucks for us, maybe I can reach some Heathers and Marys out there, some of the thousands of kids who hate themselves and think they need to be hurt and humiliated to feel good." She looked at Jason. "Making the world prettier is fine, but the ugliness is part of it. Random horror, like Terri, Byron's sadism . . . we don't do our designs on pure white paper. I needed to accept that."

"Whoa," Jason said. "You're getting worked up. It's okay now, kid. We're in the sunshine. It's all over."

Amanda felt emotions shake her by her roots. "No. It's never over. And if we don't take over the job of designing our lives, it's going to happen again. We're all so weak, and the Byrons and Helens and Lone Dogs are so strong, and it's so easy to let them have everything. . . ."

She began to fill up. He drew her close. "I know," he said softly. "Don't take it all on yourself."

She put her hands tenderly on his hot face. Her grateful eyes swept the sky, the hovering clouds, the jagged peaks and polished floor of the desert. Heat and wind aroused her skin and she pressed close to Jason. She kissed his mouth. "I love you, Jason."

"I love you, Amanda."

He looked at her, his lips unsteady. She cried openly. "I waited such a long time for it, Jason. Such a long time."

He pushed her head softly onto his shoulder as the wind blew against their faces. "Well," he said, "some designs are more difficult than others."

"And much more beautiful," Amanda said.